T0333608

The
Strawberry
Field Girls
at War

Karen Dickson lives in Dorset and used to work at her local branch of WHSmith, where she was fondly known as The Book Lady. *The Strawberry Field Girls at War* is her fifth novel.

Also by Karen Dickson:

The Shop Girl's Soldier
The Dressmaker's Secret
A Songbird in Wartime
The Strawberry Field Girls

The
Strawberry
Field Girls
at War

KAREN DICKSON

**SIMON &
SCHUSTER**

London · New York · Sydney · Toronto · New Delhi

First published in Great Britain by Simon & Schuster UK Ltd, 2024

Copyright © Karen Dickson, 2024

1 3 5 7 9 10 8 6 4 2

Simon & Schuster UK Ltd
1st Floor
222 Gray's Inn Road
London WC1X 8HB

Simon & Schuster: Celebrating 100 Years of Publishing in 2024

Simon & Schuster Australia, Sydney
Simon & Schuster India, New Delhi

www.simonandschuster.co.uk
www.simonandschuster.com.au
www.simonandschuster.co.in

A CIP catalogue record for this book
is available from the British Library

Hardback ISBN: 978-1-3985-3097-3
eBook ISBN: 978-1-3985-3098-0
Audio ISBN: 978-1-3985-3099-7

Typeset in Bembo by M Rules
Printed and Bound in the UK using 100% Renewable
Electricity at CPI Group (UK) Ltd

This book is dedicated to the memory of Arthur Cole Taylor, a brave, beautiful boy who sadly gained his angel wings on 30 November 2022. Dearest Arthur, you captured so many hearts with your beautiful smile. You will never be forgotten. Fly high above the rainbows, sweet boy.

And also to Isabella-Bleu Pioli-White, a beautiful warrior princess who continues to defy all the odds. Precious Isabella, you are such an inspiration. Keep on smiling and thriving, gorgeous girl.

And to all the beautiful children born with that extra special chromosome. You are all amazing.

CHAPTER ONE

1916

The cartwheels creaked rhythmically as the pony plodded down the winding lane, its hooves throwing up clumps of snow. Skeletal trees stood stark against the white landscape, gulls and crows wheeling overhead in a monochrome sky.

'It's very kind of you to give us a ride, Mr Turner,' Dora said, her breath billowing in the cold air.

'Yes,' said Leah. 'Thank you.'

'Like I said, I'm going into town to pick up Alice,' Mathew replied. 'It's no bother to have you girls riding along. I enjoy the company.' He sat between the two girls, holding the reins lightly in his gloved hand, his hat pulled low over his eyes, snow dusting the shoulders of his thick coat.

'It's going to be freezing in the factory this morning,' grumbled Daisy from the cart bed where she sat among sacks of turnips, huddled under a blanket, her cheeks pink with cold.

'Just be grateful you're not out in the field picking turnips anymore,' Dora told her, turning to look over her shoulder. Inside her woollen gloves, her rough, cracked fingers tingled painfully.

'Well, at least you don't have to do that anymore.'

'Sorry, Mr Turner.' She flashed Mathew an apologetic smile.

'No need to apologize,' Mathew said. 'It's backbreaking work, especially in this weather when the soil's as hard as rock. You've stuck it out for a good eighteen months or more. I don't blame you girls for wanting to better yourselves. Stephen would be proud of you, Dora.'

'Do you think so?' Dora asked, her eyes pricking with tears. It was almost two years since her father's death at his own hand. Time had eased the rawness of her grief, but there were times, such as now, when it washed over her like a tidal wave.

'I know things were difficult for you after his illness,' Mathew said quietly, 'but deep down, he was still your dad, and I reckon he'll be looking down on you now and applauding your decision.'

'I think you're dead brave, Dora,' Leah said, as Dora wiped away a tear with the corner of her handkerchief. She squeezed Dora's hand. 'I couldn't do it. I haven't the stomach for it.'

'Dora's used to it, though, aren't you, Dor?' Daisy said, adjusting her position as best she could. She was starting to get pins and needles in her legs. 'I mean, you looked after your dad all by yourself for years. Working in a hospital can't be much different.'

'I shall have a lot to learn,' Dora replied, blowing her nose. 'I must admit, I am nervous.'

'You'll be fine,' Leah assured her. 'Alice put in a word for you with the matron, so you're already on a winner.'

Dora laughed. 'She also said the matron is a right tartar. She's not someone I want to get on the wrong side of, I'm sure.'

'And why should you?' Mathew said amiably. 'You're an intelligent girl, you're not afraid of hard work and you've proved your nursing skills looking after Stephen.' He gave her an encouraging smile. 'Just do as you're told and you'll be fine.'

They lapsed into silence. It really was too cold to talk. Dora tugged her scarf over her mouth and nose, listening to the dull thud of the pony's hooves on the frozen mud. She wondered if Nate had received her letter informing him of her decision to enlist as a VAD nurse. She felt the familiar tug at her heart as she thought about him. He'd turned eighteen the previous week, an event that had gone uncelebrated in the trenches around Delville Woods. Dora had made sure to send off his parcel in plenty of time, and he'd written back immediately to tell her how much the lads had enjoyed her homemade biscuits and how grateful he was for the three pairs of thick woollen socks.

'At least they can't send me home now,' he'd concluded jokily, making Dora sigh. Enlisting at the tender age of six-teen was no joking matter as far as she was concerned, and though she'd forgiven him (how could she not?), she couldn't help the occasional twinge of annoyance when she thought of the months apart when he could have been at home, in Strawbridge, with her.

The front wheel hit a rock, jolting Dora out of her reverie. She gazed ahead to the row of factories lining the bank of the River Itchen. Water lapped against the muddy banks where groups of raggedly dressed children scavenged along the low-tide mark. The ferry was midway across the river, heading towards them, Dora noted thankfully, and Mathew guided the pony and cart to the end of the lengthy queue that had formed along the bank. From her vantage point, Dora could just make out the hulking warships anchored out at sea through the thin mist.

The ferry bumped gently against the jetty, and they boarded. Dora shivered. A cold wind blew off the choppy water, carrying the smell of dank vegetation and rotting fish. Gulls screeched overhead, their plaintive cries mingling with the nerve-jarring clatter of machinery drifting from the opposite bank.

Pale sunlight was breaking through the clouds by the time Mathew brought his cart to a halt in Lower William Street.

'Thank you, Mr Turner,' Leah said, clutching her hat as she jumped to the ground. She cursed under her breath as her foot landed in a pile of melting snow, soaking her stocking.

'It's a pleasure,' Mathew said, tipping his hat as Daisy clambered over the side of the cart.

'I'll drop you round the corner, Dora,' he added, as she made to follow Leah.

'If you're sure it's no bother?'

'Not at all.'

'Good luck, Dora,' Leah said, raising her hand in a wave. 'I'll see you in the Amble Inn tearoom at dinner time.'

'Thank you. And, yes, I'll see you then. Have a good day. You, too, Daisy.'

Raising his hat again, Mathew shook the reins, and the pony pulled away from the kerb, merging with the traffic clogging the street. Dora twisted in her seat, waving until they turned the corner.

'I don't think I'll ever get used to the stink around here,' Daisy grumbled, wrinkling her nose in distaste as they crossed the street, dodging carts and wagons. The street was lined with factories belching out foul-smelling chemicals and acrid smoke. It was much worse than the dry salters they had both worked at before war broke out.

Swept along the pavement by the tide of women arriving for the day shift, Leah and Daisy clocked in and made their way to their stations. Leah was working on lathes making depth adjusters for submarines, while Daisy was working at the far end of the factory, filling shells.

Both girls had been working at Franklin's since the winter of 1914. It had taken Leah a long time to get used to the din of the machinery. The hours were long, the work hard, but the pay was good. After paying her mother for her keep, she could afford the odd little treat for herself, as well as putting money aside for her bottom drawer. She and Harry were planning on getting married as soon as he turned twenty-one, later this year.

'Morning, Mr Butterworth,' she called out to the foreman as she donned her apron and cap.

'Good morning, Miss Hopwood. How are you today?' Brian Butterworth was a quiet, unassuming man who Leah guessed was about forty, with an owl-like face and a receding hairline.

'I'm well, thank you.' Leah had to shout to be heard above the grinding machinery. 'Any news on your Timothy?'

Brian's face broke into a smile. 'He's been given a week's leave. My boy's coming home.' His glasses misted up, and he took them off, wiping the lenses with his handkerchief.

'That's wonderful news,' Leah beamed. She was fond of Brian, and his wife, May, whom she'd met on the odd occasion his wife had popped in to bring Brian his dinner. Timothy was their only child. 'I'm hoping Harry will be given some leave soon,' she said wistfully. 'It's been almost a year.'

'Fingers crossed, hey?' Brian said, replacing his glasses as he moved down the row, pausing here and there to chat to the women. He was a good foreman, and everyone liked him. Which was more than could be said for the factory's owner, Wright B. Franklin. In his early sixties, he was a dour, rotund little man who cared nothing for his employees or their working conditions.

Leah leaned across her bench and adjusted the width of

the lathe. The work was mundane, but at least she had the other women to talk to. They were all good for a laugh, which helped take her mind off Harry. The constant worry was like a ball of lead in her chest, and she dreaded going home each day lest she find the dreaded telegram waiting for her.

The old gypsy woman's predictions had come back to haunt her many times over the past eighteen months. It was obvious to Leah that the outbreak of war was the nightmarish image Pearl had seen that had upset her so much. But what of herself and Harry? Pearl had seemed adamant that her future wouldn't be with him, and that terrified her. Dora and Alice kept telling her that whatever happened had nothing to do with Pearl's ramblings, but Leah remained unconvinced. Pearl had the gift of sight. She'd always known it, deep down, which was why she struggled so much with her nerves. She couldn't shake off the feeling that something terrible was going to happen to him.

'You all right, Leah?' Maud Fielding shouted above the din. 'You look like you've lost a pound and found a shilling.'

Leah smiled. She liked Maud. She was always up for a laugh. And weren't they all in the same boat? There wasn't a woman or girl among them who didn't have someone away fighting.

'Just thinking,' replied Leah, equally loudly.

'That's where you're going wrong,' Maud bellowed back with a grin. She was a big girl, heavily built with wavy chestnut-brown hair and dark eyes fringed by long, curling lashes. 'Don't let your mind wander. It'll take you to all sorts of dark places you're better off not visiting. Believe me, I know.'

Maud had told Leah just last week that her little brother, whom she adored, had received his call-up papers and was awaiting his posting abroad. Edward was the only boy in a houseful of girls, a much longed for son, and Maud's close-knit family were beside themselves with worry.

'It's hard not to, though, isn't it?' Leah argued, biting her lip.

'Well, this will give you something else to think about,' Maud said. Lowering her voice slightly, she moved closer to Leah. 'Our Nellie's only gone and got herself in the family way. The daft cow.'

'Oh dear,' Leah frowned in sympathy. Nellie was nineteen, the same age as Leah. Maud was two years older.

'Mum and Dad are fuming, obviously,' Maud continued, as she locked her lathe into position. 'Nellie's written to Arnie in the hope he can get compassionate leave to come home and marry her. She's almost three months gone, so they need to get a shift on. She'll be starting to show soon.'

Leah pulled off her first depth charger and replaced it with another. There had been several occasions during Harry's last leave, before he'd left for France, when they'd come dangerously close to throwing caution to the wind. It had always been Harry who pulled back at the last moment.

'I don't want to get you in the family way,' he'd said on that last night as they lay in front of the fire. The rest of the family had gone to bed, leaving them alone. 'I won't have my parents saying you forced my hand. I want to do things properly. As soon as I'm of age, I'll come back and we'll get married.'

She wondered what it would be like to have Harry's baby. The thought gave her a funny feeling in the pit of her stomach. Perhaps when they were married, and with a baby on the way, Isaac and Frances Whitworth would come round. After all, if the baby was a boy, he'd be in line to inherit the Whitworth fortune, not that it had ever been about money for Leah. It was Harry she loved, not his name or his money.

Her thoughts were interrupted by Maud shouting to her over the clatter of the machines.

'I need to spend a penny.' She switched off her machine and wiped her hands on her apron. 'If the tea boy comes round, mine's black with extra sugar.' She winked and headed off towards the lavatories at the far end of the factory.

Despite the bitterly cold February weather, the factory was uncomfortably warm. Perspiration trickled down Leah's spine and her armpits were damp, her thick flannel underwear clinging to her sweaty skin. She massaged her aching shoulders, grateful to see the tea boy approaching with his trolley.

'About time,' she called, grinning at him. 'I'm gasping.'

Suddenly an almighty explosion ripped through the air. Leah was knocked off her feet. She landed on her back. Winded, she could do nothing for several seconds except listen to the screams and cries reverberating around her. She could hear the roar of flames and the crash of glass as the windows exploded. Smoke billowed from the far end of the factory, its acrid smell clogging the back of her throat. More screams rang out, mingled with the sound of moaning.

As soon as she could draw breath, Leah dragged herself to her feet. The tea boy was crouched a few inches away from her. The tea trolley had overturned, broken pieces of china scattered on the floor, marooned in a sea of brown. She laid a comforting hand on his shoulder and raised her head. Women were running towards the flames. From far away came the strident clang of the fire bell.

'Daisy!' Leah whispered hoarsely. 'Daisy!' Her throat hurt and her voice sounded distorted to her ears, which were still ringing with the sound of the explosion. Panic clutched her chest in its vice-like grip. Daisy was somewhere in that inferno.

Pushing her way through the crying, screaming women, Leah fought her way closer. The smell of burnt flesh was nauseating, and she was forced to hold her scarf over her mouth and nose. Something lay at her feet. She glanced down and her stomach clenched at the sight of Mr Butterworth's charred body. His clothes had been blown right off him. One of the girls picked up a coat, shredded and scorched by the blast, and gently covered him with it.

'Daisy!' Leah shouted. The noise was horrendous. From beyond the flames came the screams of the women trapped by fallen debris.

'Out of the way, miss,' a voice said at her side. A gloved hand gripped her arm and moved her aside. 'Let us through,' the fireman called, his voice muffled by his breathing apparatus. From the far side of the building came the hiss and splash of water. Steam billowed like clouds as the firemen fought to bring the blaze under control.

'Stand back, ladies,' the fireman shouted, directing the women away from the flames. 'Make your way outside, please. Quickly now!'

'My sister . . .' Leah whispered, swallowing painfully.

'Wait outside, miss,' he said, not unkindly. 'Let us do our job.'

'Maud was in there,' a timid, blonde-haired girl called Edna whispered to Leah. At the sight of the blackened, smouldering rubble that was all that remained of the toilet block, bile flooded Leah's throat. She forced it down, her anxious gaze frantically searching the rubble for some sign of her sister.

CHAPTER TWO

The sound of the explosion had rocked the VAD recruitment office in the Methodist church hall. Dora rushed to the window to see plumes of acrid black smoke rising above the rooftops.

'Good heavens above, whatever was that?' one of the recruitment officers, Mavis Platt, cried, as the fifteen young women and five staff members glanced at each other in alarm.

'It sounded like a bomb, miss,' one of the girls offered, her eyes wide with fear.

'And quite close, too,' another added. 'Should we go to the shelter?'

Dora glanced round at her fellow recruits. During registration, she had learned that they ranged in age between eighteen and twenty-five and came from various walks of life. Now, they were on their feet, heading for the door. Like Dora, they, too, imagined they were about to be blown to Kingdom Come. They had all read the newspaper reports about the Zeppelin raid over Liverpool just three weeks earlier. Sixty-one people had been killed and scores more injured. Was Southampton now to suffer the same terrifying fate?

'Sit down, girls.' Mavis chewed her lip in consternation. Would it be safer to keep the girls in the hall or to send them out to seek the nearest shelter? She gazed out at the group of young women before her, all eager to do their bit for King and Country. She shuffled the papers on her desk, aware that fifteen pairs of terrified eyes were looking to her for guidance.

Suddenly the door was flung open and a middle-aged man in clerical robes burst in.

'There's been an explosion at Franklin's,' he gasped.

'An explosion?' Mavis's shoulders sagged slightly in relief. Not a bomb after all.

Several of the women with Dora had relatives who worked at the factory and they joined Dora at the edge of the crowd that had gathered across the street from Franklin's. She felt sick as she scanned the charred rubble. Voices shouted, and there was an almighty crash from inside the building, followed by screams from among the onlookers. Dust billowed from the open doorway like a cloud.

'I only came out to take Penny for a walk while my husband was between deliveries,' a voice said beside her. Dora turned to see the woman from the butcher's in Northam Road standing close by, her baby clutched in her arms. The little mite was screaming her head off as her mother looked aghast at a large piece of masonry that had landed on the pavement, narrowly missing the child's pram.

13

'Move along, please,' a matronly-looking woman in a Red Cross uniform said sternly to the swelling crowd. 'It's not safe, and we don't need any more casualties.' She turned to the young woman with the baby. 'You've had a shock. Go and get yourself a cup of tea,' she said in a kinder tone, steering her in the direction of the café across the street, well away from the carnage.

At that moment, movement across the street caused a commotion among the crowd.

'Leah!' Dora shouted, feeling a surge of relief at the sight of her dearest friend stumbling through the doorway. She was clutching the arm of a dark-haired woman who looked slightly older. Both of them were covered in a fine layer of white dust.

Dora ran across the street. A police constable had joined the woman from the Red Cross and was doing his best to get the crowds to move further back. Dora slipped past him and ran over to her friend.

'Leah, are you all right?'

Leah bent forward and coughed, clutching her throat. She held up her free hand and shook her head. Her ears were ringing, and the noise of the street sounded distorted.

'Daisy,' she croaked.

'Daisy's one of those trapped behind the rubble,' the girl with Leah told Dora, her brow puckered in a worried frown. 'We don't know if she's hurt or not.'

Leah straightened up, looking at Dora with eyes red-rimmed from the dust. She shook her head.

'Oh, Leah,' Dora said, gathering her friend into her arms. 'I'm sure Daisy will be fine,' she said, hoping against hope she was right. Women were pouring from the exit, and, gazing over their heads to where the flames still raged at the far end of the building, she wondered how anyone caught in the blaze could possibly have survived.

'Move along, ladies,' the police constable said, ushering them further away. 'There's a danger the building may collapse, so you need to move across the street.'

Dora nodded. Holding Leah by the arm, she managed to drag her across the street. She kept staring at the building, hollow-eyed. Water ran in rivulets down the road as the firemen battled to contain the fire.

A hush fell upon the crowd as the first body was brought out on a stretcher.

'Poor Mr Butterworth,' Leah murmured tearfully. 'His son's coming home. He was so excited.'

Both girls kept their gaze on the door. They hardly dared breathe as the bodies were brought out, lest the next one was Daisy.

'Leah, Dora! Oh, thank God you're all right, Leah.' Alice Roberts pushed her way through the crowd, her Red Cross uniform parting the onlookers like the Red Sea. She hugged Leah tight, the relief in her dark eyes immediately giving way to anxiety. 'Daisy?'

Mute with fear, Leah just shook her head.

'We don't know yet,' Dora said, her anxious gaze scanning the injured patients being loaded into waiting ambulances. The firemen seemed to have brought the fire under control, clouds of steam replacing the smoke drifting into the sky. Gulls screeched from the adjacent rooftops, and Leah winced.

'We've got a tea tent set up around the corner,' Alice said. 'Let's get you something warm to drink. You're shivering.'

Leah realized she'd left her coat in the factory. Her teeth were chattering but she felt oblivious to the cold. All she could concentrate on was that Daisy was inside the building.

'Come on, Leah,' said Alice softly. 'There's nothing you can do here.'

'I need to wait for Daisy,' replied Leah with a stubborn jut of her chin.

'They're searching for those missing now,' Alice pointed out gently, stifling a yawn. It was only then that Dora noticed how tired her friend looked. The skin beneath her eyes was bruised purple and her face was drawn.

'Please, Leah. You'll catch your death if you stay out here much longer.' Alice took Leah's arm and tried to lead her away. At first Dora thought Leah was going to resist, but with a sigh of resignation, her shoulders slumped and she allowed Alice to lead her round the corner to the hastily erected tent where members of the Red Cross were dispensing mugs of hot tea.

'Leah!' Mathew Turner appeared at their side. 'Thank God you're not hurt. Daisy?'

'Still waiting for news,' Alice replied wearily. 'Can I have a blanket for this lady, please,' she called to a passing volunteer.

Mathew laid a comforting hand on Leah's arm. 'Alice, let me take you home,' he said. 'You've been out all night.'

'I'm needed here, Grandfather,' insisted Alice, ushering Leah and Dora towards the tea stand. Women milled about, shell-shocked and whey-faced.

'You don't need to do everything yourself,' Mathew reminded her mildly. 'Come on, I'll take all three of you home. Hannah will need to be told.'

Alice and Dora exchanged sombre glances. Leah appeared not to hear. She was staring into space, her frigid fingers circling her mug, a blanket draped across her shoulders.

'Take Leah and Dora home, Grandfather,' suggested Alice. 'I'll stay here.'

Mathew shook his head in exasperation. He worried that Alice was doing too much. He understood it kept her busy, stopped her fretting over her lost babies and worrying about Samuel, but what was the point in working herself to a nervous breakdown? What use would she be to Samuel then, when he finally came home?

He sighed and took off his hat, running his fingers through his hair. 'Your grandmother won't be happy,' he said in a last-ditch attempt to get his stubborn granddaughter to reconsider.

'Grandma will be fine,' Alice smiled tiredly. 'I must stay as long as I'm needed.' She leaned forward and kissed Mathew's whiskered cheek.

'I'm staying, too,' Leah retorted. 'I'm not leaving until I know Daisy's all right.'

17

'I can't go yet,' Dora said. 'I haven't completed my paper-work and I still need to undergo a medical.' She shrugged. 'Perhaps you should return home, Mr Turner. Aunty Hannah will need to be told what's happened. She'll want to go to the infirmary.'

'Very well,' Mathew said with resignation. 'I can see I'm outnumbered.' He patted Leah's arm. 'I hope your Daisy is found alive and well,' he said soberly. Leah nodded.

At that moment, a triumphant shout went up. Leah and Dora exchanged glances. Leah handed Alice her mug and, clutching the blanket around her throat with one hand and picking up her skirts with the other, hurried back the way they had come. Dora followed in her wake.

They rounded the corner, coming to an abrupt halt. Several women were stumbling from the building. Medical staff hurried towards them, quickly assessing their injuries. Those who needed hospital treatment were directed towards the waiting ambulances. Leah held her breath, scanning the walking wounded for a glimpse of her sister.

Two ambulance men emerged carrying a stretcher. Leah stood on tiptoe as they carried the patient towards a waiting ambulance, and shrieked.

'Daisy!' She clutched Dora's arm briefly, her blanket fall-ing to the ground. Letting go of Dora, she pushed her way through the crowd. 'Daisy!'

Dora snatched up the blanket from the gutter, its edges soaked with melting snow, and hurried after Leah, catching up with her as she reached the ambulance.

'Daisy, it's me, Leah!' she cried, recoiling in horror. Daisy lay with her eyes closed. Her face was covered in blood. Her hair was stiff with it, and it had run down her neck, soaking into her blouse.

'Out of the way, love,' one of the ambulance men said brusquely.

'Please, she's my sister,' Leah whispered, glancing up at him. He was middle-aged with a salt and pepper beard. 'Is she . . . ?'

'She's alive,' he replied, his voice laced with sympathy.

'We're taking her to the Royal South,' his partner added. He was a younger man, not much older than herself, Leah surmised. Masonry dust covered the shoulders of his dark blue uniform.

'Thank you,' Leah nodded as they lifted the stretcher into the ambulance, closing the doors firmly after them.

'Let's find Mr Turner,' Dora said, as Leah stared after the departing ambulance. 'He can take you home. You'll need to tell your mum.'

'She'll be devastated,' Leah murmured, her own heart feeling heavy in her chest. 'She looked so still,' she whispered. She felt close to tears. 'What if she doesn't make it?' Leah looked at Dora, her blue-tinged lips trembling.

'Don't think that way,' Dora said firmly, giving Leah's cold hand a squeeze. 'Here.' She handed Leah the blanket. 'I managed to rescue it before it got too wet.'

They made their way back to the tea tent, Leah walking in a daze. The street was a bustle of activity as Red Cross volunteers tended to superficial wounds and dished out mugs of sweet tea and blankets to combat shock.

'Mr Turner!' Dora called, spotting her neighbour standing beside his pony and cart further up the street. He raised his hand in acknowledgement and ambled towards them, meeting them halfway.

'Daisy?' he asked, his brow furrowed in worry.

'She's alive,' Dora replied. 'They've taken her to hospital.'

'She'll be in good hands there,' Mathew assured Leah with a sympathetic smile. 'You're frozen, girl. Let's get you home. Alice is stubbornly refusing to leave, despite having been on duty all night,' Mathew said. He shook his head, though it was clear to Dora that behind the exasperation lay a deep respect for his granddaughter.

Dora waited until Leah and Mathew had driven away before going to find Alice.

'Oh, poor Daisy,' Alice said, her dark eyes filling with tears when Dora told her the news. 'I do hope she'll be all right.' She held two mugs of tea in her hands. 'Poor Hannah. Has someone gone to tell her?'

'Leah has gone with your grandfather,' Dora told her. Her eyes clouded. 'Poor Aunty Hannah. It's going to come as a terrible shock.'

CHAPTER THREE

'I'll put the kettle on,' Hannah Hopwood said, as the mantelpiece clock chimed eleven.

'A cup of tea would be lovely,' her friend and neighbour, Beatrice Turner, agreed, glancing out of the window. The grey clouds had cleared, leaving a cold blue sky in their wake. 'I had expected Mathew and Alice home by now,' she frowned, laying her knitting needles in her lap.

'Likely they've been delayed by the snow,' Hannah said, as she laid her own knitting aside and got to her feet. 'It's melting fast, so the roads are likely to be flooded in parts.' She paused on her way to the kitchen to throw another log on the fire.

She filled the kettle, gazing across the garden to the fields beyond, patches of snow glistening white under the wintery sky. Crocuses and early daffodils clustered beneath the apple tree. Melting snow dripped from its branches and from the eaves. Thank goodness spring was on its way, she mused, rinsing out the teapot.

It had been a hard winter, the biting cold weather made all the worse by the growing food shortages. When she'd popped into the village shop in Botley just last week, the shelves had been all but bare. By all accounts, they were starving in the towns and cities. They were marginally better off in the countryside. Isaac Whitworth had told his game-keeper, Cuthbert Ryall, to turn a blind eye to any poaching while the food crisis lasted, and there was talk of him turning the pond into a stew pond. And, God willing, come March next week, the hens would start laying again. She glanced over at the frying pan, where five freshly plucked sparrows lay under a clean tea towel. Muriel from next door had brought them round that morning. She had a surplus, she'd said. Her young lad, Simon, had devised an elaborate trap and was out early every morning to catch them. His dad was away in France, and he was clearly taking his responsibility for his mother seriously.

Hannah had accepted the offer gratefully. There wasn't much meat on a sparrow, but with some potatoes and turnips, she could turn them into a hearty stew. Fresh meat was hard to come by now that they no longer had Joshua around. She wondered briefly how Pearl was faring in this cold weather, all alone in her caravan. She knew Alice kept an eye on the old woman and often took food over to her, but still, she was very old to be living alone.

The kettle came to the boil just as she heard Beatrice call from the parlour.

'Mathew's just pulled up outside,' Beatrice said,

appearing in the doorway, looking puzzled. 'He's got your Leah with him.'

'Leah?' Hannah exclaimed, her chest tightening anxiously. She lifted the kettle off the heat and, wiping her hands on her apron, hurried into the other room. Leah was just coming in the door, her face ashen. She was wearing Mathew's coat. Mathew was right behind her, his expression sombre.

'Mathew, you look frozen to death!' exclaimed Beatrice, hurrying to her husband.

'I'm all right,' Mathew said, brushing her concerns aside. He looked intently at Hannah.

'What's happened?' she said as calmly as she could, all the while fighting the panic clawing at her throat. 'Where's Daisy?'

Leah opened her mouth to reply, but words failed her and she burst into tears.

'There's been an accident,' Mathew said, as Hannah took Leah in her arms, her frightened eyes meeting Mathew's.

'What sort of accident?' Beatrice asked quietly.

'An explosion,' Mathew replied soberly, his gaze not leaving his neighbour's face. 'Hannah, Daisy is in the hospital. You need to go to her now.'

Hannah inhaled sharply as the significance of Mathew's words registered.

'Bea, can you . . . ?'

'Of course. Leah, come here, dear.' She gently prised Leah's arms from around Hannah's waist and helped her shrug out of Mathew's heavy overcoat, before leading her to the sofa under the window. Shooing away the cat, she sat her down and, fishing a clean handkerchief from her pocket, handed it to her.

'She's in shock,' Mathew said to Beatrice, stoking the fire as Hannah pulled on her coat and hat. 'She needs some tea, hot and sweet. I think her hearing has been affected, too. She was quite close to the explosion.' His wife nodded.

'Alice didn't come back with you?' she asked.

Mathew buttoned up his coat, shaking his head. 'No, she decided to stay and help. I'll call by again on the way back from the hospital. Dora's still there, too. I can probably bring both girls back with me later.'

'I'm ready,' Hannah said, pulling on her gloves. She bent to kiss the top of Leah's head. 'I'll be back as soon as I can, love.' Leah nodded. She'd stopped crying and was staring into the fire, her eyes glassy.

'I'll get that tea,' Beatrice said brightly. She laid a hand on Hannah's arm. 'Give Daisy our love, won't you?'

Hannah nodded, her throat tightening. Her eyes glistened with tears. Mathew opened the door, and she followed him out into the cold lane where the pony was pawing the frozen ground impatiently. Across the lane, the women of the hamlet were at work in the field picking potatoes and turnips. Hannah folded her gloved hands in her lap, wishing her girls were doing the same. Factory work paid well, but was the extra money worth the risk? With her younger daughter lying in hospital, she was inclined to think that it wasn't.

'How bad is she?' she found the courage to ask as they started down the lane, the churning of the wheels and the plod of the pony's hooves accompanied by the incessant drip, drip, drip of melting snow.

'I didn't actually see her,' Mathew replied with a sideways glance. 'But Leah says there was a lot of blood and she was unconscious.'

Hannah nodded, her stomach churning anxiously.

The journey to the hospital seemed interminably long, and by the time they joined the cavalcade along the road leading up to it, Hannah was an emotional wreck. Dry-eyed, but pale and visibly shaking, she took Mathew's hand as he helped her down from the cart.

'I'll come in with you,' he said, securing the pony to a post and calling to a young boy standing nearby to keep an eye on her, with the promise of half a penny for his trouble. There had been rumours about ponies going missing, likely stolen for food by families on the brink of starvation.

Feeling her legs were about to give way, Hannah thanked him. She leaned gratefully on his arm as they made their way inside. It was between visiting hours, and the lobby was quiet. Heart thumping painfully, she and Mathew approached the front desk, behind which sat an attractive nurse, tendrils of dark hair peeking from beneath her cap. She looked up, peering at Hannah over her spectacles.

'Good afternoon,' she said, her expression neutral. 'How may I help you?'

'We're looking for someone involved in the Franklin's

explosion this morning,' Mathew said, clearing his throat. 'She was brought in about half past ten or thereabouts.'

'Name?' the nurse said, consulting the list in front of her.

'Daisy,' Hannah blurted out before Mathew could speak. 'Daisy Hopwood.' She held her breath. The seconds it took for the nurse to check her list seemed to last a lifetime.

'Ah, yes,' the nurse said eventually. 'Hopwood, Miss D.' She looked up, her brown eyes laced with sympathy. 'She's been admitted to Nelson Ward. If you'll take a seat, I'll get a doctor to come and see you.'

Hannah's shoulders sagged as she exhaled in relief. 'She's alive.'

Mathew thanked the nurse and led Hannah to one of several rows of wooden benches where a handful of people were sitting. She took off her coat, folded it and placed it on the seat next to her, laying her hat and gloves carefully on top. She sat down heavily, her relief that Daisy was alive tempered by anxiety over the severity of her injuries. Mathew sat down beside her, his coat draped over the bench opposite.

'Please don't feel obligated to stay,' she whispered.

'I'm in no hurry to go anywhere,' Mathew grunted.

'You're a good man, Mathew Turner,' she smiled. 'No wonder my William held you in such high regard.' She glanced around at the people waiting. They stared ahead, each seemingly lost in thought. A small child sat on the floor at his mother's feet. His nose was running and his dark eyes looked too big for his face. Catching Hannah watching him, he turned away, shyly burying his face in his mother's skirts.

Rubber soles squeaked on the grey linoleum and a doctor rounded the corner. Those seated on the benches stirred, eyes drawn towards him in nervous expectation. Hannah held her breath. He was tall and dark-haired, in his mid-fifties, she guessed, and handsome in a cold, austere sort of way.

'Hopwood?' He looked up from his sheet of paper, scanning the lobby.

Hannah gave an involuntary whimper and got to her feet. Her throat was so dry she could hardly swallow. The doctor gave her a cursory glance.

'I'm Dr Vincent. Follow me, please.' He turned on his heel and stalked back the way he had come. Hastily gathering up her hat and coat, Hannah hurried after him. She was vaguely aware of Mathew behind her as her mind raced, every possible scenario playing in her mind. Her stomach churned wildly, and she could feel the bile burning the back of her throat.

The doctor led the way down a wide corridor. A door swung open, emitting a uniformed orderly, and from somewhere within came the sound of someone screaming as if in horrendous pain. Hannah winced. The door banged shut, abruptly cutting the scream off. On the journey to the hospital, she'd been too numb with shock to pray, but now she kept up a litany of silent prayer as she hurried to keep pace with Dr Vincent.

They rounded a corner and moved down a narrower

corridor. Hannah saw the sign for Nelson Ward above a door. She gave a gasp as her heart plummeted. She had to grip Mathew's arm in order not to keel over. In smaller letters underneath the name of the ward was the word:

NEUROLOGICAL

Dr Vincent pushed open the door and motioned for Hannah to follow. Taking a deep breath, she forced herself to enter the ward. Most of the beds had the curtains drawn. Behind one set of curtains, someone was weeping quietly. At the bed closest to the door, a woman about Hannah's age sat propped up against her pillows. She was rocking back and forth, her eyes wide and staring. Hannah swallowed, terror for her daughter gripping her throat like a vice.

'Doctor.' A nurse seated at a desk got to her feet and came towards them.

'Sister,' Dr Vincent nodded. 'These are Miss Hopwood's relatives.'

'Good afternoon, Mr and Mrs Hopwood,' the nurse said with a sympathetic smile. 'I'm Sister Porter. I shall be responsible for your daughter's care during her stay with us.'

'Oh, no,' Hannah said. 'This isn't Daisy's father. I'm afraid I'm a widow. This is my neighbour, Mr Turner.'

'I'm afraid it's immediate family only on this ward,' Sister Porter said.

'Oh, never mind that now,' Dr Vincent snapped irritably. 'I have a busy schedule, Sister.'

'Of course, Doctor,' the sister replied demurely. 'This

way, please.' She turned to lead them down the ward. There were ten beds on either side and all but one appeared to be occupied. Halfway down the ward, the sister paused. 'This is Daisy,' she said. She held the pretty pink floral curtain aside for Hannah to step inside. As she did so, her hand flew to her mouth and she let out a thin cry.

'Daisy!' she wailed, falling into the chair beside her daughter's bed and reaching blindly for her hand. She looked so still and pale that for a moment Hannah thought she was too late. But the steady rise and fall of Daisy's chest told her she was alive. Her face was criss-crossed with lacerations and she had the beginnings of a black eye.

'The facial wounds are superficial,' Sister Porter said, her voice low as she leaned over to tuck a strand of dark hair behind Daisy's ear. 'They will soon heal and they shouldn't leave a scar.'

'It's the brain injury that's causing us a significant amount of concern,' Dr Vincent said, picking up the chart hanging at the end of Daisy's bed. Hannah glanced up at him in terror. Mathew laid a hand on her shoulder, and she gripped it forcefully.

'Daisy has sustained what is known as a brain contusion,' the doctor explained in his bland tone. 'During the explosion, she was hit hard on the head, probably by falling masonry. This has caused the brain tissue to swell.'

'Is . . . is there something you can do?' Hannah asked, tears welling. 'Some treatment?'

'Surgery is an option,' Dr Vincent said, his expression

grim. 'Whereby I would drill into the skull to relieve the pressure ...'

Hannah dissolved into tears.

'Will that be necessary?' Mathew asked.

'It depends whether the brain tissue continues to swell,' the doctor said, speaking directly to Mathew. 'In that case, surgery will very much be necessary.'

'Oh, Daisy,' Hannah sobbed quietly.

'Even if the swelling recedes over the next few days,' Dr Vincent said, continuing to address Mathew, 'Miss Hopwood may suffer permanent damage. There is the risk of blindness, paralysis, memory loss. She may experience difficulties with concentration and co-ordination.' He shrugged. 'I'm afraid only time will tell.' He looked at the nurse. 'I'm late for my appointment. Sister?'

'Thank you, Doctor. Mrs Hopwood, your daughter is in the very best hands. I shall see personally that she has the best care possible. Now, may I bring you a cup of tea?'

CHAPTER FOUR

Stifling a yawn, Alice gazed across the bleak landscape. It was the first day of March, yet it seemed winter was reluctant to relinquish its grip. Daffodils flanked the lane, their slender green stems bowed by the wind that howled across the fields. It was growing dark, the watery sun having already slipped below the tree line. The church clock struck a quarter to six and, on cue, she heard the cottage door shut and her grandfather appeared in the lane below. Putting on his hat, he headed for the church.

Alice rolled her aching shoulders. As the vicar's wife, she really should make the effort to attend evening prayers, but she was so tired. Surely Reverend Aldridge, who was standing in for Samuel while he was away at the front, would understand?

She turned away from the window and sank wearily onto the edge of her bed. She wondered how Leah and Hannah were coping. On the day of the explosion, she'd been kept busy until late in the evening serving tea to the firemen, police and civilian volunteers. During the afternoon, the factory's owner, Wright Franklin, had turned up. To the disgust of everyone within earshot, he'd shouted and sworn at the council official whose unhappy duty it had been to inform Mr Franklin that his factory would have to remain closed for at least a week until it was deemed safe enough for the employees to return to work, seemingly more concerned with the loss of income than the fact that five of his employees had been killed and another six injured, two seriously. As the covered cart carrying bodies had rumbled up the street, a gust of wind had caught the corner of the tarpaulin and Alice had glimpsed a charred, blackened limb. She'd had to turn away and be sick in the gutter.

In the week since, she'd been rushed off her feet. She cycled all over the countryside collecting donations for the Red Cross parcels to be sent to the boys at the front, and what with her shifts at the Penny Kitchen, she'd had barely any time to pop next door to see her friend and find out how poor Daisy was faring. Thankfully, her grandmother spent a lot of time with Hannah and kept Alice abreast of the news.

To everyone's immense relief, the swelling in Daisy's brain had begun to recede after a couple of days. She was awake for intervals, but her speech was slurred and she appeared very confused, at times not even recognizing her own mother. Her vision was another worry, though Dr Vincent had assured Hannah that he was confident her eyesight would improve with time. All they could do was wait and see.

She was jolted back to the present by the sound of voices downstairs.

'Alice,' called her grandmother. 'Leah's here to see you.'

'Coming.' She hastily checked her appearance in her dressing-table mirror and hurried down the stairs.

'Leah, I was just thinking about you,' she said, embracing her friend warmly. 'How are you?' she asked, as they both settled themselves on the sofa.

'I'll make some tea,' said Beatrice, disappearing off to the kitchen.

'I'm all right,' Leah said with a slight shrug of her shoulders. 'My hearing's almost back to normal now, thank goodness, and I'm starting back at work on Saturday.'

'I heard that Franklin's was reopening. That's something. Hopefully being busy will take your mind off Daisy.' Alice nodded sympathetically. 'How is she?'

Leah pulled a face. 'Mum just got back from the hospital. Apart from the actual swelling having almost gone, her overall condition remains the same.'

'I'm so sorry, Leah. I know how difficult this must be for you and your mum. I bet you're really looking forward to getting back to the factory?'

'To be honest, I'm half-dreading it. I keep thinking about those who were killed, like poor Maud and Mr Butterworth.' She met Alice's gaze. 'It was his funeral yesterday.'

'They're saying the stove exploded.' Alice took her friend's hand. 'Such a terrible tragedy.'

'I still have nightmares about it,' Leah said, drawing a deep breath and giving Alice a wry smile. 'Anyway, while I've been stuck at home fretting, I've managed to knit a dozen pairs of socks for your boxes.'

'Thank you. They are very much appreciated by our boys at the front, I can tell you.'

'I know. Harry's always telling me how things like new socks are such a luxury.' Leah's eyes clouded as she thought of her fiancé so far away. Though he kept his letters to her upbeat, she was astute enough to realize that life in the trenches must be pretty grim.

'Mum got fed up with me moping, so she insisted I stop feeling sorry for myself and do something worthwhile. I must admit, I did feel a bit ashamed of myself. At least Daisy is alive, which is more than can be said for those poor Merrifield boys.'

The hamlet had been rocked three days earlier by the news that two of publican Reuben Merrifield's sons had been killed within hours of each other. Now a black wreath hung on the door of the Glyn Arms pub.

'And of course, Leonard is eighteen next month,' Alice said as her grandmother reappeared with the tea tray. 'He'll get his call-up papers soon.'

'Poor Mrs Merrifield,' Beatrice said, pouring the tea and handing Leah a cup. 'Two sons killed, George and Sidney fighting God knows where and now she's going to lose her youngest to the war, too. I don't know how the poor woman sleeps at night.'

'Likely she doesn't,' Leah said, pursing her lips. Had any of them known a decent night's sleep since war broke out?

'I'm sure you're right, Leah, love,' Beatrice sighed. She straightened up, stirring her tea absently as she stared out over the empty fields. Alice and Leah exchanged knowing glances, both understanding that Beatrice must be thinking about her own son, Ian, who had been taken from her by her common-law husband when he was just three years old. Beatrice had only just discovered his whereabouts when war broke out. She had no idea where he was now, and the knowledge that she would never know if anything happened to him was like a knife to her heart.

'Grandma?' Alice said softly.

'I'm sorry, girls,' Beatrice said with a slight shake of her head. 'I was wool-gathering there.' She smiled brightly as she settled herself in the armchair closest to the fire. Her work basket was on the floor next to her.

'Will Hannah be round later?' she asked Leah, picking up her knitting.

'She just has a few jobs to do and then she'll be over,' Leah replied. 'Oh! I meant to bring the socks with me,' she added, noticing the brown paper parcels piled on the parlour table. 'I'll run and fetch them.'

'Thank you, Leah,' Alice said, hiding a yawn behind her hand. 'I'll take them to headquarters first thing tomorrow before my shift at the Penny Kitchen.'

'I'm worried you're doing too much, Alice,' her grand-mother said as the door swung shut behind Leah, a draught of cold air snaking round her ankles. 'You're exhausted. I don't believe you're fully recovered after losing the baby.'

'I'm well enough, Grandma.' Alice smiled, but her eyes were heavy with sadness. Her first miscarriage had occurred not long after Samuel had left for a training camp in Dorset. She hadn't told him how she'd slipped on the damp step, landing heavily on her ankle, spraining it badly, nor had she told him how the physical pain had been far outshadowed by the emotional anguish of losing a much-wanted baby a few hours later. Wanting to spare him, she had told him only that she'd been mistaken and that there had been no baby.

A month later, she'd discovered, to her delight, that she was expecting again. Over the late summer months, she had blossomed. Between knitting balaclavas and socks, her grandmother and Hannah had found the softest yarns in their work baskets and knitted tiny cardigans and booties.

The cramps had started one early December night. Alice had woken to find her nightdress soaked with blood. Her grandfather had gone for the doctor, but it had been too late. They had returned to find the tiny, perfectly formed little girl, still and silent, wrapped in a towel in a drawer on the kitchen table and Alice's sobs echoing from upstairs.

Alice's grip on her teacup tightened. Tomorrow would have been her baby's due date, and though she'd tried hard to bury her grief with work, it still reared its ugly head in her unguarded moments.

'I'm not sure you are,' her grandmother contradicted, interrupting Alice's thoughts. 'I would have thought the clerical work you do for Reverend Aldridge two mornings a week is enough,' she went on, sighing as she reached for the teapot. 'But on top of that, you have your shifts at the Penny Kitchen and your Red Cross work. More tea?' she asked.

'Thank you.' Alice held out her cup for a refill. 'I like keeping busy, Grandma,' she said. 'When I think how much our boys are suffering over in France, the least I can do is help send them a few home comforts. It's easy enough on my bicycle.'

'That's another thing,' Beatrice said, pursing her lips in concern. 'I'm not happy with you cycling all over the countryside, not with all those German prisoners working in the fields nowadays.'

'Oh, Grandma,' Alice smiled. 'I haven't even glimpsed a German yet.'

They both turned at the sound of the latch being lifted on the back door and of Hannah's voice calling, 'Coo-ee. It's only us.'

She came into the parlour, followed by Leah and Dora, who were carrying several brown paper packages, which they dumped on the table.

'That walk back from the hospital fair takes it out of me,' Hannah puffed, setting her work basket on the table alongside the packages and sinking heavily onto one of the straight-backed dining chairs.

'I'll make a fresh pot of tea,' Beatrice said, getting to her feet.

'I'll do it,' Alice said, taking the teapot from her grandmother. 'You and Mrs Hopwood can have a natter.'

'Dora has some news,' Hannah said, shrugging off her shawl and draping it over the back of her chair.

'Oh yes?' Alice and Beatrice tuned to Dora expectantly.

'I've received my call-up papers,' Dora said, rubbing her arm, which was still smarting from all the injections she'd had to have before going abroad. She swallowed the lump in her throat. Now that her call-up papers had arrived, it all seemed frighteningly real. 'I am to report to the St John's Ambulance headquarters on Saturday morning at ten o'clock,' she said, more confidently than she felt. 'I sail at four.'

'So soon?' Alice frowned.

'We knew it would be,' Hannah said, her smile looking forced. 'They're so desperate for nurses over there.'

'I'm back at work on Saturday, so I shan't even be able to see you off,' lamented Leah despondently.

'We wondered if Mathew might take Dora into town on his cart?' Hannah said, turning to Beatrice. 'She'll have her trunk.'

'I shall ask him as soon as he returns from evensong, but I'm sure he'll have no objection,' Beatrice assured her with a smile.

'I'll make that tea,' Alice said, heading into the kitchen. Leah and Dora followed.

'I can't believe you're going away. I shall miss you,' Leah said, pulling out a chair. She rested her chin on her hand, her expression glum.

'I envy you, Dora,' said Alice, spooning tea leaves into the pot. 'It will be an amazing experience, and you'll be doing something incredibly worthwhile.' She leaned against the dresser, her arms folded across her chest. 'You may borrow my French phrase book, if you'd like?'

'Oh, yes, please,' Dora said, grinning in relief. 'I was wondering how I'd manage with my limited vocabulary.'

'Do you know whereabouts you're being posted?' Alice asked, as she carried the teapot into the parlour.

'Yes, I'll be based at a field hospital outside a little village called Cambri,' replied Dora, following behind.

'You'll be pretty close to the fighting, then,' remarked Beatrice.

'Yes, I suppose I shall,' Dora said quietly. Silence fell upon the cosy front parlour as the women contemplated the enormity of the journey Dora was about to embark on. Leah cleared her throat, breaking the stillness.

'You'd better stay safe,' she said fiercely, her eyes suspiciously bright. 'Or you'll have me to answer to.'

'Don't worry about me,' Dora assured her with a shaky smile. 'I'll be fine.'

'I think you're awfully brave, Dor,' Leah said later that night as they snuggled under the covers, their bodies pressed close together for warmth.

'I'm not brave,' Dora replied, her voice low. 'I'm petrified.'

'Harry says being brave doesn't mean you're not frightened,' Leah whispered back. 'It means being scared but doing it anyway.' She put her arm around her dearest friend, Dora's warm breath fanning her cheek. They'd grown up next door to each other and were as close as sisters. After the death of Dora's father, it had seemed only natural that she would move in with Leah and her family.

'I'm ever so proud of you.'

Dora squeezed Leah's hand and blew out the lamp. The two girls lay staring up into the darkness, the only sounds their quiet breathing, until they finally drifted off to sleep.

CHAPTER FIVE

The first Saturday in March dawned fine but bitterly cold, and, despite her nerves, Dora was glad when Mathew brought the pony and cart to a halt outside the ornate building that housed the headquarters of St John's Ambulance.

She'd woken up feeling sick to her stomach and so had only managed a few mouthfuls of porridge, despite Hannah's insisting that she needed to eat.

'I can't, Aunty Hannah,' she'd pleaded. 'My stomach's in knots.'

'But you don't know when you'll next have the chance to eat something,' Hannah had argued, clearly vexed by the idea of sending Dora out into the brisk March wind without a bowl of warm oats lining her stomach.

'Well, here we are,' Mathew said, bringing Dora back to the present as he engaged the break. 'And with ten minutes to spare,' he added, glancing up at the clock tower. He alighted from the cart and came round to help Dora down.

She thanked him and waited on the pavement while he

tethered the pony, gazing up at the tall, grey stone building in front of her and shivering in the cold wind that howled down the busy street. Above the double doors, the Union Jack flag and the St John's insignia snapped in the stiff breeze. Swallowing down her nerves, Dora ran lightly up the wide stone steps and pulled the bell cord.

The door was opened moments later by a stern-looking man in full uniform.

'Name?' he barked before Dora could open her mouth.

'Webb,' Dora stammered, feeling her cheeks growing hot beneath his scowling scrutiny. The man consulted his clipboard and nodded. 'Welcome, Voluntary Aid Detatchment Nurse Webb. Warrant Officer Thompson.' He was a tall and imposing man with a receding hairline and a noticeable squint. 'You're early. I like that. Come in.' He stood aside, and Dora stepped inside, wiping her streaming eyes. The draughty entrance hall was only marginally warmer than outside, but at least she was out of the wind.

'Your luggage?'

'The small trunk on the cart,' Mathew replied, nodding over his shoulder.

'I'll send an orderly to help you bring it in,' Thompson said. 'VAD Nurse Webb, say your goodbyes and come with me, please.'

'Goodbye, Dora,' Mathew said, with an encouraging smile. 'I know you'll make a brilliant nurse. Your dad would be proud of you.'

At the mention of her father, Dora felt the prick of tears

behind her eyelids. 'Thank you, Mr Turner. Goodbye.' He gave her one last, reassuring grin and left, leaving Dora staring after him, her bottom lip trembling as the reality of her situation suddenly hit home. She was leaving her friends and everything she held dear to go to a foreign country. Quelling the rising tide of panic, she took a deep breath and followed Warrant Officer Thompson through a narrow doorway, up a flight of wooden stairs and along a dim landing to a small room where three other women about her age were standing around looking as lost as Dora felt.

'I'll leave you to introduce yourselves,' Thompson said. Turning on his heels, he retreated down the landing, his highly polished shoes clicking rhythmically on the bare floorboards.

After a few murmured 'hellos', they introduced themselves, Dora learning that the three other girls were Molly, Ellie and Clarissa. Eight months off her nineteenth birthday, Dora was the youngest. Ellie had just turned nineteen. Molly and Clarissa were both in their early twenties.

'The others are cutting it a bit fine,' Molly said, as the clock across the street chimed the hour. She was a pretty, slender girl with auburn curls and dark green eyes.

'How many more are we expecting?' asked Ellie, a stocky girl with pale skin and freckles.

'There are six of us altogether, I believe,' replied Molly as Dora wandered over to the window, which overlooked the rooftops of Southampton and the docks beyond. With a jolt, she realized that, in all probability, one of the several ships anchored out to sea would be the vessel that would carry her to France. Her stomach gave a nauseating lurch, and for one terrifying moment she thought she might be sick. She gripped the window ledge and inhaled deeply.

'It's a bit alarming, isn't it?' said a voice at her side.

Dora opened her eyes and exhaled slowly. To her relief, the wave of nausea seemed to be passing. 'It is a little overwhelming,' she nodded, feeling slightly embarrassed.

'I feel exactly the same every time I think about leaving England,' Clarissa smiled. She was very slender, or what Alice's grandmother might call 'willowy', with long hair as black as a raven's wing and sharp blue eyes. 'In fact, I'm terrified, though I wouldn't dare confess that outside this room. My mother would have me on the first train back to London.'

'Your mother doesn't support your decision to volunteer?' Dora asked.

'She didn't speak to me for two days when I told her I'd volunteered,' Clarissa laughed. She was clearly from a well-to-do background, Dora thought, judging by her well-tailored outfit and her cut-glass accent.

'What about you? Are your folks supportive?' she asked Dora.

'My parents are dead,' Dora replied.

'Oh, I'm so sorry,' Clarissa said, clearly mortified. Before Dora could reassure her, their attention was drawn by the sound of footsteps on the landing. Warrant Officer Thompson appeared in the doorway, followed by a middle-aged nurse with ruddy cheeks and a pleasant smile. By contrast, Thompson looked annoyed, and the two girls who scuttled out from behind him were white-faced and solemn. They filed into the room, barely raising their eyes.

'Punctuality is the order of the day,' Thompson said sternly, addressing the room. 'Tardiness will not be tolerated.' He glared at the two new girls. They looked so alike that Dora was certain they must be sisters. The two girls exchanged sheepish glances.

'Sorry, sir,' they muttered.

Thompson made a noise at the back of his throat. 'This is where we will sort out your identity papers and assign you your uniform. Afterwards, Registered Nurse Anderson here will escort you to the Stores, where you will purchase your camp essentials.' He let his mocking gaze rest on each girl in turn. 'I hope you're all prepared for life under canvas?'

Clarissa and Molly gave a slight moan. Dora shivered inwardly. She'd never slept in a tent before, but no doubt she'd manage. She didn't have a choice. There was no turning back now.

'I'd advise you not to dawdle over your purchases,' he went on. 'You board at three, and woe betide anyone who's late,' he said, his stern gaze coming to rest on the two girls, both of whom had the grace to look shamefaced.

After they'd all been issued with uniforms and identity documents, during which time Dora learned that the two late arrivals were sisters, Gwen and Joyce Bastable, and that Clarissa was also being sent to Cambri, they were ushered downstairs to the canteen for the midday meal. Having eaten hardly any breakfast, Dora realized she was starving and, even though the vegetable stew proved somewhat uninspiring, she was glad of the nourishment, especially as they were unlikely to eat again until much later.

After they'd eaten, Nurse Anderson led the six girls down the street to the Quartermaster's Stores, which were bustling with nurses, VADs and uniformed servicemen.

'I haven't a clue what to buy,' Clarissa confided to Dora as they drifted among shelves piled high with an array of equipment.

'Nor have I,' whispered Dora. She was starting to feel panicky, terrified she'd buy the wrong equipment or worse spend too long deliberating and end up being late boarding. At the moment, the prospect of Warrant Officer Thompson's wrath far outweighed any fear of the enemy.

'Can I help?' a shy-looking young private said, clearly having overheard their conversation. The two girls thanked him and within half an hour they had amassed an impressive array of items large and small, including a sturdy pair of gumboots each, which, the bashful young soldier assured them, would become one of their most cherished possessions.

'How will I get all this to the ship?' she asked anxiously as the quartermaster noted down her purchases. He looked at her over the rim of his glasses.

'They'll go direct,' he told her. 'You won't see them again until you reach your destination. Sign here.' He handed her a slip of paper, and she scribbled her signature. Thanking him, she waited for Clarissa and the two of them made their way to the entrance, where Nurse Anderson and Warrant Officer Thompson were waiting to escort them to the docks.

Gulls wheeled in a cheerless sky. Warships sat low in the dishwater-grey water. It was bitterly cold on the quayside. Dora rubbed her hands together, clenching her teeth in an effort to stop them chattering as she stared out over the white-capped Solent towards the mist-shrouded Isle of Wight.

'I'm glad I wore my thermal underwear,' whispered Clarissa as they waited to embark. 'I've lost all feeling in my toes.'

'Me, too,' Dora replied with a rueful grin. 'Perhaps it's warmer across the Channel.'

'One can only hope,' Clarissa said as they shuffled towards the gangplank.

CHAPTER SIX

'I hope I didn't upset you earlier,' Clarissa said, as they found a quiet corner below deck on the vast troop ship. 'When I asked about your folks? I didn't realize . . .'

'How could you?' Dora replied, swallowing. She'd been dreading the sea crossing in case she was afflicted with sea-sickness. She'd taken a draught that morning which Pearl had given her, and so far, touch wood – her fingers brushed the wooden arm of her chair – her queasiness appeared to be very mild.

'I lost my mother when I was a child. My father passed away two years ago.' She smiled sadly. 'I still miss him.'

'I know how you feel,' Clarissa said, her dark eyes clouding. 'I lost my brother last April. I miss him terribly. There were only sixteen months between us, and we were very close.'

'I'm so sorry.' Dora briefly touched Clarissa's arm.

'That's why I felt so compelled to volunteer,' Clarissa continued, a slight tremor to her voice. 'It gives me a measure of comfort to believe that Frank had someone like us at his side when he passed away. I'd like to offer the same comfort to other bereaved families.'

'Have your mother and father come to terms with your decision?' Dora asked, gazing out the porthole into the inky blackness and feeling grateful for the presence of the mighty warship she knew was cruising nearby.

'They came to see me off at the station,' Clarissa replied drily. 'That's something, at least.'

'I suppose they're worried.'

'I do understand that,' Clarissa acknowledged. 'I know Mother would rather I stayed safely at home knitting socks, but I'm afraid that wouldn't do. I need to feel useful.'

Dora yawned. 'We should be docking soon, shouldn't we?' she said tiredly.

'Another twenty minutes,' one of the young soldiers playing cards at a nearby table informed her.

Dora thanked him. Despite the reassuring presence of their escort ship, she couldn't help feeling she'd feel much better once she was back on dry land.

The port at Boulogne was bustling with disembarking troops and military vehicles. Dora barely had time to regain her land legs before the six girls were whisked away in the darkness to a small hotel tucked down a narrow side street. Tired and ravenously hungry, Dora, Clarissa and the others joined the fifteen or so other VAD nurses gathered in the hotel dining room, where they dined on bowls of hearty sausage casserole before being allocated their rooms.

Relieved to find she was sharing with Clarissa, Dora trudged wearily up the narrow, twisting staircase to the room in which they would spend the remainder of the night.

'My mother's closet at home is bigger than this,' Clarissa said, gazing round the tiny bedroom. There was just enough room to squeeze between the two single beds, and Clarissa had to remember to duck so as not to hit her head on the low beams.

'I'm so tired I could sleep on a park bench,' Dora yawned as she pulled her nightdress over her head. Her trunk was who-knew-where. They'd been told to bring only what they would need for an overnight stay. She slid beneath the covers, thankful that although the bedclothes were a little worn, they smelled clean.

'Well, we're in France,' Clarissa mumbled sleepily. '*Bonne nuit.*'

'Goodnight,' Dora replied, rolling onto her back. Despite her overwhelming exhaustion, sleep eluded her. A small skylight afforded her a view of the starlit sky, and she wondered if Nate was awake and whether he, too, was staring up at the starry sky and thinking of her. Though it was unlikely their paths would cross, it was exhilarating to know she was in the same country as him. With thoughts of Nate swirling, filling her mind, she finally fell asleep, awaking to the strident crowing of the hotel's rooster only a few hours later.

Breakfast was a hurried affair. The hotel's dingy, wood-panelled dining room was filled to capacity with VAD nurses from all over the United Kingdom and all walks of life. Tucking into her meal of bread, cheese and tomatoes, washed down by mugs of strong, bitter coffee, she listened to the ebb and flow of the conversations all around her. She'd met several of them on board the ship and found them a friendly bunch, though any acquaintances made in transit would be fleeting, for the nurses were being sent to hospitals the length and breadth of France and it was unlikely they'd ever meet again.

There was a sharp, loud knock on the open door and a hush fell over the room as all eyes turned to the rather imposing soldier filling the doorway. He carried his hat in his hand and held a cane with which he had knocked. He had thick ginger hair and an auburn moustache styled like the one sported by Field Marshal Lord Kitchener.

'Sergeant Major,' Nurse Anderson said, dabbing her lips with a serviette as she got to her feet.

'Good morning, Sister.' The sergeant major cleared his throat, his startlingly green eyes scanning the tables. 'I'm here to escort your charges to the railway station.'

'Of course,' Nurse Anderson nodded soberly. She gazed round the room at the anxious, pale faces. 'We shall be ready in five minutes.'

The sergeant major nodded again and, turning on his heel, left the room.

'Come along, ladies,' Nurse Anderson said, clapping her hands. 'Let's not keep the sergeant major waiting.'

Conversation started up again slowly as plates were cleared and mugs drained. Chair legs scraped the linoleum floor.

'I've got butterflies,' Dora whispered to Clarissa as she fumbled with her coat buttons.

'So have I,' her new friend admitted with a grin as she adjusted her cap.

Taking a deep breath to steady her nerves, Dora picked up her small overnight bag and joined the throng heading for the door.

The sun had yet to penetrate the narrow, cobbled street. Feathery clouds scudded overhead in a pale blue sky. It was a brisk, ten-minute walk through the picturesque town to the railway station, where they boarded a train heading south.

The train was crammed with khaki-clad soldiers who were only too happy to strike up conversation with the young VADs. Most of them were no older than herself, Dora noted as she listened to their cheerful banter and laughed at their jokes.

At first the journey was fun and exciting, with the girls exclaiming over the unfamiliar landscape rolling past the windows and waving to soldiers along the roadside, all of whom waved their hats and cheered in return. But it soon became tedious, with lengthy delays as troops and VAD nurses disembarked at various stations along the way. During one extended delay on the outskirts of a nondescript town Dora had never heard of, the train was boarded by a group of Red Cross nurses dispensing bread and tea.

The bread was coarse and the tea was weak and unsweetened, but Dora gulped it down gratefully. She hadn't realized how hungry she was, but, on reflection, it had been hours since she last ate. The watery sun was low over the western skyline and she had been travelling since just after nine o'clock that morning.

Darkness fell as the train continued to wend its way slowly through the French countryside. Dora let her head loll against the window, her tired eyes straining to pick out anything in the inky blackness. Only the odd star differentiated the sky from the ground. Now and then she spotted the flash of sporadic gunfire in the distance, and her stomach would roil as the reality of what she was heading into hit home once more.

When at last the train lurched into the small station at Cambri, she was half-asleep. Two small lamps cast an eerie yellow glow over the platform as Dora and Clarissa stumbled from their carriage, blinking at the sudden brightness and shivering in the blast of cold air.

Surrounded by a sea of khaki, Dora and Clarissa gazed about them in bewilderment.

'Where are we supposed to go?' Clarissa whispered, as they watched the dispersing soldiers heading for the trucks parked haphazardly to the side.

'Perhaps we should ask someone?' suggested Dora. She was about to head towards an important-looking man holding a clipboard standing near the exit when a man stepped out in front of her.

'Good evening,' the shadowy figure said in thickly accented English. He moved closer, holding his lantern aloft, and Dora could see he was short in stature with greying brown hair and a straggly beard. His heavy coat was frayed and patched. Several buttons were missing, and it gaped across his stomach. 'This way,' he said, motioning them towards a waiting ambulance car, his breath billowing in the lamplight.

After a brief hesitation, they clambered into the back of the ambulance. The man, who now introduced himself simply as Anton, tugged down the waterproof flap, plunging the girls into total darkness. Clarissa groped for Dora's hand.

'Not quite the reception I was expecting,' Dora whispered.

'Nor I,' Clarissa murmured. 'I shall be sure to leave this bit out when I write home.'

'Hopefully things will improve once we arrive at camp,' Dora said with little conviction. She was cold, tired and hungry. They felt the vehicle rock as the cab door slammed shut. The engine started, the noise rendering further conversation difficult.

It was an uncomfortable journey over rough terrain, with the ambulance bouncing over potholes in the stone-hard ground. A mile or two into their journey, they heard loud shouting and the ambulance came to an abrupt halt. The tarpaulin was thrown back and the ambulance was flooded with torchlight, illuminating the two terrified girls huddled together on the bench.

'Evening, Sisters,' a male voice said. 'Sorry to disturb you.' He dropped the flap, plunging them back into darkness. There was a loud banging on the side of the vehicle, eliciting a yelp of fright from Clarissa, and the engine roared to life.

'I guess that was a checkpoint,' Clarissa said, a noticeable quiver in her voice as the ambulance lurched forwards. As their eyes grew accustomed to the gloom once again, Dora and Clarissa exchanged frightened glances as they both caught the rattle of gunfire in the near distance.

'I wonder how close we are to the battlefield,' Dora said, thinking aloud.

'Too close for comfort, I should say,' remarked Clarissa drily. 'That's another thing I shan't be mentioning to Mother when I write my postcard home.'

It felt like they'd barely got going again when the ambulance came to a halt once more. The engine died, and they heard the cab door creak open and slam shut. The tarpaulin flap was thrown up. Dora and Clarissa braced themselves for the burst of light, but only Anton stood at the opening, holding his small lantern aloft, his weathered face a sickly yellow in the lamplight.

'Come,' he said abruptly.

Her cramped muscles screaming, Dora eased her bruised, tired body out of the ambulance. In the darkness, she could just make out the outline of military vehicles to her right. To her left was a large tent, thin light filtering through its canvas walls.

'This way.' Grabbing their overnight bags, they hurried after Anton, stumbling over the uneven ground towards a small wooden hut, which they later learned was the night-duty room.

They climbed the steps and pushed open the door, blinking in the lamplight as they stepped into the room.

'Evening, Mr Dubois,' said an attractive, blonde-haired woman, turning from the small stove she appeared to be attempting to light. 'Ah, and here are our new recruits. Welcome. Tea will be ready in just a jiffy.' She straightened up, blowing out a match. 'I'm Sister St Claire. I'm the matron here, and this is VAD Nurse Smith.' She nodded at a younger, dark-haired girl sitting on a low chair, cradling an open biscuit tin in her arms.

'Nice to meet you,' Nurse Smith said with a smile. She was a pretty girl with dark eyes and a wide, upturned mouth.

'Likewise, Nurse Smith,' Dora said. 'I'm VAD Nurse Dora Webb.'

'VAD Nurse Clarissa Arspery,' Clarissa smiled. 'Pleased to meet you, Nurse Smith.'

'Emma, please,' Nurse Smith said. 'We don't stand on ceremony in here.' She leaned forward, holding out the biscuit tin. 'Help yourself. You must be starving.'

'Thank you.' Dora took a biscuit and passed the tin to Clarissa.

'Thank you. They do look delicious,' Clarissa said, handing the tin to Anton.

'Mother sends a food parcel every other week,' Emma said. 'These are a particular favourite of yours, aren't they, Mr Dubois?' she smiled as he helped himself to a couple.

'They are indeed, Sister,' Anton agreed heartily. He grinned, showing a set of uneven yellow teeth, and settled himself on one of the upturned crates that passed as furniture. He reached for one of the newspapers littering the low coffee table. It was a week out of date, Dora noticed, sitting down in one of the four easy chairs set about the room. The springs were sagging, and it smelled of mildew. There were two more crates pushed against the slatted wall. As well as the newspapers, the coffee table held a selection of dog-eared magazines. Several well-thumbed paperback books were stacked on the floor in the corner.

'I'm afraid the stove is a little temperamental,' Matron said, spooning tea leaves into an industrial-size teapot. She shivered. 'And I apologize for the draught,' she added, noticing Dora shiver. 'It's rained a lot lately, which has caused the door to swell so it won't shut properly.' She rubbed her hands together, nudging a rolled-up rag along the bottom of the door with her foot. 'Still,' she smiled as the kettle finally began to boil, 'we mustn't grumble.' She poured the tea and handed round the mugs.

'How long have you both been out here?' asked Clarissa, wrapping her chilled hands around her mug.

'I've been here since last spring,' Matron said, stirring sugar into her tea. 'Though I had a week back home in the autumn. Emma has been here since October.' She leaned against the wall, cradling her mug of tea, her expression thoughtful. 'It's hard work and often heart-wrenching. But also very rewarding, at times.' She glanced over at Anton. His head had fallen back against the wall and he was snoring softly. 'Bless him,' she said with an indulgent smile. 'He lives in the village with his wife. He's the base handyman-cum-driver. He can turn his hand to just about anything.'

She turned her attention back to Dora and Clarissa. 'Well, there's no point showing you around the camp tonight, and anyway you must be exhausted. Drink up, and Nurse Smith will show you to your quarters. Try and get a good night's sleep. You'll need it. Tomorrow's going to be a busy day.'

CHAPTER SEVEN

Dora woke with a jolt. In the thin grey light filtering in through the tent canvas, she could just about make out Clarissa's sleeping form in the camp bed six feet away. When Emma had shown them to their tent, she'd been surprised by how roomy it was. It had also looked quite homely; the equipment they'd bought before leaving England having been unpacked and spread about. Their trunks had been placed at the foot of their beds, ready for them to unpack as soon as they had a few moments' leisure time.

She could hear the sounds of a camp coming awake. She reached for the alarm clock on the small table beside her bed and groaned. It was half past four. She'd had barely four hours' sleep. Breakfast was served from five, and her first shift started at half past.

Gritting her teeth, she threw back the blankets and, shivering in the frigid air, slid her feet into her slippers and reached for her gown.

'Clarissa,' she hissed, lighting the stove to heat water for her morning wash. 'Clarissa, wake up.'

Clarissa groaned and stirred. Her raven-black hair fanning the pillow, she opened one eye, peering at Dora through the gloom.

'It's half past four,' Dora told her, splashing water into a bowl. 'Come on. You don't want to be late on your first day.'

'All right,' Clarissa grumbled. 'I'm up.' She swung her legs over the side of the camp bed, yawning. 'I'm glad we thought to buy those extra blankets,' she said. 'It's freezing. So much for spring.' She unzipped her toilet bag and took out her hairbrush.

'Yoohoo!' a voice cried outside the tent fifteen minutes later. 'It's me, Emma. Are you decent?'

'Just about,' Dora called back, adjusting her headdress in front of the mirror. The tent flap was pushed aside and Emma stuck her head in. 'Did you sleep well?'

'Like a log,' Dora admitted. 'I was so tired.'

'Not quite the comfortable bed I'm used to,' Clarissa said ruefully. 'I'm surprised I'm not black and blue this morning.'

Emma laughed. 'Give it a few days and you'll be so exhausted you'd fall asleep on a clothesline. I'm glad to see you're up and ready, though. Matron's a stickler for punctuality and if the sisters report you for tardiness, she'll have your guts for garters.'

'She seemed nice enough last night,' Dora said, sitting on the edge of her bed to fasten her shoes.

'Oh, she is,' Emma agreed. 'But she takes her position very

seriously. Nothing gets by her, and her temper is legendary. I think even the doctors are terrified of her.' She smiled. 'The patients adore her, of course.'

'Is that bacon I can smell?' Clarissa said, going to the entrance of the tent to empty the water bowl.

'It is,' Emma replied. 'We'd better hurry if you want some.'

'I'm ready.' Dora got to her feet. With one final check of her appearance, she took a deep breath to steady her nerves and followed Emma and Clarissa out into the cold, crisp morning.

Dawn was breaking in the distance, the skyline streaked with colour. Dew glistened on the rough ground where the grass had been all but worn away. Military personnel moved among tents. A soldier perched on a low camp stool outside his tent, shaving, a towel draped around his bare shoulders. Dora glanced away quickly.

'You'll get used to it,' laughed Emma as they picked their way across the campground towards the mess tent. Dora gazed across the field. In the growing daylight, she could clearly make out the rows of tents that housed the camp orderlies and other support staff.

The nurses' tents were to the left, slightly closer to the hospital. Military vehicles were clustered at the edge of the camp. The mess tent and the hospital tents were directly ahead of her. To the right stood a row of six wooden chalets.

'That's where the doctors, Matron and the other high-ranking nurses live,' Emma said. 'The bath house is behind them. Over behind the hospital tent are the stores where everything is housed – food, medical supplies, petrol.'

Despite the early hour, the mess tent was filling up quickly. Utensils clattered and voices rose and fell, metal scraping on metal as forks scraped on tin plates.

'You'll soon find your way around,' Emma said, once they'd collected their food and found places at the long refectory table. 'It's not a very big camp. We're mostly a transit station,' she explained. 'Most of the men who pass through here are shipped off back to Blighty. Those whose wounds aren't bad enough to warrant being sent home get sent further south to the hospital there.'

She gave Dora and Clarissa a wry smile. 'It's not a Sunday picnic over here, I can tell you.'

Dora put down her fork. 'I don't expect it to be,' she said soberly. 'I was down at the docks one day when they were carrying wounded soldiers off. I'm under no illusions as to how bad it can be.'

They were distracted by a noisy group of five nurses. A mix of RGNs and VADs, they approached the table where Dora, Clarissa and Emma were sitting. Emma made the introductions as the women seated themselves along the bench. Dora and Clarissa were bombarded with questions about life back home. As Emma explained to Dora later, with everyone homesick and desperate for news, anyone freshly off the boat from England was deemed a vital source of information.

Dora couldn't help but notice a group of three nurses sitting over on the other side of the mess tent, who kept glancing over in a disdainful manner.

'Take no notice of those three,' Emma said, following Dora's gaze. 'Most of the RGNs treat us volunteers like we're one of them. Unfortunately,' she continued, raising her voice slightly to be heard above the clatter of cutlery and conversation, 'you'll always get the odd one or two, like Dawn there, who think they're better than us.'

'By the time you've been here a week,' said a tall, auburn-haired nurse sitting across the table from Dora and peering at her over the rim of her spectacles, 'you'll know as much about nursing as we do. As soon as the next convoy comes in, you'll be thrown in at the deep end and then it's sink or swim, love.' She grinned. 'I'm Justine, by the way.' She extended a pale, freckled hand.

'Dora.' They shook hands briefly.

'I'm afraid you've got Sister Ripley on duty this morning,' Justine said, pulling a face. 'Try not to get on the wrong side of her. She can be a bit of an ogre.'

'Thanks for the warning,' Dora said weakly as she and Clarissa shared a wry smile.

'You'll be fine,' Emma assured them breezily, glancing up at the clock over the serving counter. 'Come on,' she said, draining her mug. 'It's time to report for duty. Have a good day, girls. See you all later.'

Amidst a flurry of goodbyes and a few whistles from the handful of men gathered at another table, Dora followed Emma and Clarissa out into the dazzling sunshine. Despite its brightness, it held no warmth and she shivered as they hurried across the uneven ground to the vast hospital tent.

The green canvas tent, of considerable size, was divided up into various wards, with two theatres. The central part of the tent, the flaps pulled back and tied to poles, formed a reception area where a nurse sat hunched over a metal table, reading through some paperwork. She replied to their cheery 'Good morning' in a distracted manner, affording them only a cursory glance as they passed by. Though she couldn't yet see into the wards, Dora could clearly hear the groans and whimpers of men in pain, causing goosebumps to rise on her skin as she breathed in the stringent smell of disinfectant, mingled with the underlying odour of urine, vomit and the fresh sawdust that covered the wooden boards.

'Ah, Nurse.' A tall, angular nurse with a weathered face, iron-grey hair and piercing blue eyes emerged from one of the wards. 'I need you to see to the patient in bed eight. His bedsheets want changing.'

'Of course, Sister. Oh, Sister,' Emma said quickly as the nurse started to turn away. 'These are the new VADs.'

Sister Ripley paused and turned back. 'Welcome,' she said brusquely. 'I'm Sister Ripley. Come with me. You can both make a start in the sluice room.'

Shooting Emma a quick glance, to which she replied with a brief shrug, Dora and Clarissa scurried after the sister.

The wooden hut that served as the sluice room was situated behind the main tent. The smell hit Dora the moment she stepped foot in the door, a stomach-churning cocktail of human waste and blood.

'Oh, thank goodness,' said the thin, pale-faced nurse bent

over the sink, elbow deep in soapy water. 'I thought I was going to have to tackle this all by myself.' She nodded at the pile of bed pans and bowls littering the tables. 'Grab a scrubbing brush.'

Before Dora could roll up her sleeves, she heard a retching sound and turned in time to see Clarissa's breakfast make a sudden, unwelcome reappearance all over the concrete floor. It splashed the hem of Sister Ripley's skirts, and she glared at Clarissa in disgust.

'You'll have to toughen up a bit, Nurse,' she said disparagingly. 'You'll see and smell much worse than this before you're done.' She looked down at the regurgitated porridge pooling across the floor. 'Get this cleaned up,' she said, shaking her head as she strode from the room.

'I'm so sorry,' Clarissa whimpered, wiping her mouth with her handkerchief.

'Don't be,' the other nurse said with a grin, wiping her hands on a threadbare towel. 'I threw up daily for the first week or two. I'm Millie Brown, by the way.'

'Dora Webb.'

'Clarissa Arspery,' Clarissa said, leaning against the table, looking whey-faced.

'Here, I'll clear that up for you,' Millie offered. 'You sit down for a minute. Settle your stomach. Sister Ripley does it on purpose, bringing new girls in here. I think she enjoys seeing whose sensibilities will let them down,' she said, filling a metal bucket with hot, soapy water. 'You're all right, though?' she asked Dora.

'I cared for my bedridden father for several years,' Dora replied, reaching for the nearest bedpan. 'I got used to the smell.' Saying that, she thought, glancing down at the thick soup of blood-flecked phlegm congealing in the kidney-shaped dish, the sight did set her stomach roiling. Breathing in through her mouth, she tipped it down the sluice drain, trying not to watch the slimy mass slithering towards the plughole.

'I'm sorry,' Clarissa apologized again, donning an apron. 'I shall not be so feeble again. It was just the smell. It caught me off guard.'

'Believe me,' Millie said, slopping soapy water over the floor as she mopped up the mess, 'you'll have a cast-iron stomach in no time.'

They were interrupted by the shrill ringing of a bell.

'The convoy's arrived,' Millie said soberly. 'Come on,' she went on, laying the mop aside. 'It's all hands on deck now.'

Dora dried her hands and followed Millie out the door. She barely noticed the cold, such was the adrenalin surging through her veins as she hurried across the patch of dirt that separated the sluice room from the hospital tent, the sound of engines loud on the cold, crisp air.

The front of the hospital tent was a hive of activity as lorry after lorry rolled into camp. The reception area was crammed with wounded men. Those who could walk were dispatched one way, the more seriously wounded laid on the ground on their stretchers while the severity of their wounds was determined.

Dora was kept busy stripping men of their tattered,

bloodstained uniforms and washing them down. The screams of the badly wounded men reverberated throughout the hospital. Several times she caught sight of Clarissa, pale-faced and looking as though she might faint at any moment, but Dora was too busy to afford her friend more than a passing pitying thought.

All day, the acrid smell of woodsmoke hung on the cold air as vermin-ridden uniforms were burned, and Dora spent most of the afternoon scrubbing the floors with carbolic soap.

By the time she paused for a cup of tea late in the afternoon, she was weak with exhaustion. She leaned against one of the tent poles, gripping her mug with shaking hands. Several hollow-eyed young soldiers sat huddled nearby smoking. One had his hand bandaged, the other seemed to have something wrong with his foot. A pair of wooden crutches were propped up beside him. They would be back with their unit as soon as they were well enough.

Late that evening, Dora found herself drafted in to help load a convoy of soldiers bound for the train station. These were the 'Blighty cases'. On the whole, they were a jolly bunch, the thought of spending time on home soil overriding the pain of their injuries.

'I hope they send me to Dorchester,' one young man said as Dora tucked his blanket more firmly under his chin. Half his face was hidden by bandages, yet his smile was infectious. 'Then my mum and sweetheart can come and see me.'

'I'm sure they'll do their best,' Dora assured him. She gave his hand a squeeze as he was loaded into the lorry.

'I hope he makes it,' Emma said, standing behind her as the flaps were dropped. She sighed. 'They're all so very young.'

Dora nodded. Words escaped her. Seeing the wounded soldiers up close had brought the horrors of the trenches to the foreground of her mind. To think that her Nate, barely eighteen years old, could be in some field hospital like this somewhere filled her with terror, and she had to swallow hard in order to keep the tears at bay.

'Come on,' Emma said with a weary sigh, 'we're not finished yet.'

They made their way back into the tent. Lamps flickered and the men were quiet. Only the occasional wracking cough or whimper broke the stillness.

Sister Ripley was standing over a bed. At the sight of the two nurses, she came over, her expression sombre.

'The young lad in bed four won't last the night,' she said quietly. 'Will you sit with him, Nurse?' She looked at Dora.

'Yes, of course,' Dora replied. 'What are the cards for?' she asked, noticing that some of the bedsteads had red tags attached. Sister Ripley took her arm and pulled her just beyond the tent flap.

'Those are the poor lads who aren't going to make it,' she said. She bent her head close to Dora's ear and lowered her voice. 'They're too ill to be sent home. The best we can do is make them comfortable and be here for them.'

'Oh, that's so sad,' Dora whispered, her eyes sparkling with tears.

'This is no time to get all sentimental,' Sister Ripley

snapped sharply. 'Be cheerful when you deal with these boys. No tears or silliness. They don't want that. Most of them will suss the situation out soon enough. Your job is to tell them how well they're doing, even when they're not,' she added, with a pointed look. 'Bed six is free,' she said, turning away to deal with another patient being stretchered in.

Breathless with nerves, Dora hurried between the two rows of beds to where the young man lay in bed four. His eyes were bandaged and his breathing came in ragged gasps. His hands lay on top of the bedclothes, his fingers twitching convulsively. Dora pulled up a nearby stool and sat down, reaching for the man's hand. At her touch, he turned his head slightly, his dry, chapped lips moving silently. With her free hand, Dora picked up his chart. The details had been written in a hasty scrawl, and she had some difficulty deciphering the words, but she discovered that his name was Giles Lake and he was just nineteen years old. He was suffering from severe internal bleeding caused by shrapnel. He had also inhaled mustard gas.

'Nurse?' he rasped, his head moving jerkily from side to side. 'Nurse?'

'I'm here.' Dora gently squeezed his fingers. 'Try and get some sleep,' she said softly, her heart breaking for him. She could smell the decay wafting up from beneath the bedcovers as his body began to shut down. For the rest of the night, she sat with him, soothing him as spasms contorted his limbs and cradling his head when he vomited up globlets of thick black blood. Several times, he cried out for his mother and Dora laid her hand on his forehead, speaking to him in soothing tones until he quietly slipped away.

She called for Sister Ripley and stepped slowly away from the bed while the orderlies came to take him away.

She felt a firm hand on her shoulder. 'You did well,' Sister Ripley said, her eyes kind. 'Letting him think you were his mother, that was a kind thing to do.' She smiled tiredly. 'The worst is over for the time being. Not every day is like this, thank God. Go and get some breakfast and catch up on a few hours' sleep.'

'Thank you, Sister.' Numb with exhaustion, Dora stumbled out of the hospital to find the outside world a foot deep in fresh snow.

'Beautiful, isn't it?' Clarissa said, coming up behind her. Her apron was smeared crimson, and she sported dark shadows around her eyes. They stood for a moment in the stillness.

'My patient died,' Dora said, the enormity of the past few hours hitting her in the chest like a cannon ball. Clarissa draped her arm around Dora's shoulders.

'Mine, too,' she said softly. 'I've just been sorting out his effects ready to send home to his mother.' She glanced away, tears glistening on her cheeks.

'Oh, Clarissa,' Dora breathed. 'It must remind you so much of your brother, Frank.'

Clarissa shook her head, waving away Dora's sympathy. 'I'll be all right. I just need a minute.'

Dora nodded. She could hardly keep her eyes open. 'I'll see you at breakfast. I'll save you some bacon.'

'Make sure you two get a good rest,' Emma said, her breath billowing in the crisp, cold air as she ploughed her way through the snow towards Dora and Clarissa. 'There are bedpans that still need tackling later.'

'What?' Dora and Clarissa cried, looking at each other in dismay. Emma laughed.

'Come on,' she said, tucking her hand through Dora's arm. 'You both deserve a good breakfast and a long sleep first. You can worry about the bedpans later.'

CHAPTER EIGHT

'It's not the same without Dora, is it?' said Alice, reaching for the dainty rose-patterned milk jug.

'It certainly isn't,' Leah agreed as Alice poured milk into their teacups. They were sitting in the Amble Inn tearoom around the corner from Franklin's. Mr Butterworth's successor, Mr Arnold, had closed the factory early as a mark of respect for one of the clerks, Pete Brickell, who had died in the Mesopotamia campaign. Having lied about his age when he enlisted the previous year, he had been only seventeen, and Leah remembered him as a fresh-faced, cheerful lad who'd always had time for a joke and a laugh with the girls on the factory floor.

'She seems to have settled into her new life fairly well,' Alice remarked, setting down the teapot and leaning back in her chair. It was a fine Saturday afternoon in early May, and the tearoom was bustling. There were several servicemen seated at various tables.

'I received a letter from her only yesterday,' Leah said,

sipping her tea. 'She makes light of her experiences, but, reading between the lines, I'm sure it's pretty grim.'

'It must be.' Alice grimaced. 'You only need to see the poor chaps coming off the boats to realize how dire things must be over there. And Dor's on the front line.'

'It sounds like she's made some good friends, though. I'm pleased about that. It would be even more difficult otherwise.'

'How is Daisy, by the way?' Alice asked, adding a drop more milk to her tea and stirring it absently. 'I debated coming over to see her on Thursday when she came home, but I thought it best to let her settle in first. It'll be a big adjustment for her after almost ten weeks in hospital.'

Leah set her cup down with a weary sigh. 'She's coming along all right, I suppose. Her eyesight is still giving her trouble, but she's getting more movement in her fingers. The doctor's confident she will get complete use back eventually, though he can't say how long it may take.'

'So frustrating for her,' Alice commiserated.

'She's finding it really difficult. You know how Daisy likes to be busy. Not being able to read for very long or do very much is really making her miserable.'

'I must look out some more books for her,' Alice said, pursing her lips. 'I've been negligent. I'm sorry. I'm sure my stepfather has lots of books Daisy hasn't read. I'll be sure to remember to have a look on my visit this Sunday.'

'How are your family?' Leah asked, her gaze shifting to the window, where a shaft of sunlight streamed in between the red and white gingham curtains. A young woman stood on the pavement, her back to the window, a basket on her arm filled with white feathers, and Leah felt a twinge of sympathy for Alice's stepfather, James. He'd tried to enlist the previous year, but his medical had picked up a faint heart murmur, which precluded him from any active service. For the moment, he remained as headmaster at his little school in Hedge End. His two male teachers had enlisted shortly after war was declared, and several of the school's past pupils had already given their lives in the trenches.

James had recently turned forty-one, yet he looked years younger and was often a target for the young women and their feathers. James was a proud man, and Leah knew how Alice grieved to see him so shamed by such blatant accusations of cowardice.

'They are well, thank you,' Alice replied. She dabbed her lips with her napkin. 'Mother is doing so well making uniforms for the army that she's taken on another two girls.' She grinned. 'Father's complaining because they've outgrown the workroom and so they've taken over the dining room and the parlour as well. Poor Father has to make do with his study.'

'How is your father?' Leah asked, her eyes narrowing sympathetically. 'I remember when Leonard Merrifield got handed a feather last year. He hadn't even had his seventeenth birthday, bless him. He felt so humiliated that he threatened to march down to the recruitment office and enlist immediately. Thankfully his mother managed to stop him.'

'I remember you saying,' Alice said. 'Wasn't it a girl he used to go to school with?'

74

'Yes, which made it all the worse, of course,' Leah said.

'Of course,' agreed Alice. 'Well, Father has taken a post with the Red Cross. That should prevent him being targeted by the likes of her.' Alice flicked her gaze towards the young woman, who was pressing a white feather into the hand of a young lad. Tall and gangly, with acne-red cheeks, the boy looked close to tears.

'They can be so cruel,' Alice said, pursing her lips, and she shook her head. 'The poor boy's probably not old enough to enlist, otherwise he'd have been conscripted by now.' Her expression brightened. 'Oh, I haven't seen you since we heard, but Martha has been awarded her scholarship. She'll start at the grammar school in September.'

'Well done her,' Leah said, genuinely pleased for her friend's younger sister. 'Is she still determined to become a doctor?'

'Even more so, and Father is encouraging her.'

'Good for her. She's a clever girl,' Leah said as they got up to leave. They paid the bill and walked out into the warm May sunshine. The pavements were teeming with soldiers and civilians alike, but suddenly a hush fell upon the street as the rhythmic sound of marching feet filled the air. Wagons and carts drew up against the kerb, the horses whinnying softly as little children were snatched up into their mother's arms.

A small company of soldiers rounded the corner, the thud of their heavy boots stirring the dust on the street. In their wake came a large column of German prisoners, some of whom smiled cheerfully, even going so far as to wave to the jeering onlookers, but most looked down at their feet. The cavalry brought up the rear, their horses tossing their proud heads as they pranced down the street.

While Leah added her jeers to those of the crowd gathered on the pavement, Alice watched the procession in sombre silence. Her recent letter from Samuel had set her nerves on edge. A lot of what he said hadn't made sense, and she was worried that the horrors of the trenches might be affecting his mind. He was such a sweet, kind soul. He didn't write much about what he was experiencing, wanting to protect her from the harsh realities of life, as always, and, of course, the censors would only black it out anyway, but she knew it must be nothing short of hell on earth and she worried for him. It terrified her that Samuel might be irreparably damaged and she prayed every day for the war to end, though realistically it didn't seem as though her prayers would be answered any time soon.

'Oh, look, there's Tilly,' Leah said, cutting short Alice's train of thought. Alice followed Leah's gaze. Sure enough, Tilly Mullens was standing across the street, clutching a brightly coloured shawl tightly around her throat.

'She doesn't look well,' Alice whispered, taking in the hollow cheeks and the dark shadows beneath her eyes. 'I haven't been round to check on her for a week or two because I heard she'd found work in a munitions factory. Now Declan's taken the kiddies over to Ireland to live with his mother, Tilly's welfare isn't a priority anymore.' She raised her hand in a wave. For a second their eyes met and then, with a brief wave, Tilly turned away, slinking off into the dispersing crowd.

Alice linked arms with Leah. 'Have we time to pop into Cartwright's before we head for home?' she asked. 'Only I want to see if they have any pork chops for Grandfather's supper. They didn't have any at the butchers in Hedge End.'

'Of course,' Leah agreed. 'I have no plans for the evening except to write to Harry.'

'I must write to Samuel this evening, too.'

'I had planned that Harry would receive a letter from me every other day,' Leah said as they picked their way across the road, mindful of the heavy military and horse-drawn traffic. 'But he says he goes days without receiving anything and then four will arrive at once.'

'Samuel says the same,' smiled Alice. 'I date the envelopes now so he knows which one to open first. Of course, it's better when they're at their billets. It's going to be more difficult to receive post when they're in the trenches. It must be chaotic, to say the least.'

'You're home early,' Hannah said, looking up from her knitting as Leah came in the front door, bringing with her the scent of jasmine wafting in on the warm evening breeze.

'We got let out early. One of our chaps was killed last week.'

'Poor lad,' Hannah sighed, adding, as Leah's gaze went

immediately to the mantelpiece, 'No letters came today. Try not to fret. You're bound to get one tomorrow.'

Leah nodded, closing the door behind her. 'Where's Daisy?'

'Upstairs,' her mother replied, laying down her needles. 'Her head's bad today, so she's lying down for a bit.'

Leah crossed the room and laid her hand on her mother's broad shoulder. Hannah was always so resolute in her belief that Daisy would get better, but Leah had often woken at night to the sound of muffled sobbing coming from her mother's room. Hannah's careworn hand gripped Leah's.

'I'm feeling a bit out of sorts myself,' Hannah said, smiling up at her daughter, her eyes tired. 'Would you mind finishing off the potatoes?'

'Not at all, Mum,' Leah said. 'You rest. You're run off your feet.'

'Thank you, love. You're ever so kind.' Hannah sighed and picked up her needles. 'I want to finish these socks tonight so Alice can take them tomorrow.' She sat up straighter. 'Have you heard? George Merrifield is in Netley Hospital. Florence went to see him this afternoon. Both his knees are shattered.'

'Poor George,' Leah said, pausing on her way to the kitchen. 'Though it's good news in a way. At least he'll be out of the war now.'

'That's some comfort,' Hannah agreed dubiously. 'It'll be a long convalescence, though. Perhaps months before he's able to walk again.'

Leah checked the potatoes boiling on the stove, testing them with a knife. Finding them soft, she lifted them off the heat and drained them over the sink, clouds of thick steam rising into the air. The back door was open, and she could hear the chickens scratching contentedly in the dirt. They were all good layers, which was something to be grateful for now that food shortages were beginning to bite. While she mashed the potatoes with a wooden spoon, she gazed out across the garden and to the fields beyond, chewing her bottom lip thoughtfully. Harry was in the same regiment as George Merrifield, as were Reverend Roberts and Nate. She fervently hoped they were all right. Surely they would have heard something by now? The thought struck her suddenly that, should anything happen to Harry, it would be his parents, Isaac and Frances Whitworth, who would be informed, and not her. The realization struck an arrow into her heart. What if Harry had been wounded or, God forbid, killed? Would Mr Whitworth bother to let her know? She swallowed hard, the potatoes forgotten as tears spilled down her cheeks. She let out a sob.

'Leah?' The clickety clack of her mother's needles fell silent, and she heard the creak of the armchair as her mother got to her feet. Hannah appeared in the doorway, her brow furrowed. 'Leah, love, what is it?'

'What if Harry's hurt and no one's told me?' she said, crumpling into her mother's waiting arms.

'Oh, sweetheart,' Hannah soothed, rubbing Leah's back. Leah was taller than her and she stood awkwardly, her face burrowed in Hannah's shoulder. 'If anything had happened to Isaac's son, the whole of Strawbridge would know about it.'

'I suppose so,' Leah sniffed. She stepped back, ferreting in her pocket for a handkerchief, and blew her nose. 'I just worry so much, you know? I saw the telegram boy knocking at a house in Millbank Street and I can't help thinking about what happened with Pearl. What if Harry's death was what she saw?'

'Oh, Leah,' Hannah said gently. 'Pearl can't see into the future any more than the rest of us.'

'But she was right about the war. She said something black and evil was coming and she was right.'

Hannah shook her head. 'A coincidence, that's all. Now, see here,' she said, reaching for some red-edged cards propped up against the metal tea caddy. 'Some kiddies came round selling these this morning. St John's are holding a benefit concert at the end of the month. An evening out will cheer us up, and hopefully Daisy will feel up to it by then. Mrs Turner bought tickets for all her lot, too.'

The thought of the benefit concert did little to lift Leah's mood, but she forced a smile, knowing her mother was doing her best to raise her spirits.

'That sounds good,' she said, managing a faint smile as she turned her attention back to the potatoes. 'I'll just make the gravy and then I'll go up and see if Daisy's awake.'

'Thank you, love.' Hannah patted Leah's arm. 'I hope she starts improving soon,' she said in a rare moment of doubt. 'I don't know what we'll do otherwise.'

'Oh, Mum,' Leah said, 'she will get well again. She will.'

'Of course she will,' Hannah affirmed stoutly, giving

herself a little shake. 'Take no notice of me, love. I'm tired, that's all.'

'Why don't you take Mrs Turner up on her offer to sit with Daisy while you have a break?' Leah suggested, stirring the meat juices in a saucepan to make gravy. The fishy smell of the trout baking in the oven filled the kitchen. Since Isaac Whitworth had made good on his promise to stock the pond with trout, the fish had become the staple diet of the Strawbridge residents. Young Simon Culley next door and his mates seemed to have taken on the job of catching the fish every morning before school. They had become a familiar sight in the lane, dragging their wooden soap box on wheels piled high with trout, silver scales glistening in the morning sunlight.

'They're showing a new film at the Palladium,' Leah said, thinking it might be nice for them both to enjoy a bit of escapism for a while. 'Why don't we go, you and I? We could go on Saturday evening. You could meet me in town after work, and we could have a fish supper. Make an evening of it?'

Hannah smiled. 'I'll think about it,' she said.

'Do,' said Leah. 'I think it'll do us both good.' She lifted the gravy off the stove and wiped her hands on a tea towel, her gaze alighting on the tickets for the benefit concert. 'In Aid of Our Brave Boys at the Front' was emblazoned across them. She sighed, her thoughts turning, once again, to Harry.

CHAPTER NINE

Harry rested his head against the old stone wall, gazing out across the rippling meadow grass. From this vantage point, watching the grass shimmering in the sunlight as it undulated in the fragrant breeze, he could almost pretend the war was a figment of his warped imagination. Then the distant sound of exploding shells and sporadic gunfire would disabuse his tired mind of the illusion. He yawned. He hadn't had a decent night's sleep in months. In the trenches, it was impossible to snatch more than an hour at a time. Even now that his unit had been moved down the line, he found that, despite his exhaustion, sleep continued to evade him.

They were billeted in a derelict farmhouse about five miles from the front. At night, lying on his chicken-wire bed listening to the rats scurrying along the rafters, he would think longingly of his comfortable feather bed in his room at the Glyn Arms pub back in Strawbridge. And he would toss and turn, his dreams a fevered kaleidoscope of battle-scarred landscapes, mutilated soldiers, his beloved Leah. Even his parents featured, though he'd heard nothing from them since arriving in France a year earlier. He'd sent them the obligatory postcard, but they'd never replied. Christmas had passed without a word. Now, with his twenty-first birthday just weeks away, he doubted they would make contact. As long as his heart was set on marrying Leah, he was as good as dead to his parents. The thought brought a wry smile to his face. With men being mown down left, right and centre all around him, the irony was not lost on him.

He shook his head, clearing his mind. From inside the old farmhouse came the sound of whistling, and he grinned. *Good old Nate*, he thought, as his friend emerged into the bright sunshine. Always cheerful. Nothing seemed to get him down.

'There's still some coffee in the pot if you want some,' Nate said as he joined Harry on the old stone bench. Harry shook his head.

'I'm all right, thanks,' he said. He withdrew a packet of cigarettes from his breast pocket. 'Smoke?' He shook out two and handed one to Nate. Harry struck a match and lit the cigarettes, inhaling deeply. Neither of them had smoked before enlisting, but they found their newly acquired habit went some way to alleviating the boredom and calming the nerves.

'I'm worried about Samuel,' Nate said, exhaling a cloud of smoke, his gaze straying across the dancing meadow grass to where Reverend Samuel Roberts was leaning against what remained of a paddock fence, gazing out into the distance. 'He's been struggling ever since we got here, but seeing those two chaps from Hedge End getting their heads blown off right in front of him has really affected him badly.'

'You don't think he'll desert, do you?' Harry frowned.

'I bloody well hope not,' Nate scowled. 'He'd be done for.'

'I don't think he expected it to be like this,' Harry said, flicking ash onto the ground.

'Did any of us?' replied Nate with a harsh laugh. 'We were green as cabbages back then.' Beside him, Harry blushed at the memory of how he'd embarrassed himself on his first day on the front line. At the sight of the bodies scattered across the ground, their faces black and bloated by the sun, he'd thrown up his breakfast.

'I'm not sure how your Dora copes with it all,' he said now, taking a long draw on his cigarette. 'She's one brave girl, I can tell you.'

'She's a diamond,' Nate agreed, smiling as he pulled a photograph from his breast pocket. It depicted him and Dora standing before a painted background of a flowering horse chestnut tree and had been taken while he was on his embarkation leave, just days before he set sail for France. Harry had a similar photo, as did Samuel. The three couples had made a day of it, having dinner at a hotel in Above Bar after visiting the photographer's studio.

'I'm hoping to see her when I next get leave. It shouldn't take me more than a day's walking.'

'She'll be made up,' Harry said, his gaze still on Samuel.

'You're lucky your girl's over here. It's unlikely I'll get enough leave to make it back to England to see Leah.'

'Oh, I don't know.' Nate pulled a face as he sipped his coffee. 'Once we've finished bombarding Jerry to Kingdom Come, we're bound to get some time off. You should put in a request to take it over your birthday. You and Leah could be married by special licence.'

'I have been thinking about that,' Harry admitted, with a grin. 'If what they're saying is true and they expect the next phase to be a walkover, I could be on my way back to England within weeks.'

'Hey,' said a voice, as a well-built soldier with a ruddy complexion and sandy-yellow hair emerged from the latrine. 'You guys heading for the pub this evening?' he asked, adjusting his trousers. 'It's our last night of freedom.'

'Definitely,' Harry nodded, shielding his eyes against the sun's glare as he gazed up at the big South African. There was a large contingent of South African regiments stationed around Delville Woods, and Harry and Nate had fought alongside them on many occasions. Several of their units were billeted on the same farm, and Ian Foster, among others, had become a firm friend.

'Right, lads!' came the shout from within the farmhouse. 'Let's get to it. Line up.' This was followed by the sound of groaning.

'Duty calls,' Nate said, draining his mug. He extinguished his cigarette and got to his feet. 'We'll see you later, Ian.'

'Yep, see you later, chaps. Have a good one.'

Ian sauntered off, leaving Harry and Nate to join their unit lining up for roll call, which would be followed by a couple of hours of vigorous training before being assigned their duties for the day.

Ian made his way around the back of the farmhouse to his tent. Lifting the flap, he was relieved to find his roommate absent. Hanging his hat on the back of a chair, he took off his boots and stretched out on the camp bed, folding his hands behind his head. His unit had been given a few hours' down time, and he was relishing not having to do anything at all except catch up on some much-needed sleep. Something rustled in his breast pocket, and he cursed. Tugging out the folded, unopened envelope, he tossed it onto the small camping table next to his bed. Another letter from the solicitors. He really must write to his former landlady and ask her not to forward any more letters to him. He had no interest in getting in touch with the mother who had abandoned him when he was just a child.

Even now, so many years later, he still remembered the pain he'd felt when his father had told him his mother had gone and was never coming back. He remembered going away with his father. They'd travelled to Durban, where he'd been raised by a succession of nannies until he was old enough to be sent away to school. His father had eventually remarried. He'd thought Annalise was the most beautiful woman he'd ever seen, yet it soon became clear that she found the young Ian nothing more than a nuisance to be tolerated. Holidays at home were miserable, especially once his stepsisters arrived, one every two years for the next six years, and Ian had started spending holidays at the homes of his friends.

All during his high school years, his bitterness and anger towards his mother had festered, at times spilling over into bouts of violence that had seen him expelled from two of South Africa's most prestigious schools.

Finally, after his father's death, upon discovering that Howard's will left everything to Annalise and her daughters, Ian had boarded a ship bound for Southampton. He'd travelled around the south of England before finally settling in a little village in Wiltshire, where he'd been taken on by a wheelwright.

He'd been happy in Mere and had even considered finding a wife and making it his home, but then war broke out and he'd enlisted. He must have missed the first letter by days. It had followed him to his training camp in Hampshire. He'd read it with growing disbelief. His mother wanted to make contact. All his old resentment and anger had come rushing back. He'd gone out and got drunk that night and had picked a fight. He'd come off second best, and his rabble-rousing had earned him a spell in the barracks prison. After that, he'd resolved to have nothing to do with his mother.

He rolled onto his side and closed his eyes. A fly buzzed around his face, and he let out a long sigh. From the make-shift parade ground, he could hear the drill sergeant barking orders and the dull thud of marching boots.

He liked Harry and Nate. They were good chaps. The rest

of their unit were good chaps, too. The Strawbridge Pals. He smiled. He'd even grown to like the chaplain. Though he had no time for all that God stuff, he could see why Roberts's calming influence would help the lads, especially the newbies. Though lately the poor chap didn't seem to be faring too well himself. Ian pictured the way Reverend Roberts's hands shook continually. He was obviously suffering with his nerves. The Strawbridge lads were headed back down the line the following day, and he doubted the Reverend was going to be able to stand much more. Poor chap. From where Ian was standing, the poor bugger's future wasn't looking too bright.

Samuel gripped the top bar of the gate in an effort to stop the shaking, his knuckles turning white. Behind him, he could hear the rhythmic tread of marching feet. He'd been suffering a bad stomach the last few days, so he'd been excused training. He'd started a letter to Alice that morning but had given up, unable to put his tortured thoughts to paper and knowing that whatever he wanted to say would be blotted out by the censors.

Anyway, how could Alice ever understand? How could he admit to his wife that he cried like a baby every night? That he woke in the night screaming, his dreams filled with the ghosts of the dead and dying. He knew that if it weren't for Harry, Nate and Sidney Merrifield, he'd most likely have been up in front of a firing squad before now. But it wasn't that he was a coward. The day Percy Merrifield had been killed, Samuel had been one of the first out of the trench during a lull in the fighting. He'd run across no-man's-land with no thought for his own safety. Without waiting for the stretcher bearers, he'd hoisted the young lad onto his shoulder and, staggering under the dead weight, started making his way back to the trench. Percy's younger brother, Seth, had met him halfway. He'd taken a moment to look into his brother's sightless blue eyes before rushing towards the German line. Miraculously, he'd made it almost all the way across before being forced to dive into a shell hole. He'd been killed himself just three days later.

Samuel knew he wasn't a coward. But being a constant witness to such relentless inhumanity was slowly destroying his soul. At times, huddled on upturned crate, ankle-deep in slimy mud, the stench of death and decay clogging his nostrils, he found himself doubting the very existence of the God he'd served faithfully for so long.

He'd heard the Germans singing hymns on Sundays, their voices drifting harmoniously across the great swathe of no-man's-land, and he'd found himself wondering, bitterly, whose side God was on.

Now, as he shifted his gaze, he could, despite the brightness of the sun causing his eyes to water, just about make out the woods. After months of shelling, all that remained of the towering trees were blackened, jagged stumps. The area in the foreground was scorched and pockmarked with craters. Wisps of smoke coloured the horizon, and the sound of gunshots was clearly audible. Samuel's insides churned. He could feel his bowels protesting. The camp medic had put his stomach disorder down to mild food poisoning, but Samuel knew it was nothing more than a bad case of nerves. He was dreading going back to the trenches. He knew, too, that Harry and Nate were worried about him. They thought he'd do something stupid, but if he did, he wouldn't be responsible for his actions. And that was the most frightening thing of all. He'd started having blackouts. He'd suddenly find himself huddled against the side of the trench, blubbering like a baby. So far, by chance or divine intervention, Captain Ingram hadn't noticed, but Samuel knew he had to be on borrowed time. His heart sat like a lead weight in his chest. How would his beloved Alice cope should he be shot as a coward? Another shell exploded in the distance, orange flashes visible against the skyline, making Samuel grit his teeth. He held his hands in front of his face. There was a noticeable tremor. He sighed deeply, then gritted his teeth firmly again as he made the determined decision to conquer whatever it was that was causing him to behave in such a manner.

CHAPTER TEN

'Hurry up, you two.' Emma poked her head through the tent flap.

'Just coming,' Dora said, hurriedly running a brush through her hair and pinning it up. She set her cap firmly on her head, securing it with the remaining hairpins. Smiling at her reflection, she turned to face her friend. 'I want to look my best for Nate,' she said, her cheeks colouring with excitement.

'You look lovely,' Emma assured her. 'Doesn't she, Clarissa?'

'You look ravishing,' Clarissa replied.

'Don't be silly,' she laughed. 'Are you sure you won't come with us?'

Clarissa shook her head. 'I'm quite sure, thank you. I have some correspondence to catch up on.'

'We'll bring you back a slice of Madame Chevalier's cake,' Dora promised as she ducked out of the tent.

'See that you do,' Clarissa called after her.

'Come on,' Emma said, grabbing Dora's hand. 'Anton is waiting for us.'

'It's kind of him to drive us,' Dora said, as they hurried over the rough ground. She supposed that, in years gone by, the churned-up field would have been awash with wild flowers, but it now boasted nothing more than the occasional tuft of yellowed grass sprouting among the ruts.

Anton was sitting in his battered old truck, the engine idling noisily. Dora called a cheery hello as she clambered up to sit beside him. Emma followed, banging the door shut. Anton ground the gears and pressed the accelerator. As the truck lurched over the uneven ground, Dora leaned back in her seat and inhaled deeply, relishing filling her lungs with air that didn't reek of blood or decay.

The last ambulance laden with Blighty cases had left for the station over half an hour before and a recent lull in the fighting had brought a measure of calm. The only patients left were those deemed too ill to risk the journey home. The less seriously injured had been transported to the hospital at Albert.

'Bad week, huh?' Anton said.

'Yes,' Dora replied, her shoulders sagging as she thought of the young men left behind in the field hospital.

'Poor Grantly won't make another sunrise,' Emma said quietly.

Anton nodded. He knew this aspect of the job was the part that hit the girls the hardest. There were those who were so badly injured that they died upon arrival at the field hospital or soon thereafter. But it was the ones that lingered who really got under Dora's skin, she mused as the truck bounced along the road. The ones she built up a rapport with. She spent time talking to them, writing letters for them, learning about their families and sweethearts back home. Then they would be gone, and it was her job to pack up their meagre belongings to be returned to their loved ones. It was a heart-breaking task that she knew she would never grow immune to, no matter how long she did it.

In the three and a half months she'd been in France, she'd grown accustomed to every aspect of hospital life and was as skilled as any of the RGNs. Despite the sadness, she thrived on the hard work. She found she could even cope with the exhaustion and had settled quickly into the hospital routine.

The sisters ruled the wards with rods of iron. No order was ever questioned, and the doctors were treated as gods by patients and staff alike. There was one doctor in particular with whom all the nurses wanted to work. Dr Simon Walmsley was exceedingly handsome, with a shock of dark hair, olive skin and chocolate-brown eyes. Even Dora, who was steadfast in her commitment to Nate, was not immune to his charm and found herself blushing under his brooding gaze. She knew Clarissa had developed a huge crush on him.

The vehicle lurched over a pothole, jolting Dora back to the present. Her spine tingled. In just a few minutes, she would see Nate. Sitting beside her, Emma squeezed Dora's hand.

'Excited?' she whispered as their eyes met. Dora nodded. Ever since last week when she'd received Nate's letter telling her he had a few days' leave and was making his way over to Cambri, she'd been beside herself, though her excitement had been tempered by worry that something would go wrong at the last minute. She knew from his previous letters that leave could often be cancelled at the drop of a hat. She still didn't know for sure that he had arrived safely, but one of the orderlies who'd walked to the village that morning had confirmed that a young private fitting Nate's description had indeed checked in to Café Rouge.

They rounded a bend and followed the road into the village. Dora had fallen in love instantly with its narrow, cobbled streets and colourful houses with their pointed roofs and pretty wooden facades. Café Rouge was situated in the village square, nestled in the shadow of the clock tower and a stone's throw from a large stone fountain.

Dora spotted Nate immediately. He was sitting with Harry at an outside table, each nursing a pint of ale. A gentle breeze stirred the edges of the blue and white checked table-cloth, which matched the blue and white checked curtains at the lead-paned windows.

As the truck rolled across the square, they both got to their feet, smiling broadly.

'Nate,' Dora called, leaning across Emma to wave as Anton brought the truck to halt.

'Dora,' Nate grinned, almost upsetting the table in his haste to reach her.

Hastily thanking Anton, Dora scrambled out behind Emma and flung herself into Nate's arms. He spun her round and kissed her hard on the mouth, to the delight of the elderly men playing draughts at a nearby table.

'I was so worried something would happen to stop you coming,' she said breathlessly, blushing at the wolf whistles.

'Well, here I am,' Nate said. With his hand resting gently on her waist, he steered her towards the table.

'Hello, Harry.'

'Good to see you, Dora,' Harry grinned broadly, quickly pulling out two empty chairs so Dora and Emma could sit down.

'And you, Harry. This is my friend, Nurse Smith.' As the introductions were being made, the proprietor's wife, Amalie Chevalier, came bustling from inside the café.

'Ah, Nurse Webb,' she said in heavily accented English. 'Thank goodness you are here. These boys, they grow anxious.' She smiled, brushing a strand of auburn hair from her flushed face. She was an attractive woman, if a little overweight, with a smooth, unlined complexion that belied her age of forty-three. In possession of a naturally sunny disposition, only her eyes betrayed the grief she carried inside. Her husband, Claude, on the other hand, was a melancholy figure who carried his heartache on his sleeve for all to see. He was a large, overweight man with a ruddy complexion, a propensity for drink and long, greying sideburns. While his wife retained her youthfulness, Claude looked every one of his forty-five years.

He emerged from the café now, carrying two plates of steaming clams that he laid in front of the men playing draughts. He stood up, tugging on his braces. He nodded at the two nurses.

'I was just saying to Nurse Webb, Claude,' Amalie said, flapping at him with her dishcloth. 'These boys were growing anxious.'

Claude grunted. Spotting Anton sitting in his truck, he ambled over, hands shoved deep in his trouser pockets.

'We're here at the time we arranged,' Dora said, smiling at Nate.

'Madame Chevalier is just teasing,' Nate said, giving Amalie a look. 'We weren't anxious at all.'

'Of course, I only jest,' Amalie said. Hands on her ample hips, she beamed round at the four. 'Coffee?'

'Something cold, please,' Dora said.

'Yes, for me, too, madame,' Emma nodded. 'So, Private Gardener,' she said, turning to smile at Nate as Amalie hurried back inside to prepare their drinks. 'It's a pleasure to meet you at last. Dora's told me so much about you.'

'Likewise, Nurse Smith,' Nate grinned.

'And you're Harry Whitworth.' She smiled at Harry. 'I was a scullery maid at Fotherington Hall, just down the road from your house in Richmond. Your parents were regular visitors.'

'Good grief,' Harry said, squaring his shoulders. 'You know my parents?'

'I know *of* them,' Emma corrected him. 'Being stuck

down in the kitchen, I had no contact with them, but I did used to see their names on the guest list. Mrs Milton, the housekeeper, always spoke highly of Mr Whitworth. He was well liked by the staff.'

'Yes, well,' Harry said, clearing his throat. 'My father and I haven't spoken for a while. We don't see eye to eye.'

'I'm sorry to hear that,' Emma said, leaning back in her chair as Amalie emerged into the June sunshine with glasses of lemonade which she set on the table.

'Enjoy,' she said. Straightening up, she crossed her arms, gazing over to where her husband was leaning in the window of the truck's cab, chatting to Anton. 'They will talk for hours,' she said, with a rueful smile. 'Ah well.' Throwing her hands in the air, she went back inside.

'She's a bit of a character, isn't she?' Nate said, picking up his pint glass.

'He comes across as a bit morose,' Harry said. 'Cooks a decent breakfast, though.'

'Their son was killed in March,' Dora said, lowering her voice. She glanced towards the café's open doorway, but Amalie was chatting to two middle-aged women seated at one of the indoor tables.

'I noticed the black armband,' Nate said quietly. 'Verdun?'

Dora nodded. 'A week before what would have been his twentieth birthday.'

Both Nate and Harry winced. 'Poor bugger,' Harry said. 'Sorry,' he added quickly, his cheeks colouring at his blunder.

Emma laughed. 'Don't be. We hear a lot worse on the

wards, believe me. The air's positively blue at times, isn't it, Dora?'

'The lads are generally very good at curbing their language around us nurses,' Dora smiled. 'The sisters take a very dim view of swearing, but sometimes, when the lads are in terrible pain or they've just woken up from surgery to find they're missing their arms or a leg, well, you can't blame them, really, can you?'

Dora leaned back in her chair, her gaze resting on Nate. He smiled at her, the skin around his eyes crinkling as he squinted into the sun. His face had matured since she'd last seen him, and he seemed older than his eighteen years, but was it surprising? These young men had seen and done things they never would have imagined just a few short years ago.

'Where's Samuel?' she asked suddenly, glancing up at the upstairs window as if expecting to see him smiling down at them.

'He decided to spend a few days at a small monastery near Rouen,' Harry told her. He rubbed the bridge of his nose with his forefinger. 'He's been finding it difficult of late.'

'Alice hasn't said,' Dora responded thoughtfully.

'I don't think he's confided in her,' Nate replied. 'He's not said anything to us, really. It's just, well, we can see things aren't right with him.'

'I hope he finds some sort of peace there, then,' Dora said with a frown. She picked up her glass, leaning back in her chair. The blue and white striped awning had been rolled back, and the sun was pleasantly warm on her face. The church bell tolled eleven o'clock as a grey muzzled Labrador ambled across the square, pausing beside the fountain to have a good scratch. In one of the houses lining the square, a baby started to cry. A jackdaw cawed on the church roof and swallows swooped and dived in the milky-blue sky.

'I wish you didn't have to go back tomorrow,' she said, gazing at Nate over the rim of her glass.

'So do I.' He smiled ruefully. 'But we've got today. What time do you have to be back?'

'Ten,' Dora grinned. Hearing the sound of raised voices, she twisted in her seat, thinking an altercation was taking place, but it was just Anton and Claude saying their good-byes. Claude banged on the cab door, and the engine roared to life. Anton lifted his hand in a wave, and the truck lurched away from the square. Claude remained where he was long enough to light a cigar, then ambled back towards the café.

'Another beer?' he said, gathering up the two empty beer mugs with his meaty fingers.

'No, no,' Harry waved his hand. 'It's fine, thank you.'

'Perhaps we could take a walk?' suggested Nate as they paid for the drinks.

'It's a lovely village to explore,' Emma said, as they got up from the table. 'There's a small museum near the railway station if you like that sort of thing, and there's the park.'

'It's such a nice day, I vote we head for the park,' Nate said as Dora tucked her hand in his elbow.

Chatting amiably, they made their way along narrow, cobbled streets to the park. Mothers sat on the grass watching their children play. Dogs gambolled in and out of the pond, where some boys were sailing their wooden boats along the edge. Two French soldiers sat on a bench, smoking. They acknowledged Nate and Harry with friendly nods.

'I quite fancy popping in to have a look at that museum,' Harry said after they'd walked the circumference of the pond. 'Anyone else?'

'I'll come with you,' Emma said, shooting Dora a wink.

'I think I'd rather sit here and soak up some sun,' Nate said. 'What about you, Dora?'

'I think I'll give it a miss, too,' she said.

'We'll see you later, then.'

'It's nice to have some time on our own,' Nate said as he took off his tunic and spread it out on the grass.

'Yes, it is,' Dora replied. He motioned for her to sit down.

'Thank you. Matron will have my guts for garters if I get grass stains on my uniform.'

Nate leaned back on his elbows, gazing across the smooth, unruffled surface of the pond. Dora sat beside him. She drew her knees up to her chin, staring out across the park to where an elderly man was tending to one of the many flowerbeds. Not far from him, a group of British soldiers lazed in the shade of a beech tree, laughing and flirting with a couple of French girls sitting on a nearby bench.

'It's so tranquil here,' she sighed. 'I can't even hear any shelling.'

'The calm before the storm,' stated Nate matter-of-factly. 'There's something brewing. They won't tell us what, in case we get caught and spill the beans to Jerry, but I reckon it's something big. The lads think it might even bring about the end of the war. We've been shelling the blazes out of the Germans for weeks now. They must be close to giving up. Anyway.' He rolled onto his side and stroked Dora's cheek. 'Let's not spoil the time we've got left talking about the war,' he said, leaning closer to kiss her.

CHAPTER ELEVEN

'Oh, hello, Leah,' Alice said, coming in the back door of her grandparents' cottage to find Leah sitting at the kitchen table shelling peas. 'This is a surprise. Is everything all right?' she asked, setting her empty basket on the table and unwinding her scarf.

'Your gran's next door at mine,' Leah replied. 'Mrs Merrifield was in a terrible state after church, so Mum and your gran are trying to calm her down.'

'Why, what's happened?' frowned Alice, draping her damp coat in front of the range. The last week of June had turned unseasonably cold and wet. In the fields, the strawberry yield had proved very poor, with the fruit rotting on the ground before it ripened. Water had been gushing down the lane all week, flooding some of the lower cottages.

'Mrs Merrifield went to see a medium.'

'A medium?' Alice pursed her lips. 'Reverend Aldridge was preaching against that very thing in his sermon this morning.'

'That's why Mrs Merrifield is so upset. This woman, who she found through an advert in the *Echo*, seemed genuine and came highly recommended, and told her that she'd been in contact with Percy and Seth, so she was feeling much better, but now Reverend Aldridge has denounced all mediums as charlatans and fraudsters, it's plunged her back into melancholy.'

'Oh dear, that poor woman,' Alice said pityingly. 'I can't begin to imagine how she must be feeling.' She sighed and pulled out a chair, her expression grim. 'And I've just come from Tilly's,' she said glumly. 'She's expecting again.'

'Expecting?' Leah looked at her friend in surprise. 'I thought Declan had been drafted to France.'

'He has,' Alice said shortly. 'He went straight from Ireland, so he's definitely not the father.'

'Then whose . . . ?' Leah frowned.

'Who knows?' Alice said, throwing her hands up in despair. 'I had heard that she was back to plying her trade. With all the troops hereabouts, she's hardly short of customers. Honestly, she's her own worst enemy.'

'I thought she'd give up that way of life once Declan was out of the picture. What happened to her job?'

'Oh, she's still working at the sorting office for now, but they're not going to keep her on once her condition becomes common knowledge.' Alice sighed. 'She'll be applying for parish relief again, no doubt.'

'Perhaps Joshua would help.'

'Do you think he would?' Rain splattered the glass and

a brisk wind swept across the garden, rattling the raspberry canes.

'You know him better than I do. What do you think? Is it worth writing to him?'

'He's always done right by her in the past.'

'I'll have a word with Pearl about it. In the meantime, I'll put a word in for Tilly with the parish relief council. Tea?' Alice asked, pushing back her chair and getting to her feet.

'Oh, yes, please.' Leah set the pan of peas on the hob and put the empty shells aside to throw on the compost heap later once the rain eased. The kitchen was filled with the savoury aroma of rabbit roasting in the oven. The arrival of summer had alleviated the food crisis somewhat in the countryside. The stew pond was stocked to the brim with trout, and rabbits were plentiful if you could catch them. Young Simon Culley in Dora's old cottage had proved a dab hand with a catapult, and both Leah's mother and Alice's grandmother would often come down of a morning to find a still-warm rabbit laid on their back step.

'Pearl's round at ours as well,' Leah said, spooning tea leaves into the pot while Alice fetched the milk from the pantry. 'Mum invited her over for her dinner.'

'Oh good. I'll have a word before she goes. Save me tramping over to her caravan in this awful weather.'

'Dora had a nice time with Nate,' Leah said, sitting back down. 'She said Harry looked well.'

'I received a letter from Samuel yesterday,' Alice said, sitting down opposite Leah while she waited for the kettle to come to the boil. 'The few days he spent at the monastery appear to have done him good. He sounds so much more cheerful. Not that he reveals much, but reading between the lines, I can see he's finding life very difficult.' She smiled sadly. 'I have to admit, I'm beside myself with worry about him.'

Leah reached for her hand. 'It's such a shame all their upcoming leave has been cancelled. I was so looking forward to Harry coming home for his birthday. We were going to get a special licence.' She sighed. 'But all that will have to wait for now.'

'Whatever's being planned, let's hope it's the turning point of this blasted war.'

'That's what they're saying at Franklin's,' Leah said. 'The brother of one of the girls has been invalided home, and, according to him, we've been bombarding the Germans without let-up for weeks now. Whatever's being planned should see them on the run with their tail between their legs.'

'Let's hope so,' said Alice, getting up as the kettle came to the boil, sending a plume of steam into the air.

They heard voices outside and the door swung open, letting in a flurry of rain and cold air.

'What sort of weather is this for the end of June?' Hannah grumbled, ushering Pearl in through the door ahead of her into the steamy kitchen. Beatrice brought up the rear, raindrops glistening on her auburn hair.

'I've just made some tea,' Alice said, getting up for more mugs.

'Thank you, love,' her grandmother said, as the three women divested themselves of their shawls. 'I've invited Mrs Hopwood and Pearl to dinner,' she continued as she hung the woollen shawls in front of the range to dry. 'Your grandfather is dining with the Reverend. They've got church business to discuss.'

'Did Daisy not want to join us?' asked Alice, pouring the tea amidst the bustle of everyone settling themselves around the table.

'She doesn't like to socialize much these days,' Hannah said, a shadow passing fleetingly across her face. 'She prefers her own company.'

'She is getting better, though, Mum,' Leah said stoutly. 'Isn't she?'

Hannah smiled and patted her daughter's hand. 'Yes, love, she is.'

'Where's Mrs Merrifield?' Leah asked.

'Her husband came for her,' Beatrice said, donning a large apron. She opened the oven door, a cloud of aromatic steam wafting into the room. 'Poor woman. She was ever so upset.'

'There's so many of these so-called mediums about at the moment,' Hannah said, clucking her tongue in disapproval. 'Preying on people's grief. Shameful, that's what it is. Shameful.'

'You can't blame people for being curious, though, can you?' Leah said, frowning. 'I mean, if it brings them some comfort, where's the harm?'

'They're making money off of people's misery, Leah,' replied Hannah sternly. 'That's just cruel.'

'I've had some come to me,' Pearl said quietly. She looked sunken and frail sitting at the table. Leah had no idea how old she was. She doubted Pearl even knew herself. Her skin was wrinkled and weathered, and her hair was snow-white. She'd lost most of her teeth, which gave her mouth a sunken look, yet her piercing blue eyes missed nothing and her mind was still as sharp as a tack.

'I tell them I'm no medium. I can see into the future, yes, but I can't communicate with the dead.' She shook her head sorrowfully. 'It's heartbreaking to have a bereaved mother begging you to tell her that her son is all right, begging just to hear him speak. I tell them I can't do that.' Her gaze came to rest on Leah, and she opened her mouth as if she were about to say something. Leah held her breath, but Alice spoke and the moment was lost.

'Pearl, I was wondering if your great-grandson might be able to help Tilly out a bit, financially. She's got herself in a bit of a mess.'

Pearl's expression darkened. 'That girl will be the death of me,' she said sharply. 'Got herself in the family way again, hasn't she?'

'Oh, you know?' Alice said, taken aback.

'My Joshua has been sending her money ever since he's been gone.' She shook her head. 'I thought once she'd got rid of that worthless piece Declan, she'd get her life on track. Make an honest living for a change.' She gave a derisive snort.

'That didn't last long, did it? Oh, I hear things. I might be old but I've got all my faculties. I know what she's been up to, the little madam. Came to me, she did, wanting me to sort her out with one of my potions.'

'Pearl!' Alice gasped in horror. 'You didn't?'

'No, I did not!' Pearl said vehemently. 'I use my skills with the herbs for healing, not harm, and she knows that.'

'What will she do?' Alice said, biting her lip. 'Much as I dislike Declan, I think him taking the children to his mother was the best thing for them. I'm sorry, Pearl, but Tilly has never been a good mother and I worry for this baby.'

'I'll see to it she's taken care of,' Pearl said. 'I'll write to my Joshua and put him in the picture.'

'She might want to think about adoption,' Leah suggested.

'I did suggest the idea, but she was adamant she wanted to keep it,' Alice said. Her eyes clouded, and Leah knew she was thinking about the baby she'd lost. *How unfair*, she thought, *that someone like Tilly can produce babies at the drop of a hat.*

'We look after our own,' Pearl said firmly. 'Tilly will be all right. And so will the baby.'

All through the midday meal, when the conversation turned to more mundane topics like the poor strawberry harvest, Leah grew more and more convinced that Pearl had something she wanted to say to her. Ever since war had been declared, Pearl's strange behaviour of three summers before had haunted her. Pearl had seen something. She was sure of it. Something to do with herself and Harry. Something bad.

Determined to get Pearl alone, Leah offered to walk with her back to her caravan. Tugging her black woollen shawl over her white hair, Pearl paused, regarding Leah with her piercing gaze.

'Don't trouble yourself. I'm quite capable of walking back alone,' she said, pursing her thin, pale lips.

'It's no trouble,' Leah replied blithely, ignoring her mother's questioning gaze. 'I could do with some fresh air.' She snatched up her shawl and draped it round her slender shoulders. Although the rainclouds had cleared, leaving the sky a pale, washed-out blue in their wake, the wind was still cool. Before Pearl could make another protest, Leah had the door open. With a deep sigh of resignation, Pearl walked past her into the garden.

Raindrops glistened on the wet grass and a stiff breeze swept through the vegetable patch. The hens clucked loudly as they emerged from their coop, plumping up their feathers and pecking at each other in irritation.

They rounded the cottage in silence. Leah's heart was racing. Puddles of brown rainwater pockmarked the lane, which was empty apart from a dog running in the direction of the pub. The strawberry fields were deserted apart from some pheasants picking their way between the sodden rows.

'What do you want to ask me?' Pearl said, breaking the silence as they passed the church.

Leah cleared her throat as she sought to find the words. Her palms felt clammy and her pulse raced as she wondered if she was really ready to hear what Pearl had to say.

'When we came to see you that time, you wouldn't tell me what you saw,' she began, her voice shaking. She took a deep breath to steady her nerves.

'Leah—' Pearl began, but Leah interrupted.

'I realize that you must have seen the war and it frightened you,' she went on quickly. 'But you saw something else, didn't you? Something to do with me and Harry.'

Pearl stopped walking. In the pale sunlight, leaning heavily on her stick, she looked frail and weary. She let out a long, whistling sigh.

'I didn't realize what it was, of course,' she said. 'It was just a great darkness, something evil.' She shivered.

'And me and Harry?' Leah pressed. She swallowed, in an attempt to lubricate her dry throat. Pearl sighed again.

'Leah,' she said as she started walking again, 'I don't get clear pictures in my head. They're images, snippets of things.'

'But you saw *something*,' Leah insisted earnestly. 'Please tell me, Pearl,' she implored as they turned up the track. The long, wet grass brushed the hem of Leah's skirt, soaking the fabric. 'Will Harry survive the war?'

'That I can't tell you,' Pearl snapped, rounding on her crossly. 'And you shouldn't ask me.'

'But ...' Leah stammered. She felt close to tears. Seeing her obvious distress, Pearl's anger faded and her eyes filled with compassion. Balancing on her stick, she reached out and patted Leah's arm. 'Child, all I can see is that your and my great-grandson's futures are somehow entwined.'

'Joshua?' Leah blurted, taken aback. 'How?'

'I told you,' Pearl snapped, starting off along the track. 'I don't see the details.'

'But what about Harry?' Leah cried, hurrying after her.

'How many times, child? I can't see anything.'

'Does that mean . . . ?' Leah whispered, the blood draining from her cheeks.

'No,' Pearl replied sharply. 'It means I can't see anything, that's all.' She stopped again. 'I can make my own way from here,' she said. 'Look,' she added kindly, 'just because I can't see you with Harry doesn't mean anything, pet. Keep praying the boy will make it through, that's all you can do.' She looked up as a sharp bark rent the air and smiled. 'Bear knows I'm coming. He'll be wanting his scraps.' She gave Leah's hand a squeeze. 'Go home, Leah. Go home.'

Silently, Leah watched the old woman disappear into the thicket. A plume of smoke curled above the treetops, pinpointing the exact position of Pearl's caravan. Pearl had lived in the grounds of Streawberige House as long as Leah could remember, her little painted caravan tucked among the apple and pear trees, her piebald pony tethered nearby. The sturdy little pony was gone now, commandeered eighteen months earlier by the army. What had become of her since, Leah couldn't bear to wonder.

With a disappointed sigh, she turned on her heel and headed for home.

CHAPTER TWELVE

The kettle whistled loudly. Dora lifted it off the heat and poured boiling water into the cracked teapot. For now, the big guns had fallen silent and all she could hear through the open door was the chirp of crickets and the occasional hoot of the barn owl that had taken up residence in the shower block.

For days, there had hardly been any let-up in the sound of heavy artillery fire and the air had been vibrant with excitement in anticipation of the great advance. In the past week, all the men deemed fit for battle had been sent to rejoin their battalions while all Blighty cases had been hastily shipped off back to England in preparation to receive the inevitable wave of new patients.

Earlier that day, word had filtered through that the great advance had begun three days earlier. The news had been greeted with cheers from staff and the few remaining patients alike, everyone thinking the same thought: could the end of the war finally be in sight?

Cradling her mug of tea, Dora settled herself on the doorstep, gazing across the camp to where the coming dawn was merely a thin grey line on the horizon. She yawned. She'd done a twelve-hour shift, but there was no point in going to bed. Word had come through that a convoy was due in within the hour, and it would be all hands on deck. She hoped the tea would revive her enough to cope. Her stomach rumbled and she wondered if there were any biscuits left in the tin to tide her over until breakfast. She was about to get up and go look when, by the light spilling from the hut, she spotted Clarissa picking her way across the ground.

'Tea's fresh,' Dora said by way of greeting.

'Thank you,' Clarissa sighed. 'I'm gasping.'

'Bring the biscuits as well, would you?' Dora called after her, sipping her tea.

'I reckon we're in for it over the next few days,' Clarissa said, joining Dora on the step a few minutes later, a mug of tea in one hand and the battered biscuit tin in the other. She handed it to Dora, who peered into it with a disgruntled sigh.

'It's time someone got a parcel from home. These are going really soft,' she said, taking out a custard cream and dunking it in her tea. 'I believe so,' she added, replying to Clarissa's comment. 'Sister Ripley gave us a good talking to this evening. There'll be no leave for us for weeks.'

'Your Nate will be in the thick of it, no doubt?' Clarissa said, regarding her red-raw hands gloomily. No matter how often she washed them, she couldn't rid them of the smell of carbolic soap and disinfectant. It was making her very self-conscious, especially when the gorgeous Dr Walmsley would hold them to his lips. She flushed, the memory of his kisses making her feel weak at the knees as she briefly relived the stolen moments she daren't even share with Dora.

'He can't say much in his letters,' Dora replied, wondering if her friend was all right. Her cheeks were very flushed. 'But I know they're involved in this advance. I just hope he'll be safe. I hope they all will.'

Clarissa didn't reply, and Dora turned to her friend. 'Are you all right?' she asked with genuine concern.

Typhoid and dysentery were rife in the camp and the nursing staff were in no way immune to succumbing. They'd lost a young VAD nurse to typhoid just the other week. The entire hospital had needed to be scrubbed down and disinfected and the nurse's personal effects burnt.

'You're very flushed.' Dora frowned. 'Have you hurt yourself? You've got a bruise on your neck.'

Clarissa's blush deepened. 'It's nothing,' she muttered, tugging her collar over the offending mark. 'I'm perfectly well.'

Dora regarded her with a puzzled frown. She'd been worried about Clarissa for a while now. She was always sneaking off somewhere and was often late for her shifts, leaving Dora to cover for her. It was becoming wearying.

'Are you sure everything is all right, Clarissa?' she asked softly. 'If you need some time, I'm sure if you spoke to Matron, she would arrange for you to have a day to yourself.'

'You heard the sisters,' Clarissa shot back. 'No leave until things calm down.' Her smile didn't quite meet her eyes.

'I'm fine, Dora. Don't worry about me.' She appeared to be about to say more, but they were interrupted by the sound of approaching trucks.

Getting swiftly to her feet, Dora drained her mug and, wiping her mouth with the back of her hand, hurried towards them. Standing with the other nurses in the half-light of dawn, she watched in mounting horror as the convoy kept coming. The trucks and ambulances were soon replaced by wagons and carts. The cries of the wounded and the dying could clearly be heard above the cacophony of the vehicles and terrified, wild-eyed horses. Then came the walking wounded, some with a comrade slung over their shoulder, others carrying stretchers, stumbling over the rough ground, faces grim as they tried desperately to keep their charges from toppling off.

There was little time for Dora to process her thoughts as she hurried to follow the orders being barked out by the sisters trying to coordinate this mass arrival. Where would they put everyone, she wondered, as she raced to the dressing station for bandages and hot water.

Throughout the day, she worked, sweat dripping down her spine, the humidity sucking the very breath from her lungs as she moved from one screaming patient to another. All the beds were full, there were patients on the floor and still more were being laid outside where flies hovered mercilessly around their undressed wounds.

'Oh my . . .' Beside her, Clarissa gagged and clapped her hand to her mouth. Dora followed her friend's gaze. She'd just removed the makeshift bandage around a young corporal's leg to find the wound crawling with maggots.

'Are you sure you're all right?' Dora hissed, giving Clarissa a puzzled look. It wasn't as if they'd never had to deal with maggots before. It was a consequence of lying out in no-man's-land for hours under a hot sun. Wherever flies swarmed, maggots were sure to follow.

Clarissa nodded, her eyes shimmering as she fought for control. Her nostrils flared, and she swallowed hard. Holding up her hand to assure Dora she had things under control, she bundled up the filthy bandage, tossed it aside and reached for the bowl of hot, soapy water.

Satisfied her friend was coping, Dora turned her attention back to her own patient. He was a young subaltern, his freckled face smeared with blood and dirt. His eyes were closed, his breathing fast and shallow. Dora's gaze travelled along his body to the mangled pulp that was all that remained of his legs. Picking up her scissors, she gently cut away the fabric of his khaki trousers. The stench of rotting flesh was overpowering. Breathing through her mouth, she carefully peeled back the material to reveal the full extent of the young man's injuries.

'Will I lose my legs, nurse?' he said quietly. He had green eyes, she noted as they scrutinized her intently.

Dora cleared her throat. 'One of the doctors will be along shortly. He'll explain everything to you then.'

'Only I'm a footballer,' he continued sleepily. 'I was about to try out for Sunderland AFC when I was conscripted.'

He smiled, his eyelids closing. 'I'm going to be a famous footballer one day, nurse. You'll have to watch out for me. Lee Harper.'

'I shall certainly do that,' Dora said brightly, thankful that he couldn't see the pity in her eyes.

The hours passed in a blur, with more convoys arriving throughout the day. An orderly was dispatched to the village to recruit volunteers willing to house wounded servicemen in their homes or businesses. By the end of the day, wounded soldiers were being billeted in the church, several private homes and the café.

And still they came. Tents were erected around the camp, with lorries leaving for the station hourly, until finally, after days of convoys, the message came through that the boats were full and no more patients could be accepted. Wounded soldiers were being billeted in barns and out-houses, the nurses being issued with bicycles in order to do their rounds of the neighbouring area as efficiently and quickly as possible.

As July merged into August, the convoys kept coming. Boats were again transporting seriously ill patients across the Channel, which eased the situation a little, but for every wounded serviceman shipped out, there were two to take his place.

Dora lifted the dipper to her parched lips and gulped the tepid water, relishing the feel of it trickling down her throat. It was so hot and humid. She was desperate for a bath. She could smell her own sweat and her skin was itchy, making her anxious that she'd caught lice from a patient.

It was now the middle of August, and the onslaught showed no sign of abating. Her gaze drifted to the rows of wooden crosses on the outskirts of the camp. Young Lee Harper hadn't survived the surgery to amputate his legs, and it had been Dora's unhappy task to write to his mother, returning his personal effects. Another of her patients, a young corporal named Billy, who had been shot through both eyes, had left yesterday, bound for England and a lifetime of blindness. Before the war, he'd been a promising painter of watercolours. She bit back a sob, an impotent rage burning the back of her throat as she contemplated the hundreds of thousands of young men robbed of their dreams and futures. She lived in fear of seeing Nate or Harry, or any of the boys she knew from back home, coming through her hospital, and she felt a stab of envy for Leah and Alice for, while they worried constantly about their men, they were shielded from the worst of the realities. If anything happened to Nate, Dora knew she wouldn't be fobbed off with the line fed to the grieving relatives that their loved one was killed instantly and didn't suffer. Dora had seen enough suffering to last her a lifetime, yet on it went.

'Oh, Dora,' Clarissa started in surprise. 'I didn't realize anyone was here.'

'I was just having a drink,' Dora replied, holding out the ladle. 'Are you all right, Clarissa?' Her anxiety over her friend had been slowly increasing over the past few weeks. She looked pale and drawn, and there were dark shadows beneath her eyes. Of course, it could just be sheer exhaustion, but . . .

Expecting Clarissa to brush her off as she always did when Dora questioned her, she was surprised to see her start welling up.

'No,' Clarissa said, her lip trembling as a tear spilled over her lashes to roll down her wan cheek. 'Everything isn't all right at all. In fact, it's a mess.'

'Oh, Clarissa. What is it?'

Clarissa glanced around. Anyone nearby was involved in their own business and far too busy to take any notice of the two nurses.

'This way,' Dora said. Grabbing Clarissa's arm, she hurried her towards the sluice room. Checking to see they were alone, she bundled Clarissa inside, closing the door. It was hot and sticky, and the smell of dirty bedpans was almost overpowering, but it was about the only place Dora could think of where they were unlikely to be interrupted.

'Now, tell me what the matter is,' she said, leaning against the metal sink. 'Maybe I can help.'

Clarissa shook her head. 'You can't.'

'Try me.'

Clarissa sighed. 'I'm expecting.'

'What?' Dora gave a half-laugh, certain she'd misheard.

'I'm serious,' Clarissa said solemnly. 'I'm almost three months gone.'

'Who?' Dora stammered, feeling herself blush. 'Who's the father?' she asked, imagining some French farmhand.

'Simon,' Clarissa whispered. She stared at the floor, unable to meet Dora's gaze.

'Simon?' Dora frowned, her mind drawing a blank. Was he a patient? The idea seemed absurd.

Clarissa raised her gaze. Seeing Dora's blank expression, she gave a sigh of exasperation.

'Simon,' she said again. 'Simon Walmsley.'

Dora's mouth fell open. 'Dr Walmsley?' she exclaimed.

'Hush!' snapped Clarissa, her anxious gaze darting to the open window.

'Sorry, but ... how ...?' Dora shook her head in incomprehension. 'You must set a date.' Her gaze came to rest on Clarissa's still slender waist. 'Before you start to show. You and Dr Walmsley can apply for compassionate leave. You could be married here, in the magistrate's office in the village.' She tapered off as she realized Clarissa was shaking her head.

'There isn't going to be a wedding,' she said sadly.

'What?'

'Simon.' Clarissa checked herself. 'Dr Walmsley has denied the child is his. He said he could give me the name of a woman back home who'd take care of things for me.' Tears spilled down her cheeks. 'I don't know what to do, Dora.'

'Oh, come here.' Dora held out her arms and Clarissa collapsed against her, sobbing noisily into her shoulder.

'I've been such a fool,' she gabbled into Dora's neck, her tears soaking into her uniform. 'A stupid, stupid fool.'

'Can't you go to Matron? She'll be able to help you.'

'I can't tell anyone. I'm too ashamed.'

Dora bit her lip. 'You'll start showing soon. So you'll have to tell Matron soon.'

Clarissa nodded. She lifted her head, her expression bleak. 'I know. I shall have to return to England in disgrace. Oh God! What will my parents say?' she wailed as she was engulfed by a fresh wave of tears.

'We'll worry about that when we have to,' Dora said firmly. Her dad had always said she was good in a crisis, but if she were honest, Clarissa's confession had floored her. She had no idea how she was going to help her friend through this particular situation. No idea at all.

CHAPTER THIRTEEN

Alice shivered in the early evening chill as she cycled towards her grandparents' cottage. She'd spent the afternoon at her parents' house in Hedge End, catching up with the family. She was pleased that her sister, Martha, appeared to be settling in at the grammar school. Her mother, Lily, was so busy with commissions from the military that she'd had to take on two more apprentices. There were now six young girls sewing uniforms in her back room, and she was even thinking about moving to a bigger premises.

A chill swept across the fields. The strawberry harvest had been poor this year, but now, once again, the fields had been turned over to the growing of turnips and potatoes. The surrounding trees, resplendent in their autumn colours, caught the last rays of sunlight. A fox ran across her path, causing her to wobble precariously for a moment before she regained control of her bicycle. It turned to look at her before disappearing into the hedge.

She paused to catch her breath outside the Glyn Arms

pub. She was still reeling over the news that poor Leonard Merrifield had been executed for desertion and that her dearest Samuel had been forced to witness the awful miscarriage of justice.

The telegram informing Reuben and Florence of their son's ignominious death had arrived in early September, the same day Alice received word that Samuel was in hospital in Rouen being treated for severe shellshock. Harry had written to her telling her about Samuel's participation in Leonard's execution. No wonder her poor husband had suffered with his nerves, she fumed angrily after reading it. How could the army expect anyone to witness the senseless death of a friend, never mind such a mild-mannered, peace-loving man as her husband.

Light spilled from the pub windows. The black paint spelling out the word 'Coward' across the stonework had been almost erased. One of the upstairs windows, smashed when someone threw a rock through it, remained boarded up. Unable to cope with the torrent of abuse she and her husband were receiving over Leonard's execution, despite two of their sons dying honourably in battle, Florence Merrifield had gone off to stay with her parents in St Albans, where she would be closer to her eldest boy, George, who was convalescing at nearby Hatfield House. Reuben continued to open up and was well supported, his clientele consisting mainly of the older generation now that all the young men of legal drinking age were away fighting, but to Alice he seemed diminished somehow. He seldom cracked a smile and, so she had heard, he'd removed Leonard's photograph from the wall where it had once been proudly displayed alongside his four brothers.

At least her husband couldn't be accused of cowardice, Alice comforted herself. He'd remained at his post despite his declining health, and she was proud of him. She'd written and told him so.

She pushed off on the bicycle, freewheeling the rest of the way, and pulled up outside the row of three cottages. Smoke curled from the chimney pots and lamplight spilled from the crack in the curtains. She wheeled her bike round the back and leaned it against the wall. Lifting the latch, she let herself into the steam-filled kitchen.

Her grandmother stood at the stove stirring something in a pan.

'Hello, Alice,' she said, her cheeks flushed. Her welcoming smile faltered a little as she inclined her head towards an envelope propped up against the milk jug. 'You've had a letter.'

At the sight of the official-looking envelope, Alice's stomach roiled. Pulse racing, she picked it up with a shaking hand. 'It's postmarked Southampton,' she said, frowning as she slit it open with her fingernail and drew out the single sheet of notepaper.

'It's Samuel,' she exclaimed with an exhalation of relief. 'He's been sent to the Royal Victoria at Netley.' She lowered the letter with a smile. 'That's barely an hour's walk from here. I'll be able to see him as often as I want.' Feeling suddenly weak at the knees, she sank onto a chair and read the letter again. 'I can visit from tomorrow,' she said, unable to keep the elation from her voice.

'That's wonderful news,' her grandmother said, turning down the heat and leaving the bean soup to gently simmer. 'I mean, I'm sorry he's got shellshock,' she amended, wiping her hands on her apron, vividly recalling men she'd seen being unloaded at the docks, heads and hands shaking uncontrollably, eyes wide and staring. 'That can't be very pleasant for him, but at least he's on English soil and, God willing, he'll be able to come home soon.'

'Will they send him back, though, do you think?' Alice mused, biting her lip in consternation.

'I shouldn't think so,' her grandmother replied reassuringly. 'It's more likely they'll find him something to do here. But don't fret about that now. He's got to get well again first, and seeing you will be just the tonic he needs.'

The following afternoon, Alice wheeled her bicycle up the long, tree-lined drive of the Royal Victoria Military Hospital. The gravel was carpeted with fallen leaves, muffling the crunch of her footsteps as she approached. She came to a halt, pausing to take in the sprawling but impressive building, its many turrets and domes silhouetted against the sombre October sky. Despite the autumnal chill, there were several patients being wheeled across the lawn by uniformed nurses. A group of patients in dressing gowns sat on chairs in a circle, smoking. Most of them sported bandages. One stood slightly to the side, leaning on a wooden crutch. He spotted Alice and smiled, raising his free hand in greeting. Alice waved back, recognizing him as the brother of Mrs Culley, Leah's neighbour. She remembered her grandmother mentioning that he was in Netley Hospital. She was pleased he looked quite well.

She pushed her bike the rest of the way and, propping it against the wall, climbed the steps to the main entrance. With its high ceilings, columns and arches, the interior was even more impressive than the outside. Patients were seated on benches lining the wide corridors, smoking or reading. Trying not to get in the way of the nurses and orderlies bustling up and down, Alice anxiously made her way to D Block, her footsteps echoing on the tiled floor. Her heart was racing and she tried to compose herself. Though she had no idea what sort of state Samuel would be in, she had seen enough pictures in the newspaper to cause her to worry and so she approached the ward with trepidation. As she reached the door, a shrill cry rang out, causing the hair on the back of her neck to stand up. It was followed by another, sharper cry. Taking a deep breath, she pushed open the door.

Strange noises and cries rang out from the various wards. One man was screaming as though in agony, the sound chilling her blood as she anxiously searched the names above the doors for the right ward, exhaling in relief as she spotted the name above the nearest door. As she opened it, a pleasant-faced nurse got up from her desk and came towards her, greeting her.

'Good afternoon,' managed Alice, her gaze darting

nervously along the rows of beds. Most had the curtains drawn, but a handful of men were seated at a table weaving baskets under the watchful eye of a male nurse, and a few more were seated near the many windows, looking out over the grounds. She could hear snippets of conversation from behind some of the curtains, assuming correctly that there were other visitors or nurses making their rounds.

'I've come to see my husband,' she said, her voice little more than a whisper. 'Reverend Roberts.'

'Ah, yes, our Reverend,' the nurse said, her smile faltering slightly. 'He's down the end. If you'll follow me.'

Her palms clammy, Alice followed her down the ward. From behind one of the curtains came a deep, guttural groaning. The same shrill cry she'd heard earlier came again, making Alice jump.

'It's all right,' the nurse said, sensing Alice's alarm. 'It's normal. Most of these men will recover eventually.' She halted beside the last bed in the row. 'I don't want you to be alarmed, Mrs Roberts,' she said, gripping the edge of the pale blue curtain. 'Your husband will get better, but I'm afraid he's in a bad way. He has been diagnosed with neurasthenia – shellshock. Some men recover very quickly once they're removed from the battlefield, but others, like your husband, take a little longer.' She laid a hand on Alice's arm. She raised her eyebrows questioningly. 'Ready?'

Alice swallowed, her stomach churning, and nodded. 'Yes,' she managed hoarsely.

Gently, the nurse drew the curtain aside. Alice gasped.

She had assumed by his silence that Samuel was asleep, but he was lying on his back, staring wide-eyed at the ceiling.

'Samuel?' Alice said tentatively. There was no response. She looked at the nurse, who smiled at her encouragingly.

'He may not respond,' she said, 'but he can certainly hear you. Have a seat,' she said, motioning to the wooden chair beside the bed, 'and I'll bring you a cup of tea.'

As the curtain fell back into place, Alice remained standing, listening to the receding squeak of the nurse's rubber-soled shoes.

'Samuel,' she whispered. Again, there was no response. No sign at all that Samuel was aware of her presence. Tears pricked her eyelids, and she blinked furiously. She refused to cry. Samuel needed her to be strong. Taking a shuddering breath, she slowly took off her coat and lowered herself onto the chair, her coat across her lap, and took one of Samuel's hands in hers. She could feel him trembling. Suddenly his whole body jerked, as if he'd been hit by a bolt of electricity. She was about to summon a nurse when the spasm stopped as suddenly as it had begun.

'He's improved a lot since he was first taken to hospital in Rouen,' the nurse assured Alice when she reappeared a short while later with Alice's cup of tea. 'According to his notes, his tremors were continuous. The poor man could get no relief, even when he was asleep. Now they're intermittent.' She glanced down at Samuel. 'He will be starting therapy in a few days' time. We're hopeful it will make a difference to his condition.'

'How long . . .' Alice began. The teacup rattled against its saucer, and she realized she was trembling. She cleared her throat and tried again. 'How long before he can come home?'

The nurse gave her a sympathetic smile. 'That all depends, love.'

Alice stayed an hour, but Samuel's condition remained unchanged. At the end of visiting hour, she gathered up her coat and hat and slipped through the curtain. Other visitors were leaving now, too. The sound of weeping could be heard behind several curtains.

The men who had been basket-weaving were being led back to their beds, following the male nurse like docile lambs.

Not looking where she was going, she almost bumped into another woman making for the doorway.

'I'm so sorry,' she said, stepping back to allow the woman to go ahead.

'No need to apologize,' the woman assured her with a wan smile. 'My fault entirely.' She was a stout woman, in her early twenties, Alice surmised, like herself, with blue eyes and blonde hair piled up under her purple hat. The woman's rosy cheeks were wet with tears.

'It's awful, isn't it?' she said, pausing in the corridor to wipe her eyes. 'I'm sorry. I never allow myself to cry in front of him, so I'm always in floods when I leave.'

'Is it your husband?' Alice asked softly.

'My fiancé.' The woman managed another smile. 'Kitty Wheeler. Pleased to meet you.'

'Likewise. Alice Roberts. My husband only arrived here yesterday.'

'Where was he?' Kitty asked as they made their way along the corridor.

'Delville Woods.'

Kitty nodded. 'That's where Carl was.' She shook her head sadly. 'He looks so broken. Like a frightened child.' She blew her nose. 'He was such a strapping man before. Not afraid of anything.' Her smile quivered. 'He was mentioned in dispatches last March for his bravery under fire.' Her brow puckered. 'I can't understand how he's been reduced to this.'

'It must be awful for them out there,' Alice said soothingly. She couldn't understand it herself, though she had every sympathy for the men affected. She knew there were many who assumed these men were cowards or weak, but many of the men who were now suffering from shellshock had proved themselves to be brave soldiers in the past. She wondered now, as she stepped out into the main body of the hospital, whether shellshock had been the cause of poor Leonard Merrifield's desertion. She could only hope and pray that Samuel would recover from his ordeal.

'Sometimes, I think my Carl will never be completely well,' Kitty confided. 'My mother is worried he'll never be able to work and so won't be able to support me.' She pulled a face. 'My father says Carl's a pathetic excuse for a man. My two brothers are still over there. They all enlisted together, you see, Jerry, Frank and Carl.'

'He's not a coward, Kitty,' Alice assured her, stoutly. 'None of them are.'

'Perhaps I shall see you tomorrow?' Kitty said as they neared the bottom of the windswept drive, seagulls wheeling above their heads.

'Yes, I shall be coming every day,' Alice replied, straddling her bicycle.

'Oh good. Until then,' Kitty smiled.

'See you tomorrow,' grinned Alice, pushing off as Kitty hurried to hail the approaching omnibus.

CHAPTER FOURTEEN

Dora struck a match, cursing softly under her breath as it was extinguished yet again by the draught gusting under the ill-fitting door. Her fingers were clumsy, numb with cold. It was the last week of November and bitterly cold. Snow had been falling steadily all day, causing havoc with the convoys, the sub-zero temperatures only compounding the misery of the wounded soldiers. Several of her new patients were suffering from severe frostbite and awaiting evacuation to the coast, but, until the train tracks were cleared, no one was going anywhere.

'Ah,' she squawked in relief as the next match burst into flame and she managed to light the stove. Blowing out the match, she set the kettle on the stove, rubbing her cold hands in an effort to get the blood flowing. She was reaching for the tea caddy when the door flew open and Clarissa blew in on a flurry of swirling snowflakes. She slammed the door shut and leaned against it, breathing hard. Her cheeks were pink with cold, her lips pursed in a thin line. Tears sparkled on her lashes.

'I've been summoned to see Matron,' she said, her mouth trembling as her hand went automatically to her swollen belly. 'Will you come with me?'

'Of course,' Dora said solemnly. 'We knew it had to happen,' she said, spooning tea leaves into the pot. 'It's pure luck you've managed to get away with it this long.'

'I know,' Clarissa wailed. She flung herself into the nearest chair. 'I'd hoped to stay a bit longer, though.' She scowled. 'I bet it was that Dawn who told Sister Ripley. I've caught her and her cronies giggling and whispering a lot lately, and every time they see me, they shut up.'

'You can't pull the wool over Sister Ripley's eyes for very long,' Dora reminded her, as she poured boiling water into the teapot. 'If she hadn't been ill in bed for so long, she would have realized your predicament long before now.'

'I know,' Clarissa sighed.

'Is Dr Walmsley still not prepared to accept his responsibility?'

'No,' snorted Clarissa, crestfallen. 'He refuses to speak to me unless it's absolutely necessary. I can't believe I was so stupid as to believe he was in love with me.'

Dora looked at Clarissa with sympathy but said nothing. She wasn't unwise to the ways of the world, and Strawbridge had seen its fair share of hurriedly planned weddings followed by the arrival of a baby just a few months later.

'Let's have a cup of tea before we go to see Matron,' Dora suggested. 'It'll warm us up.'

They sat huddled around the tiny stove listening to the

howling wind, the walls of the wooden hut shaking with every gust, sipping their tea in silence. At length, Clarissa set her cup down on an upturned crate and let out a long sigh.

'I suppose we'd better go.'

'Better to get it over and done with,' Dora agreed.

They pulled on their coats and, braving the elements, ploughed their way through the thick snow to Matron's office.

'Come in,' she called in reply to Clarissa's hesitant knock. 'Ah, Nurse Arspery. Sit down.' She indicated the two chairs facing her desk. 'Nurse Webb, your presence is not required. You may return to your duties.'

'Please may she stay, Matron?' Clarissa spoke up as Dora made to leave.

'Oh, very well,' Matron sighed. 'Sit down.'

Dora took the chair beside Clarissa. She folded her hands in her lap. A fire burned merrily in the grate and the lamp cast a warm, buttery light over the tastefully furnished room.

'Nurse Arspery, I have been informed that you are in the family way. Is this true?' Matron said sternly.

Blushing beneath her scrutiny, Clarissa squirmed uncomfortably on her chair. She nodded. Her reply was barely audible.

'Yes, Matron.'

Matron sighed again. 'Oh, Nurse,' she said, shaking her head sadly. 'You know this means I have no choice but to dismiss you.' Matron leaned forward, her arms resting on her desktop. 'You will be relieved of your duties with immediate effect and make ready for your return to England.'

'No, please!' Clarissa cried. 'I can't go home, Matron. My parents . . . They'll be so ashamed.'

'You should have thought about that before you . . .' She shook her head. 'Is the child's father prepared to stand by you?' When Clarissa shook her head, Matron's eyes narrowed. 'Are you willing to name him? He should at least be brought to task by a superior officer.'

Again, Clarissa shook her head. What would be the point? Simon had made it perfectly clear he wanted nothing to do with her or her baby. She just wanted to put the sorry affair behind her.

'Nurse, do you not see that you suffer the disgrace while whoever it was who got you in this mess in the first place will get away scot-free?'

Clarissa nodded. 'Very well,' Matron said wearily. 'I can't force you to name him. I shall be sad to see you go, Nurse. You're a hard worker and you'll be sorely missed.'

'Can't I stay, Sister?' Clarissa begged, tears trickling down her cheeks. 'At least for a few weeks more?'

'What example would that set the other girls, Nurse?' came the sharp retort.

'Please, Matron,' she said, shamefaced. 'I can't go home. At least not yet. My parents will disown me. Perhaps once the baby is born, they may soften, but I can't go home now. I just can't.'

'I'm sorry,' Matron said, looking genuinely sympathetic. 'While I sympathize with your predicament, my hands are tied.'

'What if Clari . . . Nurse Arspery were to take a room in the village?' Dora suggested quickly. Clarissa turned to her, her eyes hopeful. 'Madame Chevalier may be persuaded to take in a lodger now her soldiers have moved on.'

'Yes,' Clarissa breathed, grasping the lifeline with both hands. 'That would be the perfect solution, Matron. I could board with the Chevaliers until the baby comes and then make plans to go home in the spring.'

In spite of her dismay, Matron found herself nodding. 'Very well. If the Chevaliers are agreeable, I don't see why not.'

'Thank you, Matron,' Clarissa said with heartfelt relief.

'A word of warning, though,' Matron said sternly. 'Of course, you will be a civilian again, so what you do is your own affair, but, for your own sake, I advise you not to let your condition become common knowledge. The people of Cambri are very conservative.'

'I will do my best not to draw attention to myself,' promised Clarissa.

'You should make your arrangements as soon as the weather permits,' Matron said, shuffling papers to indicate that the meeting was at an end. 'And if Madame Chevalier is unwilling to take you in,' she added as both girls rose to leave, 'then you will need to arrange your passage home.'

CHAPTER FIFTEEN

It wasn't until three days later that the road to the village was passable. To Clarissa's immense relief, the Chevaliers were more than willing to have her board with them until the baby was born. By Clarissa's calculations, it was due in the middle of March.

Though Dora visited Clarissa as often as her duties allowed, she missed having her around. A new VAD, Bernice Clifford, arrived and was sharing Dora's tent. Though the two nurses got on well, Dora didn't feel the connection she'd had with Clarissa. She was still very friendly with Emma and Millie and, with Christmas approaching, the three of them were involved in organizing the carol concert and party for the patients. Dawn and her cronies were still frosty and unpleasant, but most of the nurses were perfectly amiable and Dora, Millie and Emma had managed to put together a good selection of performers.

Now, three weeks later, as she balanced precariously upon a low, three-legged stool stringing sprigs of holly across one of the wards, she heard her name being called and glanced round, almost losing her balance in the process.

'Nurse Webb, there's a chap outside asking for you,' an orderly told her, hastening towards her, outstretched arms ready to grab her should she overbalance and fall.

'Thank you.' Pressing in the last drawing pin with the flat of her thumb, Dora climbed down from the stool.

'He's just outside.'

'Did he give his name?' she asked, feeling the heat in her cheeks as excitement coursed through her veins.

'No, miss, he didn't.'

It can only be Nate, she thought giddily. Tucking a few strands of escaping hair under her cap, she smoothed down her apron and hurried through to the reception. It was bitterly cold. Snow had drifted under the tent flap, forming puddles in the damp sawdust where it had melted. Barely able to contain her excitement, Dora tugged her cape around her shoulders and stepped outside to find not Nate waiting for her, but Harry.

'Oh, it's you,' she exclaimed, unable to hide her disappointment.

'I'm sorry, Dora,' Harry said. The collar of his heavy greatcoat was turned up about his ears, snowflakes dusting his shoulders. 'I didn't want to alarm you by giving the orderly my name.'

'Why are you here?' Dora interrupted. 'What's happened? Where's Nate?' Her teeth were chattering but she barely seemed to notice the cold. For Harry to have made the journey to see her, something must have happened to Nate. Her stomach filled with cold, hard dread.

'Has something happened to him?'

Harry's brow creased. 'You'll be getting the official letter soon,' he said. 'You're Nate's next of kin.'

'Oh God!' Dora's hands flew to her mouth. She bit down on her fist in an effort to keep the scream building inside her at bay. Her eyes sought Harry's. 'He's dead, isn't he?' she whispered.

'No.' Harry gripped her arms and gave her a little shake. 'No. Dora, listen to me,' he said sternly as she began to keen softly. 'He's not dead. He's not even injured. He's been taken prisoner.'

'Pardon?' Dora wiped her eyes. The raw wind and swirling snow stung her wet cheeks as it swept across the camp. From the nearby barn, a cow lowed mournfully.

'He's been taken prisoner,' repeated Harry. 'It seems he and some of the other chaps became disoriented in the chaos and got separated from the rest of us. We were organizing a search party when we got word that he was being held behind enemy lines. He'll be okay, Dora.' He tried to smile, but his lips were so stiff with cold that all he could manage was some sort of twisted grimace. 'The war's over for Nate. He'll be far away from the front line for the rest of the war.'

'But the Germans . . . ' Dora whispered, her mind conjuring up all the horrific stories she'd heard about the German army's mistreatment of prisoners and refugees. 'Oh, poor

Nate,' she wailed, shoulders slumping with the weight of her anxiety.

'I'll write to Leah tonight and ask her to get Alice on the case,' Harry said, rubbing his gloved hands together. 'She can use her contacts in the Red Cross to find out exactly where Nate has been taken and she can arrange for things to be sent to him. You'll be able to write to him.' He paused. 'It's not the worst thing that could have happened,' he said so quietly that Dora had to strain to hear him over the howling wind and the drone of approaching vehicles.

'He's alive. He'll be taken to a camp somewhere and, as long as he keeps his head down, he'll probably see out the rest of the war in relative ease.'

Despite her misgivings, Dora nodded. She hated to think of her beloved Nate being a prisoner of the reviled Germans.

'Look, when do you finish your shift?' Harry asked, stamping his feet. 'I'm with my mate. We borrowed a truck. We could drive into the village.'

'Sorry?' said Dora, realizing she hadn't been concentrating.

'A drink in the village, if you're free? My mate will give us a lift.'

'Er, yes, I'm off duty now, actually. I was helping decorate the wards. I'll just let someone know I'm leaving camp.'

Her emotions in turmoil, she ducked back inside the tent in search of Emma, finding her up a short ladder stringing Christmas cards along one of the walls.

'Is everything all right, Dora?' she asked, seeing Dora's pale face and anxious expression.

'Nate's been captured,' Dora replied, her lip trembling.

'Oh, poor love.' Emma descended the steps and came to put her arm around Dora's shoulders. 'At least he'll be away from the fighting now, though,' she said, hugging Dora warmly. 'You have to look on the bright side.'

Dora nodded and, swallowing the lump in her throat, told Emma where she was going.

'He's a good-looking chap, that Harry,' grinned Emma. 'If he wasn't smitten with your friend back in England, I'd be tempted to have a crack at him myself.'

'His heart belongs entirely to Leah,' Dora grinned back. 'I shan't be long. I was hoping for a chance to call in on Clarissa and see how she's getting on. We can run through the programme when I get back. I want us to give the chaps a decent show.'

'And we will,' Emma said. 'Go on, off you go. Give Clarissa my regards.'

Dora promised that she would and hurried back into the swirling snow to find Harry huddled next to a small olive-green truck, smoking a cigarette.

He opened the passenger door for her, and she climbed into the cab.

'Oh, hello,' she said to the soldier hunched over the steering wheel.

'Nurse Webb, my mate, Ian Foster,' Harry introduced them, clambering up after her and pulling the door shut behind him.

'Pleased to meet you, Nurse Webb,' Ian said, starting the

engine. He spoke with a strong accent. For some reason, the accent and the name Ian Foster resonated with her, but her mind was so occupied with processing Harry's news about Nate that she didn't give it any more thought as the truck lurched forward, the windscreen wipers scraping valiantly back and forth in a futile attempt to clear the windscreen of the swirling flakes.

The road into Cambri had been cleared and, as they drew nearer to the village, the snow began to ease. The truck bounced over the frozen mud, slithering to a halt near the frozen fountain in the village square. A holly wreath adorned the head of the fountain nymph and icicles had formed along the guttering of the surrounding buildings. Christmas tree lights glinted from the occasional house window and the air was full of the aroma of roasting chestnuts.

Ian engaged the handbrake and they got out of the cab and headed for the Café Rouge. Catching a glimpse of Clarissa in an upstairs window, Dora waved. Clarissa waved back, her bright smile looking forced.

The outside table and chairs had been packed away for the winter and the windows were steamed up. The bell jangled shrilly as Dora pushed open the door, leading the way into the warm, chocolate-scented fug of the café.

'Hello, *chérie*,' Amalie Chevalier called across to them as she emerged from the kitchen in her flowery apron, bearing a tray of soup and bread that she delivered to two elderly Frenchmen playing chess at a corner table.

That was the only occupied table, and Dora, Harry and

Ian settled at a table near the window. The wide window seat was scattered with plump embroidered cushions. Painted plates lined the wooden pelmet and ceramics and watercolours adorned the uneven duck-egg-blue walls.

'What can I get you?' Amalie beamed as she came over, her cheeks flushed from the warmth of the café.

'Just tea, please, madame,' Dora said. The men ordered coffee with a splash of brandy. Amalie smiled and headed back to the kitchen just as the door to the stairs opened and Clarissa peered out, her eyes searching the café for Dora.

'Ah, there you are,' she grinned, approaching their table. She was six months gone now and, despite her efforts at concealment, there was a noticeable swelling beneath her burgundy woollens.

'Join us, please,' Harry said as both he and Ian rose to their feet.

'Thank you.' Clarissa sat down heavily. She looked well, Dora noted, as Harry made the introductions. Her condition certainly suited her. Her complexion was flawless.

'I'm sorry I haven't been over to see you before now,' Dora apologized, as Amalie arrived with the drinks and an extra cup for Clarissa. 'What with the snow and practising for the Christmas concert, I've been pretty much confined to barracks.' Despite her forced enthusiasm, she couldn't make her smile reach her eyes.

'Something's happened,' Clarissa said, her eyes narrowing. 'What is it?'

'Nate's been captured,' Dora said weakly.

'Oh no!' Clarissa shot Harry a questioning glance.

'I'm afraid he has,' he said, taking a sip of his coffee. 'But like I said to Dora, in a camp somewhere far away from the front line he's better off than the rest of us.'

'As long as the Germans treat their prisoners well,' Clarissa said drily, exchanging glances with Dora.

'He'll be fine,' Ian said. He hadn't spoken up to now but had sat nursing his coffee, his blue eyes fixed on the blurred view of the square. 'Nate's a strong man. He'll get by all right.'

'You know Nate?' Dora asked, surprised. 'My Nate?'

'Ian's regiment is billeted not far from mine,' Harry told her. 'On the next farm, to be exact.'

'Where are you from?' Clarissa asked, reaching for the milk jug. 'You're not English.'

'South Africa,' Ian replied, shortly.

'South Africa?' Dora's ears pricked up. 'I thought there was something familiar about your accent but didn't make the connection. My neighbour's accent isn't as pronounced as yours, but there is a similarity. She lived in South Africa for many years.'

'Interesting,' Ian smiled lazily. 'I've lived in England since 1910, and until I joined my unit in 1915, I hadn't come across any of my fellow countrymen.'

'Apart from Mrs Turner, I hadn't met any South Africans until your unit moved in next door,' Harry grinned at him.

'Turner?' Ian repeated, frowning.

Harry raised an eyebrow at his friend's reaction. 'Dora's

neighbour. She's the one who lived out there for several years. Beatrice Turner.' He frowned. 'Do you know her?'

Ian shook his head quickly. 'No, of course not,' he said. He grinned, but his smile looked forced. 'South Africa's a big place.'

The bell jangled and a group of soldiers shuffled in, rubbing their hands and stamping their feet, melting snow pooling on the floor around their boots. They nodded at Harry and Ian, and said hello to the two girls as they made their way noisily to a couple of tables near the back.

'What can I get you, gentlemen?' Amalie asked, bustling over with her pencil and pad poised.

Clarissa pushed back her chair. 'I must see what I can do to help,' she said, getting to her feet.

'Oh, must you?' Dora said, disappointed. 'We've hardly had a chance to talk.'

'I can't expect the Chevaliers to keep me for nothing,' she whispered. 'And I enjoy helping them. They're very good to me.'

'I'll try and visit again soon,' Dora promised.

'Yes, please do.' Clarissa's smile didn't quite reach her eyes. 'My hosts are very kind, but I do get lonely.' She pulled a wry face. 'I wish I'd tried harder with my French at school.' She gave Dora's hand a quick squeeze. 'Madame,' she said, following Amalie towards the kitchen. 'What can I do to help?' The door swung shut, cutting off Amalie's reply.

'Your friend . . .' Harry said, looking perplexed.

Dora nodded. 'She will be returning to England once the baby is born.'

'The father?' Ian queried.

'Not interested,' Dora replied flatly.

'A squaddie, I take it?' Ian said as the two men exchanged uneasy glances. Several men in their unit had begun romances with local girls and at least two of them had discovered recently that they'd got an unwanted pregnancy on their hands.

'A doctor at the hospital.'

'A doctor! He should know better than to disregard his responsibilities, then,' Harry fumed on Clarissa's behalf.

'Surely he should be removed from his position?' Ian said mildly, drinking the last of his coffee.

'We can't afford to lose a doctor,' Dora replied matter-of-factly. 'And Clarissa hasn't named him, though I'm sure Sister Ripley has a fair idea who the culprit is.'

'He's a cad!' Harry declared, so loudly that several heads turned towards them.

Dora shushed him with a stern glare. 'Clarissa is embarrassed enough as it is, without us drawing attention to her,' she warned him.

'I'm sorry,' Harry said, lowering his voice. 'That sort of thing makes my blood boil. What will she do, do you think?'

'She doesn't know yet. Hopefully her family will accept the child and she can go back home,' Dora sighed. 'They are a well-respected family with good connections. It will come as a huge shock to them, I'm sure.'

Harry lifted the lid of the teapot and glanced inside. 'Another?' he asked Dora, who nodded. It was warm and cosy in the café, and she had no wish to rush back to the chaos of the hospital.

'Thank you, that would be lovely.'

'That nurse's neighbour,' Ian said as they drove away from the field hospital after dropping Dora off. 'Do you know her?' The windscreen wipers squeaked across the frozen glass as the truck bounced over the unyielding ground.

'Not well,' replied Harry, lighting a cigarette with shaking hands. 'Why?'

Ian shrugged. 'Just wondered,' he muttered. He fixed his gaze on the snow-covered terrain, but his mind was thinking about the letters he'd received. Could this Beatrice Turner be his mother? He'd hated her for so long that he'd closed his mind to any possibility of a reunion, but now ... The truck hit a rock and the vehicle lurched sideways, jolting Ian back to the present. He managed to gain control and, ignoring Harry's questioning frown, steered the truck around the bend, the wheels skidding slightly on the ice.

Perhaps, if he survived this blessed war, he mused bitterly, once they were on safer ground, he might look Harry and Nate up, get to know this Beatrice Turner and find out if she really was the mother who'd abandoned him so long ago.

CHAPTER SIXTEEN

Alice hurried along the corridor to Samuel's ward. He appeared to have improved so much over the past week that she was beginning to hope he might be home in time for Christmas. She smiled as she recalled the moment Samuel had become aware of her for the first time. He had stared at her for the longest time, the expression on his face telling her that he wasn't sure if she was real or a figment of his fevered imagination. As she'd been told by the nurses, she began to speak to him. She had seen it in his eyes, the moment he'd realized that she was real, and he'd burst into tears. She'd held him while he sobbed.

Now, pushing open the door to the ward, her hopes of a Christmas homecoming gave way to despair as she heard the commotion coming from behind the curtains that surrounded her husband's bed. Giving Kitty a frightened glance, she pushed aside the curtains and was horrified to find her husband thrashing about on the bed uncontrollably, his eyes rolling wildly in his head, as two male nurses attempted to hold him down.

'What happened?' Alice cried.

'Step aside, madam,' one of the nurses grunted, teeth clenched. Dazed, Alice took a step backwards, but she couldn't tear her eyes away from Samuel. He appeared to have gained superhuman strength as he squirmed and writhed beneath the powerful grip of the two men.

She heard the sound of running feet behind her, and a doctor was pushing his way past her.

'We need to sedate him immediately,' she heard the doctor say as she was bundled out of the way by a female nurse.

'This way, Mrs Roberts,' the nurse said kindly, leading her away. Alice craned her neck, trying desperately to see what was happening, but the curtain had fallen into place and she could see nothing. The sound of Samuel's groaning and thrashing followed her back up the ward.

'He'll be more comfortable once the doctor has sedated him,' Matron said kindly, handing Alice a cup of tea. They were sitting in her office along the corridor from Samuel's ward. A fire blazed in the grate and a handful of Christmas cards lined the mantelpiece, on which stood several framed photographs.

'My son, Patrick,' Matron said, noticing Alice's gaze straying to the photograph of a young, shy-looking man that took pride of place among the others. 'He's over in Greece.'

Alice smiled tightly. Her fingers were clenched around her cup so tightly that her knuckles were turning white. She kept seeing Samuel thrashing on the bed, a terrified expression on his face. He reminded Alice of a rabbit she'd once seen caught in a trap. It had had the same wild-eyed, terrified look on its face that Samuel had had. Her father had taken pity on the creature and had set it free. Who could free her Samuel from his torment?

'We've seen these types of setbacks before,' Matron said, sitting down in the armchair adjacent to Alice's. 'Patients make seemingly remarkable recoveries, only to relapse some weeks later. We can only guess what triggers these outbursts, but,' she paused to sip her tea, 'there is the concern that your husband may suffer these episodes for some time, perhaps all his life. He may well be able to lead a normal life once he is discharged, although one or two of our patients have been transferred to institutions.' She set her cup and saucer on the small table to her side and sat back in her chair, regarding Alice with sympathy.

'I won't put Samuel in one of those places,' Alice said quietly. Her tea was too sweet; to help with the shock, she surmised. She set the cup down and folded her hands in her lap. 'Surely there's something more the doctors can do?'

'As you know, Mrs Roberts, your husband has undergone several different therapies, and, for the most part, we're seeing a vast improvement. You yourself must recognize how far he has come? His speech is slowly returning and, although his movements are still erratic, he is able to get out of bed now; and until today, he has been enjoying spending time in the day room. It had been our plan to start him weaving baskets later this week.' Her face clouded. 'Of course, we'll need to see how much this episode has set him back.'

'But you're confident he will overcome this setback?' Alice frowned.

'Experience says yes,' Matron assured her. 'Though, of course, every case is different. Some of the men you see walking about D Block had similar episodes to your husband and they're perfectly able to function normally.' She smiled. 'I have high hopes our Reverend Roberts will recover just as well.'

'Just not was quickly as we'd hoped,' Alice finished.

'Quite.'

'Carl told me the staff are making preparations to give the patients a good Christmas,' Kitty told Alice as they boarded the tram for the city centre. 'They've got entertainers coming in and there will be a fancy dinner for those able to eat it. Families are invited in the afternoon and Father Christmas is coming. Will you come?'

'Yes,' Alice replied despondently. Thanks to the sedative, Samuel had slept her entire visit. Her disappointment at realizing her husband was likely to remain in hospital for many more months to come was acute. His improvements had been such that she'd allowed herself to hope. As the doctor had told her when she'd been allowed to return to Samuel's bedside, she mustn't expect too much too soon.

She took a deep breath. She must be patient, just for a little while longer, she told herself as she turned her gaze to the drab winter streets, trying not to feel jealous of Kitty. Carl was due to be discharged the following day.

They alighted in Lower High Street. Seagulls wheeled in

a dishwater-grey sky. The Salvation Army band were playing 'Away in a Manger' outside Holyrood Church, and a small crowd had gathered to listen. The aroma of roasting chestnuts mingled with the pungent tang of woodsmoke and horse manure.

Dodging the many wagons and carts, Alice and Kitty crossed the road, their breath billowing in front of their faces. A few flakes of snow swirled in the air, and Alice shivered as she followed Kitty into the department store.

They were going to do their Christmas shopping and have tea in the tearoom on the upper floor. Alice had been looking forward to the outing, but Samuel's setback had dampened her enjoyment a good deal.

'Look,' Kitty said, in an attempt to cheer her up as they walked through the toy department. Paperchains crisscrossed the ceiling above their heads. In one corner was a small nativity, surrounded by a group of children oohing and aahing over the painted figures nestled in the sweet-smelling straw. 'I'm sure your little brother would like those toy soldiers in his stocking?'

Alice forced a smile. 'Yes, Johnny certainly would.' She picked up the box, studying the miniature German and British soldiers snuggled inside. 'And Jimmy will like this, I think,' she said, picking up a board game she'd seen advertised in the newspaper – 'Bombarding the Zeps'. 'I'm not sure my mother would approve, but my father and brothers will love it. They like a board game to play after dinner.' She put it in her basket along with the toy soldiers.

'Now,' said Kitty cheerfully, taking Alice's arm, 'let's have a look at the wedding dress patterns.' Her joy was infectious and, as they climbed the stairs to Haberdashery, Alice felt her spirits lifting. It hadn't been too long ago that Kitty had felt the same as she did now, that Carl would never recover sufficiently. But here he was, about to be discharged from hospital, his old job waiting for him and a wedding to plan for.

Over the past weeks, Alice and Kitty had become friends. It was nice to have someone to talk to before and after her visits to Samuel. Leah tried her best to be sympathetic, of course, and she had some measure of understanding of what Alice was going through, what with her worries over Daisy (who continued to improve slowly), but with Kitty, Alice felt she could let out all her frustrations and anger without being judged. The other wives, mothers and sweethearts who visited the ward were friendly enough, of course, but Alice felt that Kitty had become a proper friend. She would miss her once Carl was discharged.

As they stepped into the haberdashery department on the first floor, Alice found herself hoping Kitty's parents would come round before the wedding, which was set for early March. So far, her father was refusing to attend, believing that Carl was a shirker and a coward and, as such, was unworthy of his daughter. Her mother, Kitty had confided to Alice, did whatever her husband told her, and she'd already warned her daughter that she would not be attending her wedding if her father forbade her.

Alice knew it was all deeply troubling for her friend, whose family had, until Carl's breakdown, been very close.

'What do you think of this one?' Kitty said, breaking into Alice's thoughts. She held up the pattern.

'It would suit you,' Alice said, joining her friend at the rack of dress patterns. 'This one's nice as well. I like the sleeves.'

'I was hoping my mother would help me make it,' Kitty said, looking downcast as they moved over to look at the bolts of fabric lining the back wall. 'But with the way my father's behaving, I doubt he'd allow her.'

The shop assistant, a tall, slender woman who looked to be in her mid-fifties, came bustling over.

'I can recommend an excellent seamstress,' she smiled, clearly having overheard Kitty's remark. 'She's very reasonable and has a sterling reputation.' She held out a card. 'This is her address.'

Kitty took the card and thanked her. 'I shall leave you to browse,' the woman said, retreating graciously. 'Do shout if you need any assistance.'

'That's my mother,' Alice whispered with a grin, pointing at the pretty scallop-edged card in Kitty's hand. Her friend looked at her in surprise.

'Really?'

'She's very busy with commissions for the military at the moment, so she's not taking on much private work, but I'm sure she will make an exception for you. I've mentioned you to her and she's always been sympathetic about Carl.'

'Do you think she would consider it?' Kitty asked hopefully. 'I mean, it would be an answer to my prayers because I doubt my father will come round, and while I'm pretty handy with a needle and thread, this,' she waved the pattern in front of Alice's face, 'is beyond my expertise.'

'I shall call in on my way home and speak to her,' Alice promised.

'Oh, thank you, Alice,' Kitty breathed. 'Oh, I do hope she agrees. It would be such a weight off my mind.'

Alice arrived at her parents' home in Hedge End just as the last of the daylight was fading.

'Alice!' her mother exclaimed in delight when she opened the door. 'I didn't know you were popping by. Come on in.' Lily ushered Alice into the warm hallway. 'What is it?' she asked sharply, her smile slipping as she noticed her daughter's strained expression.

'Oh, Mum,' Alice sighed, unbuttoning her coat. 'Samuel had such a dreadful turn today. They had to sedate him.'

'Oh, Alice,' Lily said, her face crumpling in dismay as she took Alice's coat and hung it on the coat rack. 'I'm so sorry.'

'It was awful,' Alice went on, close to tears. She had held herself together so as not to spoil Kitty's afternoon, but now, in the face of her mother's sympathy, she could do so no longer. 'I don't think he'll ever get better,' she sobbed as she fell into Lily's waiting arms.

'Oh, there, there, my love,' she said, stroking Alice's back.

'What's happened?' Alice's stepfather, James, appeared in the kitchen doorway, the anxious faces of her younger siblings peering round him.

'Samuel had a bad turn,' Lily said.

'I'm sorry to hear that,' James said solemnly. He was inordinately fond of his son-in-law and he, too, had been hopeful Samuel would be joining them for Christmas Day. 'Come on, children, let your sister compose herself in peace,' he said, ushering his children back into the kitchen.

'I'm all right now,' Alice said, disentangling herself from her mother's embrace. 'I'm sorry.' Taking out a handkerchief, she blew her nose and wiped her eyes.

'Don't be silly,' Lily said. 'You're entitled to get upset, Alice. You don't always have to be the strong one. Why don't you stay for tea? James can take you home in the pony and trap later.'

'Thank you,' Alice smiled. 'I'd like that.'

She followed her mother into the kitchen to find her family and two of her mother's apprentices gathered around the large table. A large pot stood on a trivet in the centre, emitting a delicious meaty aroma. Alice pulled up a chair.

'How is the Reverend?' Martha asked, passing round the plate of bread and butter. Since she had started at the grammar school in September, her confidence had blossomed. She'd made some good friends, and her teacher, a Mr Edwards, was fully supportive of her ambition to become a doctor.

'He was doing well until today,' Alice said, taking a slice of bread. The stew smelled good, but she had little appetite. All she could think of was her poor Samuel thrashing about in his bed.

'Likely it's just a brief setback,' Lily consoled her, ladling stew into bowls which she gave to Caroline to hand out round the table.

'My friend's brother was gassed,' twelve-year-old Jimmy piped up. 'He's come back a different man, Tommy says.'

'Elsie said the same about her uncle,' Martha agreed. One of the apprentices nodded her agreement, and the conversation veered onto the depressing topic of soldiers who had been forever altered by their experiences. Alice listened to the litany of misery, staring at her plate in despair.

'I don't think Alice needs to hear all this now,' James cut in, glaring round the table. Under his stern gaze, everyone fell silent and for a few seconds the only sounds were the scrape of cutlery on the plates and the crackle and pop of the fire in the grate.

'What about your friend's chap?' he asked Alice, spearing a slice of potato with his fork. 'The young man taken prisoner?'

Alice afforded him a grateful smile. 'I've found out he's being transferred to a camp in Germany. I've told Dora that if she writes care of the Red Cross, they'll be able to send her letters on.'

'How's poor Dora coping?' Lily asked.

'I gather from her letter that she's being very philosophical about it. She sounds so busy, I doubt she has too much time for worrying. They've certainly had a very grim time of it over there. Oh, I almost forgot, Mother. The reason I popped in was to ask a big favour. You know Kitty's fiancé is being discharged tomorrow? Well, they've set a date for March, and

I wondered if you'd make Kitty's wedding dress? Only if you feel able to, of course,' Alice added quickly.

'I'm sure we'll be able to squeeze her in,' Lily smiled. 'She sounds a lovely girl, and I'm just pleased you've made a friend in that awful place. I know these past weeks have been difficult for you and it's been a comfort to me knowing you've had Kitty for support.' She patted Alice's hand. 'You can tell her that I'd be delighted to help her out.'

'She'll be so pleased,' Alice smiled at her mother. 'Thank you.'

It was close to eight o'clock when Alice and James approached the Glyn Arms public house. The blackout curtains were pulled across the windows, preventing any chinks of light from escaping, but the sounds of music and the clink of glasses could clearly be heard from inside. The tang of tobacco smoke hung in the frosty air and the orange tip of a cigarette glowed in the darkness, where Alice could just make out a figure huddled on the bench. As they drew closer, the figure rose and moved towards them, startling the pony, which shied slightly to the left.

'Whoa,' James said swiftly, reaching over to pat the pony's neck.

'Sorry, James,' the voice said. 'I didn't mean to startle your pony.'

'Reuben?' James lifted the lantern, its pale light illuminating the haggard face of Reuben Merrifield. 'Are you all right?'

Reuben nodded. He dropped his cigarette butt on the ground, crushing it with the heel of his boot.

'I just wanted to say, Mrs Roberts,' he said, addressing Alice, 'that I'm ever so grateful to your husband for what he did for my Leonard.' His voice shook, his Adam's apple bulging in his throat. 'I heard how he spent the night with him and refused to leave his side right up to the very last minute.' Reuben blinked. His cheeks were wet with tears. 'I'll be forever in his debt. You tell him that. I know he's having a tough time of it right now, but you tell him, we're praying for him, me and the missus.'

Swallowing the lump in her throat, Alice nodded. She reached down and gripped Reuben's cold hand in her gloved one.

'Thank you, Mr Merrifield,' she whispered. 'My husband will be encouraged by your kind words.' She gave his fingers a squeeze and Reuben stepped back, allowing them to continue on their way.

'I just hope Samuel recovers enough,' she murmured to her stepfather as they pulled up outside her grandparents' cottage.

'He will, Alice,' James replied. 'It'll take time, but Samuel's a strong man. He'll pull through. You'll see.'

'I hope you're right,' Alice said wistfully as he helped her down from her seat.

The door opened, bathing them in lamplight. 'Oh, Alice, here you are. I was beginning to wonder where you'd got to. Good evening, James. Will you come in for a warm drink before you head back?'

Declining the offer of a drink, James turned the pony round.

'I'll see you soon, Alice, Beatrice.' He raised his hat. 'Good evening,' he said and started back up the lane.

'We've got good news,' her grandmother said, ushering Alice into the front parlour, where Hannah, Leah and, to her surprise, Daisy, were seated on the sofa under the window.

'Daisy!' she exclaimed. 'It's so nice to see you. How are you?'

'I'm feeling better than I have for a while,' Daisy replied shyly.

'Isn't it wonderful news?' Beatrice smiled, bustling about refilling cups of tea. 'Daisy hasn't had a headache for two days now.'

'And I managed to walk from here to the church and back without getting panicky,' Daisy said, smiling up at Alice.

'That's excellent,' Alice replied, genuinely pleased for her young friend. The past nine months had been a very trying time for Leah's family, for Hannah in particular. At least if, God willing, Daisy's headaches continued to abate, her neighbours would have a better Christmas than the one they'd been expecting. She only wished she could look forward to the same, she mused sadly.

'So, tell us?' Beatrice said cheerfully, handing Alice a cup of tea. 'How is Samuel? Will he be home for Christmas?'

'Unfortunately, no.' Alice shook her head sadly. 'He suffered an awful setback today,' she said and, taking a deep breath, related the details of her visit to Netley Hospital.

CHAPTER SEVENTEEN

1917

Dora sniffed the air in pleasure. It was late March and it finally felt like spring had arrived. The morning air was mild and the verges along the lanes as she cycled towards Cambri were awash with cowslip, primroses and wild daffodils.

It had been a winter of bitter snows and endless convoys, with Christmas Day offering only a brief respite. She'd heard from Nate several times in the three months since his capture and, while she was sure his letters were heavily censored, the cheerful nature of his words brought her some measure of comfort. At least he was well away from the fighting.

She peddled into the village square. Doves cooed up on the rooftops, and the tables outside Café Rouge were filled with soldiers and locals enjoying the fair weather. Small white clouds scudded across the sky, their shadows dancing on the cobbles as she alighted from her bike and wheeled it over to the café.

Leaning it against the wall, she ducked under the striped awning and, calling a quick '*Bonjour*' to Claude Chevalier, ran up the stairs.

Amalie met her on the landing.

'*Bonjour*, madame,' she said breathlessly. 'I came as soon as I could.'

Amalie smiled and, holding a finger to her lips, slowly pushed open the door closest to her. Dora looked past her, her gaze moving swiftly to the bed in which Clarissa lay. She was fast asleep, her dark hair fanned across the white pillow. A soft mewling sound came from a small bassinet beside the bed, and Dora gave Amalie a questioning look. The older woman smiled and nodded, indicating for Dora to enter.

Quietly, so as not to wake Clarissa, Dora tiptoed into the room. She stood beside the bassinet, looking down at the tiny swaddled infant. He had a shock of dark hair and, despite the fact that he was barely two hours old, Dora was certain he had the look of Dr Walmsley about him.

The floorboards creaked as Amalie came to stand beside her, looking down at the sleeping baby as proudly as any grandmother might. Dora felt a pang of pity for her, knowing how hard it would be for Amalie when Clarissa and the baby returned to England.

'He's gorgeous,' Dora whispered.

'Clarissa was so brave,' Amalie whispered back, her gaze not leaving the baby's face. 'He was a big boy: nine pounds, two ounces, the midwife said.' Dora winced, her gaze moving to her friend. She looked so serene.

As if sensing Dora's presence, Clarissa opened her eyes. 'Dora,' she said sleepily, stretching languidly.

'Hello, Clarissa,' Dora said, perching on the edge of the bed. 'Congratulations. He's absolutely gorgeous.'

'I shall leave you girls to talk,' Amalie smiled. With one last, lingering look at the baby, she slipped out of the room, pulling the door to behind her.

'Have you thought of a name yet?' Dora asked.

'Frank,' Clarissa said. 'After my brother.'

'That's lovely,' Dora smiled. 'That may go some way to appeasing your parents.'

Clarissa pulled a face. 'I hope so. I shall write to them today. Monsieur Claude offered to send a telegram, but I think it would be too much of a shock. I can break it to them gently in a letter.'

Dora gave her friend a wry smile. From what Clarissa had divulged about her parents, she doubted they would be willing to welcome an illegitimate grandson. 'All the girls send their love,' she told Clarissa in an attempt to cheer her up. 'Emma and Millie will be over to visit in a day or two, as soon as they get some free time. Matron gave me special permission to come today, but I can't stay long. Oh, here. I made these for Frank.' Dora pulled a tissue-wrapped parcel from her apron pocket.

'Oh, Dora, you shouldn't have.' Clarissa's eyes filled with tears as she unwrapped the dainty white woollen booties and little bonnet. 'Ah, they're adorable,' she said, leaning forward to give Dora a clumsy hug. 'Thank you so much.'

She indicated the small pile of baby clothes on the ottoman at the foot of the bed. 'Amalie has been so generous. She's given me some little cardigans and bonnets that she'd knitted and put away in the hope of having grandchildren one day.' She sighed. 'Poor woman. She'd have made a lovely *grand-mère*.'

Frank chose that moment to stir. His little rosebud mouth formed a perfect 'o' as his tiny fists fought their way out of the swaddling and beat the air.

'Someone's hungry,' Dora smiled.

'Would you like a hold?' Clarissa asked, leaning across to gather up her son. She handed him to Dora.

'Oh, Clarissa, he is so perfect,' she whispered in awe, inhaling the baby's sweet, milky scent. 'I defy your parents not to fall madly in love with him the moment they set eyes on him.'

'I hope you're right,' Clarissa said, unbuttoning the front of her nightdress. Dora handed Frank over, and he snuggled against his mother, his little mouth having no trouble latching onto the breast.

They chatted quietly while little Frank fed. Dora brought Clarissa up to date on the happenings at the hospital. She purposely didn't mention Dr Walmsley, and Clarissa didn't ask after him. She was clearly resigned to the fact that he had no interest in her or his child. Dora wondered if the news that Clarissa had given birth had reached his ears. Living and working in such close proximity, gossip spread like wildfire round the camp, and it was unlikely he would remain oblivious to the fact that he had become a father. But sadly, she doubted he'd be making the trip to Café Rouge any time soon.

Frank fell asleep as soon as he'd satisfied his hunger, and Clarissa laid him back in his bassinet.

'Sorry,' she said, stifling a yawn.

'Don't be,' Dora smiled. 'I'll leave you to rest. I'll come again as soon as I can.'

Clarissa smiled tiredly. She squeezed Dora's hand. 'Thank you,' she murmured, her eyes already closing.

If Dr Walmsley had heard the news, he gave no sign of it in the days that followed. Dora found herself working alongside him on several occasions, but he never asked after Clarissa and Dora felt it wasn't her place to question a doctor.

Dawn and her cronies, as spiteful and poisonous as ever, were relishing Clarissa's disgrace, but, on the whole, the nursing staff were sympathetic to her plight and several of Clarissa's closest friends had been to visit.

Little Frank was baptized at the little church on the square on the first Sunday of April. Dora, Amalie and Claude had been asked to be godparents. It was a beautiful spring day and Frank slept through the entire service, looking like an angel swathed in the white lace christening gown in which the Chevaliers' son, François, had been baptized.

After the early afternoon service, Dora, Emma, Millie, Matron and several other members of the nursing staff were invited back to the café for tea. While Amalie was in her element, cradling the sleeping Frank in her arms as she showed him off, Dora thought Clarissa very subdued.

Several times while she was talking to Matron, Dora glanced over at her friend to find her staring out of the window, chewing her bottom lip, a worried frown creasing her brow.

Clarissa must have felt Dora's gaze, for she glanced over, but though she smiled, Dora could tell it was forced. She wondered if her friend was finding motherhood difficult. It was early days, after all. Little Frank was only eleven days old. Of course, it would take Clarissa time to adjust. Dora gave her an encouraging smile. She hoped her father and mother would be supportive. When she'd asked a few days earlier, Clarissa hadn't received a reply to her letter. Perhaps that was what was worrying her, Dora mused, as Claude bustled over carrying a plate of little cakes.

'You've done Clarissa proud, Monsieur,' Matron said, helping herself to a cake. 'And wasn't it a lovely service? Little Frank was so good.'

'He is a little angel,' Claude smiled wistfully. 'With all that dark hair, he reminds me of my François at that age.' He glanced over to where his wife sat in the window seat, gazing adoringly at the infant sleeping soundly in her arms, and his eyes clouded. 'Perhaps if not for this war,' he said, lowering his voice, 'we could have been grandparents by now.'

'There are so many parents who have lost their chance to be grandparents,' Matron said softly, briefly laying her hand on his arm. 'It is very sad.'

Only half-listening to Claude and Matron's conversation, Dora suddenly noticed that Clarissa was trying to catch her attention. Nodding towards the stairs, Clarissa motioned for Dora to follow her. Excusing herself, she set her teacup on the nearest table and followed her friend up to her bedroom.

Nappies were drying on the clothes horse in front of the open window, the gentle breeze stirring the pink floral curtains. Voices drifted up from the square below, where a couple of elderly men were playing chess outside the café.

'You look worried,' Dora said as she joined Clarissa on the bed.

'I've had a reply from my mother,' Clarissa said by way of reply, her expression grim.

'I assume they didn't take your news well?'

'The letter arrived yesterday.' Clarissa's lip trembled. She took a deep breath, as if to steady her emotions. 'My mother refuses to have anything to do with Frank. She says naming him after my brother is a slur on his memory and that Frank would be disgusted with me.' A tear rolled down her cheek.

'I'm so sorry,' Dora said, taking Clarissa's hand. 'What about your father?'

'Mother hasn't told my father. She has told me in no uncertain terms that I am to return home immediately, alone, and my father is never to know anything about Frank.' Clarissa laughed hoarsely. 'She's talking about suitors and marriage. If I insist on keeping my baby, she will disown me.'

'Oh, Clarissa,' Dora frowned. 'What will you do?'

Her friend shrugged despondently. 'What can I do? I can't raise a child alone with no funds.'

'What about Madame Chevalier? She loves Frank and she's very fond of you. Surely you can stay here? Can't you carry on as you have been? You working in the café in exchange for board and lodging?'

'I don't know,' Clarissa sighed. 'I've been churning things over and over in my head ever since I got the letter.' She looked at Dora, her eyes heavy with sadness. 'I can't give my baby up, Dora,' she said, tears streaming down her cheeks. 'I just can't.'

'Of course you can't,' Dora said. She bit her lip in consternation. It all depended on the Chevaliers and whether they would extend their kindness to Clarissa and Frank on a more permanent basis. 'I'm sure Madame Chevalier will let you stay. Why don't you speak to them this evening, once we've all gone? Monsieur Chevalier was saying only a few minutes ago how they might have been grandparents, had their son not been killed.' Her face brightened. 'And he remarked how much Frank reminds him of François as a baby.'

Clarissa nodded. 'They have been so good to me,' she said, wiping her eyes. 'You're right. I must speak to Amalie and Claude before I make a decision.'

'It will all work out,' Dora said, leaning over to give Clarissa a hug. 'I've seen the way Madame Chevalier looks at Frank.' She drew back, smiling at her friend. 'She's smitten.'

CHAPTER EIGHTTEEN

The convoys of wounded servicemen continued to arrive at the field hospital and, for the next fortnight, Dora was kept so busy that she had no time to get into the village to see Clarissa. but she heard, via Nurse Millie Brown, that the Chevaliers had been only too happy to have Clarissa and Frank stay with them indefinitely.

'That must be such a relief for her,' Dora had said when Millie reported back to her after her visit to Café Rouge. 'Has she written to her mother?'

'Not yet,' Millie had replied, with a grin. 'I think she wants to let her stew a bit. Apparently, so Clarissa tells me, for her parents, appearance is everything. Having an illegitimate grandchild would see them ostracized by their social circle, and sadly, for Mr and Mrs Arspery, that is more important to them than their own daughter's happiness.'

She hadn't realized just how much she'd been worried for Clarissa until Millie had set her mind at ease, but now it was as though a weight had been lifted off her shoulders and Dora went about her work lighter in spirit. She'd had several letters from Nate recently, with three arriving on the same day. He was in some sort of labour camp in Germany and he wrote that while the work was hard, and it had been a bitter winter, the guards on the whole were decent chaps, unlike in some of the other camps where he'd heard that conditions weren't so bearable. He'd received his Christmas box from Dora and one from Alice via the Red Cross. He and some of his fellow prisoners had formed a football team and they often played against the guards. The cheerful tone of his letters brought her great comfort, something she needed desperately, given the gruelling nature of her job.

Writing to the parents of the young men who died in her care was still a duty she struggled with, but, despite her weariness, she tried to make each one as personal as she could. It was difficult sometimes, when the soldier in question died almost as soon as he arrived at the hospital, before she managed to learn anything about him. On those occasions, she had to rely on those who had served alongside him to give her a little background on his character. On the whole, she thought she managed to do a decent enough job of it. Several mothers and girlfriends had written back to her, thanking her for the care and kindness she'd shown to their loved one.

Now, she bent to pick up a bedsheet to hang on the line. Butterflies flitted across the rutted ground where tiny wildflowers had forced their way through the seemingly barren dirt. A breeze blew across the campsite, ruffling the hardy tufts of grass that had survived the churning of vehicles and horses.

She could hear the shelling in the distance. It sounded closer today and she straightened up, frowning at the wisps of smoke drifting above the treeline. There came a particularly loud explosion and she jumped. Black smoke coiled into the air.

Sister Ripley appeared beside her, standing with her hands on her hips as she followed Dora's gaze. Several members of staff had come out, Dora noticed, drawn by the apparent proximity of the explosions.

'This is a bit close for comfort,' someone murmured, sending a ripple of fear down Dora's spine. *Surely they wouldn't be so brazen as to attack the hospital*, she thought fearfully. Before she could follow the thought through, a grey-haired man came skidding round the corner of the latrines. Dora recognized him as one of the men who often played draughts outside Café Rouge.

'They're bombing the village!' he screamed in French, throwing his ancient bicycle to the ground and sprinting towards them, pale-faced and panic-stricken.

'Why?' someone cried in alarm. 'Why would they shell Cambri?'

'You must come,' the old man gabbled feverishly, grabbing the sleeve of the nearest orderly. 'The church and the café have both been hit. We need help!'

Dora's French was good enough for her to catch the gist of the man's words. The café had been hit.

'Clarissa and the baby,' she said, turning to Sister Ripley as she tried to keep the welling panic from overwhelming her.

'We can't go in while they're still shelling,' the sister said, biting her bottom lip. 'I'm sorry, Nurse Webb, we'll have to wait.'

Dora choked back a sob but she nodded, knowing Sister Ripley was right.

'But that doesn't mean we must stand idle,' Sister Ripley barked. She clapped her hands, looking round at the gathered nurses. 'We'll need medical supplies, blankets, water. Anything you can think of. Get everything ready so that as soon as we're able to enter the village we'll be ready.'

Glad to have something useful to do, Dora hurried off with Emma and Millie to start packing up the items they might need when they arrived at the village. She could only hope and pray that Clarissa, baby Frank and the Chevaliers were safe. Please God, they'd managed to get down into the cellar before the bombardment had started. She didn't dare consider the alternative.

The shelling didn't stop until late in the afternoon. Grim-faced and with every nerve stretched to breaking point, Dora huddled in the back of one of the four ambulances traversing the rutted lane towards the village. As the vehicles rolled to a halt at the edge of the village, she heard exclamations of dismay and shock from the driver. She got out, emerging from beneath the canvas to stand in the cool twilight, her eyes unable to believe what they were seeing.

Tears streamed unchecked down her cheeks as she took in her ruined surroundings. The narrow, cobbled streets were clogged with rubble, the once-quaint houses reduced to empty shells. On an upstairs floor, a brass bedstead teetered precariously over the jagged edge of a bedroom floor. The church was pockmarked with shell holes, its clock face shattered. One door hung off its hinge and not one of its stained-glass windows remained intact.

'Oh my God,' Emma breathed, clutching at Dora's arm. Her fingers dug painfully into Dora's skin, but she barely felt it as she stared at the mountain of destroyed masonry where Café Rouge had stood. Tables and chairs had been scattered across the square. She could see patches of blue-and-white-checked cloth fluttering among the chunks of broken bricks.

With the arrival of the medics, the villagers began staggering out into the open. The walking wounded were directed to the body of the church, which, apart from its shattered windows, was still intact, while the more seriously hurt were loaded onto the ambulances and ferried to the hospital. The dead were laid out in the small annex just off the nave.

Trying to quell her mounting panic when neither the Chevaliers nor Clarissa appeared among the survivors, Dora busied herself treating the wounded, but she couldn't help her attention wandering to where a hastily gathered search party was picking gingerly through the rubble.

Her throat was dry and her fingers felt numb as she tirelessly bathed bloody wounds and tied bandages. Her cheeks ached from forcing smiles for the traumatized children as she tried to keep them entertained while their parents prepared to evacuate.

And always there was the constant threat that the Germans might start firing again.

Shards of silvery moonlight shone in through the empty windows, illuminating the desperate villagers sat or sprawled among the dusty pews. Chunks of plaster and masonry dust still littered the area close to the front of the church, though an attempt had been made to clear the altar, which stood in front of a life-sized crucifix that had escaped unscathed.

A cold breeze whistled through the exposed rafters. Dora shivered, her concerned gaze drifting over the sleeping children laid out on the floor. The lorries were due to arrive the following morning to take them and their families to a refugee camp well away from the front line.

Startled, Dora sat forwards as she heard a shout from outside. She was just getting to her feet when Emma burst through the door, her eyes wide.

'They've heard a baby crying,' she panted, clutching Dora's arm.

'Frank!' Dizzy with relief, Dora leapt to her feet. She looked over at the sleeping children.

'Come on. They'll be fine,' Emma said, pulling her towards the door. 'Their mothers are here,' she added, nodding towards the figures hunched in the pews. 'They can deal with the nightmares.'

With one final glance over her shoulder to satisfy herself that the children were sleeping soundly, and clinging to Emma's hand, Dora dashed out into the moonlit square. The tinkle of water in the fountain seemed incongruous amidst the devastation. The entire rescue mission now seemed focused on the café. Two middle-aged village women, their homes apparently unscathed, were bringing out mugs of tea which they handed to the soldiers and orderlies milling about the waiting ambulances. Still more were scrambling among the debris. A bewhiskered sergeant shouted for quiet, and a deathly hush fell over the square. Dora held her breath. A baby's plaintive wail could be clearly heard beneath the rubble.

'Get digging, men!' the sergeant bellowed, scrabbling at the jagged bits of masonry with his bare hands. 'But go carefully. The last thing we want to do is cause a landslide.'

Dora and Emma stood to one side, their arms wrapped around each other for comfort as the men got to work.

'Oh God, I hope Clarissa's all right,' Millie said, coming to stand beside them. Her apron was smeared with blood and dirt, and her face was pale in the moonlight.

'If they all managed to get to the cellar before the walls collapsed, they'll be fine,' Dora said firmly, through teeth chattering with shock. 'Monsieur Chevalier is always bragging how strong the cellar is.'

It was slow, painstaking work, as each brick had to be removed one at a time in order to reduce the chance of the whole pile of rubble collapsing. Dawn was breaking in the east by the time the shout came. Rousing herself from her lethargy, Dora leapt from the rim of the fountain where she had been sitting, and on legs stiff with cold and fatigue hobbled across the cobbles. Emma and Millie huddled close, their hearts sinking as a grim-faced medic emerged from the cellar mouth. Dora stood on tiptoe, craning her neck to see who they were bringing out.

'Oh no!' Emma sighed wearily. 'Poor Monsieur.' Dora's heart sank as the medics laid a stretcher on the cold cobbles. Claude's face, hair and clothes were covered in a layer of fine masonry dust, but apart from a small gash beneath his right eye, he appeared unscathed.

'He suffocated when the walls came down,' one of the medics said apologetically to the stunned nurses.

'Madame Chevalier?' asked Millie. The medic shook his head.

'I'm sorry.' His gaze shifted to the cellar opening, where two of his colleagues were bringing out Amalie. 'It seems they were on their way down the stairs when the building collapsed on top of them.' He shrugged his shoulders dispiritedly. 'Another minute, and they'd have made it.'

Dora was too afraid to ask after Clarissa and the baby. It had been some time now since anyone had heard little Frank cry. So it was with huge relief that she heard a shout from below. Getting as close as they dared, the three nurses held their breath. There was the sound of banging from below and a cloud of white dust swirled up through the opening, followed by the high-pitched cry of a baby.

'He's alive!' Dora screeched, grabbing Emma in relief.

'Oh, thank the Lord,' Millie sighed. There came a shout, and the medics raced to help. Moments later, they emerged with Clarissa lying on a stretcher. She looked very pale and appeared to wince every time the stretcher was jolted. A soldier followed, cradling baby Frank. The infant's face was red and he was screaming for all he was worth.

'Clarissa!' Dora ran to the ambulance. 'Are you badly hurt?'

'I think I've broken my ankle falling down the steps,' she said ruefully, reaching for Frank as she was loaded into the back of the ambulance. 'Have you seen Amalie or Claude?' she asked, her expression growing anxious. 'They were coming down to join me when the walls collapsed, and ...' She must have read the truth in Dora's eyes, for she stopped abruptly, her eyes welling with tears.

'I'm so sorry, we lost them both,' Dora said, giving Clarissa's hand a squeeze.

'Step aside, please, Nurse,' the medic said gently. 'We need to get them to the hospital.'

'Of course.' Dora took a step backwards. 'I'll come and see you very soon,' she called to Clarissa as the tarpaulin sheet was pulled down. Then she stood in the square with Emma and Millie and watched the ambulance drive away.

CHAPTER NINETEEN

'Come in, Mrs Roberts. Have a seat.' Matron indicated one of the chairs drawn up to the desk. Alice did as she was instructed. Matron's office boasted an impressive view of the hospital grounds. She could see a group of patients seated on the lawn in chairs and wondered if Samuel was among them.

'Tea, Mrs Roberts?' asked Matron, her hand hovering over a small silver bell on the corner of her immaculate desk.

'Er, no, thank you.' She was so weighed down with anxiety that the mere thought of eating or drinking anything sent her stomach into painful spasms. The dark shadows beneath her eyes were a testimony to the many sleepless nights she had spent worrying about Samuel and whether he would ever be well again. There was no denying that his behaviour had grown increasingly erratic over the past few months. Reverend Aldridge had visited him on several occasions and, though he hadn't said much, the small knot of concern between his eyes told Alice that he, too, had noticed an alarming change in his young friend.

She had come here today fully expecting to be told that her husband would in all likelihood spend the rest of his life in an institution, so it came as a great surprise when Matron clasped her hands together and, leaning forwards, said with a beatific smile, 'Well, Mrs Roberts, I have some excellent news for you. The doctors feel Reverend Roberts has recovered enough to be able to go home.'

'Pardon?' Alice blinked. 'But I thought—' Matron interrupted her with a wave of her hand.

'It may be that the bad moods and bouts of temper continue for some time,' she said, matter-of-factly, 'but the doctors have consulted on the Reverend's case and are all in agreement that, as his physical symptoms appear to be cured, he would be better off at home.'

'I see,' Alice said, her relief at finally having Samuel back home tempered by her anxiety over whether she would be able to manage his bouts of melancholy and angry outbursts.

'I understand if you need a day or two to make arrangements,' Matron continued, 'but ideally, we would like to discharge your husband as soon as possible. As I'm sure you're aware, our beds are at a premium.'

'Of course, Matron,' Alice said, inclining her head in agreement. 'I only need today to prepare for Samuel's homecoming. I'm sure my grandfather will be able to collect him tomorrow morning.'

'That would be excellent,' Matron smiled. 'That will give me enough time to finalize the paperwork.' She got to her feet, signalling that the meeting was at an end. 'Thank you for your time, Mrs Roberts.'

'I doubt Samuel will feel up to giving sermons,' Reverend Aldridge said later that afternoon when Alice called in to the vicarage to tell him of her husband's imminent discharge from hospital. 'If you're agreeable, I'm quite happy to stay on for a few weeks more.'

'That would be most kind of you, Reverend,' Alice said, unable to keep the note of relief from her voice. She was dreading being alone with Samuel. It had become apparent over the past weeks that he wasn't the man she had married. It was impossible to predict what might set him off. They could be having a perfectly amiable conversation in the hospital, when something he perceived as a slight would set him off. Several times, she'd had to summon a male nurse to restrain him.

'Apparently, he has been much calmer this past week,' she said, setting her teacup in its saucer and resting it on her knee. They were sitting in the vicar's study, early April sunlight slanting through the bay window. She could hear Mrs Hurst humming to herself in the next room. The house-keeper's usual dour demeanour had brightened considerably on hearing the news that the Reverend and Alice would be moving back into the vicarage. Fond as she was of Reverend Aldridge, she had missed the young couple more than she could have imagined possible.

'Perhaps the doctors are right, Alice,' Walter said now,

stretching his legs out towards the fireplace. A small fire burned in the blackened hearth, for the spring sunshine held little warmth. 'Maybe once Samuel is home, in familiar surroundings, he will improve dramatically.'

'I do hope so, Reverend,' Alice said fervently. She wanted nothing more than to recapture the easy, loving relationship they'd enjoyed before Samuel had gone off to France. 'I'd better go,' she said, getting to her feet and setting her cup and saucer on the tray. 'I need to speak to my grandfather about fetching Samuel in the morning. Thank you for the tea.'

'You're welcome, my dear,' Reverend Aldridge said, standing up. 'Mrs Hurst will have the master bedroom all ready for you. Do you need a hand bringing your things over from your grandparents?'

'Thank you, but there isn't much,' Alice replied. 'Just my clothes and a few personal belongings. Grandfather will help me.'

'Very well. I shall see you both tomorrow, then,' he said, walking her to the door.

Calling goodbye to Mrs Hurst, Alice thanked Walter for his kindness and set off down the path towards the lane.

Her grandfather was in the field adjacent to the lane, supervising the planting of the young strawberry plants. The fields teemed with workers, women, children and old men. It was backbreaking work. Carts and wagons lined the grass verges, where several young lads were unloading crates of strawberry plants.

Mathew saw Alice and waved. Taking off his hat, he

wiped his forehead with his handkerchief and put it back on, turning to walk towards her.

'Alice,' Mathew greeted her with a smile. 'Your grandmother tells me Samuel is coming home. Good news indeed.'

'Yes, very good news,' Alice replied carefully.

'You're not sure?' Mathew said, detecting Alice's lack of enthusiasm.

'I'm ... apprehensive,' replied Alice after a moment's consideration.

'Your grandmother has told me of your concerns.' Her grandfather smiled. 'If the doctors didn't think it was for the best, they wouldn't allow Samuel home. It will be all right, you'll see.'

Alice smiled. Her grandfather's calm assurance was going a long way to soothing her anxiety.

'I suppose you've come to ask if I'll take you to fetch Samuel tomorrow?'

'Yes, please.'

'Of course. It will be my pleasure.' His gaze scanned the fields. 'Do you miss all this?' he asked Alice.

'Sometimes,' Alice smiled, 'though my clerical work at the vicarage takes up much of my time and, now that I'll be living there again, I'm sure I'll be kept even busier. And Samuel will need me, of course.'

'It's a shame,' Mathew said, shoving his hands in his trouser pockets, 'that so many of our local pickers have gravitated to the munitions factories in town. I'm trying to persuade young Daisy Hopwood to come back to the fields. Hannah says she's petrified of working in town. Can't say I blame her after what she's been through. She's still not quite right, poor girl.'

'She is much better, though,' Alice said, her gaze straying to the three cottages. Smoke curled from all three chimney pots, windows reflecting the clouds blowing across a pale blue sky. 'Leah says she doesn't have nightmares nearly as much now, and her hearing has improved a lot.'

'I don't think sitting about indoors all day does her any good,' Mathew remarked. 'I know Hannah means well, but since Daisy's accident, she does tend to mollycoddle her a bit. Perhaps I'll suggest your grandmother has a word. Try to encourage Daisy to give the picking a go. Anyway . . .' He turned to Alice. 'If you'll pack your things, I'll carry them over to the vicarage this evening. Mrs Hurst can arrange them for you before she leaves for the day.'

'Thank you, Grandfather.' Alice kissed his whiskery cheek. 'I'll see you later.'

'Would you like a cup of tea, Samuel?' Alice asked, tucking a blanket over her husband's knees as Mrs Hurst lit the lamp. They were in the vicarage parlour. The morning's frequent April showers had turned the sky dark, limiting the amount of natural light entering the wood-panelled room.

'Yes, I haven't had a decent cup of tea in months,' replied Samuel, 'And do stop fussing, Alice.' He slapped her hands away, crossly. 'I'm not an invalid.'

'No, of course not,' apologized Alice quickly, her eyes

smarting at the harshness of his rebuke. 'Mrs Hurst, would you bring some tea, please?' she said, keeping her tone cheerfully light.

'Yes, Mrs Roberts,' the housekeeper said, pursing her lips slightly. The young vicar had seemed out of sorts ever since he'd arrived home some twenty minutes earlier, she mused as she bustled off to the kitchen. Still, she reasoned as she filled the kettle, it was hardly surprising given everything the poor man had been through over the last three years.

'Are you warm enough?' Alice asked anxiously. 'Shall I put some more wood on the fire?'

'I'm fine,' replied Samuel brusquely. 'I've asked Mathew to pop by later,' he said. 'I'm anxious to discuss this Sunday's service with him.'

'But I thought . . .' Alice bit her tongue. 'I mean, I assumed you would like to settle in before you resume your duties?'

They were interrupted by a knock on the door, and Walter Aldridge's round, pleasant face peered round the doorframe.

'Samuel, my good man,' he exclaimed jovially, pushing the door wide and striding over to shake Samuel's hand. 'It's good to see you looking so well.'

'Thank you, Walter,' Samuel said coolly. Alice looked at him in surprise. His tone held none of the respect with which he had always used to speak to his mentor. Seemingly undeterred, Walter settled himself in the chair closest to Samuel's.

'I'll just go and ask Mrs Hurst to bring an extra cup.' Alice excused herself and hurried off to the kitchen. She returned some minutes later to find Walter on his feet, pacing in apparent agitation.

'What is it?' she asked, her gaze darting between the two men.

'I have told Walter that I am more than capable of resuming my duties and that he has until the end of the week to move out. After all, my dear, we need our home to ourselves.' Totally disarmed by Samuel's smile, Alice gave Walter an apologetic look.

'Are you sure, Samuel?' Walter asked, frowning so deeply his eyebrows met across the bridge of his nose. 'Do you not think you need a little more time?'

'No, Walter, I don't,' Samuel said, as Mrs Hurst entered with the tea tray. 'You've had the run of this parish for the last three years. And I'm grateful, but I'm back now and quite able to resume my duties.'

'But . . .' Walter spluttered, exchanging glances with Alice. She had confided in him briefly that while Samuel had been deemed physically fit for civilian life, his unpredictable mental state had resulted in his discharge from the army on medical grounds, leaving both Alice and Walter with the impression that he wasn't quite ready to return to preaching.

'Are you sure, Samuel?' Alice went to crouch beside her husband's chair. 'There's no rush. Reverend Aldridge is perfectly happy to continue for as long as he's needed.'

'That's very kind of you, Walter,' Samuel replied, accepting the cup of tea that Mrs Hurst handed to him. 'But I am quite well. I shall be presiding over this Sunday's service.

Please let Mathew know I wish to see him. I want to know how things have been progressing in my absence.'

'I can tell you that things have been going well,' Walter said, looking slightly vexed. 'Thank you, Mrs Hurst.' He took the proffered cup with a steady hand. There was dirt beneath his fingernails, noted Alice. He returned his attention to Samuel. 'Our congregation is somewhat diminished, of course, with most of our men away, but we're starting to get the migrant workers arriving.'

'Thank you, Walter,' Samuel interrupted him with a dismissive wave of his hand. 'I'm sure Mathew can fill me in on all I need to know.'

'Very well,' Reverend Aldridge said with a small sigh. 'I think I shall take my tea up to my room. I shall leave for my sister's this afternoon.'

'So soon?' Alice said in alarm.

Walter's expression was kind. 'I think it's for the best all round, don't you?'

'I've missed all this,' Samuel said, once Walter and Mrs Hurst had departed. He reached for Alice's hand, drawing her close. 'And I've missed you, my dear.' He pulled her gently onto his lap and kissed her cheek. Alice rested her head against him, her shoulders sagging in relief. This was her Samuel, the man she had fallen in love with, she thought, as he gently caressed her back, his lips warm against her neck. All at once, the future didn't seem so bleak after all.

CHAPTER TWENTY

'Nurse Webb, may I have a word?' Matron cornered Dora as she was on her way to the sluice room, her arms laden with bundles of soiled linen.

'Of course, Matron.' Dora frowned, wondering what she'd done wrong. Matron was looking severely vexed.

'Come to my office as soon as you've offloaded that lot,' she said brusquely.

'Yes, Matron.' Heart racing in trepidation, Dora hurried off. Barely five minutes later, she was knocking on Matron's door, her heart hammering in her chest.

'Take a seat, Nurse,' Matron said, once she'd invited Dora inside. The window was open to the breeze, fractured shards of May sunshine dancing on the swirly-patterned rug. She smiled, her warm demeanour instantly allaying Dora's fears that she might be in trouble.

'I'm pleased to say that Clarissa is recovering well,' Matron said, folding her hands on the desk. 'She will be on the next convoy home.'

'Oh?' Dora looked at Matron in surprise. 'But I thought . . .'

'Apparently, Mrs Arspery is meeting her in Southampton.'

'I see,' Dora frowned. Clarissa had said nothing to her about her mother's apparent change of heart. But if Mrs Arspery was prepared to accept little Frank, then Dora was pleased for her friend, though she would miss them both.

'The thing is,' Matron said, her brows knitting in concern, 'I can hardly send a young woman and a baby with a convoy of men. She will need a chaperone, and I was wondering whether you would be prepared to accompany Clarissa and Frank to England.'

'Oh!' Dora squeaked in surprise. 'This is unexpected.'

'I appreciate that, Nurse Webb, but you've been here for a year and you deserve a break. I have taken the liberty of writing to my colleague at the Royal Victoria Hospital at Netley, which is close to where you come from, I believe?' At Dora's affirmation, she continued, 'They would be pleased to have you. That is, if you wish to remain in England, of course. It goes without saying that I'd be more than happy to have you back here.'

'I think I would like to come back, Matron.'

'You have plenty of time to decide,' Matron smiled. 'I shall have your transfer papers ready for you by the time you leave. You'll be on tomorrow's convoy.'

'Tomorrow?' Dora swallowed.

'You may have this afternoon to pack your things,' Matron said, getting to her feet. 'The convoy leaves at four tomorrow morning.'

*

It was still dark when the convoy of ambulances drew up outside the railway station the following morning. The destruction wrought by the recent shelling was evident in the light of the waning moon, and Dora again felt a pang of sadness as she thought about the Chevaliers and the many others who had been killed that terrible day.

She cradled the sleeping baby Frank in her arms as Clarissa hobbled along the platform, aided by a pair of crutches. All around them, wounded men were being unloaded from the ambulances and onto the train. Dora had been disappointed that none of the nurses chosen to accompany them were girls she was particularly close to, and she'd said a regretful good-bye to Millie and Emma late the previous evening. They had all promised to keep in touch.

Dora, Clarissa and the baby had been allocated a carriage at the front, and Dora soon had them settled. Frank slept soundly in her arms as the train pulled away from the station, picking up speed. She sank against the upholstered backrest, the blacked-out windows lending a claustrophobic feel to the carriage.

'I'm scared,' Clarissa said in a small voice.

'We'll be all right,' Dora said, smiling through the darkness. 'We'll be at Boulogne and on a ship before you know it.'

'It's not being attacked I'm frightened of,' she sighed. 'I'm terrified at the thought of seeing my mother. I'm meeting her at the Royal Pier Hotel for tea. Please will you join us?'

'I don't think it would be appropriate,' Dora replied, after a brief consideration. 'Your mother hasn't invited me.'

'Oh, please, Dora,' Clarissa pleaded. 'I don't think I can face her alone.'

Dora hesitated. 'But she knows you're bringing Frank?'

Clarissa's cheeks reddened as she shook her head.

'I couldn't tell her, Dora. I'm hoping that once she sees him, she'll soften. She's his grandmother, after all, and he's so adorable, how could she resist him?'

'Perhaps you should have warned her, though?'

'She wouldn't have come,' Clarissa said shortly.

They lapsed into silence, each lost in their own thoughts as the train rushed through the darkness towards the coast.

The crossing to Southampton passed without incident and, at precisely three o'clock that afternoon, Dora followed Clarissa into the hotel, the civilians and service personnel parting like the Red Sea as Clarissa made her way laboriously across the lobby.

A tall, elegant-looking woman rose to her feet. Even from a distance, Dora could tell immediately that she must be Clarissa's mother. The family resemblance was striking. She wore a well-tailored skirt and jacket, a fox slung artfully around her slender shoulders.

She raised a gloved hand, her expression stony. Sighing deeply, Clarissa made her way towards her, Dora following meekly in her wake.

'Mother.' Clarissa kissed the woman's cheek. 'Mother, may I introduce Nurse Dora Webb. Dora, my mother, Mrs Arspery.'

Barely acknowledging Dora, Mrs Arspery's gaze darted from Frank, sleeping peacefully against Dora's chest, to her daughter.

'What is the meaning of this?' she hissed through clenched teeth. 'I thought you said arrangements had been made!'

'Mother,' Clarissa's chin trembled, 'this is your grandson, Frank.'

'Lower your voice,' Clarissa's mother hissed, glancing about the busy lobby to make sure no one she knew was within earshot. 'I thought we'd agreed you'd leave the child in France! This is no grandchild of mine, Clarissa.' For the first time, she made eye contact with Dora, who was growing more uncomfortable by the minute. Her cheeks burned and she could feel perspiration pricking beneath her armpits.

'Take the child for a walk or something,' she said imperiously. 'I wish to speak to my daughter in private.' Dora looked at Clarissa for confirmation. She nodded.

'Perhaps if you walk to the quayside and back?' she suggested.

As Dora made her way through the lobby to the entrance, she turned in time to see Clarissa being ushered into the lounge, Mrs Arspery seemingly giving her a good talking-to.

It was bracing on the seafront. The air smelled of fish and vinegar. Gulls wheeled and screamed overhead. Dora found a sheltered bench and sat down. She couldn't be too long. Frank would be ready for a feed soon. Keeping an eye on the clock on the harbour office wall, she whiled away the minutes by watching the hustle and bustle of the quayside. She gave Clarissa and her mother forty minutes, by which time Frank had woken and was growing fractious. It wouldn't be long before his whimpers escalated into a full-blown cry.

She asked for Mrs Arspery at reception and took a seat near the concierge's desk to wait. Clarissa appeared a few minutes later, her face pale. She looked as though she'd been crying.

'Oh dear, was it awful?' Dora asked, with sympathy. Clarissa didn't seem able to meet Dora's gaze.

'We had a nice walk, but he's hungry now.' Dora offered Clarissa the squirming infant.

'I can't,' Clarissa said, shaking her head.

'What do you mean?' asked Dora, puzzled. 'He's hungry, Clarissa. He's going to start screaming in a minute.'

Clarissa shook her head. 'I can't take him.' Now she did meet Dora's gaze, her expression haunted. 'It will break my heart to hold him,' she said, a single tear sliding down her white cheek.

'Clarissa?' Dora jiggled the baby in an effort to calm him. His hungry cries were reaching a crescendo, drawing the attention of passers-by.

Clarissa grabbed Dora's arm, pulling her behind a grand pillar.

'You must take him,' she said, with a determined thrust to her jaw. 'Please, Dora. Otherwise it'll be the orphanage.'

'I can't. Clarissa, I have to work. I can't take care of a baby!'

'It'll only be for a couple of weeks, a month at most. Just until my parents come round to the idea. Please?' Clarissa begged, her desperation evident in her voice. 'If you don't, I'll lose him forever.' Her eyes filled with tears. 'My mother's coming – please, say you'll take him.'

Mrs Arspery reached them before Dora could reply. 'Clarissa, can you stop that child from screaming?' she said brusquely, her cool gaze sweeping over Dora to rest on her daughter. 'People are looking.'

'He's hungry,' Dora replied, surprising herself. The old Dora would never have spoken to someone like Mrs Arspery with so little reverence, but she had seen too much horror to be cowed by the likes of her friend's mother.

'Go to the kitchens and see if they'll give you some milk,' Mrs Arspery ordered with a wave of her gloved hand. 'Clarissa, the car's here.'

'Ask the driver to wait, Mother,' Clarissa begged, throwing Dora a panicked look.

'I'll get the milk,' Dora said. She felt hot, aware of the curious glances from the other guests as Frank continued to wail and flail his little fists, his little face crimson.

The chef was less than pleased to have his routine interrupted by a request for warm milk. By the time the milk had been warmed and a bottle found and sterilized, almost twenty minutes had passed. Frank had worn himself out and had fallen asleep. Arms aching, Dora carried him and the bottle of milk back into the lobby, her gaze searching the sea of people for any sign of Clarissa or her mother. With a growing sense of unease, she hurried to the entrance, scanning the few cars parked alongside the kerb. She looked up and down the street. Hurrying back inside, she tried the ladies' rest room and peeped into the dining room, but there was no sign of either Clarissa or her mother. Dora's heart sank as the unpleasant truth sank in. In trepidation, she approached the desk.

'I'm supposed to be meeting Mrs Arspery here,' she said.

'I'm afraid Mrs Arspery and her daughter left ten minutes ago,' the middle-aged receptionist said, eyeing Dora's left hand with a knowing gleam. Dora felt herself grow red. Of course, people would assume Frank was hers. 'They left this for you.' The woman lifted a bag from behind the desk. In it were some nappies and a change of clothes. Mumbling her thanks, she hurried out into the sunshine. Feeling less conspicuous in the busy street, she made her way to a quiet bench and woke Frank. She fed him his bottle and burped him. His nappy felt heavy, but that would have to wait until she got him home. *Home.* The word stopped her in her tracks. A wave of nausea washed over her. People would assume Frank was hers. Her stomach contracted painfully. What on earth would Hannah say when she turned up on her doorstep with a baby in tow?

It was early evening by the time Dora knocked on Hannah's front door. She could hear the chatter of the strawberry pickers in the fields behind her and the sound of organ music drifting from the church.

'Dora, you don't need to knock!' Hannah said, opening the door. The rest of her words died on her lips as she noticed the baby in Dora's arms. 'Oh,' was all she said as she stood back to let Dora in.

'You've had a baby!' exclaimed Daisy in disbelief, half-rising to her feet.

'It's Frank,' replied Dora quickly as Hannah ushered her indoors. 'My friend Clarissa's baby? I've mentioned him in my letters. Well, I'm sort of looking after him for a few weeks.'

'Where is Clarissa?' Hannah asked, frowning.

'He's so sweet. Can I hold him?' Daisy asked, holding out her arms.

'Please do. My arms are killing me.' She handed Frank to Daisy. 'He needs his nappy changing, I'm afraid.' She turned to Hannah. 'It's a long story.'

'I'll put the kettle on,' Hannah said. 'And you can tell us all about it. Supper will be ready when Leah gets back. She's gone to evensong with Alice.'

'So she's just upped and left you holding the baby?' Leah said, looking incredulous. She'd just walked in the door, her initial delight at seeing her old friend after such a long time tempered by her shock at the sight of the baby.

'Yes,' Dora sighed. 'I didn't know what to do. I couldn't take the little mite to the orphanage, could I? But I'm meant to report to the Royal Victoria the day after tomorrow, if I'm staying in England. How can I work and look after a baby?'

'If it's only for a few weeks,' Hannah said, getting up to serve the evening meal, 'I can take care of him during the day. Beatrice will help, I'm sure.'

'And me,' Daisy said, looking more animated than her mother had seen her since before the accident.

'You're back in the fields,' Leah pointed out, reaching out to stroke Frank's cheek.

'Only part-time,' Daisy reminded her. She looked at Dora. 'It would be a pleasure. He's so sweet.'

'If you're all sure?' Dora said doubtfully. 'It would be such a help. And it won't be for long. Clarissa said a week or two, a month at most.'

'I hope she never comes back and we get to keep Frank forever,' said Daisy as he opened his violet-blue eyes and smiled.

CHAPTER TWENTY-ONE

The June sun was warm on Alice's cheek as she rapped on Hannah's open back door.

'Hello, Alice,' Leah said, appearing in the parlour doorway. 'Shall we go for a walk? Mum and Dora have taken Frank over to the Merrifields, and Lizzie and Nora are here visiting Daisy. Their chatter's giving me a headache.'

'A walk sounds lovely,' Alice agreed. While Leah fetched her hat, she stuck her head round the parlour door to say hello to the three girls, and then she and Leah set off down the lane. It was a beautiful day. Swallows and skylarks swooped overhead and the surrounding trees resounded with birdsong. The recent rainfall had left the air smelling fresh and clean. Being Sunday, the strawberry fields were empty but for a lone male pheasant picking his way slowly along the rows.

'Have you seen anything of George Merrifield since he was invalided out of the army?' Alice asked Leah as they rounded the corner by the church and made their way up the track. Wild garlic brushed their skirts, its pungent scent wafting into the air, and a magpie chittered noisily above their heads.

'Not really,' Leah replied, her fingers brushing at the long stalks of grass that grew up beside the track. 'Mum said he keeps very much to himself. Mrs Merrifield is quite worried about him.'

'Poor woman,' Alice said, shaking her head sorrowfully. 'She's had such a tragic time of it.'

'Does Samuel ever speak about Leonard?' Leah asked. 'I can't imagine how horrible it must have been for him. No wonder it made him ill.'

'He won't speak about his time away at all. And I don't blame him. It's affected him more than he'll let on.' Her eyes clouded. 'Oh, Leah,' she sighed, as they reached the clearing. The pond sparkled in the afternoon sunlight, the reflected foliage lending an emerald hue to the shimmering surface. The old rope swing creaked rhythmically in the breeze, and a moorhen and her chicks paddled among the gently undulating reeds.

'I thought that when Samuel returned home, we'd get back to how we used to be.' Alice tucked her skirts beneath her and sat down on an old log. Leah joined her.

'And it isn't?' she asked, tilting her face to the sun.

'No,' Alice sighed. 'There are times when he's the sweetest man and I remember why I fell in love with him. But other times, he's like a stranger. He's so cold and . . .' She hesitated. 'I know one shouldn't criticize one's husband, but at times he's almost cruel. Even Mrs Hurst has noted the change in him, and you know how much she doted on him.'

'The tone of his sermons has changed, too,' Leah remarked, turning to face Alice. She fiddled absently with the ring on her finger. Her engagement ring. An old family heirloom, it had belonged to Harry's grandmother. 'And I'm not the only one to notice,' she said, watching how the small diamonds and emeralds sparkled as they caught the light. 'Mum said people are talking.'

'My grandparents have said the same,' Alice said. 'He's so judgemental in the pulpit nowadays.'

'He is a bit fire and brimstone, isn't he?' Leah grinned. 'Oh, I'm sorry, Alice,' she said, instantly contrite at the sight of her friend's downcast expression. 'I didn't mean to upset you.'

Alice shook her head. 'No, you're right, Leah. Even the most conservative members of our congregation were looking a bit shocked this morning. But it's not just his sermons, though,' she said sadly. 'We'll be getting along so well, then I'll say or do something that annoys him and he explodes in a rage.'

'I would never have imagined Samuel could lose his temper,' Leah said, her gaze drifting towards the pond. A fish leapt out of the water, attracting the attention of a nearby grey heron. Its scales flashed silver in the sunlight as it landed with a splash, sending ripples across the pond.

'Well, no, quite,' Alice agreed. 'Of course, he's very contrite afterwards, but having to walk on eggshells around him is very wearying.'

'It sounds like he's feeling sorry for himself, like Dora's dad.'

'Mr Webb enjoyed wallowing in self-pity,' Alice pointed out. 'I don't believe Samuel can help himself. Like Reverend Aldridge said, it is early days. He's not been out of hospital very long. And we were apart for so long before that,' she went on, feeling guilty at her earlier disloyalty to her husband. 'Of course it will take time for him to adjust.'

'What do you think about Dora being lumbered with baby Frank?' Leah said, abruptly changing the subject as they watched the heron bobbing among the bulrushes. 'It's all a bit bizarre, don't you think?'

'I think it's shocking that a mother can leave her baby for so long,' Alice retorted, her own longing for a child lending anger to her tone. 'Clarissa apparently promised Dora she'd come for him within a week or two. It's been over a month.'

'It's all a bit suspicious if you ask me. Dora said Clarissa keeps coming up with excuses. Her father still doesn't know about Frank, apparently, and Clarissa is hoping that if she can win her mother round, she will persuade the father to accept the child.' Leah stretched her arms above her head, stifling a yawn. 'I heard Martha Prior and Katie Sanders gossiping about Dora in the post office the other day. I set them straight, I can tell you.'

'I'm afraid there are quite a few people like that hereabouts,' Alice sighed. 'I suppose it's inevitable. She's just come back from eighteen months abroad with a baby in tow. Tongues are bound to wag.'

'I just hope Nate believes her. She's written to him about Frank. She wasn't going to, but as Clarissa seems to be procrastinating, she feels it's only right to explain the situation to him.'

'Nate would never think ill of Dora,' Alice said, smiling. She hadn't always been fond of her half-brother, but they had formed a bond of sorts not long before he'd enlisted and, now that he was at the mercy of his German captors, she found herself regretting all the time she had wasted. Nate had only ever wanted to be her friend, yet she had rebuffed his every attempt at friendship. She hoped her weekly letters and the Red Cross parcels she sent regularly went some way to making amends.

'Of course he wouldn't,' Leah grinned. 'He's besotted with her. Anyway,' she sat up straight, an excited glint in her eyes, 'I need to speak to you in your official capacity as parish clerk.'

'Oh yes?' Alice's brows rose.

'I shall come and see Samuel myself on Harry's behalf in the next day or so, but I would very much like you to arrange the reading of our banns.'

'Oh, Leah, that's so exciting,' squealed Alice, clapping her hands. 'Have you set a date?'

'Harry's leave starts on the twenty-fifth of September. He should arrive in Strawbridge by the Thursday at the latest, so we've decided on the twenty-ninth. He only has to be back on the fifth of October, so we'll have almost four days for a honeymoon.'

'I'm so happy for you,' Alice said, her eyes glistening with unshed tears. 'You've waited so long for this. If you let me know the name of Harry's commanding officer, I'll fill out the paperwork this evening.'

'Thank you, Alice.' Leah leaned back on her elbows, the warm sun caressing her face as she closed her eyes. 'I can't afford a wedding dress, but do you think your mother might help me alter Mum's?'

'Nonsense,' declared Alice firmly. 'You know how fond Mother is of you. It would be her pleasure to make your wedding dress. It can be our wedding gift to you.'

'You're so kind,' Leah said, emotion clogging her throat. 'Thank you.'

'Don't mention it,' Alice grinned. 'Now, if I want to get that paperwork done before supper, we should start back.'

The glorious June sunshine stretched late into the evening. Midsummer was a fortnight away and, as she carefully folded the covering letter she had written to Harry's commanding officer, Alice found herself reminiscing over the Pickers' Ball, which had always been held on the Saturday closest to Midsummer. Though Isaac still put on the occasional dance in the church hall for the pickers, there had been no ball for the past two years, and she wondered wistfully whether there ever would be again. And even if there *was* a ball in the future, it would never be the same. So many of Strawbridge's young men were never coming home.

Hearing a sound behind her, she turned, smiling at the sight of Samuel standing at the open French windows, cradling the vicarage cat in his arms.

'What is keeping you so busy this evening?' he smiled amiably.

'I'm writing to Harry's commanding officer.' She smiled at him over her shoulder. 'I shall explain in a minute. Has your meeting finished?'

'Yes, we got through everything quicker than expected.'

'Mrs Hurst has left some cold meat and creamed potatoes for you in the pantry,' Alice said, pushing back her chair and crossing the room towards him. She kissed his smooth cheek. 'Shall I fetch it for you?'

'Thank you.' Samuel released the cat, which darted across the stone terrace and disappeared behind the rhododendrons. 'With some of that apple chutney, if there's any left.'

'There are still a few jars in the pantry,' Alice smiled. Samuel grabbed her hand and pulled her against him.

'You've caught the sun,' he remarked, running his finger down her cheek. 'It suits you.'

'Thank you,' smiled Alice, resting her head against his shoulder. He smelled of coal tar soap.

'So why were you writing to Harry's commanding officer?' Samuel frowned. 'Is Harry all right? I keep meaning to write to him, but . . .' He shrugged.

'He's well, as far as I know,' Alice grinned, twisting her neck so she could see Samuel's expression when she told him the news. 'He's coming home on leave, and he and Leah are getting married.'

'Well, good for them!' Samuel exclaimed. 'It's about time.'

'Obviously Harry will have to have his banns read out

wherever he's billeted, and I've already filled out the paper-work for Leah. They've set a date for the twenty-ninth of September.'

'Excellent, I must write and congratulate him. Remind me.'

'I will,' laughed Alice. She reached up and kissed him, her heart light. If only these happy, carefree moments could last, she mused sombrely as she disentangled herself from his embrace and went to fetch his supper from the pantry.

'I've been thinking,' she said a short time later, reaching for Samuel's hand. They were sitting at the table on the terrace. The low sun cast long shadows across the flagstones. The cat lay curled up on the lawn, soaking up the last of the sun's rays.

'Oh yes?' Samuel cocked his head questioningly, dabbing apple chutney from his lips with a napkin.

'I was thinking it would be nice to invite Carl and Kitty over for Sunday dinner.'

'Carl and Kitty?' repeated Samuel, laying his napkin down and regarding Alice with a puzzled frown.

'He was on your ward,' Alice reminded him, assuming his confusion was due to him not remembering the names. 'I attended their wedding back in March?'

'I know who you mean, Alice,' Samuel snapped. 'I'm not a simpleton.'

'Of course not,' Alice assured him quickly, her cheeks reddening.

'Quite frankly, I can't imagine why you'd think I'd want

to be reminded of such a dark time in my life. I hated it in that place. I certainly would not wish to spend time with anyone associated with my time there.'

'I'm sorry, I didn't mean to upset you. It's just that Kitty was a good friend to me while you were in hospital, and as I haven't seen her since her wedding, I thought—'

'I said no,' Samuel snapped. 'You have no idea what it was like for me in there, Alice. If you even had an inkling of how I suffered in that place, you wouldn't make such foolish suggestions.' He scraped his chair back, the legs squealing on the flagstones and causing the cat to raise its head, clearly annoyed at the noisy intrusion. 'I shall be in my study. I'm not to be disturbed.'

Barely able to comprehend how quickly the pleasant evening had descended into another disagreement, Alice stared after her husband with quiet dismay. With a heaviness of spirit, she got to her feet and quietly began to clear the table.

CHAPTER TWENTY-TWO

Leah stared at her reflection in awe. 'It's beautiful,' she whispered, running her hands down the delicate fabric as she met Alice's gaze in the mirror.

'You look stunning, Leah,' Alice smiled. 'You'll be the prettiest bride Strawbridge has ever seen. Your Harry will be bowled over when he sees you coming down the aisle.'

Turning, Leah craned her neck in an effort to glimpse the tiny mother-of-pearl buttons running down her back.

'Here.' Alice took a tortoiseshell hand mirror from the workbench and handed it to Leah.

'Your mother is so talented,' Leah sighed, admiring the way the soft, pearl-white satin shimmered in the pale morning light streaming in through the window. 'Thank you so much, Mrs Russell,' she breathed, turning towards the door as Lily entered with the tea tray. 'It's everything I dreamed it would be.'

'It's been my pleasure, Leah,' Lily smiled, setting the tray on the workbench. 'You look an absolute picture.'

'I shall lend Leah my veil,' Alice said, smiling as Leah turned back to the mirror. 'So that's something borrowed.'

'And I have my blue handkerchief,' Leah said, her reflection smiling back at her friend. 'And Mum's lending me her pearl necklace.' She took a deep breath, letting the butterflies in her stomach settle. It was the middle of August. Six weeks until Harry's long-overdue leave. Four days after that, she would walk down the aisle and become his wife, at last.

Her job at the munitions factory paid well and her nest egg was considerable. She would continue to live at home until the war ended, whenever that might be. When Harry finally came home for good, they would be able to afford a comfortable home to start their married life. She hoped that day would come sooner rather than later. Much as she loved her family, the cottage was becoming a trifle cramped. Frank might only be five months old, but he certainly made his presence felt.

'What was Clarissa's excuse this time?' Alice asked now, as if reading Leah's thoughts.

'Her mother's had a bad turn, so she feels she can't bother her about Frank at the moment,' Leah replied, with a sceptical lift of her brows as she sipped her tea. The wedding dress was back on its hanger and covered by a dustsheet.

'I've been thinking for a while now that she's just stringing Dora along,' Alice said, leaning against the workbench. 'I don't believe she has any intention of taking Frank back.'

'It does seem that way,' agreed Leah. 'The thing is, we're all getting so fond of the little chap that when she does come for him, it's going to be a wrench. Especially for Dora. She's fallen head over heels for him. And so has Mum.'

'It will be hard when we all have to say goodbye to him,' Alice said wistfully, her hand moving unconsciously to her stomach. There, she felt it again, the strange twinge deep down inside that gave her cause to hope. She had been late with her monthlies before, only to have her hopes dashed when they'd finally arrived, heavy and painful, as if mocking her disappointment. But this time felt different. She felt different. She hadn't said anything to Leah. She hadn't even told Samuel, unable to bear the spark of hope in his eyes only to see it crushed later.

'Alice?'

She blinked, suddenly aware that she hadn't heard a word Leah had said.

'I'm sorry,' she said with a shrug.

'I was saying,' said Leah with a hint of exasperation, 'that Nate has told Dora she needs to be firm with Clarissa and tell her that if she doesn't take Frank, Dora will write to Mr and Mrs Arspery and tell them the whole story. I mean, he's costing Dora money. In all these weeks, Clarissa's sent one postal order, and that barely covered the medicine he needed when he had croup.'

Alice grimaced. 'It's going to end in tears, whichever way you look at it. Poor Dora.'

Dora lifted the screaming baby out of his cradle. Frank's crimson cheeks were wet with tears and his skin was hot and feverish. She cradled him in her arms as he waved his little fists angrily, and then went down to the kitchen in search of the concoction Pearl had given her which she swore would alleviate his pain.

'Poor mite,' Hannah said, bustling through the back door, her wicker basket brimming with early blackberries. 'I remember how awful it was with my lot,' she said, dumping the basket on the table. 'They all had a terrible time with teething, especially Freddie.' She paused to stroke Frank's cheek. 'Are you using that teething remedy Pearl gave you?'

'I'm just about to give him a bit more,' Dora replied, balancing the baby on one hip while unscrewing the twist of paper Pearl had pressed into her hand when they'd met in the lane yesterday evening. She tried not to think what the pale chalky-white powder might contain, but whatever it was, it had certainly appeared to ease Frank's distress. For the first time in weeks, he'd slept through the night, to the relief of the rest of the household.

'Let me take him while you do that,' Hannah said, lifting Frank from Dora's arms. 'There, there,' she crooned, jiggling him up and down. 'Aunty Dor's getting your medicine, sweetie.' Frank screamed louder, shoving his little fists into his mouth.

Dora managed to administer the soothing powder, and Hannah carried him into the parlour, bouncing him up and down, then settled herself in the rocking chair. As she rocked, Frank's wails grew weaker and his eyelids began to droop. Within minutes, he'd fallen fast asleep.

'Bless him,' Hannah said fondly. 'Whatever that stuff is, it works a treat. It was the only thing that worked with my lot, too. She's very knowledgeable on all things medicinal is Pearl.'

'That sleeping draught she used to give me for Dad was amazing,' agreed Dora, crossing to the window. The strawberry fields were teeming with workers. She could see Daisy in the middle of the field. She was standing up, arching her back, her head thrown back in laughter. Her two friends, Lizzie and Nora, were laughing, too. Whatever the joke was, Dora was pleased to see Daisy looking so happy. She still suffered from the occasional nightmare but, on the whole, she was almost back to her old self. Mathew Turner had been right – getting Daisy out into the fields had done her the world of good.

'Here come Leah and Alice,' she said, spotting her friends coming down the lane. 'Judging by the way they're smiling, I'd say the dress fitting went well.'

'I wouldn't expect otherwise,' Hannah remarked softly so as not to wake the sleeping baby. 'Mrs Russell's reputation is second to none. Leah is very fortunate. I certainly couldn't afford those prices.'

Dora heard Leah and Alice say goodbye, and Leah disappeared from view while Alice continued towards the vicarage. Catching sight of Dora in the window, she waved. Dora waved back, and moments later she heard Leah entering via the back door.

'And?' Dora demanded, as Leah stood in the parlour doorway, her face glowing. 'Is it all you hoped it would be?'

'Oh, Dor,' Leah exclaimed, her cheeks pink with excitement. 'It's absolutely gorgeous. Oh, Mum, I can't wait for you to see it. It's the most beautiful dress.'

'I'm very happy for you, love,' Hannah said, smiling broadly. 'You've waited so long. I can't believe my daughter will soon be Mrs Whitworth.' She chuckled. 'Your father would be tickled pink to think of you marrying into the Whitworth family.'

'Harry's likely to be disinherited,' Leah reminded her mother, a mischievous glint in her eyes. 'So it's unlikely I'll ever be mistress of Streawberige House.'

'You may find Mr and Mrs Whitworth think differently now,' Dora said. She leaned against the windowsill, her back to the busy strawberry fields. 'I assume you have issued them an invitation?'

'Oh yes,' replied Leah. 'I wrote to them explaining that it would obviously be a very small affair, just family and a few close friends, and that they'd be most welcome. I have yet to receive their reply.'

'Whatever their attitude now,' Hannah said mildly, 'they're bound to come round once the babies start coming.'

'Mum!' Leah exclaimed, flushing in mortification.

'I'm only saying,' her mother continued unapologetically, 'that I doubt even Frances Whitworth would turn her back on her own grandchild.'

'How strange,' Dora said, her head half-turned towards the window. 'Mr Whitworth is outside now.'

'What?' Leah flew to the window, her hand at her throat.

Sure enough, Isaac Whitworth was standing on the grass verge looking up at the cottage, his expression grim. Fear caught Leah's throat. She glanced round, wild-eyed. 'Mum?'

But Hannah was already on her feet. Handing the sleeping Frank to Dora, she came to stand at Leah's side in time to see Isaac cross the lane towards them. Seeing them clustered at the window, he nodded sombrely and removed his hat. Unable to move, Leah stood rooted to the spot, and it was Hannah who went to the open door.

'Good afternoon, Mr Whitworth,' she said as calmly as she could, though her heart was racing and she was finding it hard to breathe.

'Mrs Hopwood,' Isaac nodded. 'I wonder if I might have a word with Leah?'

From inside came a low groan, and Hannah felt her own heart shatter into pieces, her daughter's agony a knife piercing her very soul. She nodded silently and moved aside to allow him into the parlour.

'I'm so sorry, Leah,' Isaac said, his voice gruff. 'Henry was killed at Ypres early yesterday morning.'

His own eyes filling with tears, he watched the girl crumple before him. She would have fallen if her mother hadn't caught hold of her.

'Come, Leah. Sit down.' Hannah gently led Leah to the sofa, where she fell against the cushions, her face white. She was shaking. Her wide blue eyes sought Isaac's, willing him to tell her that it was not true. That it was a cruel joke.

'We're getting married next month,' she whispered.

'I know,' Isaac said in a strangled voice.

'I'm his next of kin,' she said, remembering. She sat forward. 'Why haven't I had a telegram?' The brief flicker of hope that Isaac might have been misinformed was extinguished when he continued.

'You are indeed down as Henry's next of kin,' Isaac said. Even through her own haze of grief, Leah could tell how much it pained him to acknowledge that Harry had named Leah as his next of kin over him. 'And you should receive official notification tomorrow or the next day, but my contact at the War Office felt I should be informed.' He shuffled his feet, clearly uncomfortable in the face of Leah's shocked disbelief.

'I can't believe it,' she said, her voice trembling as she reached for her mother's hand.

'I'm so sorry, Leah,' Dora whispered, coming to sit on Leah's other side. Leah looked at Frank sleeping peacefully in Dora's arms and the scale of her loss suddenly felt overwhelming. She let out a choking sob and collapsed against her mother, her hot, bitter tears soaking through the thin fabric of Hannah's blouse.

The telegram arrived just after ten o'clock the next morning. Hannah kept the curtains drawn. Unable to summon the energy to get out of bed, let alone go to work, Leah had stayed home, hidden under the bed covers. Her eyes were hot and scratchy, the combination of too little sleep and too many tears. She lay in the darkened room, listening to the procession of visitors calling to pay their respects and willing them to go away. She wanted only to be left alone to wallow in her grief and misery. She clutched Harry's photograph in her hand, terrified that his features would become blurred by the passage of time and that, one day, she might be unable to recall his face. This thought brought a fresh flood of tears, soaking her pillow and making her throat ache.

Someone rapped gently on the bedroom door. She ignored them. She heard the soft creak as the door slowly swung open.

'Leah?' Alice's voice. 'I've brought you some tea and toast,' she said, the floorboards creaking as she crossed to the bed. 'I'll just leave it here,' she said, putting a tray on the bedside cabinet. 'You may feel like it later.'

There was a pause. Leah squeezed her eyes shut, willing Alice to go away. She couldn't face anyone. Not even her dearest friends. Right now, the only person she wanted was Harry, but she would never get to see him again. She let out a muffled sob.

'Oh, Leah,' sighed Alice. Leah bit her lip, willing herself to be quiet, and presently Alice left her alone.

CHAPTER TWENTY-THREE

'Nurse, nurse!' a hoarse voice called from behind the curtain.

'Just a minute, love,' Dora called back as she finished straightening the covers on the bed next door. The patient lay deathly still, his breathing shallow, his pallor as waxen as the models Dora had once seen at a travelling fair on Hamble Common. She laid her hand on his forehead. His skin was cold and clammy to the touch. The poor boy wasn't long for this world, she thought sadly, glancing towards the window. The silver sea, shimmering in the murky light, was crammed with ships. Even with the windows closed, she could hear the shrill whistle of the trains ferrying the wounded from the quayside to the hospital. The horizon was a hazy smudge in the distance, the dark clouds bringing with them the smell of impending rain. She glanced back at her patient. Hopefully his mother would make it in time, she thought with a sigh, tucking the sheet up under his chin.

'Nurse.' The voice came again. Wiping her hands on her apron, she slipped through the curtain and, plastering a cheerful smile on her face, reached for the hand of the man lying in the bed before her. According to his information chart, his name was Ian and he was thirty years old. She had no idea what he looked like, as his face was completely hidden by a thick swathe of bandages. Only his slightly parted lips, his nostrils and his eyes, an incredible blue that reminded Dora of the cornflowers that bloomed along the lane outside the cottages, were visible.

'Thirsty,' Ian whispered, his blue eyes following Dora's every move as she poured a glass of water and, holding it under his head, tilted it so he could swallow a few drops through his chapped lips. His chart told her that he'd been hit in the face and legs by shrapnel. He'd only been at the Royal Victoria for a few days. She laid his head back against the pillows and checked his chart. He had no next of kin listed, and she wondered about the man. *Is there really no one in the world who cares whether he lives or dies?* The thought filled her with sadness.

'How are you feeling today, Private Foster?' she asked, cheerfully.

'Not . . . bad, Nurse,' Ian managed, his lips contorting into a semblance of a smile. 'I . . . I'll . . . be . . .up and . . .about . . . in no . . . time.' His lips stretched, causing a pinprick of blood.

'Of course you will,' Dora smiled, dabbing his lips gently.

'Nurse, nurse,' called a voice Dora recognized as the young lad who'd been brought in with a broken back. Sighing inwardly, she straightened up, gave Ian a gentle pat on the shoulder and slipped through the curtains. The good-looking private with the broken back was as cheerful as could be. Though he faced being bedridden for several weeks with his body encased in a brace that was hot and uncomfortable, his only complaint was that his back was a little stiff and aching. She attended to his needs and then hurried down to the sluice room, where a mountain of bedpans awaited her attention.

She'd settled in well at the Royal Victoria Military Hospital in the four months she'd been there. The work was hard and the hours long, but, in comparison to conditions at the field hospital in France, it was a vast improvement. And she got to go home every day to see baby Frank. Just the thought of his little face made her heart swell. As the days went by, she was finding it harder to remember that little Frank wasn't hers. Clarissa's letters came less frequently now. The most recent had been over three weeks earlier and had been nothing more than a litany of excuses as to why she couldn't yet come for Frank. Secretly, Dora was hoping she never would. She adored the little boy. He was five and a half months old now, and his smile when he saw Dora melted her heart. He was such a happy soul, and everyone doted on him.

Oh, she was well aware of the rumours. That was one of the reasons she avoided church now. She'd grown tired of the whispering and the funny looks. She wasn't looking forward to the memorial service later. A service had been held in the Whitworth's parish church in Richmond the previous week, but Isaac, rightly understanding that the residents of Strawbridge would also like to pay their respects to the young man they had come to love as one of their own, had arranged a smaller service to be held at St Luke's later that afternoon. Ordinarily, Dora wouldn't have taken the time off work, but Harry had been a good friend to her Nate, and she was going mainly to support Leah, who had been understandably devastated by his loss.

Leah stood in the front of the mirror. Against her black dress, her skin looked even paler than usual, the dark shadows under her eyes more pronounced. She barely slept and ate little, and spent her days at the factory working on automatic pilot. She wasn't the only one at Franklin's to be mourning a loved one. At least half a dozen of the women had recently lost sweethearts or husbands. Her line manager had lost her son just a week ago.

She heard footsteps descending the stairs.

'It's time to go, love,' her mother said gently, crossing the room to stand beside Leah. Their eyes met in the mirror.

'I don't think I can do it,' whispered Leah, her eyes glistening with unshed tears.

'You can and you will, love,' Hannah said kindly, giving Leah's shoulders a squeeze. 'Mr Whitworth is doing this for you, as much as anyone. Despite whatever misgivings he may have had, he knew how much Harry loved you.'

'I miss him so much, Mum,' Leah's voice trembled.

'I know you do, love. I won't tell you it gets easier, because it doesn't. God knows, I miss your dad every day, but the pain does get more bearable over time.'

Her gaze was drawn by the sound of voices in the lane. 'Come on, people are heading for the church. We'd better go.' She gave Leah's shoulder another squeeze and released her. 'Come on, Daisy, Dora,' she called up the stairs as she put on her hat and picked up her gloves. 'Time to go.' Daisy came hurrying down the stairs.

'Dora's not here yet,' she pointed out, adjusting the cuffs of her black mourning dress.

'She can meet us at the church,' Hannah said firmly, fastening her gloves. She opened the door just as Dora came hurrying down the lane, her cheeks red from the exertion of walking so fast.

'Sorry,' she panted, hand to her chest as she caught her breath. 'Tilly wanted to talk.' She inhaled deeply.

'Frank all right being left with her, was he?' Hannah asked as she closed the door behind them.

'He was asleep when I left,' Dora replied, bending down to brush the dust of the lane from the hem of her black skirt. 'Little Cecily's crawling now.'

'She must be, what, nine months?' Hannah said, tucking her arm through Leah's. Her daughter remained silent, her gaze fixed on the ground in front of her.

'Just about, yes,' Dora nodded. 'There'll only be about eleven months between her and the next one.' She winced. Much as she adored Frank, she found it exhausting looking after one baby. Tilly would certainly have her work cut out having two so close together.

'That's Tilly for you,' Leah said bitterly. 'She'll end

up having these ones taken off her as well if she doesn't watch out.'

'Leah,' chided her mother gently. 'It's not our place to judge.'

'Oh, but Mum,' Leah protested, scowling. 'Look at the state of her. She couldn't look after her other children, why would she be any better with Cecily? Especially as Joshua's not around to keep an eye on her.'

'She's got Pearl,' Hannah reminded her. 'And us. Alice is very kind to her.'

'Alice is too soft,' Leah muttered sullenly. She sighed. It wasn't in her nature to be so spiteful, but today she couldn't seem to help herself. In the two weeks since learning of Harry's death, a dark cloud of despair had settled over her that she couldn't shake.

Mourners were streaming towards the church. A mournful melody drifted across the churchyard as Leah followed her family up the cinder path and into the cool, dim church. Aware of the looks from certain members of the congregation, Dora kept her gaze steadfastly fixed on the altar. In the absence of a coffin, a photograph of Harry in his uniform, a replica of the one treasured by Leah, stood on a low table to the side of the pulpit. The air was thick with the cloying perfume of the lilies that adorned the front of the church.

As they slid into a pew midway down the aisle, Dora felt Leah reaching for her hand. Her friend's face was devoid of colour, and for a moment Dora thought Leah was about to faint, but she managed to rally herself and, giving Dora a watery smile, sat down and bent her head, her lips moving as if in silent prayer.

The worst thing, Dora thought, was that Harry's body hadn't yet been recovered. He had no final resting place. She glanced over at the front pew. Reserved for the Whitworths, it remained empty. Mathew Turner and Reverend Roberts stood close to the altar, heads bent together in hushed conversation. All around them, the pews were filling up. She caught sight of Alice sitting near the front across the aisle. She turned and, meeting Dora's gaze, gave her a small smile. Suddenly Mathew jerked his head up and Samuel cleared his throat. Running his fingers nervously around his clerical collar, he hurried up the aisle. A deep hush descended over the congregation, and everyone rose as Isaac and Frances Whitworth made their way slowly down the aisle behind Samuel.

Leah slowly raised her gaze to watch their progress down the aisle. They walked stiffly, their backs ramrod straight. Isaac nodded to several members of the congregation, silently acknowledging their presence, but Frances just stared straight ahead. She clung to her husband's arm, her face hidden by a black veil. Always a slight woman, her drastic weight loss was clearly noticeable, her tailored dress hanging off her thin frame. Twice she seemed to falter, and Isaac had to pause to allow her to compose herself. They slid silently into the front pew, and the congregation took their seats. The organ fell silent and Samuel, resplendent in his clerical robes, took to the pulpit.

'This is a particularly difficult service for me,' he began, his gaze sweeping over the assembled mourners. 'Not only did I count Harry – Henry – Whitfield as a good friend, I also served alongside him. I will miss him.' His voice faltered and he paused to clear his throat and collect himself. Muffled sobs emanated from the front pew. Leah bit her lip, clenching her fists tightly in her lap. Dora slipped her arm around Leah's shoulders, pulling her close.

Her chest felt tight and she could hardly breathe. Swallowing the lump in her throat, Leah blinked back her tears. Samuel was reading a passage from the Bible now, but she couldn't concentrate. All she could think was that she would never see Harry again. There was a rustle from the back of the church. Turning slightly, Leah glimpsed Pearl out of the corner of her eye. This was what the old woman had seen four years earlier, she thought bitterly. She turned back to face the front. Isaac was getting to his feet. Hardly able to breathe, Leah watched as he made his way up to the altar. His face drawn, he gripped the edge of the pulpit and gazed out over the sea of mourners.

'Henry was a beloved son, a friend to many,' he began. 'He was loved by many in this parish, where he felt so at home. It was here, in Strawbridge, that Henry was happiest. It was here he formed lasting friendships, where he found love . . .' His gaze sought out Leah. Dora squeezed her shoulders, and finally the tears came. She pressed her handkerchief to her mouth in an effort to muffle her sobs. Whatever else Isaac said was lost in the overwhelming agony of her grief.

*

'I'm sorry for your loss, Mr Whitworth, Mrs Whitworth,' Leah found the courage to say as she followed the mourners filing out into the late summer sunshine. Already the trees in the churchyard were on the turn, and the grass was littered with young acorns.

'Thank you, Leah,' replied Isaac, inclining his head graciously. 'May I extend my condolences to you. I know you made Henry very happy.'

Frances turned her face away. Leah flushed and looked away, embarrassed to be so publicly humiliated by Harry's mother.

'Mr and Mrs Whitworth, my sympathies,' Hannah said, coming up behind Leah and taking her arm. 'Come along, Leah.'

'She wouldn't even look at me,' Leah muttered tearfully as Hannah led her away down the path.

'You'd think she'd be grateful Harry had a sweetheart to mourn him,' Daisy piped up, hurrying to catch up with her mother and sister.

'Mrs Whitworth never thought I was good enough for him,' Leah said. 'If it wasn't for them . . .' She faltered, hit once again by the magnitude of all she'd lost. She glanced down at her left hand, where Harry's ring glinted. She wasn't ready to take it off yet. She wondered if she ever would be. It was all she had left of him, she thought sadly. A ring and a couple of photographs.

'Leah!' Alice came hurrying towards her. 'Oh, Leah, I'm so, so sorry. I wanted so badly to come over and sit with you, but Samuel said propriety dictated I sit near the front. Oh, my dear friend. Come here.' Leah let herself be enfolded in her friend's embrace. 'You've been so brave and dignified. Harry would be so proud of you.'

Leah nodded, her tears flowing freely as she buried her face against Alice's shoulder.

'Are you going to the Glyn Arms, Alice?' asked Hannah.

'I must,' replied Alice, over Leah's head. 'Samuel expects it of me.'

'I can't face it, Mum,' Leah said, raising her red-rimmed gaze.

'No, I don't think I can, either,' Hannah said. She looked round at Dora and Daisy. They both shook their heads.

'I think I'd prefer to be quietly at home,' Daisy said.

'Me, too,' nodded Dora. 'I'll go and fetch Frank from Tilly's, and we can have a quiet afternoon at home, remembering Harry in our own way.'

'I'll see you all later, then,' Alice said. 'I'm here if you need me, Leah,' she said, giving her a final hug. 'Always – don't ever forget that.'

'I won't, Alice.' She managed a weak smile. 'Thank you.'

CHAPTER TWENTY-FOUR

Leah set her basket of apples on the step and pushed open the heavy oak doors of St Luke's Church. Breathing in the scent of beeswax, she made her way slowly up the aisle, the soles of her shoes squeaking softly on the cold flagstones.

Dust motes drifted lazily in the shaft of coloured light shining in through the stained-glass window above the altar. At the front pew, she paused, letting the quiet stillness settle around her as her eyes were drawn to the stone slab that adorned the old greystone wall above the font.

HENRY GEORGE WHITWORTH
A MUCH BELOVED SON AND FRIEND.
1895–1917

She glanced around the silent church. Satisfied she was alone, she held on to the rim of the stone font with one hand and climbed onto the plinth, carefully edging her way round in order to reach the plaque. Gently, she ran her fingers over the smooth stone, feeling the ridges of the chiselled letters against her skin.

'Harry,' she whispered, her eyes filling with tears. Isaac had commissioned the memorial stone at the same time that he'd ordered a larger, more detailed one for their parish church back in Richmond. There had been a short service the previous day to unveil the stone plaque, but it had been poorly attended by the locals. While the people of Strawbridge had been fond of Harry, he wasn't the only local boy to have given his life on a foreign battlefield, and there was some anger that his was the only death that had been marked in this way.

Leah had taken the afternoon off work to attend. Isaac Whitworth had come alone. He had sat in the front pew, a solitary figure in black, his housekeeper, Mrs Lamb, weeping quietly in the row behind him. From her seat, third pew from the front, her mother and Alice seated either side of her, Leah had kept her gaze fixed on Harry's memorial stone. Bright and new, it looked out of place among the older stones commemorating other Whitworths: Harry's grandfather, an uncle who'd died in India, a cousin who'd perished in a shipwreck off the Devon coast. So many Whitworths, and now her beloved Harry had joined them. Yesterday, she had felt unable to approach the stone; she'd only wanted to get out of the church and away from the horrors her imagination conjured up when she thought about her Harry lying on a foreign battlefield, unclaimed. Mr Whitworth's contact had told him that Harry's remains had not been found. Leah's flicker of hope that Harry might still be alive was all too brief. Several members of Harry's platoon, Isaac told her solemnly when he caught up with her in the lane, had witnessed Harry being hit.

She'd declined his offer of tea, preferring to return home, needing to be alone with her memories.

Now she had returned. She had worked through her dinnertime in order to leave an hour early, when she knew she would have the church to herself before Reverend Roberts and Mathew Turner arrived to prepare for evensong.

Standing on tiptoe, she pressed her lips to the cold stone and closed her eyes. Harry's face swam into her mind. He was so tantalisingly real, she almost smiled. The vestry door creaked, and Leah almost lost her balance. Her eyes snapped open and she would have tumbled off the plinth had Samuel not been there to catch her arm.

'Leah,' he frowned, as he helped her down. 'What are you doing clambering about up there? You could have suffered a nasty sprain if you'd fallen.'

'I'm sorry,' Leah mumbled, feeling her cheeks heating up. 'I just wanted to be closer to Harry.' Samuel's eyes clouded.

'I'm sorry for your loss, Leah,' he said softly. 'Harry was a good friend to me.' He shrugged. 'I miss him.'

Not trusting herself to speak, Leah simply nodded.

Their eyes met, united by grief. Samuel cleared his throat. 'Come on, I'll walk you home.'

Their footsteps echoed loudly on the stone floor. In the covered porch, Leah stopped to retrieve her basket of apples.

'Let me,' Samuel said, taking it gently from her. 'The last of Isaac's crop,' he said, inspecting the bruised fruit.

'I only took what was on the ground,' replied Leah defensively.

'I'm sure Isaac won't mind,' Samuel assured her with a small smile. 'They'd only be left to rot otherwise.'

They stepped out into the cool autumn sunshine. The surrounding trees groaned and creaked in the breeze, their leaves shimmering like burnished copper and gold in the low sunlight. It was cold in the shade, and Leah shivered. Samuel slid his arm around her shoulders. Leah flinched, but immediately relaxed. The pressure of his arm felt comforting, reassuring, and she found herself leaning in towards him. As she walked, she was suddenly overcome by emotion. The sobs burst from her like a hot spring.

'Oh, Leah,' Samuel said. He stopped in his tracks, turning to face her. Through her tears, Leah could see her own grief reflected in his sorrowful gaze.

'I feel as though Harry's death is the accumulation of all the horror and the nightmares I've suffered since returning from France,' he said, his voice breaking. 'I feel like no one understands how I feel.' He turned away, clenching his fists. 'Alice tries, God bless her, but how can she know what it's like to have your very soul destroyed?' He turned back to Leah. 'Do you find yourself feeling that way?' he croaked.

Leah nodded. Tears streamed down her cheeks. She knew she must look an absolute sight, but she was past caring. Her broken heart was a physical pain deep in her chest. It was a pain from which she doubted she would ever recover.

'We're a pair, you and I, aren't we?' Samuel said with an attempt at a smile. 'Two lost souls.'

A magpie watched them from on top of the churchyard wall as they approached the lychgate. Leah wiped her eyes with the back of her hand.

'Here, allow me,' said Samuel, whipping a neatly folded handkerchief from the folds of his cassock. Shaking it out, he handed it to Leah, who took it gratefully. She wiped her eyes and, turning away, discreetly blew her nose.

'Thank you,' she sniffed, stuffing the handkerchief into her skirt pocket. 'I shall wash it and return it to you.'

'No need. I have plenty.'

'I'm keeping you,' Leah said. 'You'll need to prepare for evensong.'

'There's no rush,' Samuel assured her. 'I can spare a few minutes. I find talking to you a great comfort. Shall we?' He indicated the track running adjacent to the churchyard. Leah hesitated. Her mother was waiting for the apples, but she really couldn't face going home yet and she felt so comfortable with Samuel.

'Just a short way,' she replied. 'Then I really must get back.'

The ground was soft underfoot as they made their way slowly along the track. The sun was low and the trees cast deep shadows. She could hear Pearl's dog, Bear, barking, and the tell-tale coil of smoke from her caravan rose above the trees.

They talked about Harry and about Samuel's experiences at the front. As he began to talk about Leonard Merrifield's execution, he broke down. Leah could only watch in dismay as he sank to his knees, his cassock crumpled on the damp ground, his shoulders shuddering as he wept into his hands.

'Samuel?' Leah whispered. He appeared not to hear her. His whole body shook, wracked with his sobs. 'Samuel, shush, it's all right.' Leah laid a tentative hand on his shoulder and slid clumsily to her knees beside him. 'Samuel.' She pulled him towards her, and he buried his head in her bosom, sobbing like a baby. Leah hesitated, then softly began to stroke his hair. She felt his head shift under her palm as he slowly turned his head. His tear-filled gaze met hers, and suddenly he was kissing her. Momentarily stunned, Leah drew back in shock.

'Leah,' Samuel muttered, his tears wetting her cheeks as he pulled her head towards him.

As his lips sought her again, Leah felt her resistance crumble. The warmth of his physical presence afforded her the solace she needed right now. She craved oblivion and Samuel could give it to her, even if only for a short while. With her own tears mingling with Samuel's, she closed her eyes and surrendered.

'Oh my God, Leah!' Samuel panted, staring down at Leah, his expression one of abject horror as he fiddled with his trouser buttons. 'My God,' he exclaimed again, rubbing his hand across his face. 'What have you done?' He staggered backwards away from her. Leah averted her gaze, the sudden chill on her bare skin filling her with shame. She tugged her skirts down and got to her feet.

'You can't tell anyone,' Samuel said, pacing back and forth in agitation, his black robes swirling around his legs like the wings of a large crow. 'Especially not Alice. Oh God!' he groaned. 'You can't tell Alice. Swear to me,' he demanded in panic.

'Do you think I want anyone to know what we've just done?' Leah hissed coldly. Her cheeks flamed with shame and embarrassment, but inside she felt chilled to the bone. She shivered. In a matter of minutes, it seemed, the light had been leached from the sky. The undergrowth rustled eerily in the breeze.

'I'm late,' Samuel said. 'Not a word to anyone,' he added harshly. 'You . . . Jezebel!'

The name was hurled with such venom, Leah recoiled in shock. 'Samuel!' she called after him, but he was already hurrying away from her, crashing carelessly through the undergrowth in his haste to get away from her.

Tasting bile in her throat, Leah retrieved her basket, groping in the faint grey twilight to gather up her apples, which had spilled out into the long grass. She felt hollow inside. 'Oh, Harry,' she whispered tearfully. 'I'm sorry.' A sob escaped her throat as hot tears of recrimination burned her cheeks. She wiped them roughly away and dragged herself to her feet. Feeling bruised and dirty, she slowly made her way home.

*

'Where on earth have you been, Leah?' Hannah had been watching from the window and had the door open before Leah reached the cottage. 'I was starting to get worried.' She paused, peering at Leah in the lamplight. 'Are you all right? You look very pale. Has something happened?'

'I needed some time alone after seeing Harry's memorial plaque,' Leah muttered, hoping she sounded convincing. She had rehearsed her excuse all the way home. 'I didn't realize the time. I'm sorry.'

'Oh, Leah, I'm sorry. Of course. I forgot you were popping into the church. Give me the apples. You sit by the fire. You look washed-out. Daisy, bring your sister a cup of tea, will you, love?'

'It must have been hard for you,' Dora said, looking up from her knitting. She smiled down at Frank, who lay on the hearthrug, kicking his chubby legs and babbling contentedly to himself. 'Seeing Harry's name carved in stone, I mean. It must make it so real,' she explained, as Leah took the chair opposite her. 'I've nearly finished the last pair of socks for Nate's Christmas parcel,' she continued when Leah didn't reply. 'I've used the thickest wool I could find. The winters are so bitter where he is. I do worry about him.'

'We haven't had a letter from Clarissa for weeks,' Daisy said, coming into the room with Leah's tea. 'Have we, Dora? I reckon we're going to get to keep Frank.' She flopped onto the sofa. 'What do you think about that, Leah?'

'What?' Leah blinked. She couldn't get the memory of Samuel's touch out of her head. She felt sick. What had she been thinking? What she had hoped would bring her comfort had instead made her feel a hundred times worse. Now she had guilt and disgust to add to her grief. A sudden thought struck her. Alice was one of her dearest friends. How on earth would she ever look her in the eye again?

CHAPTER TWENTY-FIVE

'Adultery!' Samuel bellowed across the heads of his congregation. A few people shuffled uncomfortably in their pews. Daisy nudged Leah and grinned, but, to her disappointment, Leah didn't smile back. Leah lowered her gaze, her cheeks burning with humiliation and shame. *Can anyone tell?* she wondered, hardly daring to raise her eyes. She felt as though she had a light above her head screaming her sin for all to see.

'Adultery is an abomination!' Samuel declared loudly, thumping the pulpit as if to emphasize his point. Leah slid lower in her seat.

In the fortnight since her encounter with Samuel, Leah had managed to avoid Alice, but they were due to meet that afternoon to pack the Christmas boxes to send to the soldiers serving at the front. She bit her lip, wishing she hadn't volunteered to help. While Reverend Roberts preached his damning sermon, she wondered briefly whether she could get out of helping by pleading a headache. Just the thought of seeing Alice was making her feel physically ill.

Daisy nudged her again. The congregation were getting to their feet to sing a hymn. Leah stood up, but kept her gaze fixed on the open hymn book in Daisy's hands. She didn't dare look at Samuel.

'Who do you think Reverend Roberts was meaning?' Daisy asked, her eyes shining with mischief. 'I wonder if it's the new blacksmith, Mr Ambrose. He and Mrs Harper seemed very cosy at the harvest supper yesterday evening.'

'Daisy Hopwood!' her mother exclaimed. 'That's how malicious rumours start. I'm sure Reverend Roberts wasn't referring to anyone in particular, though it is rather odd he would choose the sin of adultery to preach on two weeks running.'

'Well, you know he's not right in the head, don't you?' one of the women, Sally, said with a sneer. 'He likely forgot what he preached the week before.'

'I wouldn't let my granddaughter hear you say that,' Beatrice said in an undertone.

'I didn't mean anything by it,' Sally muttered. 'But everyone knows he's a bit funny since he got out of hospital ...' A door creaked, and an uncomfortable silence descended on the table as Alice appeared in the doorway, struggling with a pile of boxes.

'Here, let me help you with those,' Dora said, taking some of the boxes and placing them on the table.

'Thank you,' Alice said with a grateful smile. She set the remainder of the boxes beside them. 'It's nice and toasty in here,' she remarked, rubbing her gloved hands together.

'Your grandfather came up and lit the stove straight after church,' Beatrice told her as Alice held her hands out towards the glowing coals.

'Well, thank you all for taking the time to come,' Alice said, smiling round at the group gathered around the long table, who had already begun to sort through the assortment of knitted socks, scarves and balaclavas. 'I'm sorry I'm late,' she continued, shedding her coat and hat and joining them at the table. 'I just had those few boxes to collect at the last minute.' She smiled at Dora. 'Where's Frank? I was hoping to have a cuddle.'

'Tilly's watching him for me,' Dora replied. 'Little Cecily dotes on him.'

'She must be quite far along now,' one of the women said, with thinly pursed lips.

'Christmas time,' Dora replied.

'Another illegitimate babe for the parish,' the woman said sourly, as Dora flushed to the roots of her hair. It irked her that her neighbours would tar her with the same brush as the unfortunate Tilly, who seemed to only need look at a man to find herself in the family way.

'Nothing more from Frank's mother?' Alice asked pointedly, unwinding a ball of string. Dora shook her head.

'Nothing for weeks now.'

'I reckon you're lumbered with him, love,' Martha Prior said with a wry smile. 'What's your Nate think about it all?' she asked, lowering her voice so as not to be heard over the general chatter.

'He's puzzled how a mother can just abandon her baby,' Dora replied softly. 'But he doesn't understand what it's like for Clarissa. She has her family's reputation to consider. I'm sure she's doing all she can. The only thing is,' Dora's smile wavered, 'the longer she takes, the harder it will be giving him up.'

'Leah, I feel like I haven't seen you in ages,' Alice said, smiling across the table at her friend as she unfurled a large roll of brown paper. 'How are you?'

'I'm all right,' Leah replied listlessly. She felt sick with shame and could hardly bring herself to meet Alice's eyes.

'Is your head still bad?' Alice asked sympathetically. 'Poor you. I missed you at the harvest supper last night.'

'I just didn't feel well enough,' Leah replied brusquely. She saw the flicker of hurt in Alice's face and looked away. Her cheeks burned with mortification and she buried her head in the task in front of her. Alice regarded her friend in puzzled silence, her hand resting gently on her still-flat stomach. She was almost three months gone now. Her bouts of morning sickness had all but disappeared, and she was starting to feel hopeful. She hadn't yet told Samuel. In part, because she wouldn't be able to bear seeing his disappointment should something go wrong, but also because she wanted to cherish her secret for just a little while longer. For the moment, this little person growing inside her was hers alone and she wasn't quite ready to share him or her with anyone. She certainly wouldn't be so insensitive as to tell Leah, not when Harry hadn't even been gone three months yet. Her heart constricted for her friend as she watched her surreptitiously across the table. Leah's skin was pallid, and there were dark circles under her eyes. But she was still a lovely-looking girl. Grief in all its starkness couldn't detract from Leah's natural beauty.

Seemingly unaware of Alice's scrutiny, Leah bent her head over the table, her fingers clumsy as she attempted to tie the string around the brown paper-wrapped box. Harry's ring caught the pale autumn light coming in the window, and she felt the bile rise up her throat. She swallowed it down. She had besmirched his memory, and the thought made her sick to her stomach.

'I thought Reverend Roberts spoke well this morning,' Mrs Lamb, Isaac Whitworth's housekeeper, remarked to Alice as they stacked the packed boxes in the corner of the dusty hall ready for Mathew Turner to collect with his pony and trap later.

'You did?' Alice said, surprised. 'I mean, thank you, Mrs Lamb. He does get quite passionate on certain subjects.'

'I know we're at war,' Mrs Lamb continued primly, 'but that's no reason to allow morals to slip.' She glowered across the room to where Leah was absent-mindedly dragging a broom across the floor. 'I'll never forgive that Hopwood girl for the rift she caused between Mr Whitworth and Master Henry,' she sniffed.

'Mrs Lamb,' Alice chided her mildly. 'Leah is grieving, too. Perhaps a little compassion?'

Mrs Lamb snorted. 'I save my compassion for those who

are deserving of it,' she said. 'I must get back to Streawberige House. Mr Whitworth will be wanting an early supper if he's intending to head back to London tonight.' She laid a gloved hand on Alice's arm. 'Keep up the good work, dear,' she said with a tight smile. 'I'm sure our lads over there will appreciate your efforts.'

Alice watched her go with mixed feelings. While she found Isaac's crusty housekeeper difficult, she couldn't help feeling sorry for her. From what Samuel had confided in her, it appeared that, with Harry's death, Isaac would be spending more time in Richmond. Frances was apparently suffering badly with her nerves, to the point that Isaac was afraid to leave her alone for any length of time. From what Alice could gather, Mrs Lamb had no life beyond Streawberige House, and she wondered what would become of the woman should Isaac decide to shut up the house for an extended period. She would be lost. Making her mind up to be kinder to the woman in future, Alice finished tidying up the hall. She'd been pleased with the turnout. The amount of donations had cheered her, too. Strawbridge and the surrounding area was a poor community, yet nearly every household roundabouts had donated a pouch of tobacco, a bar of chocolate or knitted items to fill the Christmas boxes that the Red Cross would send to as many serving soldiers and POWs as possible.

Her wandering thoughts were interrupted by Hannah calling goodbye.

'Goodbye, Mrs H,' Alice replied. 'Bye, Daisy, Leah. I'm sorry we didn't get much time to talk,' she said, hurrying over. 'Perhaps you'd like to come round for supper one evening?' she smiled. To her surprise, instead of accepting, Leah shook her head and frowned.

'I'm working late shifts all this week,' she said, her gaze focused on something to the left of Alice.

'Oh, right,' replied Alice, slightly bewildered. She did hope Leah wasn't suffering with melancholy. Through her work with the Red Cross, she'd seen women who'd seemingly given up on life and she didn't want Leah to end up in the same boat.

'Let me know when you've some free time,' she said with a tentative smile.

'Sure,' Leah nodded. 'I'd better go.'

'Of course,' Alice said quickly. 'Thank you for coming.' Confused, she watched Leah shrug on her coat and head out the door.

'Do you think Leah is all right?' she asked Dora some time later as they walked down the lane leading from Tilly's cottage. 'She seems very distracted and out of sorts.'

'She's been like that at home, too,' Dora grunted as she tried to cuddle Frank, who squirmed in her arms. 'Golly, he's getting so heavy.'

'Let me,' Alice offered, taking the little boy in her arms. She buried her face against his hair, and he giggled.

'I think Leah's more affected by the unveiling of Harry's memorial stone than she's letting on,' Dora said, tugging her collar up around her neck. A chilly wind blew down the lane, sending a flurry of autumn leaves swirling into the air. 'It's since then that she's been behaving strangely.'

'Perhaps it's made Harry's death more real to her,' Alice suggested, her brow creased in concern for her friend. She couldn't even begin to imagine how Leah must be feeling. No matter how difficult her marriage might be, and while she would never dream of speaking ill of her husband to anyone, though she was sure Dora and Leah had their suspicions, she couldn't imagine being without him. She jiggled Frank on her hip. He was a bonny boy with his dark hair and wide, violet-blue eyes. He grinned, showing off the two bottom teeth which were just visible above his pink gums. He reached out, trying to grab Alice's nose. She laughed and he chuckled, kicking his legs as he bounced on her hip. Alice nuzzled the back of his neck, savouring his sweet baby scent. All being well, in six months' time, she would have a little one of her own.

'Thanks for coming with me to fetch Frank from Tilly's,' Dora said as they neared the row of cottages. Smoke drifted from the chimney pots, mingling with the scent of damp earth and rotting leaves.

'It was my pleasure,' replied Alice, prising Frank's chubby fingers from her coat so Dora could take him. 'It was nice to see Tilly.' She sighed. 'She seems happy enough. Though I can't agree with her lifestyle, I've come to understand that I have to accept that I can't make her change her ways. All I can do is support her in whichever way I can.'

'She does seem to be her own worst enemy,' agreed Dora, tugging Frank's rabbit fur bonnet down over his little ears.

The October sun was sinking rapidly below the trees and the encroaching twilight had brought with it a sharp wind. 'Ooh, this wind is cold. I'd better get Frank indoors before he catches a chill.'

'Yes, sorry. I'll see you soon, and tell Leah she's welcome to pop round anytime. Even if she's not in the mood for a chat. I'm quite comfortable with companionable silence.' She smiled.

'I'll tell her,' Dora grinned. 'Bye.'

Alice continued on towards the vicarage. An owl hooted above her head, making the hairs on her arms stand on end. The boughs of the large oak tree creaked and groaned in the wind, sending a shower of acorns raining down on her head. She ran the last few steps and let herself in the front gate. Weeds were pushing their way through the cracks in the front path. Looking at the messy flowerbeds, Alice couldn't help but feel a pang, wondering what Reverend Aldridge would think of the sight of his beloved garden being left to go to rack and ruin. She sighed. *I really must make the time to tidy it up*, she thought, turning the wrought-iron door handle and opening the heavy oak door.

'Hello!' she called, stepping into the dim hallway. 'Samuel? I'm home.'

She found him in his study, head bent over his big, leatherbound Bible. He was so engrossed in his reading that he couldn't have heard her enter, for he jumped when she put her hands on his hunched shoulders, his head snapping round, his eyes glaring.

'Gracious, woman!' he growled. 'Don't sneak up on a person like that.'

'I'm sorry I startled you, Samuel,' Alice apologized quickly. 'I did call out.'

Samuel grunted, apparently mollified, and Alice exhaled in relief. She kissed the top of his head, and Samuel reached for her hand.

'How was your afternoon?' he asked, twisting in his chair so that he faced her.

'It was a good turnout and we got all the boxes packed. Grandfather is on the way to headquarters now. With luck, they'll be delivered well in time for Christmas.'

'I'm sure our lads will be very appreciative,' Samuel said, turning back to his Bible. 'I'm popping over to see Reuben and Mrs Merrifield later,' he said, with his back to her.

'They haven't had more bad news?' Alice asked, aghast.

'Not so far as I know,' Samuel replied. 'I'm going over to talk about Leonard.'

'Is that wise?' Alice asked, biting her bottom lip anxiously.

'Oh, don't fuss, woman,' Samuel replied. 'I am perfectly well. They deserve to know the truth.'

'As long as you're sure?' Alice murmured.

'I am,' her husband replied determinedly.

'I'll make some tea,' Alice said. Pausing in the doorway, she looked back at her husband's hunched figure. 'I'm a bit worried about Leah,' she said.

'What?' Samuel spun round. 'Why? What do you mean?'

Surprised by Samuel's response, Alice shrugged. 'I think

seeing Harry's memorial stone upset her a lot. She hasn't been herself since.'

'Perhaps it's time you took a step back from your friendship with her,' Samuel said. Alice looked at him in amazement.

'Samuel, Leah is one of my dearest friends.' She searched his face, but his expression was unfathomable. 'Why would you say that?'

'I don't think she's a good influence on you,' Samuel said. 'You are a vicar's wife, after all.'

'Samuel?' Alice laughed. 'What are you talking about? Bad influence indeed!'

'Don't mock me, Alice,' Samuel snapped. 'You ask me what I'm talking about? There's your answer right there. You would never have made fun of me before I went away. I've been away too long. You've had things your own way for far too long. Well,' he said, getting to his feet, 'it's time you started treating me with respect. I'm off out,' he added, reaching for his coat. 'I'm calling in on a few parishioners before I see the Merrifields. Don't make supper for me. I'll have something at the pub.'

The cramps started soon after Alice got into bed. Samuel still hadn't returned home. Moonlight filtered through the curtains, bathing the room in its pearly light. She lay on her back, staring up at the ceiling, willing the pain to stop. It wasn't unbearable yet, just a tugging sensation deep in the pit of her stomach. She pressed her hands to her abdomen, as if, by sheer will alone, she could keep her baby safe. She tried to swallow. Her mouth was dry and she could taste the fear, like bile, rising up her throat. She heard the church clock strike nine. The pain was growing stronger. She let out a sob as she was wracked by a painful contraction that drove her from her bed. Doubled over with pain, she staggered onto the landing, the hot, wet, sticky sensation on her thighs so terrifyingly familiar.

'Samuel!' she screamed, staring in horror at the blood gushing down her legs. 'Samuel!' She fell to the floor, sobbing bitterly as her hopes and dreams died on the blood-soaked carpet.

CHAPTER TWENTY-SIX

Leah groaned and sank back on her heels, wiping her mouth with the back of her hand, her nostrils assailed by the stench of stale urine and fresh vomit. Her forehead was clammy, and sweat trickled down her spine despite the fact it was barely above freezing in the small cubicle.

There was a burst of clattering machinery as the cloakroom door swung open and someone rapped on the cubicle door.

'Just a minute,' she croaked, dragging herself to her feet. She peered into the toilet bowl and grimaced before pulling the chain. Straightening her skirts, she pinched her cheeks and slid back the bolt.

'Crikey, Leah,' said Maud Fisher. 'You all right? You look like death warmed up.' She took a step backwards and pulled a face. 'You're not coming down with something, are you?'

'I'm fine,' Leah said, pushing past her. At the sink, she washed her hands and splashed water on her face. Her reflection stared back at her, her skin ashen, her eyes dull and listless, purpled bruises a testimony to sleepless nights.

It was the first week of December, and she had been sick every morning for the past six weeks. When she'd first missed her monthlies, she put it down to the shock of Harry's death. But when they'd failed to appear the following month and the sickness had started, she could pretend no longer. She was expecting a baby. Reverend Roberts's baby. The thought sent a shiver of disgust down her spine. Alice's face swam in front of her eyes and she squeezed them shut in an effort to dispel the image. Leah was still keeping her distance from Alice. She had been ill recently and had spent a fortnight at her parents' home in Hedge End recuperating, which had made it a lot easier for Leah, but she knew she couldn't keep avoiding her friend forever. People were starting to notice. Only the other day her mother had questioned the fact that Leah hadn't spent any time at the vicarage lately. Leah had trotted out her overused excuse about working long shifts and being tired, but she knew Hannah wasn't fooled.

'You two haven't had a falling out, have you?' she'd asked, peering at Leah in the lamplight.

'Of course not,' Leah had replied, but she could tell her mother wasn't convinced.

Now she started as she heard the toilet flush. Not wishing to answer any more probing questions from Maud, she dried her hands quickly on the threadbare towel and hurried out onto the factory floor.

The racket of the machinery made her head ache, but at least the intricate nature of her job helped take her mind off her predicament, so it was only when the whistle blew, signalling the dinnertime break, that her worries and fears came crashing back down like a tidal wave.

She sat with her usual bunch, letting the chatter and jokes wash over her as her mind whirled in its search for a solution to her problem. She was two and a half months gone. She would never be able to disclose who the baby's father was. Fear clutched at her like an icy hand. She would be the talk of the hamlet, shunned and gossiped about like Tilly – and poor Dora, who Leah firmly believed had done nothing to warrant anyone's condemnation. What would her mother say? She'd be so shocked and ashamed. The tears welled, hot and bitter, scalding her cheeks. She wiped them away quickly before anyone noticed. What would she tell Alice? She could tell by the way her dear friend fussed over Frank that she was desperate for a baby of her own.

She sat upright, her uneaten bread and dripping forgotten, as she was struck by a thought. Would Samuel want the child? If he and Alice were unable to have babies of their own, per-haps he would insist she give the child up to him. It would be a solution. She certainly could not have a baby on her own, out of wedlock. She wasn't like Tilly. She cared too much about what people thought of her. Hastily arranged marriages were not uncommon in the district. There would be the knowing smiles and whispered comments when the baby arrived 'early', but as long as the child wasn't born illegitimately, it was all soon forgotten. Leah swallowed miserably, staring down at her coarse, work-worn hands. She had taken Harry's ring off, but there was still a slight indentation where it had been on her ring finger. She wore it on a ribbon around her neck. She reached for it now, but the feel of the cold, hard metal against her fingers failed to bring her the comfort it usually did. Was he looking down on her now, she wondered, despising her for what she'd done? If, by some miracle, Harry came back from the dead, he wouldn't want her now. Her stomach churned in disgust and self-loathing. She wished she could blame it all on Samuel, say that he had taken advantage of her grief, but she had hardly been unwilling. She squeezed her eyes shut, trying to erase the memory of their hasty lovemaking. What had she been hoping for? Comfort, the warmth of a man's arms after so long on her own? She couldn't remember. All she knew for certain was that she had made a terrible mistake for which she would pay for the rest of her life.

'Nurse Webb, your shift finished half an hour ago,' Matron said, coming to stand behind the chair Dora was sitting on.

'Just a few minutes more, Matron,' the patient, Ian, pleaded. 'The detective has the suspects all assembled. I shall never get to sleep unless I get to discover who the murderer is.'

Matron laughed. 'As long as Nurse Webb doesn't mind,' she said lightly. 'Not too late, though, Nurse. Your little boy needs you at home.'

'You have a child?' Ian asked, his quizzical gaze visible between the layers of bandages.

Dora laid the book face-down on her lap. 'I foster a little boy,' she said. 'You remember my friend Clarissa? He's hers.'

'I can tell by the way your face has brightened that you

are inordinately fond of him,' Ian said. His voice was muffled slightly by the bandages.

'He is a delightful boy,' Dora smiled.

'Then you must not let me detain you too much longer. How many pages have we left?'

'Barely a chapter,' Dora replied, picking up the book. She bent her head and began to read. Her voice was soft and melodious. Many of the patients had remarked on her soothing tone, and she had taken to staying a little longer after her shifts to read to those who were too ill or disinclined to read for themselves. She'd grown particularly fond of Ian. Once he had recovered from his injuries enough to converse comfortably, he'd reminded her of their meeting in France when he'd driven over with Harry to inform her of Nate's capture. Over time, he'd told her quite a bit about his early years living in South Africa, a country she knew little about. He'd been saddened to learn of Harry's death. 'He was a good bloke,' was all he'd said, but that afternoon she'd found him to be much quieter than usual.

'The end.' Dora closed the book and smiled at Ian.

His nostrils flared and what she could see of his lips appeared to be smiling. 'I was right. I knew he was the culprit all along.'

'Good for you. Now, I must be going,' she said, getting to her feet. She paused, one hand resting on the bed covers. 'Are you excited about your bandages coming off tomorrow?'

Ian shrugged his broad shoulders. 'Nervous rather than excited, I'd say.'

'Dr Boatwright doesn't seem to think the scarring

will be too bad,' she said in an attempt to allay his fears. Disfigurement was a huge worry to the men. Her heart had broken for a young corporal just the other week. He had been terribly disfigured in a shelling attack. Having lain on the battlefield for some time before being rescued, gangrene had set in, resulting in his losing much of his face. The first and only time his fiancée saw him without his bandages, she'd screamed and fainted dead away. A few days later, the corporal's tearful mother had visited to break the news that his fiancée had called off their engagement.

So it was understandable that Ian was feeling anxious. Dora didn't know whether he had a fiancée or a sweetheart, but as he had never mentioned anyone, she assumed not. It was a shame, she mused now as she left him lying on his back staring up at the ceiling. He seemed a nice man.

She retrieved her bicycle from the shed at the back of the hospital and peddled off down the frosty driveway, her breath billowing in front of her face. The crescent moon afforded her just enough light along the tree-lined road, the skeletal branches glistening with frost. She freewheeled past the gates to Streawberige House and the Glyn Arms pub, and down the lane. Alighting at the corner of her old cottage, she wheeled her bike around the back and, leaning it against the wall, let herself into the Hopwood's warm, cosy kitchen.

'Hello, Dora,' Hannah said, coming through from the parlour. 'I've given Frank his bottle and put him down.'

'Thank you, Aunty Hannah,' Dora smiled, divesting

herself of her coat, which she hung on the hook behind the door. 'Sorry I'm so late,' she said, unwinding her scarf. 'I stayed behind to read to some of the patients.'

'You're a good girl, Dora,' Hannah said, with an answering smile. 'Your supper's keeping warm,' she continued, opening the oven door and retrieving a covered plate. 'I'm afraid the meat's a bit thin on the ground,' Hannah apologized, setting the plate on the table. 'Young Simon Culley was very apologetic that he could only get such a scrawny specimen. But I've bulked it out with potatoes. Lord knows we've enough of those.'

'It smells delicious,' Dora said, her stomach growling as the savoury aroma hit her senses. 'I'll just nip up and give Frank a kiss.'

She found Leah in the bedroom the three girls shared, staring out of the window at the inky blackness.

'Hello, Leah,' Dora said softly so as not to wake the baby slumbering in his crib. 'Are you all right?' she asked as Leah turned to face her, her expression bleak. 'Were you thinking about Harry?'

'I miss him so much,' whispered Leah.

'I know you do,' Dora replied, going over to put her arms around her friend. 'It must be especially hard for you with Sidney and Joshua home on leave.' She tried not to think that, had Nate not been captured, he, too, might have been at home on leave now. Dora bit her lip thoughtfully. 'Leah, is it just Harry or is there something else?'

'What do you mean?' Leah said with a jerk of her head.

'Nothing, it's just you seem so downcast, which is understandable, of course, but I just wondered if there was something else troubling you.'

'There isn't,' Leah said resolutely. Frank stirred in his crib, and both girls stared down at him. He really was a beautiful little boy. He was almost eight months old now and just starting to crawl. Apart from a brief note enclosing a postal order which she was to use to buy Frank a Christmas present, Dora hadn't heard from Clarissa in weeks. As dangerous as it might be, she was starting to think of Frank as her own. She couldn't love him more if he were her own flesh and blood, and her loss would be unbearable when, or if, his mother did decide she wanted him back.

She stroked his rosy cheek and he settled. She leaned over to kiss the top of his dark head.

When she straightened up, Leah was staring at him with a strange look on her face.

'What is it?' she asked, frowning.

'Nothing.' Leah turned away.

'Supper's ready, by the way,' Dora said, slipping her arm through Leah's. 'Come on. You hardly eat anything these days. You're going to fade away.'

'I'm not hungry,' Leah muttered miserably, obstinately ignoring her hunger pangs.

'Well, you need to eat,' Dora replied firmly. 'Come on. After supper, we can make a start on that jigsaw puzzle Alice lent you. It'll take your mind off things.'

CHAPTER TWENTY-SEVEN

'How do you feel?' Dora stood at the foot of Ian's bed, her hands behind her back.

'I think I look quite the rake,' Ian grinned, handing back the small tortoiseshell mirror. 'Dr Boatwright says I'll be back on active duty within a week or so, but they're sending me off somewhere first for a spot of rest and relaxation. As if I haven't just spent the last two months resting up.'

'You deserve it,' Dora said, perching on the edge of his bed. 'You've been through a lot.'

His hair had grown during his time in hospital, curling boyishly around his face. He grinned up at Dora. 'What do you think about my scars?'

'They're not as bad as I'd expected,' replied Dora honestly. The scars were vivid red in colour, zigzagging across his face, the worst being along his chin and jawline. 'And they should fade with time.'

'That's what the doc said. He assures me most of them will be barely noticeable in about six months. He suggested

I grow a beard to hide the rest.' He cocked his head side-ways. 'What do you say to that? Would a beard suit me, do you think?'

'I think a beard would suit you very well,' replied Dora with a smile. 'When do you leave?'

'This afternoon.'

'So soon?'

'They need the beds,' Ian replied, his smile fading. 'I heard there's a trainload of chaps due in later today.'

'It keeps us on our toes,' Dora replied lightly. In truth, the seemingly endless trainloads of wounded young men were heartbreaking to see. At least the fact that the men had made it across the Channel and onto home soil meant they had a fighting chance. Her breath caught in the back of her throat as she thought back over all the young boys who had been so badly injured that they'd never even made it on to the Blighty list.

'I'll come and see you before you leave,' she promised Ian now, as she hurried off to attend to another patient.

As she worked through her duties, she found herself wondering how everyone was faring back in the field hospital at Cambri. She had kept in touch with Millie and Emma. Emma, like Dora, was back in England, working at a hospital in Bristol, and Millie had been transferred to a field hospital somewhere on the French/Belgian border. She had been interested to learn that Dr Walmsley, Frank's father, had also returned to England and was now working at a prestigious London hospital that specialized in rebuilding the faces of severely disfigured soldiers. Though she could never feel anything but contempt for the man who had treated Clarissa so badly, she had to admit he was working for a worthy cause. She wondered if the poor, jilted corporal from the other week would be one of the fortunate recipients.

There had been a large intake of new patients over the past few days, and Dora was kept busy assessing injuries and dressing wounds. Many of the men still bore the filth of the battlefields and had to be bathed before they could be admitted into the wards.

It was late in the afternoon by the time she paused for breath. She heard the rumble of trucks outside the window. Remembering she had promised to say goodbye to Ian before he left, she hurried up to his ward, where she found him sitting on his bed, fully dressed and ready to leave.

'Well, here we are,' Ian said.

'Yes,' Dora smiled, thinking how dashing he looked in his uniform. 'Here we are.'

'I shall be pleased to get back to my unit,' he said, running a hand through his sandy-blond hair. 'Though how many of them will be left,' he added sombrely, 'I don't know.'

'Don't think about that now,' Dora told him. 'Enjoy your convalescence first.'

Matron appeared in the doorway, and Ian got to his feet.

'It's been a pleasure getting to know you, Nurse Webb,' he said, holding out his hand. 'Your Nate's a lucky man.'

'Thank you.' Dora shook his hand. 'Good luck.'

'Time to go, Private Foster,' Matron said, beaming.

Shouldering his bag, Ian nodded. Shouts of 'Good luck, mate' rang out as he followed Matron down the ward. The doors swung shut behind them, and the ward fell quiet. With a sigh, Dora began to strip the bed.

It was cold in the sluice room. Dora had long since grown accustomed to the putrid stench of infection, but the black phlegm coughed up by some of the more seriously wounded, those with severe internal injuries, still turned her stomach. Feeling a little queasy, Dora dried her chapped hands on a towel and stepped out into the corridor. The wide, stone-floored passageway was a main thoroughfare through the hospital and was always teeming with staff, patients and visitors. Three patients sat on the benches adjacent to the sluice room, smoking. The large window framed a grey winter's day. There were still three weeks until Christmas, but sprigs of holly had begun to appear on window ledges and, on the wards, nurses and patients were busy making decorations to add a little seasonal cheer.

Amidst the hustle and bustle of the corridor, Dora was surprised to see Alice hurrying towards her, her face drawn and pale but for a crimson flush on her cheeks. Dora was just about to call out when Alice spotted her, her relief evident in her face.

'Dora,' Alice gasped, clearly out of breath. 'I'm so glad it's you. I thought I might have to go through someone in authority.'

'Why?' Dora frowned. 'What's happened?'

'Daisy told me you have a patient . . .'

'I have many,' Dora grinned as Alice broke off to catch her breath.

'Ian,' Alice said, clutching Dora's arm. 'Ian Foster.'

'Private Foster?' Dora's frown deepened. 'Oh,' she said, as realization dawned. 'Does your grandmother know him? I know he's South African, but the chance of them knowing each other . . .'

'Dora,' Alice said, inhaling deeply as she fought to remain calm, 'I believe he may be my uncle.'

'What?' Dora blinked. 'Really?'

'Grandmother had another child, a son. He was taken from her by his father when he was a child. My Uncle Charlie has been trying to trace him. We knew he had enlisted, but had no idea where he was posted or even what regiment he's in.' She sighed, taking a step back and almost colliding with a doctor. He met her apology with a look of contempt before hurrying on, muttering something under his breath.

'I know it's a long shot,' she said. 'Foster is a common surname, but Grandmother asked me to find out. Please, may I see him? Just for a moment? I won't say anything to upset him, I promise.'

'Oh, Alice, I'm sorry, he's gone.'

Alice blanched, her hand flying to her mouth as her eyes widened in shock.

'Oh no,' Dora said quickly, grabbing Alice's gloved hand

reassuringly. 'I don't mean ... He's left the hospital. He's being sent away for a few days' R&R before being sent to rejoin his unit.'

Alice stared at Dora in stunned silence.

'I'm sorry, Alice. If I'd realized ...'

'When did he leave?' Alice said, finding her voice.

Dora hesitated. 'An hour or so ago.'

'So close,' Alice murmured bleakly.

'I'm sorry,' Dora said again, feeling wretched. 'So many times, I thought I must mention him to you, just because of the South African connection. I never dreamt ...'

'No, no, of course, you wouldn't,' Alice said. 'You didn't know.'

'I did speak about your grandmother to him. Perhaps one day ...'

Alice shrugged. 'It probably isn't the right Ian Foster, anyway. There must be hundreds of Ian Fosters.'

'Now I think of it,' Dora said, 'he did favour your mother a bit.'

'Well, we'll never know now,' Alice said. She slumped against the wall, her shoulders drooping in resignation.

'I'm sorry,' Dora said again. Alice shook her head.

'Please stop apologizing, Dor. It's not your fault.'

'I'll find out where he's been sent. Perhaps you could write to him. Even if your letter arrives after he's returned to the front, they would forward it on to him.'

'Oh, Dora,' Alice beamed. 'That would be wonderful. Thank you.'

'I'll see to it straight away. Now, did you come all this way especially?' Dora asked.

Alice nodded. 'I've just come from Tilly's. She's had her baby.'

'Oh, it's a bit early, isn't it? Everything all right?'

Alice nodded. 'Another girl. She's a little on the small side but seems to be thriving. Pearl and Joshua are with her. I'm going to the parish relief tomorrow to plead her case. They'll probably take a dim view of the fact she keeps having babies with no man on the scene. Thank goodness for Joshua. Tilly would never survive without the money he sends her every month.'

'Perhaps he'll give her a bit of a talking-to,' Dora said. 'It's hardly fair on him.'

Alice shrugged. 'They're family,' she said simply. She sighed. 'Well, I'd better be getting back. Samuel will be wondering where I am.'

'I'm sorry you missed Ian, but I'll let you know the address as soon as I can,' Dora said.

Alice gave her a grateful smile. Within moments, she was swallowed up by the crowd.

CHAPTER TWENTY-EIGHT

A cold wind whistled through the apple trees as Leah slowly approached Pearl's caravan. Coils of grey smoke rose up from the small chimney, drifting away across the clearing. Against her will, her eyes were drawn to the big house, the many empty windows staring back at her like unseeing eyes. She'd heard from her mother, who'd heard it from Alice's housekeeper, Mrs Hurst, that Mr Whitworth had ordered the house to be shut up permanently. Mrs Lamb had apparently left to take up a new position with a family over near Portsmouth.

'It's a house that deserves to be filled with children.'

Leah whirled round. The old gypsy woman stood in the doorway of her gaily painted home.

'Pearl!' Leah gasped. 'You startled me.'

Pearl chuckled. Her dog, Bear, peered out to the side of Pearl's black skirt and emitted a low growl. Pearl shushed him.

'Come on in,' she said, ducking back inside. 'The water's just boiled.'

'I don't want my tea leaves read,' Leah said, climbing the wooden steps. The inside of the caravan smelled of the dried herbs hanging from the curved ceiling mingled with the scent of wet dog.

'Have a seat,' Pearl said, indicating the narrow, cushioned bench. Squeezing passed the laundry-draped clothes horse surrounding the stove, Leah perched on the edge of the bench. A folded army greatcoat took up the end of the bench, a khaki cap resting on top. Joshua's.

'Here, get this down you,' Pearl said, pressing a mug of strong, sweet tea into Leah's icy hands. Pearl wrapped her fingerless-gloved hands around her own mug and sat down opposite. 'Why have you come?' she asked, regarding Leah with a quizzical smile.

'I . . . I need your help,' Leah said, averting her gaze.

'What sort of help?'

'I'm in trouble.' Leah raised her eyes. Pearl nodded knowingly.

'You're in the family way?'

Leah nodded. Her cheeks grew warm, and it wasn't due to the heat from the stove. Shame engulfed her like a tidal wave and she had to look away, unable to bear Pearl's scrutiny.

'God knows, I'm not going to judge you,' she said at length. 'Our Tilly had her baby yesterday. Only the Lord knows who her father might be. I doubt even Tilly knows.' She shook her head. 'A girl without morals, that one. Still, her mother was no better.' She clicked her tongue, stroking Bear's coarse fur absently, her rheumy gaze staring off into the distance. Leah waited in silence, her heart thudding. She lifted her mug to her lips with trembling hands.

'Don't look so scared,' Pearl said suddenly. Leah swallowed, forcing a smile. In truth, she was terrified. She'd heard talk of Pearl's 'special' potions during her time working in the strawberry fields. She even knew one or two women who'd used them. They were women with large families, who just couldn't afford another mouth to feed. One woman had been pretty graphic in her description of the pain and the blood which had swiftly followed the drinking of the evil-smelling potion. It had done the job, though, by all accounts.

'You'll have some cramping,' Pearl said, getting stiffly to her feet. 'And you'll bleed a lot when it comes away.'

Leah nodded. Her cup rattled as she set it on the saucer.

'I'd recommend you take it just before bedtime,' Pearl said over her shoulder as she rummaged in a scuffed leather bag. 'Here.' Turning, she handed Leah a twist of paper. 'Mix the contents with half a pint of boiled water. Let it brew about five minutes.'

Wordlessly, Leah could only stare at the object in her hand, hardly able to comprehend that the small portion of whatever the paper contained would kill her unborn baby. The thought hit her like a sledgehammer, and she realized this was the first time she'd actually referred to it as her baby. Before, it had always been a problem she needed to be rid of. She raised her head, aware that Pearl was still speaking. 'If anyone asks, you never got it from me, all right?' she was saying sternly. 'I could go to prison for this.'

'Remember,' Pearl said, as she saw Leah out a few minutes later, 'if anything happens, you start bleeding bad or the pain gets unbearable, you don't mention my name.'

Leah nodded. She stumbled down the steps, the cold air hitting her like a slap in the face. Barely responding to Pearl's goodbye, the twist of paper tucked into her glove, she ran across the clearing. It wasn't until she reached the fork in the lane by the corner of the church that she realized she was sobbing. The cold wind stung her wet cheeks. She leaned one hand against a gnarled tree trunk, bending almost double as she caught her breath. She couldn't remember a time she had felt so absolutely miserable and wretched.

She sucked in a lungful of cold, crisp air. A few snowflakes swirled in the air. The surrounding landscape was still and silent. The only sign of life was a solitary crow flying over-head, a black speck in the vast monochrome sky.

She let herself in the back door, the heat from the stove making her frozen fingers and toes tingle as she unbuttoned her coat. The parlour door was shut in order to conserve the heat, but she could hear voices and her heart sank as she recognized Alice's among them.

Slipping the twist of paper containing the powder into her skirt pocket, she opened the door.

'Leah,' Hannah said, looking up from her knitting. 'Where have you been?'

'Have you been crying?' Alice asked, rising from her chair. 'Oh, you poor thing,' she said, putting her arms around Leah and giving her a hug. Leah blushed. Hot with shame, she held herself stiff in her friend's embrace. She knew how desperately Alice longed for a child, and here she was, unmarried and expecting a baby by Alice's husband. She burst into tears.

'Oh, Leah,' Hannah sighed. Setting aside her knitting, she got to her feet. 'I'll put the kettle on.'

'It's seeing the likes of the Merrifield boy back home that's set you off, isn't it, love?' Beatrice said kindly, laying her knitting in her lap.

'Of course,' Alice murmured as she led Leah to the sofa under the window. 'It's bound to make you miss Harry all the more.'

Leah sat down, tears of self-pity and recrimination streaming down her flushed cheeks. She said nothing, but inside she was screaming. She didn't deserve Alice's sympathy. Nor did she deserve to mourn Harry. She had disgraced his memory. Wherever he was, he'd be turning in his grave at what she'd done.

'It's only been four months, after all,' Daisy said, giving Leah a sympathetic smile. She was kneeling on the rug with Frank, who was amusing himself with a basket of wooden clothes pegs. Daisy had dressed a handful of them in scraps of material and was drawing faces on them, like their father used to do for her and Leah when they were little girls.

Leah blew her nose noisily, tears streaming down her face, as Alice stroked her gently between the shoulder blades. Leah didn't dare meet anyone's gaze. How could she explain that her grief over Harry was eclipsed by disgust at herself, compounded now by a tenderness for her unborn child? Now that she had the means to be rid of her baby, she was overwhelmed by a fierce desire to protect him or her.

Hannah returned with the mugs of tea.

'I've put some sugar in yours,' she said, as Leah accepted the steaming mug. 'Why don't you take it upstairs and have a lie down?' she suggested, her brow furrowed with concern for her eldest daughter. 'You look washed-out.'

'You haven't managed to shift that sickness yet, have you?' Beatrice pointed out, winding up her ball of knitting wool. 'No wonder you look so pale. You need to see the doctor, love, before you fade away.'

'I don't need the doctor,' Leah said quickly, wiping her eyes on her sleeves.

'There's no money for doctors, anyway,' Hannah said bleakly, her gaze scanning her meagre furnishings as she contemplated what they might be able to sell should Leah really need the attentions of the doctor.

'Perhaps you might ask Pearl to make you up one of her preparations?' Beatrice suggested, as Leah's blush deepened. Her tears had abated, leaving a hollow feeling in the pit of her stomach.

'I think I will lie down for a bit,' she said, getting unsteadily to her feet. She was unable to meet anyone's gaze as she made her way to the stairs.

'Try and have a bit of a sleep,' Hannah said, biting her lip, her concern for Leah evident in her eyes.

'She's really taken Harry's death hard,' Alice said softly, as her dark eyes followed Leah's progress up the stairs.

'I don't think there's anything physically the matter with her,' Hannah said. She sat back down, but her gaze was on the ceiling. The floorboards creaked overhead. 'She's always been such a sunny-natured girl. It breaks my heart to see her like this.'

'She's young,' Beatrice assured her. 'In time, she'll meet someone else.'

It was cold in the bedroom, and Leah's breath clouded in front of her as she tugged the eiderdown from the bed. Wrapping it around her shoulders, she curled up on the broad windowsill.

Snowflakes danced lazily past the icy glass. Resting her head against the wall, her fingers reaching for the ring nestled against her breast, she gazed across the darkening fields, remembering the day she'd first met Harry. How shy and sweet he'd been. She smiled sadly, her mind's eye conjuring up the memory of him standing on the haycart, pitchfork in hand, cheeks reddened by the sun and shiny with perspiration. Bitter tears stung her eyes and angry resentment curdled her stomach. If it hadn't been for Harry's parents, they could have married before he went away to war. She might have had Harry's child now. A precious son or daughter to comfort her in her loss. Instead, she was carrying the child of a man she now detested. She slipped her hand into her pocket and brought out the twist of paper Pearl had given her. Slowly, she unfurled it, revealing grains of slightly off-white powder. She licked her finger and dabbed it in the powder. She touched it to the tip of her tongue, shuddering at its sharp bitterness, one hand going instinctively to her stomach. How could she harm her baby? He or she was an innocent, entirely blameless for their parent's actions. With a sob, she scrunched the paper in her fist, specks of the powder falling to the floor, and shoved it deep into her pocket. She couldn't do it. Tears fell hot and fast down her face. She was in a hopeless situation and she had absolutely no idea what she was going to do.

CHAPTER TWENTY-NINE

'I've written to Ian at the convalescent home in Dorset,' Alice said to her grandmother as they stepped out of Hannah's cosy cottage. The snow was beginning to settle now, large flakes drifting past their faces.

'With luck, it will reach him before he's posted back to France,' Beatrice said, as they paused outside her own cottage. 'I'm trying not to get my hopes up. Foster is an extremely common surname.'

'I do hope he writes back,' Alice said earnestly. 'Even if it turns out he isn't your Ian, at least we'll know for sure. You and Grandfather are still coming for supper tomorrow evening?' she asked, as she turned to go.

'Oh yes,' Beatrice replied. Her grandmother's reply was cheerful enough, but Alice noticed the slight hesitation before she answered, and her smile didn't quite meet her eyes. Alice's cold cheeks flooded with heat. Had her grandparents noticed Samuel's strange moods? Was that why her grandmother's acceptance of her invitation was a little less enthusiastic than she might expect? Alice smiled, hiding her dismay that her husband's increasingly erratic behaviour was apparently no longer her painful secret.

'Lovely, I'll see you tomorrow, then. Give my love to Grandfather.'

'I will,' Beatrice said, letting herself into her cottage.

As she walked the few yards to the vicarage, Alice couldn't help the feelings of resentment building up inside her the closer she got to home. At once, she was flooded with guilt. It wasn't Samuel's fault, but over the past three months she'd found him more trying than ever. The slightest thing made him angry these days, and he shouted and raged at Alice and Mrs Hurst. On the odd occasion that Alice did invite her grandparents or parents for a meal, she spent the entire time on edge, not knowing how Samuel would behave. Sometimes, he was almost like his old self, playing the genial host, but then it could be something as simple as the gravy being slightly lumpy or the potatoes being a little cooler than he might like, and he would become taciturn and morose. He made her life extremely difficult. She sighed as she pushed open the gate.

In the warm, airy kitchen, she took off her damp shoes and coat, leaving them to dry by the range. The large table bore the remnants of Mrs Hurst's baking, and Alice sniffed appreciatively at the aroma of the mince pies cooling on the wire rack.

'Ah, Mrs Roberts, you're back,' Mrs Hurst said, bustling into the kitchen, an empty tea tray in her hands.

'Hello, Mrs Hurst,' Alice smiled, removing her gloves. It was snowing hard now. The windowsill was already half an inch deep. 'Is my husband in his study?'

'Yes, missus, I've just taken him his tea.'

'Thank you. I think I shall join him.' She paused in the doorway. 'Is he in want of company, do you think?' she asked hesitantly.

'The Reverend seemed in an amiable mood,' the house-keeper replied evenly.

Alice smiled and nodded.

She crossed the hallway and rapped softly on the door of Samuel's study.

'Samuel?' She turned the handle and opened the door a crack, peering into the warm room.

'My dear,' Samuel said, looking round with a smile. Alice's shoulders slumped in relief and she crossed the room towards him. Standing behind him, she kissed the top of his head.

'What are you working on?' she asked, glancing over his shoulder at the papers spread out in front of him.

'I'm writing to the parish relief council in support of Tilly's application for increased help. She has two mouths to feed now.'

'Poor Tilly,' Alice said, moving to stand to the side of him. Despite her sympathy for the girl, she couldn't help a flash of irritation at the way Tilly kept producing children when she herself seemed unable to carry a child.

'I'm going to speak to Pearl,' Samuel said. 'She needs to

talk some sense into the girl, otherwise she and her children will end up in the workhouse.'

'Surely not!' Alice gasped, pushing aside her own sorrow. 'That would be dreadful.'

'Then she needs to stop going with every man she meets,' Samuel said darkly. 'Pearl needs to take some moral responsibility here. I'm warning you, Alice, the parish relief will give up on Tilly and the workhouse will be her only option. Honestly, you women are all the same,' he snorted, scribbling his signature across the paperwork with a flourish.

'I beg your pardon?' said Alice, thinking she'd misheard him.

'You women,' Samuel said, leaning back in his chair to regard her with a look Alice could only describe as contempt. 'You're all like the woman in Proverbs who lures unsuspecting men to their doom.'

'Samuel, you don't believe that, surely? You've always been so sympathetic to Tilly's plight.'

'Yes, well, I was young and naïve. I am no longer naïve. This is the last time I will make a plea to the parish relief on her behalf. Have you seen anything of Leah lately?' he asked, startling Alice with his abrupt change of subject.

'Yes,' Alice replied, taken aback. 'I was with her a while ago. She's terribly upset. I think she's finding Harry's death incredibly difficult.'

Samuel snorted.

'Perhaps you might talk to her?' suggested Alice gently.

'Whatever for?' Samuel said, incredulous.

'You know, as a vicar. Offer her some words of comfort.'

'I believe Leah will be fine,' Samuel said dismissively. 'She'll get over Harry soon enough. She's that sort of girl.'

Alice frowned, but she couldn't face an argument. Instead, she slipped her arms around Samuel's neck and said, 'You haven't forgotten we're having my grandparents to supper tomorrow, have you?'

Samuel sighed deeply. 'I have not. I suppose we *must* have them?'

'Samuel? You always said how much you enjoyed my grandparents' company.'

'That was before,' Samuel said mutinously. 'You know how difficult I find company these days, Alice. My headaches . . .' As if to prove his point, he gripped his forehead, his knuckles turning white as he pressed his fingertips against his skull.

'Oh, Samuel, of course,' Alice cried, instantly contrite. 'I'm so sorry. I'll cancel.'

'No, no,' Samuel said, shaking his head. 'Don't let me spoil your evening. If I feel too ill, I shall simply take myself off to bed.'

'If you're sure?' Alice said doubtfully.

'Yes, yes,' Samuel said impatiently. 'Now, was there something in particular, because I really do need to work on my sermon for Sunday.'

'No,' Alice replied, hurt. 'No, nothing.' She forced a smile. 'I shall leave you to your sermon.'

With a leaden feeling in her chest, Alice quietly left the room.

'Everything all right, Mrs Roberts?' Mrs Hurst called from the kitchen door.

'Everything is fine, thank you, Mrs Hurst,' Alice assured her as she started up the sweeping staircase. It was only when she reached the sanctity of her bedroom that she let the tears come.

'Leah, there's a bloke to see you,' one of the women called as the dinner whistle shrilled across the factory floor. Leah looked over in surprise.

'Did he say who he is?'

The woman shrugged. 'He's in uniform,' she said, her eyes flashing with curiosity.

'Harry?' Leah murmured, but the brief flash of hope immediately turned to crushing disappointment as the woman continued. 'Dark-haired chap. Devastatingly good-looking.'

Glad of an excuse to escape the toxic-smelling air and deafening din of machinery, and mildly curious as to who it could be, she quickly donned her coat and hurried out to the yard, where the bitter wind had piled the snow into knee-high drifts against the dark brick wall.

'Joshua!' she exclaimed, her brows rising in surprise.

'Hello, Leah.' He was standing in the open gateway, the collar of his greatcoat pulled up around his chin. 'Have you got a minute so we can talk?'

'I'm due a break,' Leah replied hesitantly. 'What's wrong? Is it Mum?' she asked, in sudden alarm.

Joshua shook his head. 'Everyone's fine as far as I'm aware. I could do with a cup of tea. Shall we go across to the café?'

Still at a loss as to why Joshua was here, Leah simply nodded.

The café was quiet. They chose a table by the fogged-up window and sat down, making small talk as the waitress took their order for tea and toast.

'Have you taken it?' Joshua said once they'd received their mugs of tea and hot buttered toast.

'Taken what?' Leah asked, feigning surprise, although she knew exactly what Joshua was talking about.

'You know what I mean,' Joshua said, his eyes narrowing. He leaned closer, lowering his voice. 'Nan let slip you'd been to see her.'

Leah stared down at her untouched toast.

'It's okay,' Joshua said. 'I won't tell anyone.' He sighed. 'I just need to know if you took it?'

Leah shook her head. 'I couldn't,' she whispered.

Joshua let out a long sigh of relief. 'Thank God for that,' he said. 'That stuff is dangerous. I gave Nan a good talking-to. I know she's only trying to help,' he went on, pouring milk into both their mugs. 'But it can cause organ problems. One of the chaps in my regiment got a girl into trouble. She took some and died of severe kidney failure.'

Leah looked at him in horror. Her bottom lip trembled.

'I don't know what to do,' she said, her voice wobbling. Joshua reached across and squeezed her hand.

'I don't know whose kid it is, and I don't want to know, but I'm here to offer your baby a name and a father.'

'What?' Leah sat back in shock.

'You know how I feel about you, Leah.' He held up his hands. 'I know you can never love me like you loved Harry, but we're friends, aren't we? I reckon we'll rub along all right.'

Leah could only stare at him in amazement. Her mind was whirling. This would offer her a way out of her predicament. There would be the inevitable raised eyebrows and mutterings when the baby arrived early, but he or she wouldn't have to bear the stigma of illegitimacy.

'My leave ends on the thirtieth of December. I reckon if I can get a special licence, we can be married before then. I thought a registry office do. Or would you prefer a proper church wedding?'

'No,' Leah blurted out, thinking she couldn't bear the thought of saying her vows under Samuel's contemptuous glare while all the time knowing his child was growing in her belly. 'A registry office wedding will be fine.'

Joshua grinned. 'Does that mean you're saying yes?'

'I don't have much choice, do I?' Leah sighed. 'I'm sorry. That sounded ungrateful.' She smiled. 'It's all just such a mess.'

'I'm not the lad I used to be,' Joshua said earnestly. 'I've grown up a lot. Life in the trenches does that to a bloke.' He gave her a wan smile. 'I will look after you and your baby,' he promised. 'I shall sign my wages over to you. You'll both want for nothing. All I ask is that Tilly is looked after. Especially if anything happens to me.'

Leah nodded. 'Of course.' She met his gaze over the steam rising from her mug of tea. 'Thank you.'

All afternoon, as she worked at her bench, she fretted about what she would tell her family. Harry had barely been gone four months. It was far too soon for her to be contemplating walking out with another man, let alone marriage. Her mother was certain to smell a rat.

She was still deliberating over what to say as she let herself into the warm kitchen. She stripped off her coat and hat, shoving her gloves in her coat pocket before hanging it up. Her stomach roiled at the aroma of the chicken soup bubbling on the stove. She unlaced her boots and placed them in front of the range to dry, her frozen feet tingling as they began to thaw.

'Leah, love, I didn't hear you come in,' her mother said, coming down the stairs. 'I've just got Frank settled. Supper's ready when you are.'

'Where's Daisy?' Leah asked, getting the bowls from the pantry.

'She's having supper with one of her friends. They've been skating on the pond.'

Hannah lifted the lid on the large pan. 'How was work?' she asked, ladling the thin broth into bowls.

'All right,' replied Leah, pulling out a chair. She stared into her bowl of soup, seemingly mesmerized by the flecks of meat floating in the stock as she listened to her mother reciting snippets of news she'd gleaned from Beatrice, whose husband, Mathew, regularly bought a newspaper. Though the soup was thin on meat, it was swimming with vegetables and potatoes. There was no bread to mop it up, given the shortage of flour, but Leah had no appetite. She forced herself to eat to please her mother and because she knew the baby needed the sustenance. Twice, she almost opened her mouth to tell her mother about her impending marriage, but each time her courage failed her. Perhaps it would be better to tell everyone once the deed had been done, she decided, the cold, hard twist of dread inside her easing slightly as she got up to help with the dishes.

CHAPTER THIRTY

The last Saturday of the year was bitterly cold. Standing in the bleak registry office, Leah shivered, despite her heavy coat over her plum-coloured woollen dress, the small pot-bellied stove offering little in the way of warmth. Close by, Joshua was talking to the two witnesses, two chaps from his unit whom he'd simply introduced to her as Bert and Sid. They spoke in hushed tones, but their voices seemed to echo in the almost-empty room.

'Good morning,' said the registrar, as he hurried in, clutching a sheaf of papers. 'I'm sorry to keep you.' He dropped the papers on the desk. 'Would the bride and groom come forward, please?' he said, beaming at Leah. She glanced nervously at Joshua, who flashed her an encouraging smile and offered her his hand.

Standing before the registrar, her stomach in knots, she could hardly concentrate on the words. All she could think about was what her mother would say when they got home and announced that they were man and wife. Somehow, she managed to mumble her way through her vows and, in what seemed barely minutes, the registrar proclaimed them married. The register was signed, congratulations offered, hands shaken and the registrar bustled off, leaving Leah feeling rather bewildered at the swiftness of it all.

'Well, congratulations, Mrs Mullens,' Joshua said, giving her a quick kiss on the cheek. Sid and Bert shyly offered their congratulations, and the small party made their way out onto the bitterly cold street, where they bade goodbye to their two witnesses.

'Right,' Joshua said with a lengthy sigh. 'Are you ready to go home and face the music?'

The dishwater-grey sky reflected Leah's mood as he helped her up onto his little cart and started down the road, the wheels splashing through the puddles of melted snow. They were silent on the journey home. The thick snow in the lane muffled the noise of the pony's hooves, and the only sound was the creaking of the cart and the cries of the crows. Dark branches formed a knotted canopy above their heads, stark against the pewter sky. Leah's nerves increased with every plod of the pony's hooves and every turn of the wheels, and it seemed no time at all before they were pulling up outside Sunnynook Cottage.

'Here we are,' Joshua said, with an attempt at a smile. 'Best to get it over with.'

Leah nodded. She couldn't speak. Her throat was so dry that she could hardly swallow and her tongue stuck to the roof of her mouth. The door flew open as Joshua was helping her down from the cart. Her mother stood on the threshold, her face creased in worry.

'Leah, are you all right? What's happened?'

'Nothing, Mum, I'm fine,' Leah rasped.

'Why aren't you at work?' her mother asked, stepping to one side to allow Leah and Joshua into the warm parlour. Frank was sitting on the rug. He looked up as they entered and flashed them a toothy grin.

'I didn't go to work, Mum. I took the day off.'

'Took the day off?' Her mother's frown deepened. 'Whatever for?'

Joshua gave Leah's hand a squeeze.

'You might want to sit down, Mrs H,' he said kindly. Hannah shot him a look.

'Will you two just tell me what you're up to,' she said, looking vexed. Leah took a deep breath.

'We're married,' she blurted out.

'What?' Hannah said, incredulous. 'You can't be married.'

'Leah and I were married by special licence this morning,' Joshua explained, as Hannah sank into the nearest armchair, her hand to her racing heart.

'We've just come from the registry office,' Leah added in a small voice.

'I don't understand ...' Hannah looked from Leah to Joshua and back again. She lifted her hands in a gesture of helplessness. 'Why?'

Leah and Joshua exchanged glances. 'I know it must be a shock to you, Mrs H,' Joshua said, the buttons on his uniform glinting in the firelight. 'But I love Leah, I always have, and, well, with things the way they are, we need to snatch our chance of happiness when we can.'

'But ...' Hannah looked at Leah sternly. 'What about Harry? The poor lad's barely cold.'

Leah's cheeks flooded with shame.

'Of course, a part of Leah will always love Harry,' Joshua said, giving her an encouraging smile. 'But like I said, we've got to grab our happiness where we can and, I promise you, I will look after your daughter to the best of my ability.'

'I don't doubt that, Joshua,' Hannah interrupted. 'You've always been a good lad, even if you do fly a bit close to the wind at times.'

'That's all in the past, Mrs H,' Joshua said quickly. 'I'm a changed man.'

'I just wonder why you felt the need to marry so quickly and secretly?' Hannah sounded hurt, and Leah felt a stab of guilt.

'Like Joshua said, Mum, what's the point of waiting when none of us knows what tomorrow will bring,' she said. 'I'm sorry we didn't tell you, but we didn't want any fuss, Mum.'

Frank crawled across the rug and tugged at Leah's skirt. She picked him up, nuzzling his neck and making him giggle. In about six months' time, she'd have a baby of her own. The thought gave her a warm, tickly feeling inside. She just hoped that if Harry was looking down on her, he could forgive her. Joshua was a good man, for all his wild ways, and he'd be a good father for her baby.

'Well,' Hannah said at length, 'I suppose this calls for a toast. I'll get the elderflower cordial from the pantry. We can have a bigger celebration this evening when everyone gets home. No doubt they'll all be as surprised as me,' Leah heard her mother mutter as she headed for the kitchen.

'Congratulations to you both,' Alice said, giving Leah a hug. 'I wish you all the happiness in the world.'

'Thank you,' Leah replied formally, unable to look her friend in the eye. She was relieved Samuel had chosen not to join his wife in coming to offer his congratulations.

As soon as news of Leah and Joshua's nuptials had filtered through the hamlet, neighbours had been calling in to offer their congratulations.

'It's lovely to have something to celebrate for a change,' Florence Merrifield had said, gripping Leah's hands tightly in hers, her eyes glistening with tears. *No doubt thinking of the three sons she lost*, Leah thought pityingly.

Dora had been visibly shocked when she'd returned home from her shift at the hospital to the news that her dearest friend was married, but she recovered quickly, hurrying to give Leah a hug.

'I'm so happy for you. For both of you,' she said, turning to Joshua.

'When do you return to your unit, Joshua?' Mathew Turner asked, shaking Joshua by the hand.

'Tomorrow afternoon, sir,' Joshua replied.

'Not much of a honeymoon for you two, then,' he

remarked drily, causing Leah to blush crimson. Up until now, she had thought only of her wedding day. She hadn't given a thought as to what would happen after.

'Unfortunately not, sir,' Joshua grinned. They were interrupted by someone knocking on the door.

'Nan!' exclaimed Joshua as the door swung open to reveal Pearl's shapeless form standing in the doorway. She had on so many layers, she waddled more than walked into the room.

'When were you going to tell me you were married, then, Joshua Mullens?' she said, eyeing him sternly as she unwound the frosted veil from her face. 'I have to hear it from Cuthbert Ryall that my own great-grandson has gone and got himself wed!'

'I'm sorry, Nan,' Joshua apologized, his expression contrite.

'Pearl,' Hannah said, hurrying towards her. 'Let me help you with your wraps. Joshua, get your nan a mug of mulled cider.'

'I suppose congratulations are in order,' Pearl snorted, eyeing Leah across the room. 'I saw this, you know. It made no sense to me at the time. It was all jumbled up in my head, but I knew my Joshua's future was somehow entwined with yours.'

The room had fallen silent. Dora, Leah and Alice exchanged nervous glances, each remembering the day long ago when they'd gone to Pearl to have their fortunes read. Leah swallowed hard, terrified Pearl might mention the baby. She gave Leah a knowing look, but said no more, and Leah heaved a sigh of relief.

Joshua returned with the mulled cider, and Pearl seemed happy enough to sit by the fire, sipping her drink and listening to the conversation without taking part.

'Where will you live?' Daisy asked, bouncing Frank on her knee.

'Well,' frowned Leah. 'Here.'

'Of course you'll be staying here,' Hannah said quickly. 'You'll have plenty of time to find a place of your own once the war's over.'

'I'm afraid we haven't thought too much about the future,' Joshua said apologetically.

'You don't need to worry about that yet,' Hannah assured him. Leah shot him a glance. They would have to tell her mother about the baby soon. A woman at work had given her the name of a corset maker in Northam whom she promised would be able to help Leah conceal her pregnancy for several more weeks, but, the skill of the corsetier notwithstanding, her expanding girth would soon become noticeable.

'I must say I'm surprised,' Alice said, looking at Leah over her shoulder. She was at the sink, elbow-deep in washing-up water. 'It's so sudden. I didn't realize you had developed feelings for Joshua?'

The three girls were in Hannah's kitchen. Hannah was upstairs putting Frank to bed, Daisy had popped next door to borrow a book that Beatrice had offered to lend her and Joshua was seeing his nan home to her caravan.

'He's a good man,' Dora interjected quickly, seeing the look of anguish on Leah's face.

'Oh, I don't doubt that,' Alice said, drying her hands. 'It's just, well, you've never mentioned Joshua. I didn't even know you were courting.'

'It happened so quickly,' Leah muttered, averting her gaze. She hated lying to her friends, but she couldn't bear the look of concern in Alice's eyes. How could she ever tell her the truth? It would destroy her. 'And with Joshua returning to his unit tomorrow, we thought it best not to wait,' she explained, surprised at how easily the lies slipped from her lips.

Alice opened her mouth as if to reply, but they were interrupted by Hannah.

'I'll go in with Dora and Daisy tonight,' she said, frowning slightly. 'You and Joshua can take my bed.'

Leah's cheeks grew crimson. Feeling the need to escape the scrutiny of her family and friends, she grabbed the stack of dishes Dora had just finished drying and hurried into the pantry. She set the dishes on the shelf and pressed her clammy forehead against the cold stone wall. She was dreading bedtime. Surely Joshua wouldn't expect her to . . . in her mother's bed? The thought turned her insides to water. Suddenly the light dimmed, and she turned to see her mother blocking the doorway.

'Is everything all right, Leah?' Hannah said, her lips trembling. Leah nodded. She wanted nothing more than to fling herself into her mother's arms and sob her heart out, but to do so would mean the whole sorry tale coming out and the repercussions would be disastrous for all concerned, not least for Alice. Instead, she took a deep breath and, plastering a smile on her face, said, 'I'm fine, Mum. I'm sorry I didn't tell you what me and Joshua were planning, but neither of us wanted any fuss and we both felt it would be easier this way.'

Hannah sighed. 'I hope you know what you're doing.'

'I do, Mum,' Leah assured her with as big a smile as she could muster.

They both heard the latch being lifted.

'I think your husband's home,' Hannah said.

'Don't worry, Leah,' Joshua said, as he slid under the covers. Leah was sitting on the edge of the bed in her nightclothes, her gown pulled tight around her. He reached across and gently took her hand. 'I don't expect anything. I'll be gone tomorrow, and only God knows when I'll be back again . . .' He broke off, the words 'if ever' hanging unsaid between them. Joshua cleared his throat. 'Once I'm back for good, we'll take it from there.' He patted the bed. 'Come on, get in before you freeze.'

Heart beating anxiously, Leah climbed in beside him. She could feel the heat radiating from his body. She curled onto her side. Joshua blew out the lamp. The mattress creaked, and she was aware of his warm presence pressed against her back. He slipped one arm over her shoulder, holding her close. Feeling strangely comforted, Leah fell asleep.

CHAPTER THIRTY-ONE

1918

Dora sank into the nearest chair, her hand to her throat as she reread the letter. Her hand was shaking so much, the words seemed to dance before her tired eyes. She'd just arrived home after a long, gruelling twelve-hour shift at the hospital to find the letter waiting for her.

'What is it?' Leah asked, looking up from her knitting. She held the delicate little booties up to the light, examining them with a critical eye.

Despite the best attempts by the corsetier, her rounded stomach was becoming more noticeable. Her mother had greeted the news that she was going to be a grandmother with unbridled joy, all her misgivings about Leah's hasty marriage clearly forgotten at the prospect of another baby in the house. However, Leah couldn't help but wonder whether her mother's joy would be so evident when the baby arrived three months earlier than expected.

'It's Clarissa,' Dora said, her voice high-pitched in panic. 'She's betrothed and she wants to come and see me.' She fixed her anxious gaze on Leah. 'She's going to take Frank away, isn't she?'

'What does she say, exactly?' Leah frowned. There had been no word from Frank's mother for months now. He had celebrated his first birthday the previous week without so much as a card. He was so much a part of the family, his leaving now would be a huge wrench. Not to mention what it would do to the poor boy. As far as he was concerned, Dora was his mother.

'She writes that she has been courting this Gilbert Watson for several months and they are to be married this summer. There's a lot of trifling information about how they met and so forth, and how much her parents adore him – he's the son of a duke, apparently. In line to inherit titles and all sorts. She doesn't mention Frank until the last paragraph.' Dora snorted derisively. 'She asks after his health and says she is visiting her relatives in Southampton and will call in on Saturday afternoon.'

'This Saturday?'

'Yes,' Dora replied miserably. Her eyes rested on Frank, sprawled on the hearthrug, playing with a wooden spinning top. 'Oh, Leah, how will I bear to be parted from him?'

'Oh, Dor,' Leah sighed, getting up and going to perch on Dora's chair arm. 'It will be a dreadful wrench for all of us. Mum will miss him terribly.'

'I suppose I always knew this day would come,' Dora went on, trying not to cry. 'But I had hoped, once the letters stopped, that Clarissa had moved on with her life without him.' Sensing Dora's mood, Frank left his toy and crawled towards her. Grabbing handfuls of her skirt, he hauled himself up against her legs. With a shaky laugh, Dora lifted him onto her knees, where he put his chubby arms around her neck and rested his cheek on her shoulder. 'You're such an angel, Frank,' she murmured, smiling at Leah over his tousled head.

Leah smiled back sorrowfully. Two days. That was all they had left to spend with little Frank. It would be heart-wrenching for all of them.

Saturday afternoon arrived far too quickly. Hannah and Daisy had scrubbed the cottage from top to bottom, 'Why we need to bother with the bedrooms when company never ventures upstairs is beyond me,' Daisy grumbled to Alice as she dragged the hearthrug outside to beat the dust out of it.

'How is Dora bearing up?' Alice asked, adjusting her hat, which the brisk March wind seemed determined to whisk off her head. She just hoped she'd used enough hat pins to secure it.

'She's not back from the hospital yet. Mum's just giving Frank his bath.' She paused, noticing Alice's elegant attire. 'Where are you off to?'

'Oh, to some incredibly dull affair with the bishop and assorted clergy. I'd much rather be here to support Dora, but Samuel is insisting I attend.'

'Leah's annoyed she couldn't get the time off,' Daisy said,

pulling a face. 'Still, it's probably best she's not here. It's going to be a difficult afternoon, and she's a bit emotional, what with the baby and all that.'

'How is she?' Alice asked wistfully.

'She seems to be coping remarkably well,' Daisy said. 'Mum says Leah's really fortunate. She was sick every day for the whole nine months when she was expecting her.'

'She is fortunate,' Alice agreed, remembering her own bouts of debilitating morning sickness. But she'd endure any amount of discomfort, if only she would be blessed with a baby that lived. 'Anyway,' she went on briskly, 'I must go. Samuel hates to be kept waiting. Tell Dora I shall be thinking of her.'

Daisy nodded. Then she gave the carpet a good beating, almost choking on the dust that swirled from its fibres, and dragged it back indoors.

'I think it looks very nice,' Hannah said, standing with Frank on her hip as she admired their hard work. Not a speck of dust remained on any surface, the slate floor shone in the spring sunlight slanting through the open window. A bunch of egg-yolk-yellow daffodils stood in the centre of the table, which was laid for afternoon tea. There was milk for the tea, but no sugar, because the sugar ration had been used in the making of the small sponge cake that stood, slightly lopsided, on Hannah's iris-patterned cake stand. She wiped her hands on her apron and glanced at the clock.

'You go and wash your hands and face,' she told Daisy. 'Dora will be home soon.'

*

Dora ran frantically down the lane, her cape flying out behind her. Her hair had come adrift from its pins and tumbled around her flushed face in a tangled mess. She'd left the hospital later than she'd planned and had had to queue for longer than expected for the ferry. Thankfully, she'd managed to hitch a ride with a farmer's wife returning from market, who had dropped her at the crossroads about three miles out of Strawbridge.

'I'm so late,' she gasped, dashing into the cottage. 'I thought Clarissa might overtake me on the road.'

'Calm down,' Hannah smiled. 'You've got twenty minutes yet. Go and get yourself washed up.'

'Mama, Mama,' Frank cried, bouncing on Hannah's hip. He held his arms out to Dora, beaming joyfully.

Stifling a sob, Dora took him from Hannah and cuddled him. Frank chortled loudly, then stopped. As if sensing something was wrong, his toothy grin disappeared to be replaced by a frown as his eyes filled with tears.

'Dora, love, you're upsetting him,' Hannah said gently. 'There'll be time enough for tears later.'

Dora nodded. Wordlessly, she handed Frank back and hurried into the scullery to wash.

Precisely twenty minutes later, she was pacing the floor, Frank cradled in her arms. Hannah had combed his unruly dark brown hair into a side parting, and he looked very much the little cherub in his white smock.

Daisy was standing at the parlour window, watching for Clarissa's arrival.

'I think this is her now,' she said, half-turning to face Dora, eyes wide and anxious in her pale face. Balancing Frank on her hip, Dora hurried to the window in time to see a small carriage drawing up outside. Hannah came to stand behind the two girls, dread curdling her insides as the doors opened and an elegantly dressed woman of about middle age alighted, followed by a very attractive younger woman. It was clear they were mother and daughter; the similarity was striking.

'I didn't realize Clarissa was bringing her mother,' Dora murmured anxiously. She felt as though her chest was being squeezed by a giant vice, and she could hardly breathe as Hannah went to open the door.

'Mrs Arspery, Miss Arspery, good afternoon.' Hannah's voice sounded distorted to Dora's ears. She stood in the middle of the room, clutching Frank to her chest.

'I'm Hannah Hopwood, Dora's friend,' Hannah went on politely, stepping to one side and gesturing with her hand. 'Please, do come in.'

'Dora,' Clarissa breathed, smiling.

'Hello, Clarissa,' Dora croaked. Frank beamed at the new-comers, flapping his hands in excitement as he squirmed to be put down. 'Mrs Arspery.'

'Good afternoon, Dora,' Clarissa's mother said, her gaze coming to rest on Frank as Hannah quickly introduced Daisy.

'What a big boy you are,' Clarissa said, crouching down to where Frank stood at Dora's side. He giggled, burying his face in Dora's skirts and peeping at Clarissa shyly.

'Say hello to your mama, Frank,' Dora said hoarsely. Frank

293

gazed up at her, his big, dark eyes puzzled. 'Mama,' he said, tugging at Dora's skirt. Clarissa gently stroked his cheek, her expression sad.

'Can I offer you some tea?' Hannah said, hovering awkwardly in the background.

'Thank you,' Mrs Arspery said, with a haughty nod of her head. Peeling off her gloves, she sat down gingerly on one of the chairs around the table. 'Clarissa?' She indicated the chair next to her.

With obvious reluctance, Clarissa joined her mother at the table.

Dora and Daisy took their seats at the table. Frank sat on Dora's lap, eyeing the visitors warily, with none of his earlier exuberance. It was as if he had picked up on the tension in the room, thought Dora. While they waited for Hannah to make the tea, Dora chattered about Frank, telling Clarissa what a delightful, clever little boy he was, but her replies appeared stilted and awkward.

'There we are,' Hannah said with a cheeriness that sounded forced even to her own ears, as she set the teapot on the trivet. She pulled out the remaining chair and sat down. 'Dora tells me you are to be married, Miss Arspery,' she said to Clarissa, as she poured the tea. 'Congratulations.'

'Thank you, Mrs Hopwood,' Clarissa smiled.

'You're a lucky girl,' Mrs Arspery said acidly, making Clarissa blush.

'I am very fortunate,' Clarissa mumbled. 'Gilbert is a kind man.'

'Is he serving?' asked Hannah.

'He has been invalided out of the army,' Clarissa said. She turned to Dora. 'I didn't mention it in my letter, but poor Gilbert was badly wounded at Ypres. He lost a foot.'

'I'm sorry to hear that,' Dora said, with genuine sympathy. He must be a decent chap if he was willing to take on another man's illegitimate child. She said as much to Clarissa. Her smile faded and, beside her, her mother shuddered.

'I'm sorry,' Clarissa said quietly, staring at the slice of untouched sponge cake in front of her. 'You don't understand. Gilbert doesn't . . . I mean, I haven't . . .'

'Mr Watson knows nothing about the boy,' Mrs Arspery said coolly, picking at her cake with a fork. 'And he never will, either.'

'I beg your pardon?' Dora stammered. 'I understood that Frank would be going to live with you.'

'You understood wrong,' Mrs Arspery replied. Clarissa kept her head bowed. 'My husband is unaware of Clarissa's . . . indiscretion, and I'm determined he will remain so. Do you realize what a scandal there would be, should it become public knowledge that our daughter had a child out of wedlock?' Clarissa's mother's horrified gaze swept round the table.

'Well, I can understand it would be embarrassing for you and your husband, of course,' ventured Hannah.

'Embarrassing? We would never be able to hold our heads up again. And Clarissa's marriage prospects would be non-existent. Mr Watson is the son of a duke. His family would never accept another man's bastard.'

Dora instinctively held Frank tighter as she and Hannah exchanged glances.

'I instructed my husband's solicitor to draw up the papers,' Mrs Arspery went on, laying down her fork. She reached into her small bag and withdrew a sheaf of papers. 'This signs away all Clarissa's rights to the boy,' she said, handing the papers to Dora, who took them with shaking fingers. 'The child is never to know the truth about his parents.'

'Is this what you want, Clarissa?' Dora asked, frowning across the table at her one-time friend. 'He's your son, your flesh and blood.'

'I can't take him, Dora,' Clarissa said sadly. 'Gilbert would break off our engagement if he knew about Frank, and I can't bear the thought of him being sent to some terrible orphanage. He's obviously very fond of you. Please, say that you'll be his mother?'

'I will, of course,' Dora said. 'I love him as if he's my own, but are you certain you won't change your mind? I have no wish to set myself up for future heartbreak.'

'Of course she's certain,' Mrs Arspery interjected before her daughter could open her mouth. 'She's marrying the son of a duke. My future grandson will one day inherit the title.'

'*Frank* is your grandson,' Dora said. The woman batted her words away with a flick of her hand.

'This child is nothing to me. I'm grateful that you're prepared to take him off our hands,' she added, as if Frank were nothing more than an inconvenient pet. 'Now, I have arranged for a modest sum of money to be paid to you every month to provide for the child's keep until he is of age. So if you would sign the papers, we'll be on our way. We have a dinner engagement this evening, and I wish to drop these papers off at the solicitors before they close for the day.'

'Clarissa?' Remembering how heartbroken Clarissa had been when she'd persuaded Dora to take Frank initially, she felt obliged to try again. 'Are you absolutely sure this is what you want?'

Clarissa could barely bring herself to look at Dora. 'I have no choice,' she said lamely. 'Not if I wish to make a good marriage.'

Dora sighed. Having been subjected to malicious gossip, she understood only too well the stigma and shame suffered by an unmarried mother. She reached across the table for Clarissa's hand.

'Here's a pen,' Mrs Arspery said. 'If you'll sign where the crosses are.'

'I'm glad it's you,' Clarissa said, as she made to climb into the waiting carriage. 'I know you'll give him a good home.'

'I will, I promise,' Dora said, hugging Frank tight. Clarissa gently stroked his rosy cheek.

'Goodbye, little man,' she said softly. 'I'll never forget you, ever.' Her voice broke as tears filled her eyes.

'Clarissa,' her mother barked from within the carriage. 'We really must go.'

Flashing Dora a wobbly smile, she turned to allow the driver to help her into the carriage. The door closed and the coach driver swung himself up onto the seat. He flicked the reins, and the horses set off at a brisk trot. Dora raised her hand to wave, but Clarissa wasn't looking.

'Well,' Hannah said, one hand resting on Dora's shoulder. 'That was a turn-up for the books, wasn't it?'

'It certainly was,' replied Dora, giddy with relief as they watched the carriage make its way down the lane. 'It certainly was.'

CHAPTER THIRTY-TWO

As the cart creaked to a halt in front of the Glyn Arms public house, Ian Foster stretched out his left leg in an attempt to ease the cramping in his calf muscles. It was something he would have to put with his whole life, the doctors had warned him, but, on the whole, he knew he'd been lucky. The shrapnel had missed his vital organs, and the surgeons had managed to remove most of the fragments, though a few had evaded the knife, like the shard wedged halfway down his calf. For the most part, he was able to ignore the intermittent throbbing, but it plagued him more when he was tired and when the weather was inclement, which, he groused quietly to himself now as he glanced up at the dull-as-dishwater April sky, was pretty often in England.

He alighted from the cart gingerly, leaning heavily on his stick as he waited for the cramping to ease.

'There you go, mate.' The farmer, who'd kindly given him a ride from the railway station, handed him his canvas holdall. 'Good luck.'

'Thanks.' The cart trundled away and, shouldering his holdall, Ian turned to look at the pub. A few mud-splattered daffodils nodded in a wooden tub beside the stout stained-oak door. A forgotten pint glass stood on a low wooden bench. The ground beneath it was littered with cigarette ends. He glanced up and down the lane at the cottages grouped together in twos and threes, hugging the road. Two little girls were playing in the dirt. They both paused in their play to stare at him, their faces and pinafores streaked with dust. Ian smiled and raised his hand to wave, which sent them scuttling round the corner of the house out of view.

'Morning. Can I help you?'

Ian turned to see a thickset man standing at the corner of the building. He looked close to himself in age, broad in the shoulder with a mop of unruly dark hair. His breathing sounded laboured and his left sleeve flapped loosely at his side.

'Ian Foster.' Ian held out his free hand. 'I'm looking for a room.'

'Welcome.' The man shook his hand. 'George Merrifield.' He nodded at the stick. 'Medical discharge?'

Ian nodded. 'Invalided out last week. Shrapnel. You?'

'My war ended long ago, mate. Been in and out of hospital since 1916. Lost three brothers.'

Ian grimaced. 'That's tough.'

George shrugged. 'That's war for you.' He inclined his head towards the door. 'Come on in.'

Ducking his head to avoid the low lintel, Ian preceded George into the dingy pub. The air was thick with the smell of stale beer and old tobacco smoke. The ceiling was stained yellow and the carpet sticky underfoot.

A broad-shouldered man with thinning hair stood behind the bar, polishing a glass.

'We're closed,' he said, without turning round.

'Pa, got a chap looking to rent a room,' George said.

'Ah, right.' The man turned. Putting down his cloth and the glass, he rounded the bar and walked towards them, hand outstretched.

'Reuben Merrifield,' he grinned, grasping Ian's hand in his firm grip. 'Landlord of this here fine establishment.'

'Pleased to meet you,' Ian said. Though Reuben's smile was warm and friendly, Ian could see the deep sorrow in his eyes. 'Ian Foster.'

'You're not from around here, Mr Foster,' Reuben remarked, brows raised quizzically.

'No, I'm originally from South Africa,' Ian explained as Reuben poured them both a drink. 'But before the war, I was living in Wiltshire. A little place called Mere?'

Reuben shrugged. 'Can't say I've heard of it.' He slid Ian's pint across the shiny surface of the bar. 'Thought I recognized the accent, though. We've got a South African living right here in Strawbridge. Cheers!' He raised his glass and Ian did the same. George had disappeared back to whatever it was he'd been doing when Ian arrived.

Ian took a sip of his beer. It was strong and bitter on his tongue. He put the glass down, licking the froth from his upper lip.

'That wouldn't be Beatrice Turner, by any chance?'

Reuben's brows rose in surprise. 'You know Mrs Turner?'

'Not exactly,' replied Ian drily. 'But I would like to make her acquaintance.' He pulled a scrap of paper from his breast pocket. 'Nettlebed Cottage?'

'Just a way down the lane,' Reuben told him. 'You can't miss it.'

'Thanks.' Ian lifted his glass. 'Now, about that room?'

Beatrice draped the last of the laundry over the clothes maiden and set the empty wicker basket on a nearby stool. Hopefully the heat from the stove and the fresh air blowing in through the open doorway would combine to dry the washing, she mused, glancing out the window at the grey sky.

Wiping her hands on her apron, she went into the pantry to fetch the ingredients to make a start on the evening meal. Alice and Samuel were coming for supper and, though she was looking forward to seeing Alice, she had her reservations. She and Mathew seldom had them round as a couple. Samuel found social situations difficult, so Alice often came on her own and, while her granddaughter always appeared to be her usual warm, chatty self, Beatrice was astute enough to realize that all was not well at home.

If only the poor girl would get herself in the family way, she fretted, dumping her meagre rations of flour and butter on the table. Thank God the hens were laying well and – she smiled at the plump grouse lying on a sheet of newspaper, plucked and oven-ready – thank the good Lord for young

Simon Culley, who had become quite the expert with his catapult.

She was still thinking about Alice as she rolled out the pastry a short time later. Though Alice seldom mentioned her desire for a baby, she knew that Alice was distressed by the fact that Leah was expecting a baby so soon after her marriage. Beatrice wouldn't be surprised if Leah was expecting twins, she was that large, and only four months gone.

She carefully laid the pastry in the greased pie dish. The grouse was roasting in the oven, filling the whole cottage with its delicious aroma. She was trimming the edges of the pastry, humming softly to herself, when she heard the knock. She looked up in surprise, wondering who would come knocking at the front door on a Monday morning.

Of course, Hannah often popped in with Frank for a cup of tea and a natter, but she always used the back door.

Wiping her floury hands on her apron, she hurried through to the parlour. Taking a moment to check her appearance in the mirror, she lifted the latch and opened the door.

'Hello?' She smiled up at the tall man silhouetted against the pale grey light. His features were in shadow, but she felt there was something familiar about him.

'Mrs Turner? Mrs Beatrice Turner?' The man's accent sent a shiver of recognition down her spine. A vision of her common-law husband, Howard, swam before her eyes, causing her to take a step backwards. She gripped the door frame, fearing her knees were about to give way.

'Who ... who are you?'

'I'm Ian. Ian Foster. Howard Foster was my father.'

Her face drained of colour. 'Ian?' She hardly dared breathe. 'My Ian?' She clapped her hands to her face as tears welled. 'I never imagined ... I wrote so many times,' she blurted out. She realized she was trembling. 'You got Alice's letter?'

Ian frowned. 'I don't recall receiving a letter from an Alice. It may have gone astray. I've no doubt it will catch up with me eventually.'

'My granddaughter. She wrote to you at your convalescent home. Well, never mind.' Beatrice said nervously. 'You're here now.'

'Yes, I am,' Ian responded drily. 'May I come in?'

Weakly, Beatrice moved aside. Ian seemed to fill the room. He stood in the middle of the parlour, his hat in his hands, as if uncertain what to do next.

'Please, sit down,' Beatrice stammered, collapsing into the nearest armchair as her legs finally gave out. 'You never replied to my letters,' she said, hating the slight accusatory edge to her tone.

Ian sat down slowly. He leaned his stick against the chair arm, stretching out his injured leg.

'You're wounded,' Beatrice said anxiously when she realized no answer to her accusation was forthcoming.

'It's nothing,' Ian responded brusquely, brushing aside her concern. 'Enough to get me kicked out of the army, but nothing that I can't live with.'

A heavy silence settled on the room. Beatrice could hear the blood rushing in her ears and wondered if she were about to faint. She gave herself a mental shake. Her son was sitting opposite her. In her wildest dreams, she had never imagined this moment would ever happen, yet here he was. He was taller than she had imagined, his fair hair cropped short. His skin was tanned, yet there was a thin pale strip above his lip where he'd obviously shaved off his moustache. His eyes were Howard's, yet he had a look of her about him, too, she was pleased to note. She leaned forwards.

'You said Howard "was" your father?' she queried.

'He passed away some years ago,' Ian said. He spun his hat in his hands, his eyes drifting about the room.

'I'm sorry.'

Ian shrugged. 'He wasn't much of a father,' he said, his words laced with bitterness. 'I didn't see much of him once I was sent away to school.'

'I'm sorry,' Beatrice said ineffectually.

'Abandoned by both my parents,' Ian said with a bitter laugh.

'I never abandoned you, Ian,' Beatrice cried. 'It was your father. Howard took you from me when you were three. I would never have left you.'

'That's not what he told me,' Ian drawled.

'I knew he would lie to you,' Beatrice said. 'That's the sort of man he was.' She laughed humourlessly. 'It was your third birthday,' she said, gazing off into the distance. 'We arranged to have your photograph taken and meet for dinner. When I arrived at the hotel at the prearranged time, neither you nor your father were there. The hotel manager told me there was no dinner reservation. By the time I managed to arrange transport back to the farm, you were gone.' Her green eyes shone with tears. 'My heart shattered that day.' Her smile trembled. 'I'm so glad you've come.'

'I almost didn't,' he said grimly, wondering whether he'd been mistaken all these years about his mother. His father had proved to be a cold, unfeeling man, but he hadn't made up his mind about Beatrice yet.

'But you did,' Beatrice persisted. All the emotion she'd been holding in check since Ian had turned up on her doorstep so unexpectedly suddenly threatened to overwhelm her. Not wanting Ian to see her reduced to a sobbing mess, she rose to her feet and, telling him she was going to put the kettle on, hurried into the kitchen.

In the cool pantry, she crouched on the low, three-legged stool she used to reach the top shelf and sobbed silently into her apron. Like a dam bursting its defences, all the pent-up angst going back over forty years poured out of her. The grief that had started with the loss of her infant daughter, Lily, when she was just sixteen had been impacted by the loss of Ian some twelve years later. It hurt her that he was so cold towards her, but she knew that was down to Howard. She couldn't bear to lose her son again. She had to win him round. She had to. The alternative was too awful to contemplate.

'I kept all your letters,' Ian said, setting his teacup in its saucer, balancing it on the chair arm. 'My neighbour forwarded them on to me.'

'I'm glad you kept them,' Beatrice said. She was feeling calmer now. It was surreal, sitting in the parlour, sipping tea with her son. She almost wanted to pinch herself to make sure she wasn't dreaming.

'I don't know why I did,' replied Ian truthfully. 'I used to read them in the trenches.' He gave a hoarse laugh. 'Anything to provide a distraction.'

Beatrice tried not to feel hurt. 'Then you must understand that I never left you,' she responded earnestly.' Howard, your father, took you from me.'

'It was Nurse Webb who persuaded me to come,' he said after another lengthy pause.

'Dora?' frowned Beatrice. 'Yes, of course, she nursed you at the Royal Victoria.'

'She spoke highly of you,' Ian said, with a hint of a smile. 'I decided I would look you up after the war, but then fate had other ideas and, while I was recovering on the Isle of Wight, I thought, what the heck. I've nothing to lose. I may as well see this place Strawbridge for myself and see whose account of Beatrice Turner is the truth: Nurse Webb or my father.'

Beatrice held her breath. 'And?'

'It's too early to say,' Ian replied with a lopsided grin. 'But I'd say it's looking promising.'

Beatrice smiled. 'Alice is coming for supper this evening. Will you join us?'

'Whoa!' Ian held up his hands. 'You don't think it's too soon to be meeting all the family?'

'Of course,' Beatrice said, unable to hide her disappointment.

'I'll think about it,' Ian relented. 'If I decide to come, what time should I arrive?'

'Six o'clock?' suggested Beatrice.

Ian nodded. 'Don't expect me.' He drained his cup and got to his feet. 'Now, I must be going. The landlord of the Glyn Arms has invited me to dine with him.'

'Reuben Merrifield's a good man,' Beatrice said, walking him to the door. 'He lost three of his boys over in France, you know. And then there's poor George.'

'Yes, I met him briefly at the pub earlier,' Ian told her. 'The Merrifield boys were stationed not far from my unit. I didn't know them personally, though I did hear about the young lad who was executed.'

'Oh, that was terrible,' Beatrice said. 'Poor Leonard. He was just a boy. A dreadful miscarriage of justice, as far as I'm concerned.'

Ian turned his collar up against the chill wind and hesitated. 'It was good meeting you,' he said, with a nod.

Beatrice beamed. 'That invitation for supper still stands,' she said by way of reply.

Ian nodded again and set off up the road.

Beatrice lingered on the doorstep, watching him go. Once he was out of sight, she turned her gaze to the fields opposite. They were teeming with workers readying the soil for the spring planting. She spotted Mathew on the far side. And Daisy and Leah. Leah had only recently given up working in the factory to return to the fields. While the pay was less, she'd been concerned about how the chemicals might affect her unborn baby.

Bursting to tell Mathew her news, Beatrice grabbed her shawl and hurried out into the field, her cheeks glowing with excitement. Strawbridge was a small place, and gossip spread fast. By nightfall, everyone in the district would know that the good-looking stranger staying at the Glyn Arms was Beatrice Turner's long-lost son.

CHAPTER THIRTY-THREE

Dora freewheeled down the lane, her thoughts very much on Nate. After having no word from him in weeks, yesterday she'd received a pile of letters from him. Though the tone of his letters was cheerful, she could tell life in the POW camp was getting him down. She had taken to reading the newspapers left in the staff common room at the hospital for snippets of good news, anything she could pass on to Nate to give him hope that the war might soon end. But recently, there had been very little in the way of good news.

She was so lost in thought, she didn't notice the man walking along the lane until she was almost upon him. Swerving wildly, she careered across the lane and into the hedge, landing on her side in the lane.

'Nurse Webb,' Ian shouted in alarm as he ran to help her up. 'Are you hurt?'

'I don't think so,' Dora said, getting gingerly to her feet and brushing dust from her skirt. 'Which is more than can be said for my bicycle.' She looked in dismay at the bent wheel.

'I'll sort that out for you,' Ian said. 'Here, let me.' He picked the bike up. 'Where are you headed?'

'I'm on my way home,' Dora said. She frowned. 'But what are you doing here?' She noticed the stick. 'You're wounded again?'

'Shrapnel,' Ian said with a wry smile. 'Got me a medical discharge. So,' he grinned, 'finding myself with plenty of time on my hands, I decided to pay a visit to this Strawbridge that Harry and Nate were always talking about.'

Dora put a hand on his arm. 'You've been to see Mrs Turner?'

Ian nodded. 'I have.'

'I felt so bad because I didn't realize who you were. Alice was very upset. She came to the hospital, you see, to see you, but you'd already been discharged. But, of course, you know this. She wrote and told you as much.'

'So Beatrice told me. I haven't yet received her letters. Top notch as the postal service is, letters do occasionally go astray, and I have moved about a lot since I returned to France.'

'What was it like, seeing Mrs Turner?' Dora asked with genuine curiosity.

'It went well.' Ian cleared his throat and gazed out over the fields. 'Even though we're strangers to each other, I think I feel a connection. That's where I'm headed right now. Mrs Turner invited me to supper.'

'Then we can walk together,' Dora smiled. 'I live next door.'

With Ian wheeling the bike with its bent wheel, they walked companionably side by side down the lane.

311

'So, Nurse Webb, are you still smitten with your Nate?' Ian asked cheekily.

'I am,' replied Dora primly. 'In fact, I received several letters from him only yesterday.'

'How is he bearing up?'

Dora shrugged. 'He's cheerful enough,' she replied. 'But I get the feeling, reading between the lines, that it's all getting a bit much.'

'I can imagine. But you and he can both thank your lucky stars he's not over in France. It sounds pretty grim over there right now. They're saying in the pubs in town that the tide may be turning against us.'

'Oh, surely not?' Dora gasped in dismay. 'We can't lose! Not after all we've been through. All the young men we've lost. If we lose, it will all have been for nothing.'

'Don't fret,' Ian said. 'It's just talk. Pay no attention.'

They continued down the lane, feeling rather subdued. *What will happen to Nate should England and her allies lose the war?* wondered Dora anxiously.

A shaft of pale moonlight broke through the clouds, bathing the lane and the hedgerows in its milky glow. The buckled bicycle wheel squeaked rhythmically in time with the dull thud of their footsteps.

'Well, here we are,' Dora said, as they came to the row of three cottages. 'It's been nice to see you again, Mr Foster.'

'Ian, please,' Ian grinned. 'It's been nice talking to you, too, Nurse Webb.' He touched the brim of his hat. 'I expect I'll see you around.'

'I expect you will,' Dora smiled back. She glanced at the bike.

'I'll have this sorted out for you by the morning,' Ian promised.

Dora thanked him and, lifting the latch, went indoors.

Ian leaned the bicycle against the cottage wall and rapped on the door. Beatrice must have been waiting for his knock, for the door swung open immediately.

'You came!' she beamed. Silhouetted in the soft lamp-light, her features appeared softer and she looked younger. Something stirred in his memory. He blinked as he realized Beatrice was talking.

'I'm so pleased you decided to accept my invitation,' she was saying, as she ushered him into the cosy parlour. 'Let me take your coat. Everyone's in the dining room. They'll be so pleased to meet you.' As Beatrice took his coat and hat to hang up, a well-built, pleasant-faced man emerged from what Ian assumed was the dining room. His neatly trimmed dark hair and beard were streaked silver and his complexion was weathered. He held out his hand.

'Mr Foster, I'm Beatrice's husband, Mathew Turner. Welcome to our home.'

'Thank you, Mr Turner,' Ian said. The man's smile was infectious, and he couldn't help but grin back.

'Come on and meet my granddaughter,' Mathew said, pointing the way. Ducking his head, Ian followed him into the dining room.

'My granddaughter, Mrs Roberts,' Mathew said, indicating

the very attractive young woman with rich, chestnut-brown hair seated at the oval dining table. 'And her husband, the Reverend Samuel Roberts.'

'Samuel!' Ian exclaimed in surprise.

'Ian Foster, as I live and breathe!' Samuel bellowed, leaping to his feet. 'I wondered if it could possibly be you.' The two men shook hands warmly. 'Alice, this man was a good friend to me in France.' His smiled faded a little. 'You've obviously been discharged, like me?'

'Nothing too serious,' Ian assured him. 'Shrapnel in the leg. Well, all over, really, but they managed to get most of it out, apart from this stubborn bit in my calf. I got off lightly, though, in comparison to some of the poor chaps.' He laid his hand on Samuel's shoulder. 'I'm sorry for what you went through, mate. Having to witness a friend's execution. Shouldn't have been allowed.'

Alice tensed as she saw Samuel swallow hard, his Adam's apple bobbing up and down his throat. A statement like that could set him off. She cast a quick glance at her grandmother, who was watching anxiously from the doorway.

'At least I wasn't one of the poor buggers pulling the trigger,' was all Samuel said as he retook his seat.

'Oh, Ian, you're sitting here,' Beatrice said, seeing Ian casting his uncertain gaze round the table. 'Next to Alice. Her mother, Lily, is your half-sister. I thought it best not to overwhelm you with all the family at once, but,' she bit her lip nervously, 'if you're planning on staying a while, it would be nice for you to meet her.'

'I've taken a room at the Glyn Arms,' Ian said, pulling up his chair. 'I'm not sure how long I shall stay.' He turned to Alice, who was appraising him coolly with her dark eyes.

'Mrs Roberts,' Ian said. 'I'm pleased to make your acquaintance.'

'Likewise, Mr Foster,' Alice said pleasantly. 'I didn't realize you knew my husband.'

'We were billeted on neighbouring farms,' Ian explained. 'I got to know quite a few of the chaps from round here. Especially Nate, Harry and your husband.'

'Nate's in a POW camp in Germany,' Alice said.

'So Nurse Webb told me.'

'Here you go, Ian.' Beatrice set a plate of game pie, potatoes and gravy in front of him. As the meaty aroma hit his senses, he was rather pleased he'd made his excuses to Reuben.

In the kitchen, Beatrice caught sight of her reflection in the dresser mirror. Her cheeks were flushed from the heat of the stove, and a few wisps of greying auburn hair had come loose from her bun. She tucked them behind her ear, smiling to herself. Her son was sitting at her dining table – she could hardly believe it. She carried her plate into the dining room and took her place at the table, savouring the warm feeling in the pit of her stomach.

Samuel, Ian and Mathew spent the evening discussing current events, the church and the history of Strawbridge, the latter of which Ian seemed to find particularly interesting. Though she tried to tell herself not to be foolish, she couldn't help but hope that Ian might one day make his home in Strawbridge, or at least nearby. He didn't seem to have a tie to this place he'd lived in Wiltshire, though he did speak fondly of his former neighbour. As she was the one who had forwarded Beatrice's letters to Ian, she felt quite amenable to the woman herself.

Mathew was interested to hear about Ian's life in Africa, and Beatrice reacted with shock and dismay to hearing that Howard had left his estate to his children by his second marriage – not that he and Beatrice had been legally married, she reminded herself wryly.

'Will you return to South Africa, do you think?' Alice asked, pouring custard on her apple crumble. 'My Uncle Charlie lives out there. It was he who engaged the firm of solicitors that helped us discover your whereabouts.'

'I see. It all depends when this blasted war is over,' Ian replied. He blushed. 'I beg your pardon, ladies. I mean, obviously travel is out of the question for the foreseeable future. I had a thriving business in Mere. I may go back, though I could start up again just as easily somewhere else.'

'I believe Strawbridge would benefit from the services of a wheelwright,' Beatrice blurted out.

'Now, now,' her husband reprimanded her mildly. 'Don't pressure the lad.'

'It's all right, Mr Turner,' Ian said. 'I've been somewhat adrift since being discharged from the army. I'm not sure where I shall end up.'

'Well, while you're here, you must join me for a game

of dominoes,' Samuel said amiably. 'I'm sure you owe me a rematch.'

'I believe I do,' Ian grinned.

Alice smiled fondly at her husband across the table. Samuel had been in a jovial mood all evening. It had been so long since they'd enjoyed an evening out together where he didn't get upset or angry that she had quite forgotten what it was like to enjoy herself and not feel on edge, terrified that someone might say or do the wrong thing. Ian appeared to be good therapy for him and, not least for her grandmother's sake, she hoped he would decide to stay for quite some time.

CHAPTER THIRTY-FOUR

Leah sat back on her heels and massaged her aching back. She glanced up at the azure-blue sky. There had been no rain for over a week, and the soil was dry and crumbly between her fingers. The strawberries gleamed brilliant red among the green leaves, plump and juicy.

Wiping her juice-stained fingers on her apron, Leah got awkwardly to her feet. Her basket was barely half full, but she found she didn't really care. She'd felt tired and listless all day. She'd forgotten to bring her hat, and the hot July sun beat down on her bare head, making it ache. The baby was sitting uncomfortably low in her belly and every movement felt like an effort. She knew her time was close, and the thought of giving birth terrified her. Suddenly dizzy, she reached out. Finding her sister's arm, she gripped it tight.

'Leah, are you all right?' Daisy asked, scrambling to her feet. She'd thought Leah didn't look at all well, which was the reason she'd chosen to work close by today instead of joining her friends a few rows over.

'I think so,' Leah whispered. She closed her eyes, waiting for the dizzy spell to pass. 'I'm all right now,' she said, opening her eyes and sucking in a deep breath of hot, dry air. High above them, a buzzard soared lazily on the thermals, its haunting cry echoing over the fields.

'I might just go and sit in the shade for a while,' she said. She was about to take a step when she was hit by such a powerful contraction that she doubled over.

'Leah!' Daisy shrieked, eyes wide open in fear, grabbing her sister by the arms.

'Looks like the baby's coming,' one of the women working close by said knowingly.

'Bit early, isn't it?' her companion remarked, sitting back on her heels and regarding Leah with a quizzical look. 'Mind you, it's a big bugger.'

Breathing deeply as she rode out the pain, Leah took no notice. She'd done her best to ignore the sniggers and whispers. She'd even caught her mother looking at her suspiciously over the last few weeks as her stomach expanded. *Well, let them talk,* she thought now, gritting her teeth against another contraction. It was no one's business but hers.

'You'd better get her home, Daisy,' the woman said. 'The speed those pains are coming, the baby won't be long.'

'I can't walk,' Leah spat, gasping for air.

'Well, unless you want to give birth in the middle of a strawberry field, you'd better try,' the woman fired back unsympathetically. She'd given birth to five children, all with relative ease.

'I'll go for your mum,' one of the younger girls said, getting hastily to her feet. Daisy gave her a grateful smile. Brushing soil from her skirts, the girl took off across the fields. She called something to Mr Turner, but her words were lost to Daisy as she attempted to get Leah to move.

'Come on, love,' Daisy coaxed her gently. 'Let's get you home.'

The pain had eased, so, leaning heavily on Daisy, Leah took a few tentative steps across the rough terrain. Out of the corner of her eye, Daisy could see Mathew Turner watching them, shielding his eyes against the sun's glare. Many of the women and girls working the fields had also paused to watch Leah and Daisy's agonisingly slow progress across the field.

'Leah!' At the sound of her mother's voice, Daisy heaved a sigh of relief. Her sister was growing quite heavy, making their journey across the uneven terrain quite difficult.

'Where's Frank?' Daisy asked, as Hannah grabbed hold of Leah's left arm.

'Bea's got him. Come on, Leah, let's get you home and into bed.'

Between the two of them, they managed to get Leah into the cottage and up the stairs. She sank back against the pillows, a sheen of perspiration coating her skin as she moaned in pain.

'Daisy, run and get Pearl. Tell her Leah's baby is coming.'

As Daisy hurried away, Hannah fetched a damp cloth and gently bathed Leah's forehead. 'There, there,' she crooned softly. 'It'll all be over soon.'

'It hurts,' wailed Leah as she was gripped by another strong contraction.

'I know, sweetheart, but the speed the pains are coming, baby won't be long.' She got to her feet. 'Now, I just need to get a few things ready. I won't be long. Just shout for me if it gets too bad.'

While she waited for Pearl to arrive, Hannah busied herself boiling water and fetching clean towels from the airing cupboard. She laid them in a pile at the foot of the bed and stroked Leah's clammy forehead. Her daughter looked pale and wan, her hair fanned out across the pillow. Hannah had had her suspicions for a while now that Leah was much further along than she'd let on. If her suspicions were correct, the baby wasn't Joshua's, that much was certain. She sighed. She'd thought she'd brought her daughters up to know better, but these were difficult times. And who knew how badly Leah had been affected by Harry's death? Grief could make you do daft things, and knowing the baby wasn't Joshua's only increased her respect for her son-in-law. She just hoped and prayed he'd survive the war so he could come home and look after his little family.

Her thoughtful meanderings were interrupted by the clatter of footsteps on the stairs, and she looked up in relief as Pearl entered the room, followed closely by Daisy. She couldn't help but smile at Daisy's terrified expression.

'How close are the contractions?' Pearl asked calmly as she approached the bed.

'There's barely any time between them,' Hannah replied. 'The poor girl's exhausted.'

'I can't . . .' Leah whispered hoarsely.

'Now, now,' Pearl chided her in a brisk, business-like fashion. 'You can and you will. You've got work to do. There'll be plenty of time for resting afterwards.'

Leah squeezed her eyes shut as Pearl got to work down at the business end of things. She could feel her hands, rough and prodding, but any embarrassment she felt was instantly blotted out by the next contraction.

Leah felt as though she was floating on an endless sea of pain. Waves of agony crashed over her one after the other, with barely a moment's reprieve between them. She was dripping with sweat and her throat was hoarse from screaming when at last Pearl gave a triumphant shout.

'I can see the head! Only a few more pushes now, girl, and that will do the trick.'

Leah bit down on her lip. She let out a long, primeval scream that seemed to Daisy to bounce off the walls, and the baby slithered out into Pearl's waiting arms.

'It's a boy,' she said, holding the slippery infant aloft for Leah to see. 'A healthy baby boy. About a nine-pounder, I'd say,' she continued, reaching for one of the waiting towels.

Hannah helped Leah sit up, and Pearl handed her the baby. She stared down at him in wonder. He had a shock of dark brown hair and, even still covered in blood and vernix, he was the most beautiful thing Leah had ever laid eyes on. She searched for some resemblance to Samuel, but could see nothing. She exhaled slowly in relief.

There would be talk, of course. It was inevitable in a small place like Strawbridge, but, in time, people would forget. Joshua's name would be on the birth certificate and, for all intents and purposes, he would be the baby's father.

'Do you have a name?' Pearl asked, washing her hands at the washbowl on the nightstand.

Leah looked at her mother. 'I thought I'd call him William, after Dad.'

Hannah's eyes sparkled with tears. 'I think that's a lovely gesture, love,' she said, coming to perch on the edge of the bed. 'Your dad would be dead proud. May I hold him?'

'Of course.' Leah carefully passed the swaddled infant to her mother. He made a small mewling sound and pursed his pink lips.

'He's probably hungry,' Pearl said. 'I'll give him a wash in a minute, and then perhaps you should try feeding him.'

'I must write to Joshua and let him know,' Leah said anxiously.

'There's plenty of time for that when you're rested,' her mother said, handing baby William to Pearl. 'I'd better nip next door and relieve Beatrice of Frank. Lord knows, she's had him all afternoon.'

'Oh, she'll have loved every minute of it, Mum,' Daisy said. 'I wonder how he'll take to another baby in the house.'

'He'll love him to bits, I shouldn't wonder,' Hannah replied. 'Right, I'll be back in a bit. Daisy, make Pearl and Leah a cup of tea. Lord knows they've earned it.'

William wasn't fond of being bathed and was still crying lustily as Daisy climbed the stairs with the tea a short while later.

'Thanks, dear,' Pearl said, wrapping the squirming infant in the softest towel and handing him to Leah. He continued to scream loudly, red-faced, as Leah stared down at him, at a loss as to what to do.

'He wants feeding, pet,' Pearl said. Fumbling clumsily with the buttons of her nightdress, Leah manoeuvred William so that his face was at her breast. To her surprise, he seemed to know exactly what to do and latched on immediately, sucking noisily.

'There you go,' Pearl beamed. 'He's happy now.'

They heard the back door. Darkness was falling, and Pearl drew the curtains while Daisy lit the lamp. Moments later, Hannah appeared in the doorway, Frank in her arms. He squirmed, wanting to get down.

'Bea's given him his tea,' she said, setting him down on the floor. He toddled over to the bed, plucking at the bedclothes with his chubby fingers.

'Let him up on the bed,' Leah said. 'Let him see William.'

Daisy hoisted Frank up onto the bed. He gazed at the suckling baby for a few seconds before deciding it was nothing to warrant his attention and slithering to the floor. The flickering shadows cast by the lamp soon caught his attention, and he giggled as he tried to catch them.

'He'll find the baby more interesting when he's a bit older,' Hannah said, smiling at Leah's disappointment. 'Bea sends her congratulations, by the way. She said she'd let Alice know.'

Leah blanched, the joy in her newborn son suddenly tainted with guilt. How could she stand by while Alice fussed over William, knowing how badly she had betrayed her friend?

'You look tired, Leah,' Hannah said, mistaking Leah's woebegone expression for exhaustion. Leah attempted a smile. Her mother wasn't far wrong. She felt utterly physically and emotionally drained.

'We'll leave you in peace now.' Hannah leaned over and smoothed the hair away from Leah's forehead. 'When you're done feeding the little lad, try and get some sleep yourself. I'll only be downstairs if you need me.'

Leah nodded and closed her eyes, relishing the gentle tug at her breast. *He's a hungry little chap,* she thought with a smile. Soon it became clear that William had fallen asleep, and she gently eased his mouth away from her nipple. Tucking him carefully into the crook of her arm, she softly stroked his smooth cheek and closed her eyes.

When Hannah peeped in on them a few minutes later, both mother and baby were fast asleep.

CHAPTER THIRTY-FIVE

'Can you manage another potato, Samuel?' Alice asked, holding up the blue-and-white-striped dish.

'Thank you.' Samuel leaned over and speared the last remaining potato with his fork. 'I must say, Mrs Hurst has excelled herself with this pigeon pie. That young Culley boy must be earning himself a few bob if he's supplying the whole of Strawbridge with fresh meat.'

'He's certainly a crack shot with the catapult,' Alice agreed, taking a sip of water. With food shortages and rationing, they were grateful for the frequent additions of game to supplement their menu. Rumour had it that Isaac Whitworth had told his gamekeeper, Cuthbert Ryall, to turn a blind eye to any poaching as long as the food shortages lasted. Between Simon and the well-stocked stew pond, the residents of Strawbridge hadn't fared too badly. Unlike their town- and city-dwelling cousins. Alice saw daily the depths of deprivation and starvation that affected the poorer of Southampton's communities. Children were left to fend for themselves while their mothers worked to supplement their widow's pensions or separation allowances, which were nowhere near adequate enough to live on. The free kitchens and soup kitchens were overrun, so much so that Alice was often terrified that they would run out and she would have to turn hungry people away. For many, it was their only hot meal of the day.

Even now, Mrs Hurst was delivering a food parcel to Tilly, who, yet again, had found herself in the family way. Despite Samuel's best efforts, the authorities had stopped Tilly's parish relief. *A rather upside-down way of looking at things*, Alice thought now, fuming quietly at the inhumanity of the decision. It had been done as punishment for Tilly's loose morals, but the ones who suffered the most were her two little children.

It broke Alice's heart to see them so hungry and cold, and she had suggested to Samuel that they take little Cecily and Polly into their home, just until Tilly got her life straight, but he'd refused point-blank.

'That's what the workhouse is for, Alice,' he'd replied coldly. 'Look what happened to your friend Dora. She took on Frank as a favour and now she's stuck with him. I'm not having that happen to us.' He'd stalked off to his study, leaving Alice staring after her husband in dismay. The old Samuel would never have been so callous.

Now, watching him tucking into his meal, she wondered if he felt even a spark of guilt that a lot of families not too many miles away would be going to bed hungry tonight.

'Did you and my Uncle Ian have a pleasant afternoon?' she asked, in an effort to engage her husband in conversation. Meal times could be quite tedious if he was in a taciturn mood. Though, this evening, he did seem more mellow than usual. Ian seemed to have a calming effect on him, for which she was grateful.

In the two and a half months that Ian had been in Strawbridge, he and Samuel had become good friends, spending a couple of afternoons a week in the snug at the Glyn Arms enjoying a pint over a game of dominoes. Occasionally, if the pub was quiet, which it usually was on a weekday afternoon, Reuben and George would join them.

'Thank you, yes,' Samuel said, fork poised midway between his plate and his mouth. 'He's spending the next few days with your mother and family, did you know?'

'Grandmother said so, yes. I'm so pleased my mother and he get on so well. Grandmother is over the moon, of course. Having him here is doing wonders for her. I hope he stays a long time.'

'I believe he may wish to remain in Strawbridge for quite some time,' Samuel said with a sly smile.

'Oh?' Alice responded curiously. 'What makes you say that?'

'He appears to be a bit smitten with the younger Hopwood girl.'

'Daisy?' Alice's brows shot up in surprise. 'Daisy's only just nineteen. Ian is what, thirty, thirty-one?'

'It's only a twelve-year age gap,' Samuel replied mildly.

'There were fifteen years between my grandparents, and they muddled along reasonably well.'

'I'm just surprised.' She chewed thoughtfully. 'Do you know whether Daisy returns his affections?'

'They've been for a couple of walks, apparently. They seem to get on well enough.'

Alice was still ruminating on the news that her uncle was walking out with her best friend's younger sister when Mrs Hurst appeared in the doorway.

'Oh, Mrs Roberts,' she said, slightly breathless. 'I've just bumped into your grandma. The Hopwood girl has had her baby.'

'Oh, goodness!' Alice said, frowning. 'It's early.'

'Nine pounds, according to your grandmother,' Mrs Hurst said with a sceptical smirk as she left the room.

'That's very puzzling, don't you think, Samuel? I mean, Leah's only been married six months ...' She broke off. 'Samuel?' Her husband was staring into space, a peculiar expression on his face. 'Samuel,' she repeated. 'Is something the matter?'

He pushed back his chair with such force that it clattered to the floor. Uttering a low, guttural sound in the back of his throat, he strode quickly from the room. Perplexed, Alice rose to follow him, but sank back onto the seat as the sound of his study door slamming shut reverberated through the vicarage.

What could have brought about such an outburst? she wondered, as a small knot of unease began to form in the pit of her stomach. The icy finger of dread traced its way down her spine. Surely Samuel had nothing to do with Leah's baby? The idea was preposterous. She put her fingers to her throbbing temples. Samuel would never do such a thing. They had their difficulties, but he'd never be unfaithful, would he? Leah was her dearest friend. The icy cold fingers now clutched at her heart as she recalled how Leah's attitude towards her had changed in recent months. She couldn't pinpoint the exact moment she'd realized there was something amiss in their friendship but, if she was honest with herself, she could almost be certain it was about nine months earlier. She had put it down to Leah's grief over Harry making it difficult for her to be around her married friend, a painful reminder, perhaps, of all she'd lost, but now she thought about it, could the reason be because Leah was ashamed and embarrassed to be around her?

Alice began to feel faint. She was breathing too fast. She took a deep breath and exhaled slowly in an effort to get her emotions under control. If Samuel was the father of Leah's baby, what would become of *her* child? Her hands moved instinctively to her stomach.

She had missed her last two courses and, despite her anxiety, had a gut feeling that this baby would survive. She had been tempted to go and see Pearl, but the fear of bad news stopped her.

If her worst fears were realized and Leah's baby was Samuel's, their children would be siblings. She picked up her glass with a shaking hand. *My husband is an adulterer,* she thought dully as she took a sip. The thought was like a knife slicing through her heart. How could she bring herself to be a wife to him now? How would she be able to look Leah in the eye, knowing what she'd done?

'Shall I clear the table now, Mrs Roberts?' Alice jumped at the sound of Mrs Hurst's voice.

'Oh, yes, please,' she stammered, quickly wiping her eyes. She hadn't even realized she was crying. 'Thank you,' she said with as much dignity as she could muster. 'I have a bit of a headache. I think I shall retire early.'

'Very well, Mrs Roberts,' Mrs Hurst said, tactfully averting her gaze from her mistress's tear-stained face. 'I'll see you in the morning, then.'

Alice lay awake in the darkness, listening to the rhythmic ticktock of the grandfather clock in the hall below. It chimed every hour, and still Samuel didn't come to bed. She heard the clock chime five before she finally fell into a fitful doze, only to wake two hours later to find Samuel's side of the bed empty and cold. He hadn't come to bed at all.

At breakfast, Samuel was his usual indifferent self. He'd had a lot of paperwork to deal with and had ended up falling asleep in his chair, he told Alice brusquely when she enquired as to why he hadn't come to bed. Of his strange behaviour at dinner the previous evening, no mention was made.

'I shall be in my study,' Samuel said, excusing himself as soon as he'd swallowed his last mouthful of tea. 'I am not to be disturbed.'

Alice sat back in her seat, her heart as heavy as a piece of lead in her chest.

'I expect you'll be over to see the new baby this morning?' Mrs Hurst said as she cleared the table.

'I suppose so,' Alice said with a wan smile. She would have to go. It would look strange if she didn't, but the prospect gave her no pleasure. She left the dining room and wandered out into the garden. Without Reverend Aldridge's green fingers, the vicarage rose bushes had been left very much to their own devices. Now, donning her wide-brimmed hat and a pair of grubby gardening gloves that she found in the shed, Alice grabbed the pruning shears and spent the next hour tackling the rose bushes. Taking a handful of long-stemmed lemon-yellow roses indoors, she arranged them prettily in a vase, standing them on a low table in the front hall. The grandfather clock chimed eleven o'clock. She could put it off no longer.

She washed her hands and changed her dress. She paused outside the study door, debating whether to tell Samuel where she was going but deciding against it. Instead, she called to Mrs Hurst in the kitchen, telling her she'd be back in time for dinner.

Her heart thumped painfully in her chest as she walked the few yards from the vicarage to the row of cottages. She ducked round the side of her grandparents' cottage and crossed their garden. She glanced in through the open door in case her grandmother was about, but saw no one. The back door of Sunnynook Cottage stood open, and Hannah was just coming out with a basketful of wet nappies.

'Hello, Alice,' she said with genuine pleasure. 'Go on up. Leah will be so pleased to see you.'

Alice smiled thinly. She made her way up the stairs, her heart sinking with every step. She found Leah in Hannah's bedroom, sun streaming in through the window. She was sitting up in bed, her dark blonde hair fanned out against the pillow, her baby cradled in her arms.

'Alice,' Leah said nervously. She smiled brightly, but Alice had seen the flash of fear that had crossed her face the moment she'd spotted Alice hovering in the doorway.

'Hello, Leah. Congratulations.' Even to her own ears, her words sounded forced. She focused her gaze on the baby. Her eyes searched for any resemblance to Samuel. William had dark hair like Samuel's, but, she consoled herself, that was proof of nothing. Joshua had dark hair.

'Would you like to hold him?' Leah asked tentatively. She held her breath as Alice nodded and moved closer to the bed. Alice took the sleeping baby in her arms. The tension in the room was palpable. Alice met Leah's gaze, and she blushed furiously and looked away, confirming Alice's worst fear. She swallowed hard.

'He's a lovely-looking little chap,' she said, finding her voice. 'Joshua must be very proud.' She gave Leah a hard look. Leah's immediate thought was, *She knows!* She looked away, shame washing over her like waves.

'Have you told him yet?' continued Alice, settling herself on the corner of the bed.

'Who?' Leah looked up in alarm.

'Joshua, of course,' Alice said, a slight edge to her voice. 'Who else would I mean?'

'Of course,' Leah replied, flustered. 'Mum posted my letter this morning.'

Alice nodded and turned her attention to the baby. William was a comforting weight in her arms, and she couldn't help imagining what it would be like to hold her own baby. By her reckoning, she was due early in the new year. She tried not to dwell on how she would feel if she lost another baby.

William squirmed and opened his eyes. He looked at her with his unfocused gaze, his little mouth making soft sucking noises.

'I think he's hungry,' she said.

'Not again,' Leah sighed, taking him back. 'He's insatiable.' She unbuttoned her nightdress and settled William to feed. 'Mum says he will eventually go longer between feeds.' She adjusted her position against the pillows. 'Daisy seems quite taken with your uncle,' she said, in an attempt at conversation.

'So my husband tells me,' Alice replied, the emphasis on the word 'husband' making Leah wince.

A heavy silence settled upon the room. The sound of voices drifted in from the strawberry fields, and they could hear Hannah humming to herself as she hung up the laundry. She broke off to say something to Frank, who responded with a gleeful yell. The creak of wagon wheels sounded in the lane below, punctuated by the slow, heavy thud of horse's hooves.

As she watched Leah suckling her baby, Alice felt a heavy sadness descend upon her. How she would have loved to confide in Leah that she, too, was expecting. But she couldn't summon the enthusiasm to do so. Their babies would be close enough in age to be friends. Instead, they would be siblings. Though neither of them would ever admit it out loud, their friendship had been irrevocably changed.

The church clock struck noon, and Alice got to her feet.

'I must go,' she said with an inward sigh of relief. 'I told Mrs Hurst I'd be home in time for dinner.'

'Of course,' Leah said, with a stricken expression. 'Thank you for coming.'

Alice paused in the doorway, looking back at Leah over her shoulders. There passed between them a look laden with regret and sorrow. She could read the silent plea for forgiveness in her friend's eyes, but Alice was not yet ready to forgive.

'Goodbye, Leah.' With a last, wistful look at baby William, she left the room. At the sound of Alice's receding footsteps, Leah sank back against the pillows and began to cry.

CHAPTER THIRTY-SIX

In the days that followed William's birth, the newspapers carried the news that, in Russia, Tsar Nicholas and his whole family had been murdered, but more important to the residents of Strawbridge was the news that, for Britain and her allies, the tide finally appeared to be turning.

Though Nate's letters home were heavily censored by his German captors, reading between the lines, Dora got the gist that many of the guards at the prison camp had lost their appetite for war. Mostly young men, all they wanted to do was to return home to their families.

Wounded soldiers arriving from the front were bursting with stories of German defeats and told how whole units had surrendered. She'd seen for herself the parties of captured German soldiers being marched through the city streets accompanied by the boos and jeers of the watching crowds.

'Mama.' Her thoughts were interrupted by Frank tugging at her skirts. She put down the bowl of peas she was shelling and lifted him onto her lap and cuddled him. He was sixteen months old now and as bonny as could be with his dark hair and large brown eyes. She'd taken him to the photographers on Above Bar Street and had their picture taken. One she'd given to Hannah, who'd put it in a frame on the mantelpiece, and the other she'd sent to Nate. She'd been relieved that he seemed to accept Frank's presence in their lives with perfect equanimity. But then, her Nate was a kind man and Frank wouldn't want for a better stepfather. One of the nurses at the hospital who'd been widowed in the first months of the war had recently remarried, and she was always complaining to Dora about the strife between her new husband and her three children.

'It's such a warm day,' Hannah said, sitting back on her heels and wiping the perspiration from her brow. 'Just watch Frank doesn't get too hot.'

'It's fine here in the shade,' Dora assured her, but she ran her finger under the collar of Frank's smock just to make sure he didn't feel too warm.

'It's thirsty work, this weeding,' Hannah said, getting stiffly to her feet and brushing the soil from her fingertips. 'I'll fetch us a cold drink.'

'Thanks, Aunty Hannah,' Dora said, shielding her eyes against the sun's glare. Frank squirmed to be let down, and she lowered him onto the grass where he proceeded to pluck at the daisies.

'I'll see if I can persuade Leah to come out for a bit. The fresh air will do her good.'

'Yes, do,' Dora urged her. 'There's plenty of room here under the apple tree.'

Hannah rinsed her hands in the bowl in the kitchen and climbed the stairs, feeling troubled. In the ten days since William's birth, Leah had seldom left her room. She'd heard that some women suffered severe bouts of melancholy after having a baby, and she was in two minds as to whether to send for the doctor, though it was an expense she could well do without. She wondered, briefly, whether Pearl had any herbal remedies she could give her daughter. She was Leah's great-grandmother-in-law, after all.

'Leah?' The bedroom door was ajar. Hannah knocked softly and peered into the darkened room. Leah was sitting against the pillows, nursing baby William. Looking at her, Hannah was reminded of a painting of the Madonna and Child she'd seen in a museum once. She looked radiant.

Leah tilted her face towards her mother.

'I wondered if you might like to come out to the garden for a bit?' Hannah said, going to sit on the bed. She smiled down at her grandchild, her eyes full of adoration. She'd loved every one of her five children with a fierce, overwhelming love, yet nothing had prepared her for the depth of the love she felt for William. The strength of it was so overwhelming that at times she felt as though her heart would burst.

'A bit of fresh air would do William good, and you, too. You're looking a little peaky.'

'I might,' Leah replied listlessly.

'We should start thinking about a christening,' Hannah said, tracing the contour of the baby's cheek with her fingertip. 'It'll give you something to focus on.'

'No,' Leah said firmly.

'What?' Hannah looked at her in surprise. 'You've got to have the little lad christened, Leah!'

'I don't want to,' Leah said with a mutinous glare.

'Whyever not?' Her mother looked so shocked, Leah almost laughed. 'You have to, Leah. You're already the subject of gossip. If you refuse to have him christened, why, people will be scandalized. He won't be able to attend services or get married in the church.' Hannah frowned. 'Look, I know Reverend Roberts can be difficult, but . . .'

'No!' Recoiling at the vehemence in Leah's voice, her mother could only stare at her open-mouthed.

'What has got into you, girl?' she demanded, clearly perplexed.

'I don't want him anywhere near William.'

'Who? The Reverend?' Hannah blinked. Leah looked away, two red patches glowing on her cheeks.

'I don't understand why . . .' Hannah's face paled. Her hand shot to her mouth. 'Oh, Leah,' she whispered, her eyes widening with shock as realization slowly dawned. 'You're not saying . . .' Leah kept her gaze fixed firmly on the wall. 'Leah Hopwood! The vicar?' The curtains stirred and Hannah quickly got to her feet. 'How could you?' she hissed, closing the window. 'He's married to one of your best friends. And what on earth was he playing at?'

'It was a mistake,' Leah mumbled, hot tears spilling down her cheeks. 'Neither of us meant it to happen.' She turned her ravaged gaze on her mother. 'You must believe me.'

'Does Alice know?' Hannah stood at the foot of the bed, her arms folded across her heaving bosom. She was having a hard time comprehending what Leah was saying.

Leah nodded miserably. 'I think she suspects.'

'Oh, Leah,' Hannah sighed. Her shoulders slumped. 'Does Joshua know?'

Leah shook her head.

'Well, I never thought . . . I imagined it was some chap at work who'd turned your head, but . . . Samuel?' She shook her head. 'Poor Alice.'

'Poor Alice! What about me, Mum?' Leah cried, wiping away the tears with her sleeve. 'I'm the one married to a man I don't love. I've likely lost one of my best friends . . .' She began sobbing in earnest.

Hannah sighed. Careful not to crush the feeding baby, she leaned over to give Leah an awkward embrace.

'I'm afraid you've made your bed, love. You'll be all right with Joshua. He's a decent man. Once he's home for good, things will get better. You're fond of him, aren't you?'

'We're friends, that's all,' Leah hiccupped.

'Well, there you are, then. Friendship's as good a starting place as any.'

'What about Alice?' Leah sobbed. 'Do you think she'll ever forgive me?'

Hannah sat back and sighed. 'I don't know. Only time

will tell.' She patted Leah's hand. 'Come on, love. Dry your eyes. I'm getting me and Dora some blackcurrant cordial. Will you have a glass?'

Leah nodded.

'Come on downstairs. It won't do you or the baby any good sitting up here moping.'

Reluctantly, Leah followed Hannah downstairs.

'Oh, I'm glad you came down,' Dora said, looking up from the bowl of peas on her lap. Frank gave a squawk of delight at the sight of his Aunty Leah, pausing momentarily in chasing the chickens around the garden to flash her one of his beautiful smiles. Leah couldn't help but smile back. Frank was such a tonic.

She sat on one of the kitchen chairs Hannah had brought outside, settling William on her lap. After ten days cooped up in her mother's bedroom, it was actually quite pleasant to be outside. Snippets of conversation drifted from the strawberry fields, and two magpies squabbled noisily on the top of the lichen-crusted wall. Butterflies flittered among the clumps of lobelia that sprouted from the cracks in the rough, grey stone.

'He's such an angel,' Dora said, nodding at William, who was sleeping peacefully in Leah's arms. 'I don't remember Frank being such a contented baby.'

'Don't speak too soon,' Hannah said, emerging from the cottage with three glasses of her homemade blackcurrant cordial. 'It could be the calm before the storm. Our Freddie was the easiest baby in the world until he was three months old.' She handed a glass to Leah and Dora and set the tray on the ground at the foot of the apple tree. 'It was like an imp had come in one night and left a changeling in his place. I don't think I had a decent night's sleep until he was about three.'

Leah managed a small laugh. 'Oh, don't say that, Mum.'

'He's an absolute darling,' Dora said, giving Leah an encouraging smile. 'I'm sure he'll be the perfect baby.'

Leah smiled back. She wondered what Dora thought about William's unexpectedly early arrival. Her friend was no fool. She would have worked out that William couldn't possibly be Joshua's. While she knew Dora would never judge her – after all, her Frank was the result of an illicit liaison – she must be curious as to who William's father was. Hopefully, as her mother had, she would assume it was someone she'd met at work. The fewer people who knew the truth, the better.

Dora was telling them about one of her patients, a sad story about a young man who'd lost both his legs, when they were interrupted by a shouted 'Hello!' and Daisy rounded the corner. She was nineteen and, having always viewed her as her younger sister, Leah was suddenly aware that her sister was, in fact, a very attractive young woman. With her face flushed from a day spent out in the summer sun, tendrils of thick, dark hair framing her face, she was extremely striking. *No wonder she caught Ian Foster's eye*, Leah thought with amusement.

'You're early,' Hannah remarked with a frown.

'I've only popped home for a minute to let you know I'm going walking with Ian after work,' replied Daisy.

Hannah's brows arched. 'Are you indeed?'

'If that's all right with you?' Daisy said. 'Is there any of that left?' she asked, eyeing the glasses of cordial. 'I'm parched. Hello, Frankie, sweetheart. Are you going to give your Aunty Daisy a kiss?'

'I'll fetch you a glass,' Hannah said, pursing her lips as she got heavily to her feet.

'Thanks, Mum.' Daisy swung Frank into the air and blew raspberries on his neck, making him giggle. 'And how's little William?' she asked Leah, holding Frank on her hip.

'Asleep,' Leah said. 'Where are you and Ian going walking, then?'

'I'm going to show him the pond,' Daisy said. 'And then he's going to buy me supper at the Glyn Arms. I'll be home by eight at the latest, Mum, I promise,' she added, as Hannah returned with her glass of cordial.

'With this light, you could be working until at least nine,' her mother said drily.

'Oh, Mum.' Daisy pulled a face. 'I've done so much overtime this week. I've hardly seen Ian.'

'Well, mind you make it up tomorrow,' Hannah said. 'We need the money now Leah's not working anymore. I know, I know.' She held up her hands to Leah. 'I know you get Joshua's pay and your separation money, but out of that you're supporting Pearl and that good-for-nothing Tilly.' This last was said with a snort of derision. 'You should be making the most of these long evenings while the weather holds, Daisy. In fact, I'm thinking of doing the odd shift in the fields myself. You can have Frank during the day, can't you, Leah?'

'Yes, I suppose so,' Leah said hesitantly. Much as she loved

Frank, he was at the age where he was into everything and needed watching constantly. *Like now*, she thought drily, as Dora leapt to her feet just in time to prevent him eating an earthworm one of the chickens had dug up.

'It's just until you feel able to go back to work,' Hannah said. 'Then I'll stay home and mind the kiddies.'

'Right,' Daisy said, draining her glass. 'I'd better get back to work. I'll see you all later.' She gave Frank a peck on the cheek and disappeared off around the side of the cottages.

There was no denying that Daisy had come out of her shell a great deal since Ian Foster started showing her some attention, and, watching her leave, Leah was unable to quell her envy. *There's something special about being in the throes of new love*, she thought with a jealous sigh. Sitting in the shade with William in her arms, she couldn't help but feel old before her time. It was almost a year since Harry had been killed. Perhaps she might have been falling in love again. She felt weighed down by self-pity.

'While I'm not completely at ease with this budding romance,' her mother said, going back to her gardening, 'it does my heart good to see Daisy almost back to her old self. She's not been the same since the accident.'

'Love does that to you, Aunty H,' Dora said with a grin. 'No matter how grim Barbie-Jean and my dad made my life, just knowing that Nate loved me made everything so much easier to bear.'

'Your Nate's a good man,' Hannah said, smiling at her over her shoulder.

'Does he ever hear anything from his mother?' Leah asked, brushing away a fly that was trying to settle on William's sleeping face.

Dora shrugged. 'If he does, he never mentions it. He knows there's no love lost between us.'

'She was a nasty piece of work,' Leah snorted.

'Oh, Hannah,' a voice called from an upstairs window of the cottage next door. 'Have you heard the news?'

'What news, Bea?' Hannah got to her feet, wiping her hands. Dora and Leah exchanged glances.

'Wait there,' Beatrice replied. 'I'll be right down.'

'What can have happened?' Leah wondered aloud.

'I don't know,' Hannah sighed, taking a long swallow of her cordial. 'I hope it's good news, whatever it is. I'm not sure I can take much more.'

Only the previous week, Southampton had been rocked by the news that an Australian hospital ship transporting wounded soldiers from France had been torpedoed in the English Channel. She had taken two hours to sink, and over a hundred people had lost their lives.

Beatrice came hurrying from her kitchen. With one hand she held up her skirts, in the other she clutched a folded newspaper.

'Look at this,' she panted, dropping her skirts and shaking out the newspaper so that they could all see the headlines.

'Thousands of Germans taken prisoner!' Leah read with a gasp.

'British and Allied forces make massive advances into

German territory,' Hannah read out loud. 'German soldiers surrendering in droves.' Tears sparkled in her eyes. 'You don't realize just how tired you are until there's a spark of hope,' she said, her voice trembling.

'I think most people feel the same,' agreed Beatrice. 'We're all just so exhausted by war. At times, it's hard to believe we'll ever know peace again, but then you get news like this, and you're right. It allows you to hope again.'

CHAPTER THIRTY-SEVEN

In the days and weeks that followed, the newspapers reported victory after victory. The feeling of lethargy had been replaced by a general mood of optimism, which was significantly bolstered on the twenty-ninth of September when Bulgaria signed an armistice with the Allies.

Life in Strawbridge continued in its usual vein, but there was a definite air of anticipation, and talk in the fields was generally of when the war would end, rather than if.

Listening to them talk, Leah found herself wondering what her life would be like once Joshua returned home. The thought of living together as man and wife terrified her. She was thinking about that now as she gazed out of the bedroom window. The field opposite teemed with workers. Her mother had started back in the fields three weeks earlier, leaving Leah in charge of Frank and William. She found she enjoyed her days. Frank, for all his boisterous nature, was an easy-going child, and she seldom had to reprimand him. William was the most contented baby, and she found she could waste many minutes just watching him sleep. She also found herself scrutinizing his features for any resemblance to his father, but so far, to her continued relief, she could see nothing of Samuel in him. Even despite the dark hair, her son was pure Hopwood.

'Leah? Leah?' Her mother's voice snapped her out of her reverie. She'd been so lost in thought that she hadn't noticed her mother returning to the cottage.

'Up here,' she called, turning from the window. 'I've just put Frank down for a nap,' she said, meeting her mother on the landing.

'Bless him,' Hannah smiled. As far as she was concerned, Frank was just as much her grandchild as William was. No matter that Dora wasn't her daughter; she'd known her since she was a newborn baby, so Dora was family and so was Frank.

'I was talking to Beatrice,' she said over her shoulder as she led the way back downstairs, where William was sleeping contentedly in his cradle. 'She said Alice and Samuel are away next weekend. They're going to visit Alice's aunt in London. Reverend Aldridge will be taking the services on the Sunday.'

At Leah's frown of incomprehension, Hannah sighed. 'I thought you could have William christened then,' she said impatiently. 'That way, you won't have to face Reverend Roberts.' She walked over to the cradle and stood gazing fondly down at her grandson. 'Though Lord knows I find it hard to bring myself to be civil to him these days.' She clicked her tongue in derision. 'All those long-winded rants on adultery. Hypocrite, that's what he is.'

'Mum, please,' Leah whispered.

'I'm sorry, love, I don't mean to rub it in, but he should be ashamed of himself. He stands up at that pulpit, week after week, preaching hell and damnation and Lord knows what, while all the time he's ...' Noticing her daughter's stricken expression, Hannah fell silent. 'I don't suppose you've seen anything of Alice, have you?' she asked kindly. Leah shook her head.

'Dora says she asks after us both when she sees her, but other than that, no. I can't say I blame her.' Leah gave her mother a sad smile. 'If it was the other way round and I suspected Alice of sleeping with Harry, I'd never speak to her again.'

'It's a shame,' her mother commiserated. 'You were such good friends. Perhaps, as it's only a suspicion, you may be able to patch things up in time.'

'I hope so,' Leah sighed. 'I miss her.'

Ten days later, Leah and her closest friends and family gathered in the cool, dim church for William's christening. She had chosen Dora, Daisy and Mathew Turner as godparents. Pearl watched from the back of the church, her beady eyes missing nothing as she recalled the events she'd read in Leah's tea leaves all those years before. She had known that somehow her great-grandson's future would be wound up with the girl, but back then it hadn't been clear how. The baby wasn't

Joshua's. Any fool could see that, and hadn't Leah come to her for something to make the child come away? She'd known at the time that the girl wouldn't go through with it. Which was why the powders she'd given her were nothing more potent than a simple herbal remedy to ease toothache.

The old woman smiled to herself. She'd always known her Joshua and Leah belonged together. Theirs was a love that would grow over time, she was certain of it.

She flexed her aching shoulders and a shudder ran through her body. She knew she wasn't long for this world. This coming winter would be her last, and so she was glad Joshua was settled and she no longer needed to worry about him. Her daughter and granddaughters had all been feckless good-for-nothings. Joshua had been barely weaned when his mother had left him with Pearl. She'd done her best by him, of course, but there was no denying he'd lacked the discipline of a father's hand. Still, from what she could tell, he'd grown up a lot since he'd been away, and no doubt Leah would keep him on the straight and narrow.

It was Tilly who really concerned her. The girl was her own worst enemy. If ever there was a case of the saying 'like mother, like daughter' being true, this was it. Tilly was as feckless as her mother and her grandmother before her. Pearl rummaged among the folds of her black skirts for a hand-kerchief and dabbed at her eyes. Ever since she'd tried to read Tilly's future a few days before, a cold dread had settled in her chest. For she could see nothing but darkness. Just as she had for Harry when she'd read Leah's tea leaves the year before the war broke out. She desperately hoped she was wrong, but in her heart of hearts, she knew the truth. Like her aging great-grandmother, this coming winter would be poor Tilly's last.

After the short ceremony, they all went back to Hannah's for tea, where Frank scampered about, getting underfoot until Daisy took him out into the garden to run off some of his pent-up energy.

'He really is a bonny boy, isn't he?' Beatrice said, coming up behind Leah as she laid William in his crib.

'I think so,' she smiled, gazing at her son with motherly pride.

'Wasn't he good?' Beatrice went on. 'Not a peep out of him all through the service, not even when Reverend Aldridge poured the water on his forehead.'

'He was very good,' Leah agreed, tracing William's rosy cheek with her fingertip. 'But then, he's a very contented baby.'

'You're very fortunate, Leah,' Beatrice said. Leah wondered what her neighbour's assumption was as to who William's natural father was. She knew her mother hadn't confided in her friend, and Beatrice would never dream of asking.

'I'll go and brew up a fresh pot of tea,' Beatrice said. 'Oh, by the way, did Alice tell you she'll be staying on in London for a few weeks? No? Well, you know Alice is expecting again?'

Again, Leah shook her head, regret as sharp as a rose thorn piercing her chest. Had things been different between them, she would have been one of the first to know.

'Well, her aunt Eleanor, my Lily's half-sister, has invited Alice to stay for a while. Alice has obviously confided in her about her previous miscarriages, and Eleanor is insisting she see her doctor on Harley Street. I seem to recall Lily saying Eleanor had some difficulty when she was expecting Benjamin and the doctor was excellent.' Beatrice's face fell. 'I do hope he can help Alice. I'm not sure she can bear another disappointment. And Samuel so desperately wants a son, as does any man.'

Leah felt her face flame, but Beatrice didn't appear to notice. She gave Leah's arm a quick squeeze. 'Alice's baby is due at the end of January. All being well,' she said, injecting an optimistic note into her tone. 'He or she will be a little playmate for young Frank and William.' Her smile faltered. 'I'll just keep on praying all goes smoothly for her this time,' she said.

'I will, too, Mrs Turner,' Leah promised meekly. As she stared after Beatrice's retreating back, she couldn't help but wonder how Alice must feel, suspecting that Leah had given birth to her husband's child while she seemed unable to give him the son he apparently wanted. *How it must irk Samuel*, she thought, *to know that his son is living just up the road, yet he can never acknowledge him.* For the first time since that unfortunate day, she felt a stab of pity for Samuel. She wondered if Alice had forgiven him and, if she had, would her friend ever be able to forgive her?

CHAPTER THIRTY-EIGHT

Alice laid down her book and stared out of the upstairs window. It was the end of October and the trees in the park across the street from her aunt's elegant townhouse were resplendent in their autumn colours. A group of children making their way home from school kicked the red, brown and golden leaves that carpeted the pavement. One child held a stick, which he ran along the railings, the noise causing Eleanor's small dog, Pepé, who was in the front garden, to leap at the fence, barking furiously.

Fond as she was of the little French bulldog, Alice found his high-pitched bark jarring. Opening the window, she called down to him, scolding him for the noise. He looked up, seeming surprised to see her leaning out the window. With one final bark aimed at the children, who had entered the park and were shuffling their way towards a giant horse chestnut tree, he raced round the corner, disappearing from view. Alice knew from experience that within minutes, he would come bounding up the stairs and sit whining at her door until she opened it for him.

In the three weeks since Samuel had returned to Strawbridge without her, Alice found she had regained some of her old joy. She hadn't realized just how much she had been walking on eggshells around him. Having to weigh every word before she spoke and tiptoeing round him when he was in one of his dark moods had taken its toll on her health, physically and emotionally. She had been utterly exhausted, but now she felt like a weight had been lifted off her shoulders.

She was six months along now and, thanks to the excellent care she had received from Eleanor's doctor, she felt better than she had in a long time. He'd recommended plenty of rest, which Eleanor made sure she adhered to, and lots of fresh air. Each morning, Alice and her aunt, along with Pepé, would walk the circumference of the boating pond in the park. Sometimes, they might stop at the little café for a mug of hot chocolate or a cup of tea. Most times, though, especially if the weather was inclement, they would return home and sit in the cosy front parlour until her Uncle Arthur returned home for his dinner, when he would bring them up to date on the latest news. It was looking increasingly likely that the war would very soon be over, and Alice was overjoyed at the prospect that her baby might never know the horrors of war.

Now, she smiled as she heard the familiar whine at the bedroom door. She got up and crossed the room, opening the door to the little dog. Pepé jumped at her skirts, making funny little grunting noises as she patted his silver-brown head. Then he leapt up onto the bed and curled up on her pillow, nose resting on his paws, one eye open as he watched her move about the room.

Like the rest of the house, it was elegantly furnished. The four-poster bed was swathed in pale blue. The bedspread had pale blue swirls on a white background, the matching pillow cases were edged with fine lace. The carpet was thick and luxurious, its tone slightly darker than the blue on the bed-spread and curtains. The furniture was dark cherry wood. A fire burned brightly in the small fireplace, above which hung a painting of Bay Willow House, her Aunt Eleanor's childhood home.

Alice glanced at the small carriage clock on the man-telpiece. It was just after a quarter to four. She was due to join her aunt in the drawing room for tea at four. She felt the baby kick and smiled, placing her hand gently on her swollen belly. She even embraced the occasional backache, the swollen ankles and the heaviness in her breast. As long as the baby was kicking, all was well, the doctor had assured her only the previous day.

She ran a brush through her hair and pinned it back up before going downstairs, where she found her aunt reading a letter from her eldest son. Benjamin was at a training camp in the east of the country, and Alice knew her aunt was feverishly hoping the war would come to an end before he was transferred abroad.

'Alice,' she said, laying the letter aside and rising to her feet with her arms out. 'Are you well rested?' she asked, as the two women embraced warmly.

'I am, thank you, Aunt,' Alice replied. She had no sooner sat down than the door opened and Gloria, the maid, entered with the tea tray. She was a middle-aged woman with grey-ing brown hair, Eleanor's two young housemaids having left two years earlier for better-paying jobs in the munitions fac-tories. She'd told Alice that their gardener had enlisted early in 1915 and had been killed soon after arriving in France. Now the small garden was tended by Gloria's husband, a retired dock worker called Bill.

'I must say, I have noticed a vast improvement in your demeanour since you've been here,' Eleanor said once the maid had left. 'It can't be easy for you, what with Samuel suffering as he is.' She poured the tea and handed Alice a cup.

Balancing the delicate rose-patterned cup and saucer on her lap, Alice gave a long, weary sigh.

'Oh, Aunt Eleanor, I think Samuel has been unfaithful.' There was a noticeable tremor in Alice's voice and her eyes immediately filled with tears.

'My dear,' Eleanor exclaimed, aghast. 'He wouldn't do that, surely?'

'I don't know for certain,' Alice admitted. 'But he's not the man I married.' A tear snaked its way down her cheek and she wiped it away with her hand. 'The war damaged him in some way.' Her lips trembled. 'I'm frightened for him. He's so angry all the time, and . . .' She broke off, unable to say any more for the tears streaming down her face.

'Oh, my dear,' Eleanor cried, hurrying to sit beside her.

Taking her niece in her arms, she rocked her gently, soothing her like she used to do when her boys were young and upset.

'You say you're not sure. Have you asked him?'

Alice drew back in horror. 'I wouldn't dare,' she croaked.

'As you know,' Eleanor cleared her throat, 'my father was unfaithful to my mother. But they didn't have a happy marriage. You and Samuel are different. He loves you. If he has been unfaithful, I'm sure it was a momentary lapse of reason. He loves you, Alice.'

'I have to believe he does,' Alice sighed, wiping her eyes. 'But it's so hard.'

'Marriage *is* hard,' her aunt smiled. 'Much as I love Arthur, we've had our differences. I didn't speak to him for three days after he insisted the boys were sent away to school, and there have been many other times in our marriage that I've wanted to strangle the man.' She chuckled and Alice managed a weak smile. 'You'll get through it, Alice, you will. Things will get better.' She laid a hand on Alice's stomach. 'And once this little one comes along, you'll see, Samuel will be swept away with love for the baby.'

'I hope so,' Alice said, blowing her nose. 'I do love him so much.'

'I know you do, and it will all work out. I'm sure of it.'

At supper that evening, her Uncle Arthur, who had a minor role at the War Office, appeared greatly animated.

'I can't say much,' he said, reaching for the gravy boat. 'But let's just say that I have it on good authority that another of the Central Powers will soon be signing an armistice.' He peered at the thin brown liquid with dismay. Since living in London, Alice had discovered that the food shortages and rationing had impacted even the wealthiest of people – though, of course, it was always the less well-off people who suffered the most. She had accompanied her aunt to some of the poorer parts of the city to help in the soup kitchens and had been appalled at the poverty she'd seen. Somehow, poverty in the capital city appeared worse than anything she'd seen back home.

'Anyway,' her uncle continued, putting down the gravy boat and raising his glass of port, 'with her allies dropping like flies, I do believe Germany may surrender as early as the new year.'

'I do hope so,' Eleanor sighed. 'I'm so weary of it all.'

'Aren't we all, my dear?' her husband smiled. 'So, Alice, have you had a pleasant day?'

'I have, thank you,' Alice replied, helping herself to another potato. Being pregnant had certainly increased her appetite. 'I had thought I might take the tram into the city tomorrow and see the sights, but my aunt has cautioned against it.'

'I would agree with her, my dear,' her uncle said solemnly. 'This influenza is worse than anything we've seen for a long time. People are dropping like flies. The last thing you want is to become ill yourself, not in your condition.'

'Of course,' Alice concurred. She had read in the newspapers about the flu spreading across the country over the summer, but so far, Southampton and the surrounding villages hadn't been too badly affected.

'I also think it wise that you both give up the soup kitchens,' Arthur went on, refilling his glass. 'Germs breed like wildfire in places like that.'

'I agree,' Eleanor said. 'It would be foolhardy to risk your health, Alice, and the baby's.' She smiled at her husband across the table. 'We shall have to find something else to occupy our time.'

CHAPTER THIRTY-NINE

On Monday, Dora turned up at the hospital for her shift. She was carrying a load of bedpans down to the sluice room when suddenly the bells in the hospital chapel began to ring. Ship hooters sounded and the foghorn blared across the damp, autumn grounds. Puzzled, she hurried to the closest window. A group of soldiers, taking advantage of the mild weather to get some fresh air, were cheering. One of them threw his crutch in the air. Two nurses ran down the corridor towards Dora, tears streaming down their faces as they laughed.

'It's over!' one of them shouted, grabbing Dora's arm. She looked almost giddy with joy. 'The war's over!'

'Are you sure?' Dora asked, scarcely able to believe it.

'Definitely,' the other nurse beamed. 'Can't you hear the cheering?'

Sure enough, shouts of joy emanated from every part of the hospital. Doctors and nurses congregated in the corridors. Total strangers hugged each other. Even the most seriously ill patients appeared brightened by the news.

Finding herself hugged and kissed by doctors and patients alike, foremost in her mind was the thought that Nate would be able to come home. She could hardly contain her joy.

In Strawbridge, church bells had begun to ring out just after eight o'clock. By mid-morning, Reuben had set up a table outside the Glyn Arms, offering free jugs of mulled cider to all. The workers had left the fields and the lane thronged with people, all laughing and talking in excited voices. Leah stood across the lane, William in her arms, watching with mixed emotions as Beatrice draped bunting around the cottage door and downstairs windows.

She was overjoyed that the war was over, that went without saying. Her son wouldn't have to grow up knowing the horror of war, but her joy was tinged with sadness for all those who had given their lives. Like her beloved Harry, lost on some foreign battlefield, and the Merrifield boys. Her gaze drifted up the lane to where Reuben was dispensing cider to the growing crowd. How was he feeling right now, she wondered, with three of his five sons dead? And out of the remaining two, only one had survived the war unscathed.

'I can't believe it's finally over,' her mother said, coming to stand beside her. 'Frankie!' she shouted to the little boy who was tearing up and down the lane, buoyed along by the excitement of the crowds. He paused to look back at his adopted grandmother, grinning cheekily.

'Go steady, young man,' Hannah shouted over the hubbub of the passers-by. 'I don't want to be patching up another pair of trousers.' Frank ran off down the lane, almost bumping into young Beth Culley from next door.

'I'll get him, Mrs H,' she called over her shoulder, as she took off after the giggling child.

Beth's father, Dan, returning from his shift just after midday, told how the city had erupted with joy at eleven o'clock, with hooters blasting out from ships and factories. People had poured out of shops and factories, taking to the streets in celebration.

Daisy and Hannah carried the parlour table out into the street. Many of their neighbours were doing the same, women delving into pantries in search of offerings for an impromptu celebration meal. One neighbour wheeled out her piano, and another arrived with his accordion. Dora arrived home after her twelve-hour shift at the hospital to find her friends and neighbours dancing in the lane.

'The war's over!' Leah called, her face flushed with excitement.

'I know!' Dora called back. Frank came running towards her, and she stooped down to pick him up. 'It's bedlam at the hospital. No one can quite believe it. Thank you.' She accepted a mug of mulled cider and took a big gulp, breathing hard. 'I practically ran all the way home, I was that excited,' she grinned, her cheeks glowing pink. 'I wonder if Alice knows,' she said, nodding at the figure of Reverend Samuel Roberts.

'She's bound to, being in London,' Leah replied reluctantly, following Dora's gaze. Samuel stood against the wall, clutching a pint of cider. In the midst of the merry-making, she couldn't help but think he looked a little lost. As if feeling Leah's eyes on him, he turned his head in her direction and their eyes briefly met before Leah quickly averted her gaze.

'He must be missing Alice,' Dora mused aloud, unaware of her friend's discomfort. 'On such a momentous day, you want your nearest and dearest close.' She sighed, wondering whether Nate had been told that the war was over. And if so, how long would it be until she saw him again?

Nate waited anxiously. Not long after roll call that morning, the men had been summoned from their jobs and made to stand in rows in front of their bunkhouses. The Germans who stood guard appeared subdued. They stood with their heads bowed as the camp commander strode briskly down the steps of the command hut. He spent a moment fiddling with the metal buttons at his cuffs, as if wanting to put off what he was about to say. The POWs began to shuffle their feet in impatience. They knew that something momentous had happened; Nate could feel it in the frigid air. A crow cawed overhead, and he glanced up at the bleak November sky.

'Gentlemen,' the commander said in a hollow voice. 'Today, Germany signed an armistice. The war is over. You are free men.'

There was stunned silence. Nate couldn't believe his ears. He slid a sideways glance at the man next to him.

'Did you hear me, gentlemen?' the commander asked grimly. 'You are free to go.'

The men, Nate included, erupted into wild cheering. Hats were flung into the air as they hugged each other, slapping each other heartily on the backs. Once the initial celebrations had abated slightly, Nate found a quiet spot on the edge of the camp and sank to his haunches. He buried his face in his hands. After almost four years, he was going home.

Alice stood at the window of her uncle's office watching the crowds thronging Trafalgar Square. At eleven o'clock, church bells had rung out across the city and ships and factories sounded their hooters. The all-clear had sounded from Nelson's Column to the rousing cheers of the watching public. Though there was an air of celebration in the street below, many faces were streaked with tears and there were many among the crowds who sported black armbands and veils.

Standing with her aunt and uncle, Alice placed her hand on her stomach. As she had hoped, her baby would be born in peacetime. She just wished Samuel was with her. It seemed wrong, celebrating without him. She missed him, she realized with a pang. Despite the mood swings and, at times, unreasonable behaviour, she loved him and she wanted to be with him. Once they returned to her aunt's house, she would speak to them about returning home. She was six and a half months along now and, as long as she continued to follow the doctor's advice, there was no reason this baby shouldn't continue to thrive.

CHAPTER FORTY

'Nate's coming home!' Dora shouted, bursting in through the door, waving the letter at Leah. 'Frankie,' she cried, picking up the little boy and hugging him to her. 'Daddy's coming home!'

'Take your coat and boots off, Dor,' Hannah chided laughingly, coming out of the kitchen. 'You're dripping melting snow all over the floor.'

'Sorry,' Dora grinned. Setting Frank on his feet, she unbuttoned her coat. 'I'm just so excited. He's at some transit camp in Poland at the moment but, all being well, he says he should be home next week.' Her cheeks shone with a combination of cold and inexpressible joy.

'Oh, how lovely!' Hannah clapped her hands in delight. 'Just in time for Christmas.'

'I got a letter from Joshua this morning, too,' Leah said, with slightly less enthusiasm. 'He's been demobbed and is on his way home, too.' She jiggled five-month-old William on her lap. He smiled gummily and waved his chubby fists in the air.

'I'm looking forward to seeing Nate and Joshua again,' Ian said, emerging from the kitchen. 'Hello, all.' He grinned, his eyes finding Daisy's across the room. She smiled back, her cheeks reddening. Despite her mother's misgivings about the twelve-year age difference, Daisy found that she had grown extremely fond of the big, burly South African. He was often a guest at Hannah's dinner table, and she had dined at Beatrice's on a couple of occasions. That in itself was not unusual, as the two families often dined at each other's houses, but on these two occasions, only she had been invited, as Ian's guest.

Ian still kept a room at the Glyn Arms, despite his mother's entreaties that he move into her spare room. Much as their relationship was going from strength to strength, having lived alone for so long, he felt the need to have his own space. He was still undecided about his future, although he was becoming increasingly certain that wherever his plans took him, they would include Daisy. He only hoped she felt the same. He cleared his throat.

'I was wondering whether you might like to go skating, Daisy?' he asked now. 'The pond has frozen over, and it looks pretty thick. There were quite a few people skating when I came past.'

'I'd love to,' Daisy said, jumping up to grab her coat. 'I do so enjoy skating.'

'Just go careful,' warned Hannah sternly. 'Mind you test it first. We don't want any accidents.'

'I'll make sure it's perfectly safe before I let Daisy anywhere near the ice, Mrs Hopwood,' promised Ian sincerely. 'We'll only be about an hour or so. It's too cold to stay out longer than that.'

'I'll have some cocoa warming on the stove for when you get back,' Hannah said as they left.

'Daisy's certainly come out of her shell since Ian's been paying her attention,' Dora said, stretching her stockinged feet towards the fire. 'It's been almost eight months. Do you think he's serious about her?'

'He certainly appears to be,' Leah said, a little sourly. Ian was a good-looking man and perhaps if she wasn't married to Joshua, he might have noticed her instead of her younger sister.

'Daisy deserves to be happy,' Dora said, holding out her arms. Frank toddled over with his book of Mother Goose nursery rhymes. 'And he's such a nice man. I thoroughly enjoyed our chats when he was in the hospital,' she went on, pulling Frank onto her lap.

'I think you have quite a soft spot for him,' Leah teased.

Dora smiled. 'I'm very fond of him, but Nate's the only man for me.' She turned her attention to Frank's book and for a while it was quiet in the parlour, the only sounds the crackle of the burning wood, the rhythmic ticking of the clock and Dora's melodious voice as she read to Frank.

Leah leaned over to check on William, who was sleeping soundly in his crib beside her. Ever since she'd received Joshua's letter, her emotions had been in turmoil. She'd known this day must eventually come, but now that it was imminent, the reality of her situation had hit her hard. She was married to a man she barely knew anymore. They had courted once, but that had been years ago, before she'd known Harry. Would they be able to get back to how they had once been? she wondered, chewing thoughtfully on her bottom lip. She would always love Harry – she knew that for certain. The pain of his death had receded over the past year, but there were still times that her grief would catch her unawares and the tears would flow again.

At a knock on the door, Leah and Dora exchanged glances.

'Who could that be?' Hannah said, laying down her darning as Leah went to the door.

'Oh!' she said, her mouth falling open in surprise at the sight of her husband standing on the doorstep surrounded by swirling snowflakes. 'I wasn't expecting you.'

'So it would seem,' Joshua grinned. 'Are you going to ask me in? Or am I to freeze to death on your doorstep?'

'Come in,' Leah said quickly, stepping aside.

'Joshua, what a lovely surprise,' Hannah said, already on her feet. 'Have you walked from Botley? You must be frozen!'

'I'm warm enough, Mrs H,' Joshua said, rubbing his hands and stamping his boots on the mat. 'I walked quickly.' Leah closed the door behind him, leaning against it, her mind whirling.

'How did you get here so soon?' she asked, as Hannah disappeared into the kitchen to heat up the cocoa. 'I only just got your letter.'

'I was lucky enough to be on one of the first boats home,'

Joshua grinned, shrugging off his heavy coat. 'Then it was straight to the railway station and home. I called in to see Nan on the way.' His smile faltered. 'She's looking more frail than I remember.'

Leah hung his coat on the rack. 'She must have been over the moon to see you,' she said awkwardly as she faced him. 'Umm, this is William,' she blurted, motioning the cradle. Joshua's grin broadened as he bent his head over the crib.

'Hey, little chap,' he said softly. 'He's a bonny one, isn't he?'

'He is,' Leah agreed, swelling with maternal pride.

'And look how this young man has grown since I last saw him,' he said, turning to Frank, who was watching him warily from the safety of Dora's lap.

'Hello, Joshua,' Dora smiled. 'Frank, this is your Uncle Joshua, back from the war.' She looked up at Joshua. 'He was only a baby last time you saw him.'

'He's a lovely-looking lad,' Joshua said, reaching down to pat Frank's head. 'Hello, little man.'

'Here we go, hot cocoa all round,' Hannah said, bustling in with a tray of steaming hot mugs. 'Help yourselves,' she said, setting the tray on the parlour table. 'There isn't any sugar, but hopefully it'll be sweet enough.'

'Thank you, Mrs H.' Joshua took his mug and settled himself on the edge of the hearth.

'You all right there, Joshua?' frowned Hannah. 'There are plenty of chairs.'

'I'm just fine, thank you.' He sipped his drink, his dark

eyes smiling at Leah over the rim of the mug. Her stomach lurched nervously. She wasn't ready to be a wife to him. She wasn't sure she ever would be, but it was too soon. The thought made her feel physically ill, the cocoa sloshing ominously in the pit of her stomach.

'I'm going to take a room at the Glyn Arms,' he said, as if reading her mind.

'There's no need for that,' Hannah said slowly. 'You're welcome to bunk down in the kitchen.'

'No offence, Mrs H,' Joshua chuckled, 'but I've had my fill of bunking down on floors and such like. A proper bed is what I want, with proper sheets and blankets.' Aware that Hannah was about to protest, he held up his hand. 'It's just until me and Leah get to know each other again.'

Leah's shoulders sagged in relief, and she found herself smiling back at him.

'I'm sure that's a very sensible idea,' Hannah conceded. 'Ah, that sounds like Daisy back,' she said, at the sound of the back door latch being lifted. Voices sounded in the kitchen, and Daisy burst through the door, red-faced from cold and exertion. She was followed by Ian, who almost collided with her as she came to an abrupt halt in the doorway.

'Joshua! What a surprise!'

'Hello, Daisy.' Joshua got to his feet. 'Ian.' He held out his hand. 'Good to see you again.'

The two men fell into conversation.

'You may as well ask Ian to stay for supper,' Hannah

whispered to Daisy as she got up to begin preparing the evening meal. 'Leah, pop next door and see if the Turners would like to join us. We can make it a bit of a celebration.'

As Ian and Joshua set off up the lane towards the Glyn Arms later that evening after a particularly enjoyable supper, they were surprised when Mathew Turner came hurrying out after them.

'Might I have a quick word, Ian?' Mathew said, his breath clouding in the frosty air.

'Certainly,' Ian frowned.

Joshua slapped him on the back. 'I'll see you back at the pub,' he said, trudging up the lane, head bent against the cold wind. It was a clear night. Frost sparkled in the moonlight. Snow glistened along the hedgerows, blown into drifts by the biting wind.

'Look, Ian,' Mathew said, thrusting his gloved hands deep into his coat pockets, 'I'm not speaking to you as your step-father, rather as a friend.'

Ian's frown deepened. 'Go on.'

'It's not escaped our notice that you seem to be rather fond of young Daisy.'

'I am,' Ian agreed. 'I'm very fond of her.'

'Your mother and I thought as much.' Mathew cleared his throat. 'As Daisy doesn't have a father, your mother felt it appropriate that I have a word with you to find out your intentions with the girl. You must realize, Daisy has led a somewhat sheltered life and you, well, you seem to be a man of the world. And, of course, Daisy suffered that awful accident. It affected her badly for a long time.'

'She's told me all about that,' Ian replied. He shivered and pulled his collar higher around his neck. The tips of his ears tingled from the cold. 'I assure you, sir, my intentions towards Daisy are entirely honourable.'

'It's just that your mother says you're unsure of your plans?'

'I haven't quite decided where I wish to settle. I'm going to resurrect my wheelwright business, that's for certain.' He shrugged.

'Strawbridge could do with a reliable wheelwright,' Mathew said with a grin.

'We'll see.'

'As long as you're not leading Daisy on,' Mathew said, his tone serious once more.

'I'm not, Mathew. I promise you.'

Mathew nodded and extended his hand. 'Good luck to you,' he said. 'I wish you well, wherever you end up.'

Ian grasped his hand warmly. 'Thank you, Mathew. I appreciate it.'

The two men parted, Mathew to the warmth of Hannah's parlour and Ian to the warm fug of the Glyn Arms snug and the pint of bitter he knew would be waiting for him.

CHAPTER FORTY-ONE

With one hand, Dora clutched her hat as the rush of the train hurtling into the station threatened to whip if off her head. With her other, she held tightly to little Frank, as he squirmed and wriggled in excitement at the sight of the train, belching clouds of steam like one of the fire-breathing dragons in the picture book his Aunty Daisy had bought him from the church jumble sale.

Dora's heart thumped against her ribcage as she struggled to hang on to Frank while scanning the disembarking passengers, ghost-like figures moving through the swirling steam.

'Dora!'

'Nate!' she screamed, standing on tiptoe to catch a glimpse of him. The steam cleared and she could see him, fighting his way through the crowds towards her. Dragging Frank along, she hurried down the platform towards him. Under the station clock, they fell into each other's arms. She was still clinging to Frank's hand, even as Nate was kissing her.

'Mama, Mama!' Frank tugged at her coat. They broke apart. Laughing through her tears, Dora lifted Frank onto her hip.

'This is Frank,' she said, anxiously searching Nate's face for his reaction. 'Frankie, this is Uncle Nate.'

'Uncle?' Nate frowned. 'If I'm to be bringing him up, I'd sooner be called Dad,' he said.

Dora smiled. 'Are you sure?' she asked hesitantly.

Nate grinned. 'Definitely. You've told me so much about him in your letters, I already feel like he's mine.' He tickled Frank under the chin. 'Hello, young man. I'm your dad.'

Frank grinned. 'Dada, Dada!' he shouted, making them both laugh.

'Come on,' Nate said, shouldering his bag. He held out his arms to Frank, who went to him willingly. 'Let's go home.'

The Salvation Army band was playing 'Silent Night' as they passed through the cavernous entrance, and the streets were thronged with shoppers. To Dora, it felt as though everyone was determined to enjoy their first peacetime Christmas for four years.

'What will you do first, now you're home?' Dora asked as they hurried to catch the omnibus that would take them as far as the Northam ferry.

'Well, first thing tomorrow, I'm going to see about getting my old job back,' Nate replied. 'And then I'm going to speak to Samuel about having our banns read.'

Dora stopped walking. 'Do you mean that?'

'It's all I've thought about for the past two years,' Nate

grinned. 'I can't wait to make you my wife.' His expression turned sombre. 'That's if you still want me, of course?'

'Of course I do, silly.' Dora punched him playfully on the arm, making Frank laugh.

'I'm glad we've got that clear,' Nate said. 'Come on, we'd better get a move on or we'll miss the omnibus.'

In the vicarage parlour, Alice placed a final sprig of holly on the mantelpiece and stood back to admire her handiwork. She'd spent hours making paperchains, which she'd got Mrs Hurst to string across the ceiling. Garlands of holly and pine cones were strung around the fireplace and a huge wreath hung on the door. She threw another pine cone into the flames, savouring the spicy scent that wafted into the room as she sank heavily onto the sofa. She rested her head against the back of the sofa and closed her eyes. She was in her eighth month now and relished the swollen ankles, the backache, the pressure on her bladder, even the sleepless nights when she couldn't get comfortable because the baby was kicking so much. She welcomed the discomfort because it meant her baby was alive.

She must have dozed off, because when she woke, the parlour was dark but for the light from the fire. She heard her husband calling for her and realized that was what had woken her.

'In here,' she called sleepily, stifling a yawn as she stretched her arms above her head in an effort to relieve a kink in her spine.

'Hello, my dear,' Samuel said, sweeping into the room. He frowned. 'Why are you sitting in the dark?'

'I fell asleep,' Alice replied.

'Don't get up,' Samuel said as she made to rise. 'I have something I wish to speak to you about.' He lit the lamp and walked over to the window, drawing the curtains on the cold December night.

Alice tucked her feet under her skirt and moved her hands over her swollen belly. She could feel the baby kicking and smiled, imagining the day when she would get to hold her little baby.

Samuel sat beside her and took her hand. Alice tensed. Things had been a little better between them since her return from London, but she was always on edge, lest he erupt in a rage. She gave him a nervous smile.

'What is it you wish to speak to me about?' she asked.

'I want to go away,' Samuel said. Alice sat up straight.

'What do you mean?' she demanded, her heart thudding painfully. Was he leaving her? Her thoughts flew to Leah. Surely he wouldn't . . .

'I mean, I wish to go on retreat,' he clarified. Alice exhaled slowly in relief. He rubbed her hand with his thumb. 'I bumped into an old friend from theological college this afternoon. He's running a retreat in the new year for men struggling with shellshock and other conditions brought on by their experiences during the war. It sounds just what I need, Alice.' His face grew sorrowful. 'I know I haven't been a good husband to you. I want . . . I want to do better, for you and for our baby. I feel I need to do this, if I'm to have any hope of being the husband you deserve.'

He looked so full of remorse that Alice's heart went out to him.

'Of course you must go, Samuel,' she said softly, running her hand through his thick, dark hair. 'When is it?'

'The second to the twenty-eighth of January, in Salisbury.'

'Samuel,' Alice frowned. 'The baby is due on the thirty-first. What if it comes early?'

'Send me a telegraph and I will get the first train home,' Samuel promised. Alice studied his face. His desire to change seemed genuine.

'Very well,' she said. 'I assume Reverend Aldridge will be moving back in?' she asked reluctantly. She didn't relish the thought of moving back in with her grandparents. She'd been looking forward to preparing for her baby's birth in her own home. But Samuel's reply surprised her.

'No,' he said, with a hint of annoyance. 'He's going on holiday. The vicar from St Marks has offered to cover for me. Services will be a bit later, but it can't be helped. I'll be a better vicar when I come back, I'm certain of it. It'll be worth the inconvenience.'

'I'm sure no one will mind too much,' Alice assured him. 'Now, I need to speak to you about Christmas Day. My mother wants to know what meat we shall be bringing and has reminded me that we need to ask Mrs Hurst if she will be joining us for Christmas dinner or if she'll be visiting her sister as usual.'

CHAPTER FORTY-TWO

1919

Dora stood in front of Alice's full-length mirror, staring at her reflection in awe.

'Is that really me?' she said in a tremulous voice.

'Of course it's you,' Alice laughed, then winced. The baby was lying uncomfortably low today. 'You're a beautiful young woman, Dora. Nate will be blown away when he sees you walking down the aisle.'

Dora turned to look at Alice over her shoulder. 'It was so kind of your mum to make me this dress.' Her eyes glistened with unshed tears of gratitude. 'I've never owned anything so exquisite, ever.'

'It was her pleasure,' Alice told her, easing herself out of the easy chair. 'At least you've picked a fine day for it.' She waddled over to the bed and opened a cardboard box. Moving aside the pale blue tissue paper, she lifted out a white fur cape and held it up for Dora to see.

'It's gorgeous!' she gasped, fingering the soft fur.

'It's your wedding gift from my Aunty Eleanor,' Alice informed her, motioning to Dora to let her drape it over her shoulders.

'Oh my,' Dora breathed. She'd never had any illusions about her own prettiness. An aunt had once described her as 'plain' and, as far as Dora was concerned, she wasn't wrong. But today, wearing the beautiful white silk wedding dress that Alice's mother, the talented Lily Russell, had created for her, along with the fur cape, she had to agree that she looked, if not beautiful, then at least pretty. Not that Nate cared. He loved her for who she was, not what she looked like.

'Are you ready, Dora ... oh my goodness!' Hannah's hands flew to her mouth. 'Dora Webb, you look absolutely beautiful! Nate isn't going to believe his eyes when you walk down that aisle.'

'Let me see,' said Daisy, squeezing past her mother into the room. 'Golly, Dor, Mum's right. You look absolutely gorgeous.'

'Thank you,' Dora smiled shyly.

'I came to see if you were ready to go,' Hannah said. 'It's almost eleven o'clock.'

Dora took a deep breath. 'I am.'

'Mathew's waiting downstairs. We'll see you in the church. Come on, Daisy.'

'I'll see you in the church, too,' Alice said, once Daisy and Hannah had gone. She gave her a quick hug. 'I wish you all the luck in the world, Dora. You deserve it.'

379

Left alone, Dora walked over to the window. From Alice's bedroom, she had a perfect view of the church grounds. There were Hannah and Daisy, hurrying up the cinder path. Leah and Joshua were already inside with the children. She saw Beatrice Turner pause by the lychgate, a smile on her face. A moment later, Alice came into view. She was walking slowly, her progress hampered by her heavy belly. Dora watched as the two of them shared a laugh before linking arms and walking into the church.

She heard the clock in the hall chime eleven. She swallowed hard. Her stomach churning with nerves, she stepped out onto the landing.

Mathew Turner was waiting at the foot of the stairs as she descended, a look of rapt awe on his face.

'You look fantastic, girl,' he said gruffly, making Dora blush. 'Your dad would be so proud of you today.' She blinked back a tear at the thought of her poor dad and smiled. After the ceremony, she would lay her little posy on his unmarked grave on the north side of the church.

With her hand resting on Mathew's arm, they walked the short distance from the vicarage to the church. Though cold, the last Saturday in January was bright and sunny. The sky was a perfect cornflower blue as Dora made her way to the entrance, where Reverend Keats was waiting. He was an older man, with greying fair hair and glasses that he was continually having to push back up his nose with his index finger.

The organist began to play and the small congregation rose to its feet as Dora, clinging tightly to Mathew's arm, started to walk down the aisle to where Nate was waiting for her, a look of rapture on his face. As she reached him, he broke into a huge smile. Throughout the ceremony, his eyes never left her face, and when the vicar pronounced them husband and wife, he took her in his arms and kissed her so tenderly that she almost wept.

Afterwards, they made their way up to the Glyn Arms, where Reuben and Florence had laid on a modest wedding breakfast in their back function room. The air smelled of stale beer and the carpet was pockmarked with cigarette burns, but Dora was far too happy to take much notice of her surroundings.

'I propose a toast to Mr and Mrs Gardener,' Ian said, raising his glass. The others followed suit, and Dora laughed.

'Mrs Nathaniel Gardener,' she whispered to Nate. 'I like the sound of that.'

'So do I, Mrs Gardener,' Nate whispered back. 'I have some exciting news, too,' he said in a low voice so only Dora would hear. 'I was speaking to Dan Culley last week. His mother isn't very well, so he's moving back to Winchester. Their cottage will be vacant from the end of next week. I've spoken to Mathew, who's spoken to Mr Whitworth, and it's all been agreed. We move in next weekend.'

'What?' Dora stared at him. 'You mean, I get to live in my old house again?'

'Yes, really. I signed the tenancy agreement this morning.' His smile faded a little. 'I wasn't certain you'd be keen, given what happened there.'

'That cottage holds some very sad memories for me,' Dora

said with a wistful smile, 'but I've got so many happier ones, like from before Dad got sick and you coming to stay.'

'I doubt you've got any good memories about my mother, though,' Nate said with a snort.

'You still haven't heard anything from her?'

Nate shook his head. 'I doubt I ever will now,' he said, with no trace of resentment. 'She's a nasty piece of work, and we're better off without her. Ah, Joshua, Leah!' He got to his feet as Leah and Joshua approached their table.

'Just wanted to say congratulations again, mate,' Joshua said, sticking out his hand. Nate shook it warmly.

'Yes, congratulations, Dor,' Leah said, leaning in to give her friend a hug. 'I wish you all the best.'

'Thank you, Leah,' Dora beamed. She squeezed Leah's hand. She'd missed having Leah at home since she had moved into her new cottage at the other end of Strawbridge, but soon she would be moving out, too. She and Nate were honeymooning in Bournemouth for a few days, and when they returned, they would be moving into Woodpecker Cottage. It was only next door to where she lived now, but it seemed like the end of an era.

'Look at us,' she said to Leah, as she watched Alice making her way clumsily towards them. 'We're not girls anymore. We're wives and mothers.'

'We've been through a lot the past four years,' Leah said quietly, tensing slightly as Alice approached. She glanced at Joshua, but he was talking with Nate and hadn't noticed her discomfort.

'Dora,' Alice said. 'It was a wonderful ceremony, and you were so calm and steady.'

'I was a jumble of nerves inside,' Dora laughed.

'How's little William?' Alice asked Leah, not quite meeting her eyes.

'He's well, thank you,' Leah replied, unable to keep the pride from her voice. 'Mum's taken him home for a nap.'

'When is Samuel due back?' Dora asked, seemingly ignorant of the tension between her two friends.

'On Tuesday.'

'Are you all right, Alice?' Leah said in alarm as Alice suddenly staggered backwards. A sheen of perspiration broke out on her face.

'Yes.' She gave a nervous laugh. 'I just came over a bit dizzy. I've done too much today. That's what I came over to tell you, Dora,' she said. 'I'm going home for a lie-down. I'm sorry to rush off on your special day, but I feel really exhausted today.'

'I'm not surprised,' Dora replied with genuine sympathy. 'You look fit to drop. Have you someone at home with you?'

'Mrs Hurst is staying overnight while Samuel is away, just in case the baby decides to come early, though everyone tells me first babies are usually late.'

Leah and Dora watched her make her way back through the pub, pausing occasionally at a table to speak to someone.

'I hope everything goes well for her,' Dora said. At the adjacent table, Ian got to his feet, tapping his glass with his knife.

'Ladies and gentlemen,' he said, turning to grin at Nate and Dora. 'Will you join me in raising a toast to the bride and groom, Dora and Nate.'

Nate took Dora's hand, and they got to their feet, Dora blushing prettily as her friends and neighbours rose to toast their future. It struck her in that instant that she had no family here, no one related to her by blood, at least. But as she gazed out at the sea of smiling faces, she realized that these people *were* her family. Hannah, standing in the doorway, a wide-awake William in her arms, Leah and Daisy, who were like sisters to her, Alice, the Turners ... the list was endless. Leaning against Nate as he proceeded to thank everyone for celebrating their day alongside them, she knew that whatever the future brought, this would always be where her heart belonged.

CHAPTER FORTY-THREE

Alice stared anxiously out of the window. Storm clouds had been gathering all afternoon. Her grandmother had called in a few hours earlier on her way home from Dora's wedding to make sure Alice was all right. Alice had assured her that, apart from feeling extremely tired and the slight twinge at the base of her spine, she felt perfectly well.

'Well, you've got Mrs Hurst with you should anything happen,' Beatrice had said, only slightly mollified. 'Send her to call for me if you need anything.'

Alice had promised that she would and had gone to lie down. Before long, the storm clouds had begun to gather, bringing with them howling winds and stinging rain, which had now turned to snow. It was now not quite eight o'clock, and snow was falling thick and fast, blanketing the vicarage garden and the lane in its powdery whiteness.

She could hear Mrs Hurst across the landing, going quietly about her bedtime routine, and the knowledge that her dependable, no-nonsense housekeeper was close by went some way to assuaging her mounting anxiety.

She hadn't had much appetite at supper and now just the thought of food made her feel queasy. Her mug of cocoa sat on the bedside cabinet, cold and untouched. She let the curtain fall and made her way over to the bed. She was just climbing under the covers when she felt the first contraction. She gasped, doubling over as pain ripped through her with the sharpness of a knife. It passed as swiftly as it had come, and she lay back against the pillow, panting softly, waiting with bated breath for the next one.

She must have dozed off, because when she opened her eyes a while later, the fire had died down and the room was chilly. She got stiffly out of bed and made her way over to the fireplace to throw a shovelful of coal on the fire. As she replaced the shovel in the coal scuttle, she cried out in agony as a fierce contraction again tore through her body. She bent double, fighting to catch her breath as she waited for the pain to abate. Footsteps sounded outside her door, followed by a soft knocking and a loud whisper.

'Are you all right, Mrs Roberts?'

Alice could only groan as she was hit by another contraction. The door opened and Mrs Hurst came hurrying into the room.

'Oh, my dear Mrs Roberts, let's get you into bed.' Taking Alice by the arm, she led her back to bed and helped her climb under the covers. 'You stay put while I get everything I need,' she said in her no-nonsense voice, which Alice found strangely reassuring.

She lay back on the pillow and closed her eyes. She dozed on and off, vaguely aware of Mrs Hurst bustling about at the foot of the bed.

'I've helped birth five nieces and nephews,' she said cheerfully, as she lugged a heavy bowl of steaming water into the room and began scrubbing her arms up to the elbows.

As the hours ticked by, the storm worsened. The wind howled under the eaves, rattling the windows in their frames.

'There's no going out in this,' Mrs Hurst said, biting her lip. 'We'll have to manage on our own.'

Alice groaned. The contractions were coming in waves now, and she felt an overwhelming urge to push.

'Baby's coming, Mrs Roberts,' Mrs Hurst said excitedly. 'I can see the head. My, it's got a lovely head of dark hair.' Alice felt her hands between her legs, pushing and pulling roughly. She felt a wet, slippery sensation between her legs, and then silence.

Alice pushed herself up on her elbows to see Mrs Hurst holding the baby, a worried frown on her face.

'It's a boy,' she said, in a monotone.

'What's wrong with him?' Alice cried, trying to quell her rising panic.

'Baby's not breathing,' Mrs Hurst said. Quickly, she turned the baby upside-down and slapped its little bottom with such force that Alice jumped. But it did the trick. Alice sighed with relief as his lusty cries filled the room.

'Give him to me,' she said, holding out her arms, her exhaustion forgotten in the joy of seeing her newborn son.

Mrs Hurst hesitated.

'Give him to me,' Alice said again, her smile faltering at the expression on her housekeeper's face. 'What is it?'

'Oh, Mrs Roberts,' Mrs Hurst said sorrowfully. 'I don't think he's right.'

'What do you mean?' Alice demanded fiercely. 'Give him to me, now!'

The woman laid the swaddled baby in Alice's arms. Immediately, Alice noticed the almond-shaped eyes, the low-set ears, the thick neck. She'd seen a child with Down Syndrome before, when volunteering at the soup kitchen. She'd seen the stares, heard the comments. Looking down at the beautiful boy in her arms, her heart was filled with a fierce, protective love that almost overwhelmed her.

'You'd be best putting him in an institution, Mrs Roberts,' Mrs Hurst said, shaking her head. 'He'll be better off with his own kind.'

'An institution?' Alice's eyes narrowed angrily. 'This is my son, Mrs Hurst. I'll thank you never to suggest such a thing again.'

'The Reverend won't want a son who's not right in the head,' Mrs Hurst muttered, turning away to begin the chore of tidying up.

'Please leave, Mrs Hurst,' Alice said firmly.

Her housekeeper looked at her in surprise. 'I beg your pardon?'

'I want you to leave. Not in this storm, obviously, but as soon as you can. I will pay you a month's wages in lieu of notice, but I want you gone from this house as soon as possible.'

'Mrs Roberts . . .' The housekeeper stared at her in dismay. 'I've been housekeeper here for over twenty years. Where will I go?' Her bottom lip trembled, and Alice's anger abated slightly.

'Very well,' she said, in a tone that surprised even herself. 'You may stay, but you will never speak about my son in a derogative manner again, do you understand?'

Mrs Hurst nodded. Satisfied that the woman looked suitably chastened, Alice turned her attention to her baby son. He was sleeping peacefully in her arms, dark lashes resting on pink cheeks. He was beautiful. She smiled, knowing in that instant that, without a doubt, she would be prepared to kill and die for this precious little boy.

She didn't know how long she slept, but the storm was still raging when she was woken by Mrs Hurst knocking on her bedroom door.

'What is it?' she hissed, not wanting to wake baby Arthur sleeping soundly in the crook of her arm.

'Mrs Roberts?' Mrs Hurst came in, biting her lip in concern. 'It's Pearl, she's here and . . .' She broke off.

'What?' Alice whispered impatiently. 'Why is Pearl . . .' The words died on her lips as the old gypsy woman pushed her way into the room. She was swathed in so many layers as to be shapeless. Snow had settled on the brim of her hat and her woollen shawl was crusted with ice.

'You haven't been out in the storm, Pearl?' Alice gasped. 'Come over by the fire, warm yourself.'

'I've come from Tilly's,' Pearl said, her tone bleak. She moved closer to the fire, but her hands remained hidden beneath her thick shawl. The snow was starting to melt, droplets of water glistening in the firelight. Tears crept along her wrinkles as her mouth moved wordlessly.

'Pearl, what is it?' Alice asked, moved by the woman's obvious distress. 'Mrs Hurst, bring Pearl some warm milk, would you?'

Mrs Hurst looked as though she might argue, but did as Alice asked, muttering under her breath as she left the room.

'Tilly died this evening,' Pearl said, sitting heavily in the chair next to the bed.

'Oh, Pearl.' Alice reached for her hand. 'I'm so sorry.' Pearl nodded. Then, from beneath her many layers, came the distinct cry of a newborn baby. Alice's eyes widened in surprise as Pearl brought out a tiny baby. It was so swaddled that Alice could only see its face.

'My Tilly gave birth to a little girl just before she died.' Pearl sniffed. 'My cousin is taking the other two girls, but she won't have this one. I heard you screaming as I went by the church, so I knew you would be having your little 'un very soon. I thought you might be persuaded to take her . . .' Her voice faltered. Tears pouring down her crumpled cheeks, she held the baby girl out to Alice.

'You know my husband would never agree,' Alice replied, frowning at the old woman in disbelief.

'You could tell everyone you had twins,' Pearl insisted. 'No one need ever know the truth, apart from the two of us and Mrs Hurst, of course.'

Alice frowned. 'What you're suggesting is preposterous. I can't lie to Samuel. I won't deceive him,' she said. *But didn't he deceive you?* said a mocking voice in her head as Mrs Hurst reappeared with two mugs of warm milk.

'I added a drop of brandy to yours,' she told Pearl as she set the mugs on the nightstand. 'What the . . . ?' She stared at the baby in Pearl's arms in amazement. 'Where did that come from?'

'It's Tilly's,' Pearl said. She let out a long sigh of defeat. 'She's gone, my Tilly.' Her mouth trembled. Despite the heat from the fire and her many layers, Alice noticed that Pearl was shivering.

'Oh, Pearl,' Mrs Hurst said, placing a hand on the old woman's shoulder. 'I'm sorry for your loss.'

'Pearl is asking me to take Tilly's baby and raise her as my own,' Alice said, deciding it was better to be truthful with her housekeeper. It wasn't like she was going to go along with Pearl's harebrained scheme.

'I think that's the perfect solution for the poor motherless child,' Mrs Hurst surprised her by saying.

'Mrs Hurst,' Alice said curtly. She hadn't forgiven the woman for her earlier unkindness towards Arthur. 'Do you honestly believe the Reverend will accept Tilly's child and raise her as his own?'

'Why does he have to know the truth?' the housekeeper

said sharply. 'Even if he leaves directly he receives your telegram tomorrow, providing the storm eases enough for me to get to the post office, he won't be back before tomorrow evening at the earliest. You and Tilly have similar colouring.' She snorted. 'He'll be none the wiser.'

The baby in Pearl's arms started to cry.

'She's hungry,' Pearl said. 'She needs feeding if she's to survive.'

Alice stared at the two women in dismay. Arthur stirred in her arms, a small frown on his little face.

'I'll feed her,' she said firmly, unbuttoning the front of her nightdress. 'But that's all. You must take her to the authorities as soon as the storm clears.'

Pearl and Mrs Hurst exchanged glances. 'What?' Alice demanded, holding out her arms for the infant.

'Nothing,' Pearl replied, handing her the baby.

But as soon as Alice held the tiny girl in her arms, she knew she wouldn't be letting her go anywhere. Without opening her eyes, the baby searched for the nipple, her little rosebud mouth latching on with ease. Sighing, Alice leaned back against the pillows, savouring the sensation of the baby suckling.

'Does she have a name?' she asked with an air of resignation.

'Tilly was wanting to call her Isabella.'

Alice nodded. 'Isabella,' she whispered, gazing down at the little girl. In her other arm, her little boy stirred. 'Arthur and Isabella,' she said, louder. 'Mrs Hurst, you will have to swear that you will never tell anyone the truth about Isabella. You, too, Pearl.'

'We promise,' Pearl said quickly. 'Don't we, Mrs Hurst?'

The housekeeper hesitated.

'I doubt it would cross the Reverend's mind to suspect they're not both his. Lord knows you were big enough to be carrying two. But yes, my lips are sealed. It will be our secret.'

'Thank you.' Alice yawned, suddenly overwhelmed by tiredness. When Isabella had finished feeding, Mrs Hurst laid the two babies in the crib. Their colouring was so similar, they could easily pass as brother and sister.

'Goodness,' Mrs Hurst exclaimed as the hall clock chimed four. 'It's almost morning. Mrs Roberts, you need to get some rest. Come on, Pearl, I'll make you a bed up in the kitchen.'

Left alone, Alice closed her eyes, but she couldn't sleep. She lay awake in the darkened room, listening to the gentle snuffling of the two babies in the crib beside her bed. She stretched out her arm, her hand resting gently on the two small, warm, swaddled bundles, her mind in turmoil as she wondered how Samuel would react, firstly to the idea of twins, but also to the fact that he would have to come to terms with a son who would, in the eyes of the world, always be regarded as lacking. With these troubling thoughts swirling round her head, she finally drifted off to sleep.

CHAPTER FORTY-FOUR

'Alice, Samuel has arrived,' Beatrice said, turning from the window, a broad smile on her face. She was thoroughly revelling in her role as great-grandmother. 'You look radiant,' she said, taking in the tableau of her granddaughter sitting up in bed, her dark hair fanned across the lace-edged pillows, a baby in each arm. Alice had changed her nightgown and, after a good afternoon nap, was feeling much rested and more confident in her new role. Her only worry was whether she would be able to keep up the pretence in front of Samuel.

The storm had dissipated around six that morning, and soon after eight, Mrs Hurst had hurried to the post office to send off the relevant telegrams. Samuel had sent an immediate reply, saying he would catch the next train home. Alice's mother had also replied, saying she would be coming to visit the following afternoon. Alice was looking forward to it. More than anyone, she felt she needed her mother right now.

Footsteps sounded on the stairs, and Alice steeled herself to greet her husband.

'Alice?' He came to a halt in the doorway, an uncertain expression on his face as he met Alice's gaze. 'Are you well?' he asked in a hoarse voice.

Alice smiled. 'I am very well,' she said. She patted the bed. 'Come in. Come and see your babies.'

'I had no idea,' he said, cautiously approaching the bed. 'Two for the price of one,' he joked nervously, perching on the edge of the bed. He stared down at the two sleeping babies.

'Meet Arthur and Isabella,' Alice smiled anxiously. 'Your children.'

'They're . . .' His smile faded. 'The boy,' he said, his eyes widening. 'He's . . .' His gaze searched Alice's, as if looking for reassurance.

'He's our son,' Alice said firmly. 'And we love him.'

Samuel's expression softened as he nodded and cleared his throat. 'Of course,' he said. He gently stroked Arthur's soft cheek, then Isabella's. 'I like the name you chose for her,' he said.

'Well, you always said if we had a son, you'd like to call him Arthur, and that I could choose our daughter's name.'

'It's a pretty name for a pretty girl. She will grow up to be as beautiful as her mother,' he said, tears filling his eyes as he brushed a strand of hair from Alice's face. Neither of them noticed Beatrice leave the room, closing the door softly behind her.

'Things are going to be different around here now,' he said solemnly.

Karen Dickson

'I should think so, with two babies in the house. We'll certainly be kept on our toes,' agreed Alice with a shaky laugh.

'No, I mean us,' Samuel said earnestly. 'You and I. I'm better, Alice,' he said. 'I've beaten my demons. I've done some terrible things and treated you badly, and for that I am truly sorry. I need to confess something to you . . .'

'Shush.' Alice pressed her finger to his lips. 'I don't need to know,' she said softly. 'It's a new start.' She looked down at the babies. 'For all of us. A new beginning.'

'Thank you,' Samuel whispered, kissing her hand. 'Thank you for never giving up on us. I know I was an absolute horror to live with and I will spend the rest of my life making it up to you, I promise.'

As Alice smiled up at him, she felt the tension slip from her shoulders and found that she no longer held any anger towards him. She loved him and was ready to build a new life together with him. She didn't need him to confess his secret. She had forgiven him. After all, she thought with a smile, gazing down at baby Isabella as she slumbered in her arm, now she had a secret of her own.

EPILOGUE

Summer 1920

A warm breeze wafted across the deserted strawberry fields
and up the lane, rustling the veils and skirts of the sombre
crowd gathered around the stone memorial. Ten feet high, it
had a wide plinth and a sloping column, which ended in an
intricately carved stone cross. On the plinth were carved the
names of the dozen or so Strawbridge men who had given
their lives in the recent conflict.

Leah shifted from foot to foot, rocking her baby daughter,
Tabitha. William, now a stout two-year-old, sat solemnly
astride his father's shoulders, sporting a black armband.

'How are you holding up?' Joshua asked softly, turning to
Leah. She smiled and nodded, not trusting herself to speak.
Harry's name was on the plinth, of course. That was the
reason Isaac had forked out the money for the memorial.

He and Frances had arrived just a few minutes earlier. They
were stood at the front of the small crowd, Isaac in a black

suit, his bare head bowed. Frances stood beside him, swathed in black, her face hidden by a thick veil. *Blimey, she must be sweltering*, Leah thought, not without sympathy. Despite their differences, she could empathize with the woman's grief. She had lost her only son, after all. Leah couldn't imagine how she would cope if anything ever happened to William or Tabitha. Her children were her life.

Using one hand to support his son, Joshua pulled Leah against him. She rested her head on his shoulder, grateful for his strength and support. Despite her initial misgivings over her marriage, she and Joshua had melded together very well and, over time, her feelings towards him had blossomed into something akin to love. It would never be like the love she had felt for Harry, and still felt deep down, but it was comfortable and sustainable. He had proved to be a good provider and a wonderful father. He loved William as his own son and had never, in all their two and a half years of marriage, questioned Leah about his real father, for which she was grateful. Yet she couldn't quell the deep-seated niggle that one day the truth would come out.

She'd seen the wistful way Samuel looked at William. As much as he loved his eighteen-month-old twins and, according to Alice, was fiercely protective of little Arthur, there was no denying that the boy would always find life a bit of a struggle, and Leah couldn't shrug off her fear that Samuel might one day decide to publicly acknowledge William as his own. Which was why she was relieved that she, Joshua and the children would be leaving Strawbridge that very afternoon.

Pearl had passed away in her sleep in the spring of the previous year, and Joshua had been itching to leave Strawbridge ever since. He'd been offered a job as head gardener of an estate in Wiltshire and, after discussing it with Leah, had accepted. The estate was set on the edge of the village of Wilton, just outside Salisbury, and came with a three-bedroom cottage. They would have left a week earlier, but she had wanted to be here for the commemoration of the memorial. She owed Harry that much, at least.

She spotted Dora edging her way through the sea of black towards her, clutching on tightly to three-year-old Frank. Nate followed in her wake, carrying their eight-month-old daughter, Molly.

'Sorry we're late,' Dora whispered. 'Have we missed anything?' She stood on tiptoe in an effort to see over the crowd.

'No,' Leah whispered back. 'The Whitworths have only just arrived. I don't think Samuel's here yet; oh yes, I see him, over there with Alice's family.'

Leaving the two men to mind the older children, Leah and Dora pushed their way over to where Alice was standing with her parents, grandparents and siblings. Isabella hung onto her Grandma Lily's skirt, a solemn little figure in her black dress, a black velvet ribbon holding back her thick, chestnut-brown tresses. Beatrice jiggled Arthur on her hip, and he beamed toothily at Leah and Dora as they approached. Leah reached out and tickled his cheek. He giggled throatily. *He really is the most delightful child*, she thought, trying to push aside the knowledge that he was William's brother.

Alice was about to speak when a ripple of expectation ran through the crowd and a hush fell as Samuel made his way to a small lectern that had been set up to the side of the memorial. He cleared his throat. She could see his hands were shaking and her heart ached for him. He had been dreading today and had spent much of the night pacing the floor of his study, sleep eluding him until the early hours.

'Ladies and gentlemen,' he began, his voice gruff with ill-concealed emotion. 'Today, we are gathered here to remember those who made the ultimate sacrifice. Let us pray.'

Alice bowed her head, but found her mind drifting back over the past eighteen months. Samuel had, it would appear, come back from the brink. Since the birth of the twins, he had reverted to the man she had fallen in love with, the kind, loving man she had married. He never spoke about what had happened at his retreat, but whatever methods his old classmate had used, they had certainly worked. She couldn't have been happier these recent months.

It was only occasionally that she felt a twinge of sadness when she saw the way Samuel looked at William. There was no doubt in her mind that he loved Arthur dearly, but already the boy was several paces behind Isabella in his development. And her heart ached for her son, for she couldn't help but wonder whether, when he was older and unable to do the things a father might want to do with his son, Samuel might hanker for the boy he could never call his own.

She heard Leah sniff softly into her handkerchief and

gently touched her sleeve. She wasn't quite sure when she had forgiven her. It had been a gradual awakening, rather than a specific decision. One day, she had woken up and realized that she no longer held any animosity towards her old friend. They often gathered at each other's homes, bringing their mending or knitting, and spent a pleasant hour or so chatting, the children playing at their feet.

She would miss Leah dreadfully, but in her heart she knew it was for the best, for both of them.

Samuel cleared his throat again, drawing her attention back to her husband. His face was pale and drawn, and there were dark shadows beneath his eyes.

'Now I shall read the roll call of our glorious dead,' he said hoarsely.

'Arnold, Bert. Carter, Ronald ...'

Leah caught sight of her mother and gave her a surreptitious wave. She was standing with Ian and Daisy on the other side of the memorial. They had recently become engaged and were standing arm in arm. Ian had tears running down his face. Leah noticed that several of the men were crying. Most of the women were openly sobbing as Samuel continued to read through his list.

'Merrifield, Leonard.' A murmur of dissention rippled through the crowd. There had been those who felt Leonard's name shouldn't have been included, but Isaac Whitworth had insisted, and as he was footing the bill, no one argued. Leah cast a glance at Reuben Merrifield. He stood ramrod-straight with his back to her, so she couldn't see his face. Florence stood beside him. Leah could tell she was sobbing by the way her shoulders were shaking.

'Merrifield, Percy,' Samuel read, his voice cracking ever so slightly.

'Merrifield, Seth.'

Leah felt a vice around her chest so tight that she couldn't breathe.

'Whitworth, Henry.' Leah swayed. Instantly, she felt Alice and Dora's arms around her shoulders. Tears slid down her cheeks as she swallowed the lump in her throat.

Harry had been the last. Samuel uttered a final prayer and stepped away from the lectern, wiping his eyes. A heavy silence descended over the assembled mourners. Isaac and Frances paused to lay a wreath on the plinth, then quietly walked to their car and drove away.

'Do you want to go closer?' Dora asked Leah, as people crowded the stone cross, eagerly searching for their loved one's name. She shook her head.

'I've said my goodbyes to Harry,' she replied shakily. 'May he rest in peace, wherever he is.' She glanced back at Joshua. He was watching her anxiously. She gave him a reassuring smile. 'I'd better get back to my husband,' she said. 'We've got a train to catch.'

'Thank you,' Leah said, as the porter hoisted the heavy trunk into the baggage car. The hands on the large station clock stood at a quarter to three. Five minutes until her train was due to leave. She glanced along the empty platform. The other passengers had already boarded, and only Leah, Joshua and the children still lingered.

Her eyes were still red from saying goodbye to her mother. Not one for emotional scenes in public, Hannah had said her goodbyes at the house. Though she'd kept her emotions in check at the time, Leah knew Hannah would be sobbing her heart out right now, and her own tears threatened.

Joshua glanced up at the clock and then at the station building. 'I'll get the children on the train, Leah,' he said, gently taking Tabitha from her. 'And find us a carriage.'

Leah nodded, her anxious gaze darting back and forth. She saw the guard check his watch. He raised his flag, tapping it against his side.

'Leah! Leah!' At the sound of Dora's voice, she whirled round in relief as Alice and Dora, holding their skirts above their ankles, came running onto the platform. They fell upon Leah, taking it in turns to hug her, both talking at once.

'Wait, wait,' Leah laughed. 'I can't understand a word you're saying.'

Dora took a deep breath. 'We're so sorry we're late,' she said, glancing over at the guard, who made a show of checking his pocket watch. Leah looked up at the clock. Three minutes. 'Some farmer decided today would be a good day to move his sheep,' Dora continued. 'There must have been hundreds of them.'

'They completely blocked the lane,' said Alice. 'We had no choice but to follow on behind them. Thankfully, they turned off at the crossroads.'

'I'm just thankful you made it,' Leah said. Her bottom lip trembled. 'I'm going to miss you both so much.'

'We'll miss you, Leah,' Dora said, hugging her again.

'Promise you'll write,' Alice said, embracing her warmly.

'I will, and you must, too, both of you.'

The guard looked at his watch again, and this time blew his whistle.

'I have to go,' Leah said with a tearful smile. She gripped Dora and Alice's hands.

'Hurry, Mama, hurry!' William shouted, standing on the seat so he could lean out of the open carriage window. Joshua was standing beside him, Tabitha cradled in his arms.

'I'm coming, my love,' Leah said with a smile. Hugging her friends one last time, she climbed the steps and joined her family. She kissed William's soft, dark curls and waved as the train began to move.

'Goodbye, goodbye!' she called, waving frantically to Dora and Alice, who hurried along, keeping pace with the train until they reached the end of the platform. The train snaked round a corner and her friends disappeared from view. Leah sank down on the seat, pulling William onto her lap.

'Are you sorry to be leaving?' asked Joshua, sitting down beside her and bouncing Tabitha on his knee. Leah didn't answer straight away. Instead, she turned to look out of the window.

'Leah?' Joshua said softly.

'It's a wrench, leaving everyone and everything I've ever known,' she said truthfully, turning her face towards him.

'But I'm excited, too.' She placed her hand on his. 'I'm excited to see what the future has in store for us,' she said, smiling up at him.

Joshua grinned. 'I love you, Mrs Mullens.'

'I love you, too, Mr Mullens,' replied Leah. And she meant it.

Acknowledgements

As always, my greatest thanks go to my agent, Judith Murdoch. Thank you for seeing something in my writing that you felt was worth pursuing.

Also, thank you to my editors, Molly Crawford and Mina Asaam, and the whole team at Simon & Schuster. There is so much work that goes into a book between the manuscript landing on the editor's desk and the finished product, so thank you, everyone.

Thanks to my husband, John, and all my family and friends for their ongoing love and support. And last but not least, thank you to my readers. I hope you enjoyed the book.

For more from Karen Dickson . . .

The Strawberry Field Girls

The strawberry harvest is finally ready. The delicious fruit makes up the main source of income for the small hamlet of Strawbridge. Good friends Leah, Alice and Dora are ready to spend their summer months working on Isaac Whitworth's farm.

But when Leah takes a fancy to young farm hand Harry and Alice catches the eye of the curate's son, the two girls find themselves falling fast. This leaves Dora on the outside, struggling with the weight of being her family's sole breadwinner and caring for her sickly father.

But the summer months are long and the surprises are far from over . . .

AVAILABLE NOW IN PAPERBACK AND EBOOK

**SIMON &
SCHUSTER**

A Songbird in Wartime

Shaftesbury, 1936. Mansfield House Hotel has been
a refuge for Emily ever since she was orphaned at the
age of 16. Not only did they give her employment as a
chambermaid, but it's also where she met her fiancé Tom.

When theatre agent Roland stays at the hotel and hears
Emily singing, he is determined to take her away to Bristol
and make her a star. But knowing she'd never leave her
fiancé, he hatches a plan to get Emily away from Tom.

Six years later, Emily has made a name for herself as
'The Bristol Songbird'. Her love for Tom is still as strong
as ever, but she's not heard from him since that fateful
night so long ago. And with the world enveloped in a
war, it seems unlikely the two will ever meet again.

**Will Emily and Tom ever find their way
back to one another? Or will the war – and
Roland – succeed in keeping them apart?**

**AVAILABLE NOW IN PAPERBACK
AND EBOOK**

**SIMON &
SCHUSTER**